NICOLA CORNICK

HOUSE
of
SHADOWS

**GRAYDON
HOUSE**

LOOK FOR NICOLA CORNICK'S NEXT NOVEL
THE PHANTOM TREE
AVAILABLE SOON FROM GRAYDON HOUSE BOOKS

HOUSE
of
SHADOWS

**GRAYDON
HOUSE**

ISBN-13: 978-1-525-81138-8

House of Shadows

BookClubbish.com

Printed in U.S.A.

Recycling programs
for this product may
not exist in your area.

To Andrew, who has lived with my obsession with Ashdown House and William Craven for many years. All my love, as always.

Let your life lightly dance on the edges of Time.

—Rabindranath Tagore

PROLOGUE

London, February 1662

She dreamed about the house on the night before she died. In the dream she felt as insignificant as a child; a miniature queen clad in a cream silk gown embroidered with gold. The collar prickled the nape of her neck as she craned her head to gaze up, up at the dazzling white stone of the house against the blue of the sky. It made her dizzy. Her head spun and the golden ball that adorned the roof seemed to plunge like a shooting star falling to earth.

Beyond the walls of her bedchamber crouched the city; filthy, noisy and seething with life. But in her dreams she was far from London; she had followed the wide ribbon of the Thames upriver, past the hunting ground at Richmond and the great grey walls of Windsor, to a place where two rivers met. She took the narrower path through drowsy meadows thick with daisies and the hum of bees, for in her dream she was a summer princess, not a winter queen. The river became a chalk stream that bubbled up from springs deep in the dappled woods until finally she burst out of the shade and onto the highlands, and there was the house in a hollow of the hills, a little white palace fit for a queen.

Her lips moved. One of her women, weary, anxious, attentive, bent to catch the whisper. It could not be long now.

"William."

It caused consternation. She had sent him away, her cavalier, told her servants to bar the door against him.

"Madam…" The woman was uncertain. "I don't think—"

The Queen's eyelashes flickered. Her eyes, blue-grey, were clear, imperious.

"At once."

"Majesty." The woman curtsied, ran.

The room was hot, windows and doors closed, fire roaring. She drifted between sleep and waking, on the fringes of shadow. Outside, dawn was breaking over the river, the water rippling with a silver wake. It was unseasonably mild for February and the air felt heavy, waiting.

He came.

She heard the stir, felt the cool shift of the air before the door closed again, sealing them in.

"Leave us."

No one argued, which was good because she was too tired for arguments now. Her eyes would not open. In the silence she could hear everything, though; the hiss of the fire as a log settled deeper in the grate, the creak of the floorboards beneath his boots as he crossed the room to her side.

"Sit. Please." It was an effort to speak. There was no time for discussion now, or apologies, even if she had wished to make them, which she did not.

He sat. Now that he was close she could smell on him the night cold and the scent of the city. She could not see him but she did not need to. She knew every plane of his face, each line, each curve. It was as though they were written on her heart, an indelible picture.

There was something she needed to tell him. She fought for the strength to speak.

"The crystal mirror—"

"I will get it back. I swear it," he replied instantly. A second later his hand grasped hers, warm and reassuring but still she shook her head. She knew it was too late.

"It will elude you," she said.

He had never understood the power of the Order of the Rosy Cross or its instruments, though perhaps he did now, now that the damage was done.

"Danger to you—" She tried one last time to warn him. "Take care or it will destroy you and your kin as it did me and mine." She was gasping for breath, frightened.

His fingers tightened on hers. "I understand. Believe me."

She felt the knot inside her ease. She had to trust him. There was no alternative. Her life was unravelling like a skein of wool. Soon the thread would run out.

"I want you to take this. Keep it safe, hidden." With an effort she opened her eyes and unclenched the fingers of her right hand. A huge pearl spilled into her lap, glowing with baleful fire in the subdued light. Even now, looking on it for the last time, she could not like it, for all its ethereal beauty. It was too powerful. It was not the fault of the jewel, of course, but of the men who had sought to use it for their own wicked purposes. Both mirror and pearl had once been a force for good, strong and protective, until their power had been corrupted through the greed of men. The Knights had been warned not to misuse the instruments of the Order and they had disobeyed. They had unleashed destruction through fire and water, just as the prophecy had foretold.

She heard the catch of Craven's breath. "The Sistrin pearl should be given to your heir."

"Not yet." She was so very tired now but this last task must be completed. "You need to break the link between the pearl and the mirror. One day the mirror will return and then it must be destroyed. Keep the pearl safe until that is done."

Craven did not refuse her gift or tell her that he had no time for superstition. Once he had scorned her beliefs. No longer. She watched him scoop up the pearl on its heavy gold chain and stow it within his shirt. His face was grave and set, as though he was facing battle, such was the weight of her commission.

"Thank you." Her smile was weary. Her eyes closed. "I can sleep now."

There was a sudden commotion. The door swung back with a crash and a protesting creak of hinges. Voices; loud, commanding. Footsteps, equally loud: her son Rupert, come to be with her at the end, always hasty, always late.

There was so little time now.

She opened her eyes again. The room swam with shadows and the red and gold of firelight but she felt cold. She looked on Craven for the last time. Grief was etched deep into his face.

Old, she thought. *We have had our time.* The loss cut her like a knife. If only…

"William," she said. "I am sorry. I wish we had another chance."

His face lightened. He gave her the smile that had shaken her heart from the moment she had first seen him.

"Perhaps we shall," he said, "in another life."

She forgot that her time could be measured in breaths now, not hours or even minutes, and tightened her grip urgently on his hand.

"The Knights of the Rosy Cross believed in the rebirth of the spirit," she said, "but it is against the Christian teaching."

He nodded. His eyes were smiling. "I know it is. Yet still I believe it. It comforts me to think that we shall meet again in another time."

Her eyes closed. A small smile touched her lips. "It comforts me too," she said softly. "Next time we shall be together always. Next time we shall not fail."

1

Palace of Holyroodhouse, Scotland, November 1596

King James paused with his hand already raised to the iron latch. Even now he was not sure that he was doing the right thing. A spiteful winter wind skittered along the stone corridor, lifting the tapestries from the walls and setting him shivering deep within his fur-lined tunic.

The pearl and the mirror should be given to Elizabeth, that was indisputable; they were her birthright. Yet this was a dangerous gift. James knew their power.

The Queen of England had made no show of her baptismal present to her goddaughter and namesake. In fact it was widely believed that Mr Robert Bowes of Aske, who had stood proxy for Her Majesty at the christening, had brought no gift with him at all. It was only after the service had been completed, the baby duly presented as the first daughter of Scotland and the guests had dispersed to enjoy the feast, that

Aske had called James to one side and passed him a velvet box in which rested the Sistrin pearl and the jewelled mirror.

"These belonged to your mother," Bowes had said. "Her Majesty is eager that they should be passed to her grand-daughter."

For diplomacy's sake James had bitten back the retort that had sprung to his lips. Trust the old bitch of England to present as a gift those items that were his daughter's by right. But then he could play this game as well as any; he had paid Elizabeth of England the compliment of naming his firstborn girl after her. It was outrageous flattery for his mother's murderer, but politics was of more import than spilt blood.

"Majesty?"

He turned. Alison Hay, the baby's mistress-nurse was approaching. Her face bore no trace of surprise or alarm, although he could only imagine her speculation in finding King James of Scotland dithering outside his baby daughter's chambers. He should have thought to send for one of the Princess Elizabeth's attendants rather than to loiter like a fool in cold corridors. But Mistress Hay's arrival had brought with it relief. There was now no cause to knock or to enter this realm of women. James' insides curdled at the thought of the stench of the room, of stale sweat and that sweetly sour smell that seemed to cling to a baby. The women would all be grouped about the child's cradle, fussing and smiling and clucking like so many hens. Thank God that soon they would all be departing for Linlithgow where the Princess would have her own household under the guardianship of Lord and Lady Livingston.

He groped in his pocket and his fingers closed over the black velvet of the box.

"This is for the Princess Elizabeth. A baptismal gift." He held it out to her.

Mistress Hay did not take the box immediately. A frown creased her brow.

"Would Your Majesty not prefer to give it to Lady Livingston—"

"No!" James was desperate to be rid of the burden, desperate to be gone. "Take it." He pushed it at her. The box fell between their hands, springing open, the contents rolling out onto the stone floor.

He heard Mistress Hay gasp.

Few men—or women—had seen either the Sistrin pearl or the jewelled mirror. The pearl had never been worn and the mirror had never been used. Both were shaped like teardrops. Both shone with an unearthly bluish-white glow, the one seeming a reflection of the other: matched, equal, alike.

The pearl had been born of water, found in the oyster beds of the River Tay centuries before and had been part of the collection of King Alexander I. The mirror had been forged in fire by the glassblowers of Murano, its frame decorated with diamonds of the finest quality and despatched as a gift to James' mother, Mary, Queen of Scots, on her marriage. Mary had delighted in the similarity of the two and had had the rich black velvet box made for them.

Yet from the first there had been rumours about both pieces. The Sistrin pearl was said to have formed from the tears of the water goddess Briant and to offer its owner powerful protection, but if its magic was misused it would bring death through water. There were whispers that the Sistrin had caused King Alexander's wife, Sybilla, to drown when Alexander had tried to bind its power to his will. The mirror was also a potent charm, but it was said that it would wreak devastation by fire if it were used for corrupt purposes. James was a rational man of science and he did not believe in magic, but something about the jewels set the hairs rising on his neck. If he had been of a superstitious disposition he would have said that it was almost as though he could feel their power like a living thing; crouched, waiting.

Alison Hay was on her knees now, scrabbling to catch the pearl before it rolled away and was lost down a drain or through a crack in the floor. James did not trouble to help. He did not want to touch it. The mirror lay where it had fallen, facing up, miraculously unbroken.

Alison grabbed the pearl and struggled to her feet, flushed, breathing hard. In one hand she had the box, the pearl safely back within it, glowing with innocent radiance. In the other she held the mirror. As James watched, she glanced down at its milky blue surface. Her eyes widened. Her lips parted. James snatched it from her, bundling it roughly face down into the box and snapping the lid shut.

"Don't look into it," he said. "Never look into it."

It was too late. Her face was chalk white, eyes blank pools.

"What did you see?" James' voice was harsh with emotion. Terror gripped him, visceral, setting his heart pounding. Then, as she did not reply: "Answer me!"

"Fire," she said. She spoke flatly as if by rote. "Buildings eaten by flame. Gunpowder. Death. And a child in a cream-coloured gown with a crown of gold."

"Twaddle." James gripped the box as though he could crush the contents; crush the very idea of them. "Superstitious nonsense, all of it." Yet even he could hear the hollow ring of fear in his voice. Before magic, cold reason fled.

"Lock them away," he said, pushing the box back into the nurse's hands. "Keep them safe."

"Majesty." She dropped a curtsey.

It was done. From behind the closed door he heard the thin wail of a baby and the murmur of female voices joined in a soothing lullaby. James turned on his heel and walked away, heading for the courtyard and the fresh clean air of winter to chase away the shadow that stalked him. Yet even outside under a crystalline grey sky plump with snow he was not free of guilt. He had given the Sistrin and the mirror to his baby daughter, as the Queen of England had commanded, but it felt that in some terrible way he had cursed her with it.

2

Wassenaer Hof, The Hague, autumn 1631

There was a full moon and a cold easterly wind when the Knights of the Rosy Cross came. The wind came from the sea, crossing the wide sand dunes and whipping through the streets to curl about the corners of the Wassenaer Hof, seeking entry through cracks and crannies.

Elizabeth watched the Knights' arrival from her window high in the western wing of the palace. The moonlight dimmed the candles and fell pitilessly bright on the cobbles. In that white world the men were no more than dark cloaked shadows.

She had thought that such folly was over. The Order of the Rosy Cross belonged to a time long ago. It had been a dream borne of their youth. She and her husband, Frederick, had been so passionate about it once. They had been possessed of a desire to change the world, to spread knowledge, science and wisdom. Their court at Heidelberg had been a refuge for scholars and philosophers.

Now she felt so very different, drained of faith, betrayed, as flimsy as the playing card for which she was named the Queen of Hearts.

She was a pale reflection; an echo fading into the dark. Men had called her union with Frederick the marriage of Thames and Rhine; a political match between a German prince and an English princess destined to strengthen the Protestant cause. She had not cared for such things. She had not been educated for politics then. It had been simple; one look at Frederick and she had fallen in love. They had wed in winter but she had felt blessed by light and fortune. Frederick's ascent to the throne of Bohemia had been the final glory. The future had been so bright, but it had been a false dawn followed by nothing but grief and loss. Bohemia had been lost in battle after only a year, Frederick's own lands overrun by his enemies. They had fled to The Hague to a makeshift court and a makeshift life.

Elizabeth rested one hand on her swollen belly. After eighteen years of marriage and twelve children, people spoke of her love for Frederick in terms of indulgence, never questioning her devotion. They knew nothing.

Tonight she was so angry. She knew why Frederick had summoned the Knights. There was new hope, he said. Their long exile would soon be over. The Swedish King had smashed the army of the Holy Roman Emperor and was sweeping through Germany in triumph. Frederick wanted the Knights of the Rosy Cross to scry for him, to see whether Gustavus Adolphus' victory would give him back his patrimony. He had taken both the Sistrin pearl and the crystal mirror with him to foretell the future; the Knights demanded it. But the treasures were not Frederick's to take; they were hers.

Elizabeth felt restless. Her rooms were noisy. They always were; her ladies chattered louder than her monkeys. She was never alone. Tonight, though, she was in no mood for music or masques or cards. Suddenly the repetition of her life, the sameness, the tedium, the hopes raised and dashed time and again, made her so frustrated that she shook with fury.

"Majesty?" One of her ladies spoke timidly.

"Fetch my cloak," Elizabeth said. "The plain black."

They bustled around her like anxious hens. She should not go out. His Majesty would not like it. It was too cold. She was with child. She should be resting.

She ignored them all and closed the door on their clucking. Down the stairs, along the stone corridor, past the great hall with its gilded leather, where the servants were sweeping and tidying after supper, out into the courtyard, feeling the sting of the cold air. She passed the stables and as always the scent of horses, leather and hay comforted her. Riding—hunting—made her life of exile tolerable.

She looked back across the yard at the lights of the palace winking behind their brightly coloured leaded panes. She had never considered the Wassenaer Hof to be her home, even though she had lived in The Hague for over ten years now. They still called her the Queen of Bohemia, but in truth she reigned over nothing but this palace of red brick with its jostling gables and ridiculous little towers.

The building was swallowed in shadows. Here in the gardens there was the sharp scent of clipped box that always caught in her throat and the sweet smokiness of camomile. The gravel of the parterre crunched beneath her feet. She could never walk here without thinking of the gardens Frederick had designed for her at Heidelberg Castle, with their grottoes and cascades, their orange trees and their statuary. All had been on a grand scale that had matched Frederick's ambition. All gone. She had heard that an artillery battery now stood on the site of her English Garden. As for Frederick's ambition, she had believed that had been crushed too, struck down at the Battle of the White Mountain, buried under the losses that had bruised his honour and his fortune alike. But then, tonight, he had sent for the Knights of the Rosy Cross and brought them here, to the water tower, to tell him if his fortunes would rise again.

He had taken their son too. Charles Louis was a mere thirteen years old, but Frederick had said it was time his heir should see what the future held for him. That had angered Elizabeth too. She had already lost one son and kept Charles Louis close. He was too precious to put in danger.

She drew the hood of the cloak more closely about her face. The scrape of the metal latch sounded loud in her ears; the wall sconce flared in the draught. She closed the door softly behind her and started to descend the stone steps to the well, taking care to make no noise. It was odd that for all that the old tower was dry and the stair well lit, she felt as though the water had seeped into the very stones and now lapped around her, inimical and cold. She had hated water ever since it had taken the life of her eldest son two years before. Even now, his drowning haunted her dreams. She could not shake the belief that in some way she and Frederick had brought the loss upon themselves through the misuse of the Sistrin pearl's magic. Her father had warned her of its power and told her it should never be used for personal gain.

Elizabeth shivered, clutching the edge of her cloak closer to ward off the cold. Below she could hear the sound of water now; when the well was full the overflow from the Bosbeek, the forest stream, flowed through an arched drain and out into the Hofvijver Lake. Tonight it sang softly as it ran. The music of the water was a good omen. Frederick would be pleased.

Another step and she passed the guardroom on the left. Shadows shifted behind the half-open door. She held her breath and trod more softly still, down towards the sacred well.

At the bottom of the spiral stair the space opened out into a room with a vaulted ceiling held aloft by stone pillars. It was familiar to her, as were the items on a table to the right: a bible, a skull, an hourglass, a compass and a globe, the tools of the Knights' trade. Flames burned high in a wide stone fireplace, the golden light rippling over the water of a star-shaped well in the opposite corner of the room. The Knights were kneeling around the edge. The well had a shallow inner shelf and Elizabeth knew they would have placed the Sistrin pearl on that ledge, in its natural element of water. They were waiting for the jewel to exert its magic and reflect the future in the crystal mirror.

Light fractured from the crosses each man wore, some silver, some a soft rose gold that seemed to glow with a radiance of its own. Elizabeth could see the mirror in Frederick's hand, the diamonds shining with the same dark fire as the crosses. She did not look at the reflection in the glass itself. She feared the mirror's visions.

The heat was overpowering and the air laden with smoke and the sweet-woody scent of frankincense. The sun, moon and stars on the Knights' robes seemed to spin before her eyes. Her head ached sharply. Caught off guard, Elizabeth took a step back. She put out a hand to steady herself against one of the stone pillars but met thin air.

Someone caught her from behind, his hand over her mouth, one arm about her waist, pulling her out of the room, swinging the door shut behind them. It was sudden and shocking; no one touched the Queen, least of all manhandled her. Instinct took over; instincts she did not know she possessed.

She bit down hard, tasting the tang of leather against her tongue, and he released her at once, though the bite could not have hurt and nor could her feeble attempts to lash out with boots or elbows.

"Hellcat." His voice was deep and he sounded amused, as though her puny efforts were pitiful. She was the one who was angry and she allowed herself to indulge in it.

"You fool." She spun around to face him. She was shaken, ruffled, more than she ought to have been. "Don't you know who I am?"

She saw his eyes widen, hazel eyes, which held more than a hint of laughter. In the flaring torchlight she could see he was of no more than average height, which still made him several inches taller than she. He looked strong, though, and durable. His hair was a rich chestnut, curling over the white lace of his collar, his nose straight, a cleft in his chin. And even in this moment of stupefaction, even as he recognised her, there was still amusement in his face rather than the deference he should be showing her.

"Your Majesty." He bowed.

She waited, haughty. His lips twitched.

"Forgive me," he said smoothly, after a moment. Nothing more, and it did not sound like a request, still less like an apology.

He was young, this man, a good deal younger than she was, possibly no more than two- or three-and-twenty. Elizabeth thought she recognised him, though she did not know his name. She could see he was a soldier not a courtier. Unlike the Knights of the Rosy Cross he was clad plainly in shirt, breeches, cloak and boots. There was a sword at his side and a knife in his belt.

Heat and sudden tiredness hit her again, making her sway.

Perhaps her ladies had been right, damn them. She was six months pregnant and should have been resting.

The expression in his eyes changed from amusement to concern. He took her hand, drawing her forwards.

"Come into the guardroom—"

"No!" She hung back. "I don't want anyone to see me…"

"There is no one here but me."

She allowed him to usher her through the door into the small chamber. It was Spartan, with a bare floor and one candle on a battered table. A meagre fire glowed in the grate. It was no place for a queen but there was a chair, hard and wooden, and Elizabeth sank down onto it gratefully.

"You are guarding the ceremony alone?" she asked.

"I am." He looked rueful. "Badly, it would seem."

She smiled at that. "You could not have anticipated this."

"That the Queen herself would choose to come and watch?" He shrugged, half turning aside to pour her a cup of water from the carafe on the table. "I suppose not."

"I am a member of the Order of the Rosy Cross," Elizabeth said. "I have every right to be here."

His hand stilled. He turned back, dark brows raised. "Then why not exercise that right openly? Why creep in like a thief?"

Few things surprised Elizabeth these days. Few people challenged her. It was one of the privileges of royal blood, to be unquestioned. "Never explain, never complain" was an adage that her mother, fair, frivolous Anne of Denmark, had taught her. This man evidently thought that a commoner might question a queen.

All the same she chose to ignore his question, tasting the water he passed her instead, which was warm and brackish but not altogether unpleasant.

"I don't believe I know you," she said.

He bowed again. "William Craven. Entirely at your service."

Many men had said those words to her over the years. The court was crowded with young men such as this William Craven; men who dedicated themselves and their swords to her service. She knew that some saw her as a princess in distress, others as a martyr to the Protestant cause, unfailingly courageous in the face of adversity. Sometimes she wanted to tell them that there was no place for romantic gallantry in either war or politics. The years of exile had taught her that war was brutal and dangerous, and that politics were corrupt and ground on tediously slowly. But, of course, she never said so. They all maintained the pretence.

"Lord Craven," she said. "Of course. I have heard much about you."

His mouth turned down at the corners. "I too have heard what men say about me at the court."

She met his gaze very directly. "What do they say?"

He smiled ruefully and she saw the lines deepen around his eyes and drive a crease down one lean cheek. He still looked young, but not as young as before. "That my father was a shopkeeper and my grandfather a farm labourer; that I bought my barony; that I owe my place in the world to my father's money and your brother's need for it." Despite his ruefulness he sounded comfortable with the malice. Or perhaps he had heard it so many times before that it had ceased to sting.

"Charles is perennially in need of money," Elizabeth said. "As am I myself."

Craven's eyes widened at that, then he laughed, deep and appreciative. "Plain dealing," he said. "From a queen. That is uncommon."

So they had both surprised the other.

Elizabeth put the cup of water down on the flagstone by her chair. "What I actually meant was that I had heard Prince

Maurice speak highly of your talents as a soldier. He said you are loyal and courageous."

Craven shifted, the table creaking as he leaned his weight against it. "Prince Maurice said I was reckless," he corrected gently. "It's not the same."

"He spoke of your bravery and skill," Elizabeth said. "Take the compliment when it is offered, Lord Craven."

He inclined his head although she was not sure whether it was simply to hide the laughter brimming in his eyes. "Majesty."

There was no doubt, the man lacked deference. As the grandson of a farm labourer he should not have had a manner so easy it bordered on insolence. Yet Elizabeth found she liked it. She liked the way he did not flatter and fawn.

The silence started to settle between them. It felt comfortable. She knew she should go before the ceremony ended; before Frederick came looking for her. She had told him she wanted no part of the ceremony tonight and to be found here would invite questions. Yet still she did not move.

"You are not one of the Order?" she asked, gesturing towards the door to the water chamber.

He shook his head. "Merely a humble squire. I don't believe—" He broke off sharply. For the first time she sensed constraint in him.

"You don't believe in the principles of the Order of the Rosy Cross?" Elizabeth asked. "You don't believe in a better world, in seeking universal harmony?"

His face was half-shadowed, his expression difficult to read. "Such ambitions seem worthy indeed," he said slowly, "but I am a simple man, Your Majesty, a soldier. How might this universal harmony be achieved?"

Ten years earlier, Elizabeth might have told him it would be through the study of the wisdom of the ancient past, through philosophy and science. She had believed in the cause then, believed that they might build a better world. But the words were hollow to her now, as was the promise that the Order of the Rosy Cross had held for the future.

"...scrying in the waters." Craven's voice drowned out the clamour of her memories. He sounded disapproving. "Sometimes it is better not to know what the future holds."

Elizabeth agreed with that. If she had known her future ten years ago she was not sure she would have had the strength to go forwards towards it.

"The Knights have powerful magic." She could not resist teasing him. "They can read secret thoughts. They can pass through locked doors. They can even turn base metal into gold."

She thought she heard him snort. "As the son of a merchant, I know better than most how gold is made and it is not from base metal."

Their eyes met. Elizabeth smiled. The silence seemed to hum gently between them, alive with something sharp and curious.

"Are you wed, Lord Craven?" she asked on impulse.

Craven looked surprised but no more so than Elizabeth felt. She had absolutely no idea as to why she would ask a near stranger such an impertinent question.

"No, I am not wed," Craven answered, after a moment. "There was a betrothal to the daughter of the Earl of Devonshire—" He stopped.

A Cavendish, Elizabeth thought. He looked high indeed for the son of a merchant. But then if he was as rich as men said he would be courted on all sides for money, whilst those who sought it sniped at his common ancestry behind his back.

"What happened?" she said.

He shrugged. "I preferred soldiering."

"Poor woman." Elizabeth could not imagine being dismissed with a shrug and a careless sentence. That was not the lot of princesses. If they were not beautiful men pretended that they were. If they were fortunate enough to possess beauty, charm and wit then poets wrote sonnets to them and artists had no need to flatter them in portraits. She had lived with that truth since she was old enough to look in the mirror and know she had beauty and more to spare.

"Soldiering and marriage don't mix," Craven said bluntly.

"But a man needs an heir to his estates," Elizabeth said. "Especially a man with a fortune as great as yours."

"I have two brothers," Craven said. His tone had eased. "They are my heirs."

"It's not the same as having a child of your own," Elizabeth said. "Do not all men want a son to follow them?"

"Or a daughter," Craven said.

"Oh, daughters..." Elizabeth's wave of the hand dismissed them. "We are useful enough when required to serve a dynastic purpose, but it is not the same."

His gaze came up and caught hers, hard, bright, challenging enough to make her catch her breath. "Do you truly believe that? That you are the lesser sex?"

She had never questioned it.

"I heard men say," Craven said, "that King Charles believes he gets better sense from you, his sister, than from his brother-in-law."

Insolence again. But Elizabeth was tempted into a smile.

"Perhaps my brother is not a good judge of character," she said.

"Perhaps you should value yourself more highly, Majesty." His gaze released hers and she found she could breathe again.

"History demonstrates the truth." Craven had turned slightly away, settling the smouldering log deeper into the fire with his booted foot. "Your own godmother, the Queen of England, was a very great ruler."

"I think sometimes that she was a man," Elizabeth said.

Craven looked startled. Then he gave a guffaw. "In heart and spirit perhaps. Yet there are plenty of men lesser than she. My father admired her greatly and he was the shrewdest, hardest judge of character I know." He refilled the cup with water; offered it to her. Elizabeth shook her head.

"Did not the perpetrators of the Gunpowder Treason intend for you to reign?" Craven said. "They must have believed you could be Queen of England."

"I would have been a Catholic puppet." Elizabeth shuddered. "Reign, yes. Rule, most certainly not."

"And in Bohemia?"

"Frederick was King," Elizabeth said. "I was his consort." She smiled at him. "You seek to upset the natural order of things, Lord Craven, by putting women so high."

"Craven!" The air stirred, the door of the chamber swung open and Frederick strode in, his cloak of red swirling about him. In contrast to Craven, austere and dark, he looked as gaudy as a court magician. Craven straightened, bowing. Elizabeth felt odd, bereft, as though some sort of link between them had been snapped too abruptly. Craven's attention was all on Frederick now. That was what it meant to rule, even if it was in name only. Frederick demanded and men obeyed.

"The lion rises!" Frederick was more animated than Elizabeth had seen him in months. Melancholy had lifted from his long, dark face. His eyes burned. Elizabeth realised that he was so wrapped up in the ceremony that he was still living it. He seemed barely to notice her presence let alone question what she was doing alone in the guardroom with his squire. He drew Charles Louis into the room too and threw an arm expansively about his heir's shoulders.

This is our triumph, his gesture said. *I will recapture our patrimony.*

"The lion rises!" Frederick repeated. "We will have victory! I will retake Heidelberg whilst the eagle falls." He clapped Charles Louis on the shoulder. "We all saw the visions in the mirror, did we not, my son? The pearl and the glass together prophesied for us as they did in times past."

A violent shiver racked Elizabeth. The mirror and the pearl had shown Frederick a war-torn future. She remembered the flames reflected in the water, turning it the colour of blood.

"The lion is the Swedish King's emblem," she said. It was also Frederick's heraldic device but she thought it much more likely that it would be Gustavus Adolphus whose fortunes would rise further whilst Frederick would lie where he had fallen, unwanted, ignored. He was no solider. He could not lead, let alone retake his capital.

She caught Craven's gaze and realised that he was thinking exactly the same thing as she. There was a warning in his eyes, though; Frederick was frowning, a petulant cast to his mouth.

"It was *my* emblem," he said, sounding like a spoilt child. "It was my lion we saw."

Craven was covering Elizabeth's tactlessness with words of congratulation.

"Splendid news, Your Majesty," he said smoothly. "Do you plan to raise an army to join the King of Sweden's forces immediately?"

"Not now!" Elizabeth said involuntarily. The room seemed cold of a sudden, a wind blowing through it, setting her shivering. Her hand strayed to her swollen belly. "The baby..." she said.

Frederick's face was a study in indecision. "Of course," he said, after a moment. "I must stay to see you safely delivered of the child, my dear." His kiss on her cheek was wet, clumsy. It felt as though his mind was already far away. "I will write to his Swedish Majesty and prepare the ground," he said. "There is much to plan."

The cold inside Elizabeth intensified. She tried to tell herself it was only the shock of their fortunes changing after so many impotent years, but it felt deeper and darker than that. She knew with a sharp certainty that Frederick should not go. It was wrong, dangerous. Although she had not seen the future, she felt as though she had. She felt as though she had looked into the mirror and seen into the heart of grief and loss, seen a landscape that was terrifyingly barren.

"The winter is no time for campaigning." Craven was watching her face. There was a frown between his brows. "Besides, there is much to do before we may leave. Troops to send for, supplies to arrange." He stopped, started again. "Your Majesty—"

Elizabeth realised that he was addressing her. The grip of the darkness released her so suddenly she almost gasped. It felt like a lifting of a curse; she was light-headed.

"We should get you back to the palace, madam," Craven said. "You must be tired."

"I am quite well, thank you, Lord Craven," Elizabeth snapped. She was angry with him. She had thought she had seen something different in him, yet here he was fawning over Frederick like every other courtier she had known. And for all his compliments to her earlier, he spoke to her now as though she was as fragile and inconsequential as any other woman.

Immediately his expression closed down. "Of course, Majesty."

"Frederick," Elizabeth said. "If I might take your arm…"

Frederick was impatient. Elizabeth could feel it in him, in the deliberation with which he slowed his steps to help her up the spiral stair, in the tension in the muscles of his arm beneath her hand. He wanted to be back at the Wassenaer Hof, writing letters, planning a conqueror's return to Germany. She held him back, with her pregnant belly and her woman's fears. He was solicitous of her, masking his irritation with concern, but she had known him too long to be fooled. War was coming and that was man's work.

Charles Louis trailed along behind them through the scented garden, scuffing his boots in the gravel, his expression sulky. He appeared to have caught none of his father's excitement. Elizabeth could hear Craven talking to him. Their voices were too low for her to hear the words, but soon Charles Louis' tone lifted into animation again. His quicksilver volatility was not easy to control and Elizabeth admired the way Craven had been able to distract him.

The Knights of the Rosy Cross had gone. The gardens were empty; a checkerboard of moon and shadow. Frederick was still talking, of the fall of the city of Leipzig to Gustavus Adolphus, of the destruction of his hated enemy the Spanish general Tilly, of the visions in the mirror, the lion rampant, the walls of Heidelberg rising again, of their future, suddenly so bright.

Elizabeth crushed her doubts and followed her husband into the Wassenaer Hof. The light enveloped them; for a second there was a hush and then Frederick's blazing enthusiasm seemed to flare like a contagion through the crowds of courtiers and everyone was talking at once, laughing, lit by feverish excitement even though they did not know why they were celebrating. It was then that the cold came back to her, like the turning of a dark tide, setting her shaking so that she had to clutch the high back of one of the chairs to steady herself. The wood dug into her fingers, scoring the skin.

Frederick had not noticed. He was too busy thrusting his

way through the crowd, turning to answer men's questions. It was Craven who was watching, Craven who gestured impatiently for some of her women to come forwards to help her.

"Lord Craven." Elizabeth put her hand on Craven's arm to halt him when he too would have hurried away.

"Madam?" She could not read his expression.

"You are an experienced soldier." Elizabeth spoke abruptly. "Watch over my husband for me. Keep him safe. He does not know how..." She stopped before she betrayed herself, betrayed Frederick, too far, biting back the words on her tongue.

He does not know how to fight.

"Majesty." Craven bowed, his expression still impassive.

"Thank you," Elizabeth said.

He took her hand in his, kissed it. It was a courtier's gesture, not that of a soldier. His touch was warm and very sure.

He released her, bowed again. She watched him stride away through the throng of people. He did not look back.

3

Holly was asleep when the call came through on her mobile. She had been working all day and most of the evening on pieces for her latest collection of engraved glass and she was exhausted. She had left her little mews studio and workshop at ten o'clock, had grabbed a quick sandwich and gone to bed.

She swam up from the depths of a dream, groping for the phone that lay on the bedside table. The bright light of the screen made her wince. Normally she switched it off overnight, but she must have forgotten. She and Guy had been quarrelling over her work again. He had stomped off to the spare room, slamming the door, making a theatrical performance of his annoyance. Usually, Holly would have lay awake and fretted that they were arguing again. Just now she was too damned tired to care.

The icon on the screen was her brother's picture. The

time was two seventeen in the morning. The phone rang on and on.

Frowning, Holly pressed the green button to answer. "Ben? What on earth are you doing calling at this time—"

"Aunt Holly?" The voice at the other end of the line was already talking, high-pitched and breaking with fear, the words lost between sobs and gulps. It was not Ben but his six-year-old daughter, Florence.

"Aunt Holly, please come! I don't know what to do. Daddy's disappeared and I'm on my own here. Please help me! I—"

"Flo!" Holly sat up, reaching for the light, her hand slipping in her haste as her niece's terror seeped into her consciousness and set her heart pounding. "Flo, wait! Tell me what's happened. Where's Daddy? Where are you?"

"I'm at the mill." Florence was crying. "Daddy's been gone for hours and I don't know where he is! Aunt Holly, I'm scared! Please come—" The line crackled, the words breaking up.

"Flo!" Holly said again, urgently. "Flo—" But there was nothing other than the rustle and hiss of the line and then a long, empty silence.

"Are you mad?"

Guy had emerged from the spare room two minutes previously wearing only his crumpled boxer shorts, bleary-eyed, his hair standing on end in bad-tempered spikes.

"You can't shoot off to Wiltshire at this time of night," he said. "What a bloody stupid idea."

"It's Oxfordshire," Holly said automatically. She checked the clock, pulling on her boots at the same time. The zip stuck. She wrenched it hard. Two twenty-seven. She had already wasted ten minutes.

She had rung back repeatedly but there had been no reply.

The mill house, Ben and Natasha's holiday cottage, did not have a landline and the mobile reception had always been patchy. You had to be standing in exactly the right place to get a signal.

"Have you tried Tasha's mobile?" Guy asked.

"She's working abroad somewhere." Ben had told her but Holly couldn't remember exactly where. "I left her a message." Tasha had a high-powered job with a TV travel show and was frequently away.

"Ben's probably turned up again by now." Guy sat down next to her on the bed, putting what she supposed was meant to be a reassuring hand on her arm. "Look, Hol, don't panic. I mean maybe the kid got it wrong—"

"Her name's Florence," Holly said tightly. It irritated the hell out of her that Guy seldom remembered any of her family's or friends' names, mostly because he didn't try. "She sounded terrified," she said. "What do you want me to do?" She swung around fiercely on him. "Leave her there alone?"

"Like I said, Ben will have turned up by now." Guy smothered a yawn. "He probably crept out to meet up with some tart, thinking the kid was asleep and wouldn't notice. I know that's what I'd be doing if I was married to that hard-faced bitch."

"I daresay," Holly said, not troubling to hide the edge in her voice. "But Ben's not like you. He—" She stopped. "Ben would never leave Flo on her own," she said.

She stood up. The terrified pounding of her heart had settled to an anxious flutter now, but urgency still beat through her. Two thirty. It would take her an hour and a half to get to Ashdown if there was no traffic. An hour and a half when Flo would be alone and fearful. The terror Holly had felt earlier tightened in her gut. Where the hell was Ben? And why had he not taken his phone with him wherever he had gone? Why leave it in the house?

She racked her brains to remember their last phone conversation. He'd told her that he and Florence were heading to the mill for a long weekend. He'd taken a few days off from his surgery in Bristol. It was the early May Bank Holiday.

"I'm doing some family history research," he'd said, and Holly had laughed, thinking he must be joking, because history of the family or any other sort had never remotely interested her brother before.

She was wasting time.

"Have you seen my car keys?" she asked.

"No." Guy followed her into the living room, blinking as she snapped on the main light and flooded the space with brightness.

"Jesus," he said irritably. "Now I'm wide awake. You're determined to ruin my night."

"I thought," Holly said, "that you might come with me."

The genuine surprise on his face told her everything she needed to know.

"Why go at all?" Guy said gruffly, turning away. "I still don't get it. Just call the police, or a neighbour to go over and check it out. Isn't there some old friend of yours who lives near there? Fiona? Freda?"

"Fran," Holly said. She grabbed her keys off the table. "Fran and Iain are away for a couple of days," she said. "And the reason I'm going—" she stalked up to him, "is because my six-year-old niece is alone and terrified and she called me for help. Do you get it now? She's a child. She's frightened. And you're suggesting I go back to bed and forget about it?"

She picked up her bag, checking for her purse, phone and tablet. The rattle of the keys had brought Bonnie, her Labrador retriever, in from her basket in the kitchen. She looked wide awake, feathery tail wagging.

"No, Bon Bon," Holly said. "You're staying—" She stopped; looked at Guy. He'd forget to feed her, walk her. And anyway, it was comforting to have Bonnie with her. She grabbed Bonnie's food from the kitchen cupboard and looped her lead over her arm.

"Right," she said. "Let's go." In the doorway she paused. "Shall I call you when I know what's happened?" she asked Guy.

He was already disappearing into the bedroom, reclaiming the space she had left. "Oh, sure," he said, and Holly knew she would not.

Holly rang Ben's number every couple of minutes but there was never any reply, only the repeated click of the voice-mail telling her that Ben was unavailable and that she should leave a message. Eventually that stopped too. There was no return call from Tasha either. Holly wondered about calling her grandparents in Oxford. They were much closer to Ash-down Mill and to Florence than she was, though the car was eating up the miles of empty road. The mesmerising slide of the streetlights was left behind and there was nothing but darkness about her now as she drove steadily west.

In the end she decided not to call Hester and John. She didn't want to give either of them a heart attack, especially when there might be no reason to worry. Even though she was furious with Guy, she knew he might be right. Ben could have returned by now and Florence might be fast asleep again and, with the adaptability of a child, have forgotten that she had even called for help.

Holly had not wanted to call the police for lots of reasons ranging from the practical—that it could be a false alarm—to the less morally justifiable one of not wanting to cause problems for her brother. She and Ben had always protected each other, drawing closer than close after their parents had been killed in a car crash when Holly was eleven and Ben thirteen. They had looked out for each other with a fierce loyalty that had remained fundamentally unchanged over the years. Their understanding of each other was relaxed and easy these days, but just as close, just as deep. Or so Holly had thought before this had happened, leaving her wondering what the hell her brother was up to.

She pushed away the unwelcome suspicion that there might be things about Ben that she neither knew nor understood. Guy had planted the seed of doubt, but she crushed it angrily; she did know that Ben and Tasha were going through a bad patch but she could not imagine Ben being unfaithful. He simply wasn't the type. Even less could she imagine him neglecting his child. There had to be some other reason for his disappearance, if he had actually vanished.

But there was Florence, who was only six, and she had been alone and terrified. So it was an easy decision in the end. Holly had called the local police, keeping her explanation as short and factual as possible, sounding far calmer than she had felt. If anything happened to Florence and she had not done her best to help, she would have failed Ben as well as her niece.

The sign for Hungerford flashed past, surprising her. She was at the turn already. It was twelve minutes to four. Ahead of her the sky was inky dark, but in her rear-view mirror she thought she could see the first faint light of a spring dawn. Perhaps, though, that was wishful thinking. The truth was that she didn't feel comfortable in the countryside. She was a city girl through and through, growing up first in Manchester and then in Oxford after her parents had died, moving to London to go to art college and staying there ever since.

London was a good place for her glass-engraving business. She had a little gallery and shop in the mews adjoining the flat, and a sizeable clientele.

At the motorway roundabout she turned right towards Wantage then left for Lambourn. She knew the route quite well, but the road looked deceptively different when the only detail she could see was picked out in her headlights. There were curves and turns and shadowed hollows she did not recognise. She was heading deep into the countryside now. A few isolated cottages flashed past, shuttered and dark. She took the right turn for Lambourn and plunged down into the valley, the car's lights illuminating the white-painted wooden palings of the racehorse gallops that ran beside the road. The little town was silent as she wove her way through the narrow streets. As the stables and houses fell away and the fields rolled back in, Holly had the same feeling she always had on approaching Ashdown; a sense of expectancy she had never quite understood, a feeling of falling back through time as the dark road opened up before her and the hills swept away to her right, bleak and empty, crowned with a weathercock.

She and Ben had raced up to the top of Weathercock Hill as children, throwing themselves down panting in the springy grass at the top, staring up at the weathervane as it pierced the blue of the sky high above. The whole place had felt enchanted.

Ben. Her chest tightened again with anxiety. She was almost there. What would she find?

The lights picked out a huge advertising hoarding by the side of the road. The words flashed past before she could make out more than the first few:

"Ashdown Park, a select development of historic building conversions..."

Trees pressed close now to the left, rank upon rank of them

like an army in battle order. There was a moment when the endless wood fell back and through the gap in the trees Holly thought she saw a gleam of white; a house standing tall and four-square with the moonlight reflecting off the glass in the cupola and silvering the ball on the roof. A moment later and the vision had gone. The woods closed ranks, thick and forbidding, swallowing the house in darkness.

The left turn took her by surprise and she almost missed it even though she had come this way so many times before. She bumped along the single-track road, past a bus stop standing beside the remains of the crumbling estate wall. The old coach yard was off to the left; it seemed that this was where the majority of the building work was taking place, behind the high brick-and-sarsen wall. Even in the dark Holly could see the grass verge churned up by heavy machinery and the crouching shadow of a mechanical digger. There was another sign here, a discreet one in cream with green lettering, giving the name of the developers and directing all deliveries back to the site office on the main road.

The lane turned left again, running behind the village now, climbing towards the top of the hill. A driveway on the right, a white-painted gatepost flaking to wood beneath and a five-barred gate wedged open by the grasses and dandelions growing through it.

Ashdown Mill.

She stopped on the gravel circle in front of the watermill and turned off the engine. Bonnie gave a little, excited bark. Holly could hear the thud of her tail as the dog waited impatiently to jump out of the back. There were two other cars on the gravel, a small saloon car and Ben's four-by-four. The exhaustion and relief hit Holly simultaneously. Her shoulders ached with tension. If Ben was here and it had all been a big misunderstanding she would kill him.

She opened her door and slid out, her legs stiff, an ache low in her back. Outside the car the air had a predawn chill to it. The daylight was growing slowly, trickling through the trees and washing away the moon.

Bonnie was running around with her nose to the ground, released from the captivity of the car, a bounce in her step. She chased around the side of the whitewashed mill and disappeared from view. Holly slammed the car door and hurried after her, pushing open the little gate in the picket fence and running up the uneven stone path to the door, calling for Bonnie as she went.

All the lights were on inside the mill. The door opened before she reached it.

"Ben!" she burst out. "What the hell—"

"Miss Ansell?" A uniformed policewoman stood there. "I'm PC Marilyn Caldwell. We spoke earlier." She had kind eyes in a pale face pinched with tiredness, and there was something in her voice that warned Holly of bad news. Her heart started to thump erratically again. A headache gripped her temples.

She noticed that one of the door panels was splintered and broken.

"We had to break it to get in." There was a note of apology in PC Caldwell's voice. "The handle is too high for Florence to reach."

"Yes." Holly remembered that the door had a heavy, old-fashioned iron latch. So Ben had not been there when the police had arrived and there was no sign of him now. Her apprehension was edged with something deeper and more visceral now.

She fought back the terror; breathed deeply.

"Is Florence OK?"

"She's fine." Marilyn Caldwell laid a reassuring hand

on Holly's arm. She shifted a little so that Holly could see through into the mill's long living room. Florence was sitting on the sofa next to another female police officer. They were reading together, although Florence's eyes were droopy with tiredness and puffy with her earlier tears.

Holly's heart turned over to see her. She took an involuntary step forwards. "Can I go to her, please—"

"Just a moment." The note in PC Caldwell's voice stopped her. "I'm afraid we haven't found your brother, Miss Ansell." She was looking at Holly with forensic detachment now. "We've searched the house and the woods in the close vicinity, also all the roads nearby. There's no sign."

Holly was taken aback. Fear fluttered beneath her breastbone again. This was not right.

"Is that Dr Ansell's car outside?" PC Caldwell asked.

"Yes." Holly rubbed her tired eyes. "He can't have driven anywhere."

"Perhaps a friend came to pick him up," PC Caldwell suggested. "Or he walked to meet someone."

"In the middle of the night?" Holly said. "Without his phone?"

PC Caldwell's expression hardened. "It's hardly unknown, Miss Ansell. I imagine he thought Florence was asleep and slipped out. Perhaps he's lost track of the time."

"That would be ridiculously irresponsible." Holly felt furious and tried to rein herself in. She was tired, worried. She had driven a long way. She needed to calm down. Evidently PC Caldwell thought so too.

"We fully expect Dr Ansell to turn up in the morning," she said coldly. "When he does, please could you let us know? We'd like to have a word."

"You'll have to stand in line," Holly said. Then: "I'm sorry. Yes, of course. But…" Doubt and fear stirred within her again.

The emotions were nebulous but strong. Her instinct told her that Ben had not simply walked out.

"He left his phone," she said. "And all his stuff's scattered about. It doesn't look as though he planned to go out."

PC Caldwell was already signalling discreetly to her colleague that it was time to leave. She seemed completely uninterested.

"We've traced Mrs Ansell," she said. "She's on her way back from Spain but might not make it until tomorrow night. Apparently she's been," she checked her notepad, "helicopter skiing in the Pyrenees?" She sounded doubtful.

"Very probably," Holly said dryly. "Tasha works for a travel show—*Extreme Pleasures*?"

"Oh, yes!" Marilyn Caldwell's face broke into a smile. "Wow! Natasha Ansell. Of course! How exciting. Well—" She stopped, realising that the situation did not really merit celebrity chit-chat. "We'll be back tomorrow," she said. She turned on an afterthought. "Do you know what your brother was doing here, Miss Ansell?"

"It's his holiday cottage," Holly said. "We co-own it." She rubbed her eyes again, feeling the grittiness of them. Suddenly she was so tired she wanted to sleep where she was standing. "He was down here with Flo whilst Tasha was away working," she said. "He said he was doing some research. Family history. It's quiet here. A good place to think."

PC Caldwell nodded. "Right," she said. Holly could see her wondering how on earth someone as glamorous as Tasha could be mixed up in a messy situation like this with a man whose idea of fun was family history research.

"Well," the policewoman said. "We'll call back to chat to Mrs Ansell tomorrow."

I bet you will, Holly thought.

She felt utterly furious, livid with PC Caldwell for being

more interested in Tasha's fame than in Ben's disappearance, angry that Tasha hadn't even bothered to ring her to make sure it was OK for her to look after Flo until she got back, and most annoyed of all with Ben for vanishing without a word. The anger helped her, because behind it the fear still lurked, the sense that something was wrong and out of kilter, that Ben would never voluntarily disappear leaving his daughter alone.

Bonnie, picking up on Holly's mood, made a soft whickering noise and Holly saw Florence look up from the storybook. Her niece's eyes lit up to see them and she scrambled from the sofa.

"Aunt Holly!" Florence rushed towards her, arms outstretched. "You came!" Holly scooped her up automatically, feeling the softness of Florence's cheek pressed against hers, inhaling the scent of soap and shampoo. Florence clung like a limpet, her hot tears scalding Holly's neck. Holly could feel her niece's fear and desolation and her heart ached for her. Security was such a fragile thing when you were a child. She understood that better than most.

"Hello, Flo," she said gently. "Of course I came. I'll always come when you call me. You know that."

"Where's Daddy?" Florence was wailing. "Why has he gone away?"

"I don't know," Holly said, hugging her tighter. "He'll be back soon. I'm sure of it." She wished she were.

Later, when Florence had finally fallen into an exhausted sleep, Holly carried her niece upstairs in the pale light of the May dawn and put her gently on the big double bed in the main bedroom with her toy rabbit cuddled up in her arms. Then Holly went over to the window seat and leaning her head back against the panelled wall, closed her eyes for a moment.

Although as children she and Ben had shared the smaller bedroom next door, this was the room she had been drawn to every time. She loved the way the light poured in from the high windows.

So early, the room was still full of morning shadow. Ben's stuff was scattered all around; a shirt discarded over the arm of the chair, his watch on the chest of drawers, the bed half-made. It looked as though he had just stepped out for a second and would be back at any moment and that disturbed Holly more than it reassured her. This was all so out of character.

Nostalgia and a feeling almost like grief caught her sharply in her chest. She remembered how, as children, she and Ben would imagine the bed as a flying carpet taking them to faraway lands. They had told each other stories more spectacular, adventurous and exciting than any they had read in books. It had been magical. There had even been a little compartment hidden beneath the cushion on the window seat where they would leave each other secret messages...

The breath stopped in her throat. Softly, so as not to wake Florence, Holly slipped off the seat and lifted the cushion up. The little brass handle she remembered was still there. She pulled. Nothing happened. The box lid seemed wedged shut. She tugged a little harder.

The wood lifted with a scrape that she was afraid for a moment would wake Florence, but the child did not stir. Holly knelt down and peered inside.

There was nothing there except for a receipt for some dry-cleaning, a dead spider and a misshapen yellow pebble.

Holly felt an absurd sense of disappointment and loss. What had she imagined—that Ben would have left her a secret message to explain where he had gone? No matter how wrong it felt to her that he had simply vanished into thin air, she had to believe that the police were correct. Come morning Ben would walk in full of anxiety for Flo and apologies and relief, explaining... But here Holly's imagination failed her. She could not think of a single reason why he would do what he had done.

Eventually, when she felt calm enough, she went and curled up next to Florence on the big double bed. She didn't sleep but lay listening to Florence's breathing and felt a little bit comforted. After a while she fell into an uneasy doze, Bonnie resting across her feet.

She was woken some time later by an insistent ringing sound. For a moment she felt happy before the memory of what had happened rushed in, swamping her consciousness. She stumbled from the bed and down the stairs, making a grab for her bag and the phone, wondering if it was Guy calling to see what had happened.

But it wasn't her mobile that was ringing. She found Ben's phone halfway down the side of the sofa and pressed the button to answer the call.

"Dr Ansell?" It was a voice she didn't recognise, male, slightly accented, sounding pleasant and businesslike. "This is Espen Shurmer. My apologies for calling you so early but I wanted to catch you to confirm our meeting on Friday—"

"This isn't Ben," Holly said quickly. "I'm his sister."

There was a pause at the other end. "My apologies again." The man sounded faintly amused. "If you would be so good as to pass me over to Dr Ansell."

"I'm sorry," Holly said. "He's not here. I..." She could feel herself stuttering, still half-asleep. She wasn't sure why she had answered the call and now she didn't know what to say. "I'm afraid he's disappeared," she blurted out.

This time the silence at the other end of the line was more

prolonged. Just when she thought Espen Shurmer had hung up, and was feeling grateful for it, he spoke again.

"Disappeared? As in you do not know where he is?" He sounded genuinely interested.

"Yes," Holly said. "Last night." She was not sure why she was telling this man so much when he was probably no more than a business acquaintance of Ben's. "So I'm afraid I don't know if he'll be able to make your meeting... I mean, if he comes back I'll tell him, but I can't guarantee he'll be there..." She let her voice trail away, feeling an absolute fool.

"Miss Ansell," the man at the other end said, "forgive me for not introducing myself properly. My name is Espen Shurmer and I am a collector of seventeenth-century artefacts, paintings, glass, jewellery..." He paused. "I had arranged to meet your brother on Friday night at 7.30pm after a private view at the Ashmolean Museum in Oxford. He contacted me a couple of weeks ago to request the meeting."

"Oh." Holly was at a loss. "Well, I'm sorry I can't be of more help, Mr Shurmer, but I have no idea what Ben wanted to talk to you about. Actually I'm very surprised he got in touch. Art isn't really his thing..." She stopped again, realising she was still babbling even if what she was saying was true. Ben had zero interest in the arts. He had always supported her engraving career and had even bought a couple of her glass paperweights for his surgery, but she had known it had only been because she had made them herself. She had loved him for it but she was under no illusions about his interest in culture.

"I know what it was that your brother wished to discuss, Miss Ansell," Espen Shurmer said. "He wanted some information on a certain pearl, a legendary stone of great worth."

Holly sat down abruptly. "A...*pearl*?" She said. She thought she had misheard. "As in a piece of jewellery? Are you sure?

I mean..." It was possible that Ben might have been buying a gift for Natasha, but she was certain he would have bought a modern piece rather than approaching an antiques collector. Such an idea would never even have crossed his mind.

"I think we should meet to discuss this," the man said, after a moment. "It is most important. If your brother is unable to keep the appointment, would you be able to come in his place, Miss Ansell? I should be extremely grateful."

Holly hadn't even thought about what would happen beyond the next few hours, let alone on Friday. "I don't think so," she said. "I'm sorry, Mr Shurmer, but Ben will probably be back by then and anyway, this is nothing to do with me."

"Seven thirty at the Ashmolean Museum in Oxford," Shurmer said, cutting in so smoothly she barely noticed the interruption. "I should be greatly honoured if you choose to be there, Miss Ansell," he added with old-fashioned courtesy.

The line clicked as the call went dead.

Holly put the phone down slowly, found her bag and grabbed her tablet. She typed in the name Espen Shurmer and the time, the date and the name of the Ashmolean Museum. The information came up at once—a lecture and private view of portraits and artefacts from the court in exile of Elizabeth, the Winter Queen, sister of King Charles I, which preceded a major new exhibition starting at the end of May. Espen Shurmer, she read, was a Dutch collector of seventeenth-century painting and glass, and he had donated a number of items to the museum.

She felt a pang of regret as she closed the tablet. She would have loved to see an exhibition of seventeenth-century artefacts and talk to a renowned expert. But there would be no need. Ben would be back soon, she was sure of it. She had to be sure because there was Flo to console and there were her own fears to fight. The longer Ben was absent, the more those shadows grew like monsters, the fear that Ben would never come back and she would be alone again, totally alone this time, like they had been after their parents had died, only so much worse...

She fought back the panic. It was important to keep busy. She needed to make breakfast for Flo, then they could both take Bonnie for a walk, and by then Ben would be home...

But Ben had not come back by lunchtime when Holly drove down to the deli to fetch sandwiches, nor was he back by three when they came back from another walk in the woods with Bonnie. All day Holly had felt her anxiety rising and squashed it down relentlessly, but it grew inside her, filling the empty spaces, filling her mind so she found it almost impossible to concentrate on anything. When she heard a car coming up the track towards the mill she had to restrain herself from running outside to see if it was Ben.

"It's Mummy!" Flo had none of Holly's reticence and had bounded up from the painting they had been doing to rush out of the door, Bonnie at her heels. Holly followed them more slowly. She and her sister-in-law had always had a brittle relationship. Ben had been a link between them, but now he was missing, and Holly felt suddenly wary.

Tasha, looking as elegant as though she was stepping onto the catwalk, slammed the door of her little red sports car and came hurrying across the gravel on her vertiginously high heels.

"What the fuck is all this about?" she demanded without preamble, meeting Holly by the gate. "I've had to come all the way back from Spain! Where is he, the stupid bastard?"

Holly blinked. Tasha seemed to notice Flo for the first time and bent down to pick her up. "Hello, darling." She held Flo and her sticky painting fingers a little bit away from her. "Don't worry, sweetie, I'm here now." She gave Bonnie a vertical pat, designed as much to push her away as greet her. Tasha was not a pet person.

"Let's go inside," Holly said.

"I don't want to stay," Tasha said, taking off her sunglasses and fixing Holly with her big blue eyes. "I'm going home to Bristol. I'm not hanging around here waiting for Ben to turn up when he feels like it. Have you got Flo's bag?"

"It's not packed," Holly said coldly, "since you didn't let me know you were coming." She was too exhausted for tact. She and Tasha had never been close; she had tried to like her sister-in-law but it had proved very difficult.

"Sorry." To Holly's surprise Tasha seemed to deflate all of a sudden like a pricked balloon. "I really do appreciate you coming down, Holly, and looking after Flo. But I'm just so bloody *angry*! It's just not on for Ben simply to walk out on all his commitments—"

"Wait." Holly put a hand on Tasha's arm. "What do you mean? Surely you don't think he's just upped and gone?"

"That's exactly what I think," Tasha said fiercely, scrubbing at her eyes. She pushed the dark glasses firmly back down on her nose. "He was spending all his spare time down here. He's probably got another woman, for all I know."

"He was doing family history research," Holly protested.

Her sister-in-law gave a look of such searing scorn that she blushed.

"Yeah, and I'm Marilyn Monroe," Tasha said.

"I don't believe it!" Holly said. She was so outraged she forgot that Flo was listening, taking it all in with her blue eyes wide, so like her mother's. "Hell, Tasha, you *know* Ben would never do a thing like that! He'd certainly never leave Flo alone! And besides, where would he go? He'd never disappear without telling anyone!"

"You mean you think he'd never vanish without telling

you," Tasha said, a hint of pity in her voice now that set Holly's teeth on edge. "Oh, Holly…" She shook her head. "I know you think the two of you are really close but you don't know Ben that well. Trust me." She took Flo's hand. "Come on, sweetie, let's go and get your stuff."

Holly watched them walk up the path together and into the mill. Desolation swamped her, along with a terrible fear that her sister-in-law might be right. Secretly she had always believed she knew Ben better than anyone, even his wife. Had Ben hidden the truth of deeper fissures in his marriage? Holly could not believe it.

The sun, sparkling on the millpond, dazzled her eyes. Suddenly she felt close to tears. It felt as though she was trapped in a world where nothing was what it seemed and she was the only one trying to keep a tenuous faith. Beside her, Bonnie stood tense, her head tilted to one side, picking up on her mood once again.

"Come on, Bon Bon," Holly said, suddenly fierce. "I know this isn't right. I don't care what everyone else says."

Back in the mill she could hear Tasha moving about upstairs. The floorboards creaked and then Tasha and Flo appeared at the top of the stairs, Flo looking sulky and bumping her suitcase on each step. Tasha had Ben's holdall in one hand and a cross expression.

"I'm sure he'll turn up, Holly," she said as she reached the bottom step. "Don't worry."

"I know there's something wrong," Holly said doggedly.

"Look." Tasha put the bag down with a thump. "Don't think I don't understand. I do. You've always been a little bit clingy where Ben was concerned, haven't you?" Then, before Holly could open her mouth to give her a blistering put-down: "Oh, I understand why. I know about losing your parents and all that, and I don't mind. Really." She gave Holly a little, patronising smile as though she had given Ben full permission to pander to his neurotic sister's neediness. "But this has all happened before, hasn't it? There was that time when you thought Ben had disappeared and he'd simply gone off for a weekend with his mates."

Holly's face flamed. "That was years ago and it was totally different!"

Tasha shrugged. "Whatever. The truth is you have a rather idealistic view of your big brother and you worry about him rather a lot. My advice would be to calm down. Like I say, he'll turn up in a few days." She glanced around the living room. "Send on anything I've missed, won't you," she said.

Holly took a deep breath and counted to ten. Then she surreptitiously slid Ben's phone into her back pocket.

"Of course I will," she said.

4

The mill was as quiet as a sepulchre after Tasha and Flo had gone. The silence was so loud it hurt Holly's ears. It was three thirty and she felt unbearably weary, but restless at the same time. Time felt irrelevant, suspended. She found she was waiting for her phone to ring or for a knock at the door, or for the sound of a voice, something, anything, that might herald Ben's return.

She took her phone and went outside to try to get a better signal. She rang Guy's mobile number but there was no reply. She could not get him on their landline either. He had not called her to find out what had happened or make sure she was OK. The knowledge that he didn't care seemed unable to hurt her. Nothing penetrated the numbness and isolation that wrapped around her like a shroud.

She thought about ringing her grandparents but she didn't want to worry them about nothing. She knew that if Ben had been with them he would have been in touch long before now. It was such a strange, frustrating, suspended place in which to find herself, one minute eaten up by worry, the next so furious with her brother she wanted to scream at him. In the end, since no one else seemed to be doing anything she thought the best thing she could do would be to go out and search the woods herself. She needed to be out in the fresh air again. She needed to be active. Claustrophobia pressed down on her. She felt sick. She pulled on her thin fleece jacket and went out, leaving Bonnie, who seemed disinclined for yet another walk, snoring on the sofa.

It was a bright day with a clear blue sky. Holly didn't really know where to start so she set off down the track to the village, turning right over the bridge, past a bus stop where a girl stood, her long blonde hair blowing in the wind. She looked to be about nineteen, tall, too thin, wrapped in a long stripy scarf, smoking a cigarette and looking bored. She turned her head briefly as Holly walked past and nodded a hello, then dropped the cigarette and ground it out beneath her shoe.

The crumbling estate wall rose on Holly's left and behind it was the old coach yard. This was where the majority of the building work was taking place, and Holly could hear the whine and bleep of a mechanical digger.

A hundred yards further on was the car park and courtyard where Fran had her deli café and tea room. A dozen cars were parked in the cobbled yard and an ice cream sign swung by the shop door. Holly thought about dropping in but then she remembered Fran wasn't back until the morning. She felt odd and disoriented. She had already been into the deli once that day, only a few hours ago, and yet it felt like it had happened weeks ago. She was so tired.

There was a small flyer on the telegraph pole by the side of the road. A dog named Lucky had gone missing and his owners were offering a reward for his safe return. Looking at the sad little furry face, Holly thought she could make up posters of Ben and stick them up about the place. It might jog the memories of people who could have seen him out and about in the woods. After all, he could have gone out for some fresh air and felt ill, or fallen over and knocked himself unconscious, or any number of other accidents. He could have a broken ankle and be unable to hop home. She knew the police had said they had searched the woods in the close vicinity but she suspected it had been a cursory search at best.

Although the sun was warm she felt cold. It took her aback to find the place so busy with bank holiday tourists. For some reason she had expected it to be quiet. She strolled along the path towards the wood, following several groups of visitors, families with children dragging their heels, couples hand in hand. Holly saw them all as though she was looking through one of her pieces of engraved glass, clear but slightly distorted. They ambled with no intent, admiring the view over the Downs where the weathercock pierced the sky and the dreamy curve of the hills broadened to fill the horizon. Holly felt shockingly lonely.

Her phone rang.

"Hol?" It was Guy. He sounded hung-over. "What's going on? Why the seven thousand calls? What gives?"

"Ben's still missing," Holly said bluntly. "He hasn't come back since last night."

"What?" Guy sounded puzzled, affronted even. "Well, where is he?"

"I don't know," Holly said. "That's the point. No one knows. Tasha says—" She stopped abruptly but it was too late.

"He's got another woman," Guy finished. There was glee in his tone. "Good for him."

"I'm sure she's wrong," Holly said.

Guy ignored that. "Are you heading back then?" he said. "If Tasha's been to pick up the kid—"

"No," Holly said. "I'm staying here until Ben turns up."

There was a silence. "What?" Guy said. "Why on earth would you want to hang around?"

"In case something's happened to him," Holly said. "I wondered if you wanted to come down?" She could hear the plea in her voice and hated herself for it. Whatever Tasha had said, she wasn't normally so needy, but today it felt as though all her defences had been stripped away. It wasn't that she particularly wanted Guy, she realised, just company and comfort. She wanted to share the burden of Ben's disappearance. It was horrible feeling so alone.

She thought she heard Guy swear. "Hol," he said, "you're overreacting. Your brother's not a child. He can take care of himself. For God's sake come back—"

"I'm worried," Holly said flatly. "I know something isn't right."

This time Guy definitely did swear. "For fuck's sake, Holly! You're not his keeper!"

"Forget it," Holly said swiftly. "Forget I asked you to come down. And don't expect me back either." She snapped the phone shut, cutting off Guy's spluttering.

The brief flash of anger had lifted her spirits but they fell again immediately. She felt lost as soon as she stepped into the woods. The canopy of trees closed overhead, shutting her into green darkness. In all directions paths veered off and criss-crossed, losing themselves. She went two hundred yards along one and stopped, realising that she hadn't even put her walking boots on. She felt tears of frustration and anger well up in her throat. She made her way back down to the road feeling shaky and upset.

What was she trying to do? She was one person trying to prove a point in the face of what seemed like massive indifference. No one else seemed to think that there was anything wrong and it was frightening to be wavering on the edge of believing it herself, thinking she was mad or deluded.

A wedding had just finished at the church by the little stone bridge. As the clock on the tower struck quarter to four, the church door opened and the wedding party spilled out into the churchyard, laughing and talking. Holly paused by the gate. A sudden breeze was plastering the bride's veil against her lipstick and snatching at the guests' coats like a demanding child. It picked up the confetti and whirled it around Holly's head like blossom, and it tugged the bouquet from the bride's hands, bowling it along the ground to land at Holly's feet.

Holly bent slowly to pick it up. It was a posy of pink rosebuds, scentless.

Suddenly the wedding guests were all around her and the bride had come hurrying down the flagstone path towards her, laughing.

"Thank you so much! I don't know what I'd have done for the photographs otherwise!"

Holly handed the bouquet over, smiling. Her face felt a little stiff, as though it would not bend in the right places. No one seemed to have noticed, though. They were all wrapped up in happiness. They didn't know how out of touch she felt, how cut off. They went back towards the church door, where the photographer tried to arrange them in the neat rows required for the official pictures. At the same time she was aware of a sharp pain lodged beneath her breastbone. She did not begrudge these people their happiness but it made her loneliness feel suddenly unbearably acute.

"Are you OK?"

Holly blinked. She was not the only onlooker. A man was standing to the side of the lychgate. Youngish, thirty-two or three—she was bad at guessing ages. She felt a flash of recognition, sharp and sure, as though she knew him, but as he came closer she realised that he was a stranger.

He was tall, dark and durable looking in a battered jacket, brown moleskin trousers and boots. His eyes were very dark, as dark as the hair that fell across his brow. An expensive-looking camera hung about his neck. Holly thought he was probably a tourist, out walking in the woods and attracted by the wedding as she had been. She forced a smile.

"I'm fine, thanks. I just stopped to watch."

He smiled back, but his dark gaze was keen. "If you're sure? You look a bit...shaken."

Behind them the group was rearranging itself for yet an-other photograph. Holly put her hands in the pockets of the fleece and turned away.

"Don't let me stop you taking your pictures—"

The man grinned, obviously recognising the brush-off. "The sun's in the wrong place. Besides, it's too organised for me. I like spontaneity."

Holly frowned a little. "Spontaneity. Yes. That's nice. Ex-cuse me..."

She had only gone twenty yards from him when she had to slow down because the tears were running down her face and dropping off her chin, and she couldn't see where she was going. She felt bewildered and acutely embarrassed. She stumbled a little on the path, heard a step behind her and felt his hand on her arm.

"Look, can I help—"

"No!" Holly turned and glared at him and his hand dropped to his side. He took a step back.

"Okay." His voice was quiet, oddly soothing. "Well... Take care—"

"Oh, God, I'm sorry." A shred of conventional manners

stirred in Holly and she scrubbed her hands across her face, wiping away the tears. "I really didn't mean to be rude—"

His lips twitched as though he was about to smile. He had a striking face, thin and brown, with high cheekbones and dark, watchful eyes beneath strongly marked brows. Holly found she wanted to go on looking at him.

"Please don't apologise," he said easily. "I'm the one making a nuisance of myself—"

Holly started to cry again. "Don't be so nice about it—"

"Look, this is silly. Why don't we go and get a cup of tea until you feel a bit better? There's a tea room just down the road, isn't there?"

"Yes, but—" Holly felt horribly vulnerable. She didn't want anyone to see her looking like this. But they were already at the courtyard and he was guiding her to one of the outside tables where she could sit in a corner, partially sheltered from view.

Holly sat down and watched as he went inside, to emerge a few minutes later, carrying two big blue and white striped mugs. The steam from them floated sideways. She wrapped her hands around hers and drank deeply. It was scalding hot, but comforting.

"Thank you so much," she said. "What do I owe you?"

"Don't worry about it." He raised an eyebrow. "In case you don't take tea with complete strangers, my name's Mark."

"Holly." She considered shaking hands and decided against it.

"Nice to meet you, Holly." Mark sat back in his chair. "So do you want to talk about it?"

"What?" She stared at him, confused for a moment. Her eyes were smarting slightly. "Oh, no, thank you."

"All right," Mark said equably.

They sat drinking their tea in silence. Holly appraised

him with an artist's eye; his face was hard lines of cheek and jaw, like a stylised angel... He turned his head and their eyes met and again she felt that jolt of recognition, exciting, dangerous. Normally she would have run a mile from such instant attraction but today she felt different. Everything felt different.

She nodded towards the camera.

"That's a nice piece of kit. Did you get any good shots today?"

Mark smiled. "Yes, thanks. There's plenty of potential around here. Are you interested in photography?"

"Yes, I like it. I take pictures and sometimes I'm lucky. That's different from being good, though."

Mark inclined his head. "So what do you do for a living?"

"I'm an engraver. Glass." Holly realised she didn't want to talk about herself. "What about you? Is photography your job?"

Mark grimaced. "Unfortunately not. I'm just an amateur. I used to work as a civil engineer, but I've done some travelling lately."

Holly drained her mug. "Where've you been?"

"I was working in Asia for a bit, Norway. My sister lives there, so I stayed for the winter, crewing her husband's fishing boat."

Holly looked at him in surprise. She had seen enough TV programmes to know that was no job for amateurs.

"Are you a good sailor then?"

"No." Mark smiled. "A very bad one. But I had to do something to pay my way." He stood up, a little abruptly and Holly sensed that with him too there were barriers he didn't want to cross.

"Are you ready to go? I'll walk you to your car."

"Oh." Holly realised he thought she was a tourist too. She

hesitated, suddenly aware of how weird she felt. Everything felt odd, distorted in her mind, not quite real.

"I'm staying near here," she said.

"I'll walk you back then."

Holly was not sure that she really wanted company. "There's no need—"

Mark slanted a smile down at her. She liked the lines that fanned out from his eyes when he smiled and the crease that ran down his cheek. She noticed these things about him quite objectively and yet at the same time not objectively at all.

"I daresay you'd rather be alone," he said, "but I'd rather know you were OK. Call me overprotective if you like..." He shrugged. "I could walk a few paces behind, if you prefer."

The breeze was strengthening now and the day cooling down into evening. They left the car park and the tourists behind, passing the tiny village green with its scatter of cottages and the little stream. After all the noise and bustle the silence sounded loud. They did not speak.

Whenever Mark drew a little ahead of her, Holly watched him move; the easy, economical movements of someone comfortable in their own skin. His gaze was abstracted now as it rested on the path ahead, his face a little distant in repose. There was a tight knot in Holly's stomach as she watched him. It felt a little like pain, but it was something different, hot and fierce, that curled inside her.

At the gate of the mill she stopped. Mark looked up and seemed to register for the first time where they were. He turned towards her, frowning.

"Are you staying here?"

"Yes," Holly said. "Would you like to come in?"

She felt his puzzlement, saw the slight narrowing of his eyes as they rested on her face. Much now depended on his interpretation of the invitation, and she had the feeling that

Mark had probably had plenty of practice in that. She shifted slightly, keeping her gaze fixed on his. He was so cool, so distant. She needed to bridge that gap. She needed him. The thought of him turning away now and leaving her was unbearable. She wondered if he could feel her desperation.

He took her hand. His fingers interlocked strongly with hers, and still she did not know the answer and felt quite faint with the need to know. She stepped over the threshold and gently tugged his hand; he followed.

There was a message from Fran on the mat. It said: "I've just got back. Call me."

Holly read it upside down, stepped over it and turned back to Mark. She could smell his skin, the faint scent of fresh air. He was cold to the touch. She pulled him inside, slammed the door and reached up to kiss him. After a second he responded and she felt sharp desire and such relief that she trembled. The loneliness, the fear, faded.

She kissed him again, driving out thought, losing herself in sensation, drawing back only so that she could lead him towards the stairs. She could feel his presence behind her, close as a whisper. She was still holding his hand. The late afternoon sun was streaming in at the big bedroom window, the line of the hills spread out before them. Mark was watching her face.

"Holly, what's this about?"

She felt his breath feather across her skin. She could see the shadow of his eyelashes, spiky against the hard line of his cheek. His lips brushed her jaw. Again she felt that fierce rush of desire. She turned her head and Mark's mouth was suddenly on hers again, one hand tangled in her hair, the other low on her back. Sensation flared. Mark's hand brushed the thin cotton of her shirt, his palm against her breast. He was still kissing her. Such urgency. She had never even imagined it could be like that and she was fiercely glad; glad she was not alone any more; glad she could forget for a little while. She pulled him down onto the bed beside her and lost herself in him.

There was a distant ringing sound in Holly's ears. She struggled awake to find the room full of daylight. Her body felt relaxed for the first time in days and her mind was as clear and sharp as a cut in a piece of glass. She could remember every detail of the night. They hadn't slept much. They hadn't talked at all.

She turned over. Mark lay beside her, curled on his side, sleeping peacefully. The lines of his face were softened. Something pierced Holly's detachment and made her breath catch in her throat. She looked at him for a moment, then got out of bed and tiptoed over to the wardrobe. She almost tripped over the clothes piled on the floor. Turning the key in the door she took out an old paisley robe of Ben's she had borrowed the last time she had come down.

Light was streaming into the long living room and her phone was full of messages. She ignored them. It was the doorbell that was ringing, on and on. Bonnie was agitated, waiting by the door, tail waving. All Holly could think was that if Ben had timed his arrival back now it would be difficult to work out which of them had the more explaining to do.

She opened the door and found Fran on the step, shivering inside her jacket. It was another sunny morning but they were standing in the shade of the building and the shadows were cold.

"Holly!" Fran's eyes were puzzled, her voice full of concern. "Thank goodness! I thought you'd disappeared too. Are you ill or something? I heard about Ben—"

"You already know?" Holly blinked in shock.

"The whole village knows," Fran said. "You can't keep secrets around here." She bit her lip. "Look, I'm sorry if I caused a problem for you but when I couldn't get you last night I called your grandparents. I thought perhaps you might have gone over to Oxford. Oh, and I rang Guy as well. What the hell happened there? He told me you had broken your engagement—"

Normally Holly could cope with Fran's ramblings but this morning her head hurt. "You rang Gran?" She felt a sick, swooping sensation in her chest. She could not imagine how Hester and John had felt to hear that Ben had vanished and that Fran couldn't get hold of Holly either. No wonder she had hundreds of messages on her phone. She was surprised they weren't there, hammering on the door.

Fran's gaze dropped to her note, still resting on the mat at the bottom of the steps. She frowned. "Didn't you see my message? We've been worried about you."

Holly drew her robe more closely about her throat. "I'm sorry. I'll ring Gran straight away and let her know I'm OK."

Fran was watching her as though she knew there was something wrong but could not quite work it out. "Are you feeling ill? Has it all been too much for you? I'm so, so sorry about Ben. Has there been no word? I just don't understand it. It's not like him."

There was a sound upstairs. Fran started to say something else but Holly spoke quickly.

"I'd better go and get dressed. I'm really sorry, Fran. I'm feeling a bit weird about it all to be honest. I'll come and see you later."

Fran huddled deeper in her jacket. "You poor thing! No wonder you haven't got up yet. Look, do you want me to come in and make you a cup of coffee? We could talk—"

There was another sound from upstairs, too loud to ignore. Fran frowned. "Holly, is somebody here already? What's going on?"

Holly shivered. "Sorry, Fran, it's not really convenient to talk right now."

"Has Ben come back?" Fran demanded.

"No," Holly said.

"Then did Guy come down after all? Because last night he said—"

"No," Holly said again.

She saw the moment that the penny dropped in Fran's mind, the widening of her eyes, the look of comical shock on her face. Fran clapped a hand to her mouth. Her gaze roved over Holly's tumbled hair, her bare feet. "Oh, Holly," she said, "What have you done— Oh my God, you haven't... Say you haven't. What's happened to you? You *never* do things like that!"

Holly caught her arm urgently. "I can't talk now. Please, Fran, it's a bit complicated."

Fran looked torn between stunned horror and concern. "Holly, you're in shock. I've read about this. When people go missing their relatives can suffer from something called suspended grief, not knowing whether someone is dead or not—"

"Thanks, Fran," Holly said. Despite herself she could feel a flicker of a smile starting and some sense of normality returning. Fran's monumental lack of tact had always been cheering rather than anything else. "I'll talk to you later," she said. "Really, I will. I've got things to sort out."

"I can imagine," Fran said dryly. Then she looked past Holly's shoulder. Holly saw her expression freeze before Fran rearranged her face into ultracasual indifference.

"Mark," she said brightly. "Hi. How are you?"

Holly spun around. Mark, fully dressed, was standing in the doorway. He nodded to Fran.

"Hi, Fran."

Holly felt her stomach dip as though she was on a roller coaster. The previous day she hadn't spared a single thought for who Mark was or what he was doing at Ashdown. Now, though, she realised that far from being a random tourist who would disappear in the morning, he must live there and would be going precisely nowhere. Her stomach tightened and panic fluttered in her throat.

"You've heard about Ben?" Fran had waited for Holly to speak and then, when she hadn't, had rushed in to fill the awkward silence as best she could.

"Just now," Mark said. His gaze was on Holly's face, dark and inscrutable. "What happened?"

"He's missing," Holly said. "He vanished a couple of nights ago." It felt ridiculous, surreal, to be standing here like this politely discussing her brother's disappearance when she had neglected to mention it before.

"Holly didn't tell you—" Fran began, then saw the expression on Holly's face and gulped. "Well, anyway, I'd better..." She waved her hands about in mute confusion. "I'll be at home later so give me a ring, Holly... Or call round. Whatever." She was edging away down the path as she spoke. "Take care."

She hurried off towards the gate and Holly went back inside. Mark stepped back to allow her to pass him. She could feel his gaze on her face and she felt the heat burn beneath her skin. Suddenly the paisley robe felt far too flimsy and she felt far too vulnerable.

"I'm sorry," she said quickly, before Mark had the chance to say anything and the situation became even more excruciating. "I should have told you, but..." She stopped. She had no excuses. She couldn't even connect with how she had felt the day before, how isolated, how desperate she had been not to be alone.

"That's OK," Mark said. His tone was level but she had an unnerving conviction that he was angry. "I knew you were upset, I just didn't realise—" He ran a hand through his hair. "I'm sorry to hear about Ben," he added. "Are the police looking for him?"

"No," Holly said. "They think he's just gone off somewhere and that he'll turn up." Her eyes were burning and it felt as though something sharp was wedged in her throat. She could not believe how right everything had felt whilst she had been with Mark and how wrong it all felt again now. That was the trouble with forgetting, she thought. It didn't last long before everything crowded back in worse than before. She should have realised; realised she couldn't lose herself, realised she couldn't escape her fears about Ben.

"I wouldn't want you to think…" She stopped. Mark waited. She felt a spurt of anger that he wasn't making it easy for her.

"I didn't mean to use you," she said. "I don't usually do this sort of thing."

Mark shrugged. "I heard what Fran said." He picked up his jacket off the back of the sofa. "Just for the record, neither do I. Except that we both did."

There was another sharp silence then Mark sighed.

"I don't want to leave you if you're upset," he said. "Holly, please, talk to me."

The look in his eyes was gentle and it made Holly feel more angry. She remembered his tenderness the previous night and how she had driven it out with need. She didn't want it now either. She couldn't deal with it.

"I'm fine," she said. She drew the robe tight about her throat. "Thanks."

"Right," Mark said. He reached for the latch pausing for a second as he was about to open the door. "It might help to know," he said, "who you are…"

"Oh!" Holly jumped, the colour flooding her face again. "Holly Ansell. Ben's sister."

"And who is Guy?"

Holly hesitated a second. "Guy is…was…my fiancé."

She saw Mark's expression harden. "Okay. I get it. Well, I'll go then."

Holly didn't try to stop him. She heard the door slam behind him and felt the silence of the house press in on her. She fumbled on the dresser for her phone. She needed to ring her grandmother. Guilt swamped her. Everything else could wait. She didn't need to think about it now.

She pressed the button to call her grandparents' number. Hester answered on the second ring.

"Gran," Holly said. "I'm so sorry not to have called before—" And submitted quietly to her grandmother's scolding, hearing the fear beneath her words of reproach.

5

The palace was in chaos. Light spilled across the cobbles, torches flared, men hurrying, women calling with an edge of panic to their voices. As William Craven rode through the arched gateway into the courtyard, Dr Rumph, the Queen's chief physician, loomed up out of the dark and caught his reins, causing the horse to shy. Cursing, Craven brought it under control and Rumph stepped back, his long face growing even longer.

"Your pardon." He spoke stiffly.

"It's no matter," Craven said. He jumped down and handed the reins over to a groom. It had been a long ride from Frederick's campaign lodgings at Hanau and he had letters for the Queen but what he wanted most was a meal and some hot water. Judging by the disquiet in Rumph's face, however, he seemed destined to have neither.

"What can I do for you, doctor?" he said.

"We have lost the Queen!" Rumph said.

For one shocking moment Craven thought Rumph meant that Elizabeth was dead. It would not be so surprising. The winter had been notably wet and mild, encouraging all manner of fevers, and the Queen had been taken with an ague that had confined her to her bed for several weeks. But then he realised what the doctor meant. The chaos, the men milling around, the air of panicked confusion...

"Her Majesty has disappeared?" he said.

"That is what I'm telling you," Rumph snapped.

"You have searched the palace?"

"Of course." Rumph fell into step beside him, his long black robe flapping agitatedly as he walked. "She was last seen in her chamber several hours ago. Her ladies say she was in a melancholy frame of mind. We were afraid..." He hesitated. No one would articulate it but they feared that the Queen, borne down by fear and loneliness whilst her husband was on campaign, might commit the heinous sin of taking her own life.

"Nonsense," Craven said. It was easy in such a febrile atmosphere to imagine the worst. Rumour spread panic like a contagion. Yet he knew that the Queen would never abandon her cause.

He had left The Hague with Frederick six weeks before and they had made slow progress towards a meeting with the Swedish King Gustavus Adolphus at Hochst. During that time Craven had taken a number of letters back and forth between the King and his wife. It had not taken him long to see which of them had the greater heart, spirit and stomach for the fight. Frederick would always be a broken reed. Elizabeth would always be the stronger.

"Have you searched the gardens?" he said.

"Yes." Rumph sounded offended to be asked so obvious a question.

"Stables? Outbuildings?"

Rumph's look said quite clearly what he thought of the idea of the Queen of Bohemia hiding in an outbuilding.

"Our Lord took refuge in a stable," Craven said mildly, and was rewarded with a glare.

"You mock the scriptures, my lord?"

"Of course not," Craven said. "What about the water tower? Have you looked there?"

There was a pause, a minute hesitation. Craven glanced at the physician. Rumph knew full well what ceremonies had been held in the water tower and disapproved of them. Or perhaps, Craven thought, he was superstitious, scared. Physicians sometimes were. Rumph would not like to think that the Queen would dabble in dangerous occult practices. If it came to it, Craven felt much the same himself, although for different reasons. He deplored the use of magic.

"The tower is locked," the physician said.

"But the Queen would have access to a key."

Silence.

"We have not looked there," Rumph admitted.

"Then let us waste no more time."

By the time they had crossed the garden to the tower they had gained a motley retinue; pages with lanterns, ladies holding up their skirts in order not to dirty them on the gravel, gentlemen with hunting dogs. Craven put his hand to the door of the tower and it swung open silently. He took a torch from one of the servants.

"I'll go down alone," he said.

The faces around him swam in the flare of light; avid, speculative, malicious. Craven felt a wave of disgust. God protect Her Majesty from such ghoulish curiosity. It was no wonder she sought solitude, surrounded every moment by such a crowd.

Rumph blocked his way. "It would not be seemly for you to be alone with the Queen, my lord."

"Forgive me, doctor, but His Majesty the King insists no layman should enter the tower that holds the secrets of the Order of the Rosy Cross," Craven said, an edge of steel to his tone now. "Does anyone wish to gainsay him?" He let the question hang.

It was enough. A ripple of disquiet went through the crowd like wind through corn. No one wanted to incur the wrath of the Knights of the Rosy Cross. Only Rumph's face bore indecision.

"I must insist—"

"Be assured, sir—" Craven laid a hand lightly on his arm, "that I will call for you at once should Her Majesty be in need of medical assistance."

He started down the stone stair. There was absolute silence below and darkness that fell about him like a shroud. The air was still and musty. It made him want to sneeze. He could almost feel the layers of dust tightening his chest. This was an unwholesome place. Even if a man did not believe in necromancy and its secrets it was impossible not to feel a shudder of repulsion.

"Your Majesty!" His voice sounded loud, met by nothing but the muffling darkness. He reached the bottom of the stairs and carefully opened the door into the water chamber.

There were no Knights in black and gold tonight. At first Craven thought the room was completely empty and he felt a rush of relief mingled with respect for Elizabeth that she should not cheapen herself with foolish superstition. Then he saw the torchlight falling on the quiet waters of the pool in banners of orange and black. It glanced off the arched spans of the roof and the tall pillars of stone. Shadows rippled, then one of them formed into a figure, small, slight, kneeling at the side of the pool.

Craven's heart jumped. He almost dropped the lantern in his haste to reach her side. "Your Majesty!"

She made no response, no movement.

"Madam!" He dropped down on one knee beside her. He had never thought her a small woman before, yet she seemed as insubstantial as air tonight, a ghost in a white gown, huddled over the water as she wove her spell.

He saw it then, the pearl shimmering on a ledge at the edge of the pool. He felt a deep visceral coldness, as though the marrow were freezing in his bones. It was not fear he felt but anger. Frederick was weak and needed the magic of soothsaying to prop him up. He was its puppet. But Elizabeth should have been too strong to require the comfort of such illusions.

He snatched the pearl from the water and threw it aside. He heard the clatter as it bounced off the stone pillar and wondered if it was lost. He hoped so.

Elizabeth jumped to her feet and spun to confront him. "You forget yourself, Craven." Her voice cracked like a whip. Her skirts were soaked. Water gleamed on her bare arms. She looked like a creature of magic herself, all light and fire, her hair flowing loose about her shoulders. He had never seen her like this, never expected to see her like this.

"Who are you to interrupt the mysteries of the Knights of the Rosy Cross?" Elizabeth demanded.

"One who would not see you bend to superstition," Craven said grimly, adding a perfunctory "madam." It sounded more derisive than he had intended and he saw her expression harden. For a moment he thought she might strike him.

"Be careful that you do not trip over your own self-importance," Elizabeth snapped. "Why should I care about *your* judgement, milord? You have no education. You are no more than a soldier. I do not need your permission or your approval for what I do."

"All men's opinions matter when a kingdom is at stake," Craven said. "Do you want the world to think that you cast spells like a witch because you do not believe you will regain your patrimony any other way?" He straightened up. A glimmer of iridescence caught his eye; in the corner of the chamber the pearl gleamed mockingly. Elizabeth made a rush for it but Craven was before her, grabbing it, holding it out of her reach. As soon as he touched it all colour seemed to leach from it. It looked a dull grey, sulky and malevolent. It was a toy, a chimera. He detested it.

He raised his gaze to Elizabeth's face. "If you call on the pearl they will think you weak," he said softly. "They will dismiss you as a tool in the hands of the magicians. Or they will seek to burn you for witchcraft."

Shock flared in her eyes. He had spoken harshly on purpose because he wanted her to understand. The Holy Roman Emperor and his allies would use every means available to discredit her. She was putting herself in danger and suddenly he was fearful for her.

He could feel the tension wrapping about them, thick as cobwebs, and then Elizabeth gave a sigh and her shoulders slumped. She looked so young and vulnerable all of a sudden, fragile in the white gown. The torchlight cast its slanting shade across her cheek and deepened the warm curve of her mouth. Her blue eyes were shadowed and dark. In that instant Craven could see why hard-headed soldiers and romantic fools alike dedicated themselves and their swords to her service. She was both gallant and beautiful.

Craven remembered Ralph Hopton telling him once of how he had carried the pregnant Queen ahead of him on his horse during the retreat from Prague after the Battle of White

Mountain, of how she had ridden mile after mile without complaint whilst her husband had shed bitter tears over the loss of his kingdom. Such courage commanded men's respect as well as their love.

"Don't you see—I need certainty?" He could hear the plea for reassurance beneath Elizabeth's defiant words. "I need to know if Frederick will win," she said. "I need to know if our lands will be restored or whether..." She let the words trail away before she betrayed herself too far.

"You will not find truth in magic, only deception." Impatience made him short. Frederick would not win. Craven needed no soothsaying to tell him that. He wanted to be honest with her, to state the facts baldly:

"Your husband is no soldier and men will die because of him."

But that was needlessly cruel, and in making her face up to her lack of belief in her husband he would commit an unforgivable act of treachery. Besides, he had chosen his loyalty. He had pledged himself to Frederick's cause. The least he could do was honour that pledge until he was released from it.

"Frederick took the mirror with him." She spoke softly so that Craven had to draw nearer to hear her words. A fold of her gown brushed his leg. For a moment he smelled the scent of the orange flower perfume she wore. She glanced up at him, almost shy. "We agreed; he would have the mirror and I the pearl. Two halves of a whole." Her voice dropped still further. "They do not work so well apart. The pearl would not reveal itself tonight without the mirror as its foil."

Craven knew the Winter King had taken the mirror. Barely a day passed without him peering into its depths for some pointer to his future fortunes. It was pitiful. He clenched his fists and, in doing so, realised that he still held the pearl. He resisted the urge to throw it into the pool and let the waters of the Bosbeek wash it away.

There were sounds from above now, footsteps on the stone stairs and the flaring of torches. Clearly Rumph had decided he had been absent long enough and had come to find out what was happening.

"They are looking for me." He saw Elizabeth straighten. She reached for her cloak, smothering the white gown in darkness. Her tone had changed. The doubt, the desolation had gone. She had shown her weakness to him but now she was a queen again.

Her gaze fixed on him, formal now. "I did not ask what you were doing here, Lord Craven. I suppose you are come from Hanau with letters from His Majesty?"

"I am." He was put neatly back in his place, a messenger boy.

"Then present them to me in an hour in the Great Chamber." She held out her hand for the jewel.

Craven looked at it again. It was instinctive, that glance downwards. He expected to see nothing but a big fat pearl that should have been locked away, or reduced to what it truly was; no more than an insignificant part of a royal collection of jewels. Yet in that second, as he stared at it, the pearl was transformed. It glowed, radiating a soft light that should have been warm and yet felt as cold as the winter sea. The surface shifted like clouds covering the moon and then he saw. A bedchamber cloaked in death, the royal standard of the lion rampant hanging limp and still. He could feel the heat of the room and smell the stench of sickness. He could hear the voices of the attendants and the murmurings of a priest.

"Craven?" Elizabeth's voice called him back. He shuddered, a cold sweat breaking out on his brow. The pearl burned his palm. He handed it gently to her.

"What did you see?" she asked. As she took it from him their fingers touched.

"I saw nothing," Craven lied. "Nothing at all."

6

When Holly reached the Ashmolean Museum that evening she found huge posters flanking the entrance, proclaiming the forthcoming exhibition of artefacts from the Court of Elizabeth Stuart, the Winter Queen. It was, the poster proclaimed, an extraordinary showcase for an outstanding collection of the finest seventeenth-century glass, china and portraiture.

The curator on duty at the door was reluctant to let Holly in until she mentioned her name and that she was meeting Mr Shurmer, whereupon he stood back with what was almost a bow and directed her to the second floor. The door of the lecture room stood wide; Holly could see the detritus of canapés and empty wine glasses strewn about. The guests were still chatting, however, and the roar of conversation was like a wall of noise.

She didn't want to go in, to engage in conversation, to try to find Espen Shurmer in the crowd. Instead she turned away and immediately felt the shock of quietness fall about her. The roar of voices faded. There was nothing but the faint tap of her footsteps and beyond the floor to ceiling windows at the end of the corridor, the tumble of Oxford roofs, spires and towers and the glitter of the city lights.

Holly loved Oxford. She had grown up in the city and she loved the crackle of excitement, the same sense of opportunity in the air that she felt in London. It felt like a city of limitless possibilities as well as a place steeped in history. Tonight though it just felt lonely and the bright white walls and bare spaces of the museum made it all the more stark.

At the end of the corridor a thick red rope now blocked the entrance to the exhibition. Holly had been to similar events in London and knew that earlier in the evening, all the guests would have wandered through, exchanging professional opinions on the rarity and quality of the collection. Now the gallery was empty and she could see the gleam of glass in the display cases. It beckoned to her, forbidden, tempting. She slipped past the rope and went in, ignoring the portraits and the other objects, concentrating solely on the engraved glass.

As always when she saw such exquisite workmanship Holly felt her heart quicken. This was the long tradition she worked within. She had wanted to be a glass engraver almost from the moment she had started to study the decorative arts. Here she was looking at masterpieces of her craft. There were slender wine flutes in the Venetian style and fat goblets engraved with scenes from Dutch life. There were glasses shaped like inverted bells with stems of twisted spirals and broad bowls embellished with flowers.

A stunning floor-length picture of the Winter Queen dominated the far wall and seeing it, Holly felt a tug of memory. Her grandfather had told her stories of Elizabeth Stuart when she had been a little girl. Elizabeth had been a Scottish princess by birth and Holly, born in the North of England, had felt a sense of affinity with the child who had left behind her roots and travelled so far from home. The idea of a Winter Queen had caught her childish imagination; she had visualised Elizabeth spun from icicles, cold as snow, like the White Witch in the Chronicles of Narnia. But those stories had felt magical, unreal. Here was the story of Elizabeth's life told through items she had touched and held.

Slowly now Holly walked between the display cases, taking in all the artefacts that she had previously ignored because she had been overwhelmed by the beauty of the glass. There were letters from Elizabeth to her husband Frederick of Bohemia, an astrolabe showing the celestial sphere with the earth at its centre, an engraved gold medal celebrating the couple's marriage, a dagger enamelled and set with diamonds.

On a bed of blue velvet nestled two miniatures, one of Frederick and the other of Elizabeth. Leaning closer, Holly saw that the portraits had been painted in 1612, just before their marriage.

"Miss Ansell? How do you do? I am Espen Shurmer."

Holly jumped. Just for a moment she had forgotten that she had come to the Ashmolean to meet Espen Shurmer and talk about Ben.

Shurmer was standing on the other side of the display, hands in the pockets of his beautifully cut suit, smiling at her confusion with benevolent amusement. He stepped forwards and held out a hand.

"Am I to assume that your presence here means that Dr Ansell has not returned?" he asked. His English was almost accentless.

"Mr Shurmer." Holly felt self-conscious and only just managed not to wipe her palms down her dress before she shook hands. "Yes, I'm afraid Ben is still missing."

"My sympathies," Shurmer said gravely. "I imagine that is very difficult for you."

"Thank you," Holly said. "Yes, it is a little difficult." She thought about her grandparents and the stoicism they were displaying in the absence of any news. When she had arrived earlier that afternoon, her grandmother had hugged her tightly for a long, long time as though she was afraid that Holly might vanish too. Her grandfather had told her he had spoken to the police and was trying to encourage them to open a formal investigation now that Ben had been gone over 48 hours without contact.

"I'm sorry I didn't make myself known to you when I arrived, Mr Shurmer," Holly said. "I..." She hesitated. "I had an urge to see the exhibition."

"Of course." Shurmer smiled. "You are welcome." His eyes were a vivid blue. His face bore lines of humour and experience. It was impossible to guess his age although Holly thought he must be in his late sixties, or older. His English was slightly clipped and old-fashioned which only added to the charm.

"Why would you not wish to see it?" he said. "All these items are so very beautiful."

"Yes." Holly hesitated again. "I'm a glass engraver, you see, and these—" She gestured towards the display cases, "well, I've never seen anything quite so stunning." She found that she had put out a hand towards the nearest cabinet as though wanting to touch the glass within. It was a rose-coloured goblet with a hunting scene engraved on it in gold foil. She knew it was called gold sandwich-glass and that it was so precious and expensive that it had probably been a gift and never actually used.

She saw Shurmer's eyes widen momentarily in surprise. "A glass engraver," he said slowly. "Yes, I see."

"It's wonderful to see the glass in the context of other items from Frederick and Elizabeth's court," Holly said. "On its own it is exquisite but seen alongside some of their other possessions it has so much more meaning. I can almost imagine stepping into the palace of the Wassenaer Hof and seeing the table set for a banquet..." She tailed off, thinking she sounded impossibly naïve, but Shurmer's shrewd blue gaze had sharpened with interest.

"So you know about the Wassenaer Hof? About Elizabeth and Frederick's court in exile?"

"A little," Holly said. "I've been to The Hague but, of course, the palace has gone now. As for Elizabeth and Frederick, my grandfather told me about them when I was a child. He was a wonderful storyteller."

"The Winter Queen is not well known in this country," Shurmer said, "even though she was the daughter of King James I."

"She was known as the Pearl of Britain," Holly said. She looked at Elizabeth's portrait. "She looks heartbreakingly lovely. So young as well."

It was an unusual portrait, she thought. In it Elizabeth's auburn hair was loose about her shoulders rather than piled up in some elaborate arrangement, and the long flowing tresses complemented the bold orange and black striped gown she wore. She was a true Scottish rose with creamy white skin and pale blue eyes.

"As does Frederick," Shurmer said. Holly thought he sighed softly. "So young and eager. It is fortunate they did not know at that stage what was to come—betrayal, loss and exile."

The Winter King looked no more than a boy, handsome and clean-shaven. His dark eyes were lustrous and his dark hair had a jaunty curl. Holly could see why he and Elizabeth had apparently fallen in love with each other on sight. Their good looks, hopes and expectations would have been a mirror each for the other. Everything must have seemed so wonderful in the beginning.

Then she remembered that Elizabeth had lost her brother only months before her marriage to Frederick. Even then there had been dark clouds. Unconsciously she wrapped her arms about her, warding off the darkness.

"I'm sorry," she said. "I'm sure you did not invite me here to discuss this."

Shurmer smiled. "On the contrary, Miss Ansell. In order to understand what it is that your brother wanted from me, it is necessary to know of the Winter Queen. But it seems that you already do." His gaze was intent, as though weighing up just how much she did know. "Has Dr Ansell already told you about his researches?" he asked.

"No," Holly said. "I'm afraid not."

"So," Shurmer said. "Why did you decide to come?"

Holly did not answer immediately and he did not prompt her. There was a quality of patience, of stillness, about Espen Shurmer that was unusual, she thought. It felt as though he would always be prepared to wait as long as was needed to get what he wanted.

"I'm not sure," she said honestly, after a moment. "I think I came because I thought it might have something to do with Ben's disappearance, or at least help me to work out what has happened to him."

Shurmer nodded slowly. "It is important to you to find him."

"Very," Holly said.

Silence fell again. She waited for Shurmer to say something reassuring. Almost everyone she had met in the past 48 hours had told her they were sure Ben would turn up soon. She knew it was intended to help, to make her feel better, even though it didn't. But Espen Shurmer said nothing.

"When we spoke you mentioned something about a pearl of great value," Holly said. "I must admit it surprised me. That really doesn't sound like Ben. He's not into antique jewellery or history of any sort, to be honest. He's too—" She paused. "He's more about the present rather than the past."

"Indeed?" A frown touched Espen Shurmer's brow. "Yet he was researching your family history?"

"I only heard about that recently," Holly said. "It seemed weird—totally out of character." She looked at him. "I'm astonished he told you about that too. Did it have something to do with his questions about the pearl?"

She saw a shadow of something flicker in Shurmer's eyes. "Perhaps." His tone was non-committal. "I do not know. All I know is that Dr Ansell wanted me to tell him all I knew about the Sistrin."

"The Sistrin," Holly said, and as she said the name she felt something shift inside her like the faintest of echoes, as though she had heard the word before. "That is the name of the pearl," she said softly.

"It is," Shurmer said. "But before I tell you about it, Miss Ansell, we must go back a little." He gestured to her to sit beside him on one of the museum's wide leather benches. "You will humour an old man, I hope."

It felt something of a royal edict. Holly sat.

Espen Shurmer waved a hand towards the cabinet that was closest to them. "You see the crystal mirror, here? What do you think of it?"

Holly followed his gaze. The same display case that held the rose-coloured engraved glass also held a number of other objects, but amongst all the gorgeously extravagant glassware they had been all but invisible to her. Now she saw them: a signet ring, a sapphire necklace set in dull gold and a small mirror in a wooden frame that was studded with diamonds. It was shaped like a teardrop with a worn handle at the base. It was beautiful, a piece of workmanship so delicate it looked as though it would be too fragile to hold. The glass shone with a milky bluish radiance. Yet there was something about it that Holly did not like.

"It's a stunning piece of work," she said carefully.

"It is Murano crystal," Shurmer said, "and was a gift to Mary, Queen of Scots when she wed Francois II of France. It is pretty, is it not?"

That was something of an understatement, Holly thought. The mirror was exquisite. Yet there was also something malevolent about it. She did not want to look into it though she was not exactly sure what it was about it that scared her.

"Mary was Elizabeth's grandmother, wasn't she?" she asked. "Did she bequeath it to her?"

The lines deepened about Shurmer's eyes as he smiled. "After a fashion," he said. "It was stolen by Elizabeth I of England when she had Mary put to death. Later Elizabeth sent it back to Scotland as a christening gift for Elizabeth Stuart, who was her goddaughter. It was, however, something of a cursed gift."

"Cursed?" Holly said. She didn't believe in the supernatural. She had never liked things she could not explain: ghosts, the Loch Ness monster, even the placebo effect. Even so, she felt the goosebumps creep along the back of her neck.

"The mirror became a tool for necromancy," Shurmer said. "Soothsaying," he added, in response to Holly's enquiring glance. "After Frederick lost his throne he became obsessed with the need to know whether he would ever regain his patrimony. He was a member of the Order of Knights of the

Rosy Cross. They were said to have the power of foretelling the future and they used the crystal mirror in their magic."

"I remember reading about the Knights of the Rosy Cross years ago," Holly said. "Some people thought them healers rather than magicians. And some said they were charlatans in league with the devil."

"Very good, Miss Ansell." Shurmer was nodding his approval. "The Knights of the Rosy Cross were many things to many men." Then as she smiled, he said: "Forgive me. I sound like a teacher, I know, but it is rare to meet someone who has heard of the Order of the Rosy Cross." He sighed. "Legend has it that the Knights used a number of tools in their scrying, but that the jewelled mirror was the most important because it had the power to reflect the future. It had been forged in fire, you see, and it was said that as from fire it had come, so into fire it would lead its enemies."

Holly gave a little involuntary shiver. She found she did not want to look directly at the mirror now, but paradoxically it almost felt as though it was willing her to turn, beckoning her gaze. Very deliberately she shifted so that her back was towards it.

"The mirror was said to have caused the death of Henry, Lord Darnley, in an explosion and fire," Shurmer said. "It was also rumoured to have foretold the Gunpowder Plot. On the very day of the Princess Elizabeth's christening, her nurse saw a vision of hellfire and flame in the mirror and the child upon the throne of England."

"I know that the plotters planned to set Princess Elizabeth up as a puppet queen," Holly said, "but since the Gunpowder Plot didn't actually succeed, technically it can't be said that the mirror predicted the future."

Shurmer's eyes gleamed with amusement. "I see that you are a most logical person, Miss Ansell."

"I try to be," Holly said.

Shurmer's smile deepened. "Then I doubt you will believe for a moment the tales of the Knights and their sooth-saying," he said. "Or a mirror that can destroy its enemies through fire."

"It's certainly a great story," Holly said. "How did the mirror come into your collection?"

"That was by fortunate chance," Shurmer said. The bright white lights of the exhibition cases threw the shadows of his face into stark relief. Suddenly he looked frail, the skin stretched too taut across his cheekbones, his eyes tired.

"For many years the mirror was missing," he said. "It was believed buried with Frederick, but Frederick's tomb was lost during the Thirty Years War. Then the mirror miraculously reappeared in the late twentieth century at a car boot sale in Corby in Northamptonshire."

Holly almost choked. "Forgive me," she said, "but you do not strike me as the sort of man who spends his time attending car boot sales."

Shurmer laughed. "What I should have said is that I was alerted to the fact that there was a very old, very fine mirror for sale. An…associate of mine bought it and mentioned it to me. He knew that I was interested in seventeenth-century artefacts, particularly those from the Bohemian court."

"I suppose it had no provenance?" Holly said.

Shurmer shook his head. "Naturally not. But it matches the known descriptions and pictures of the Murano crystal mirror."

"Did you have it authenticated?" Holly asked. It would be the natural thing to do; call in a group of experts to assess the mirror and confirm its age and origin. Yet Espen Shurmer was shaking his head again and she sensed that his belief in the mirror and its myth was so strong that either he believed it absolutely without the need for proof or he did not want to question it too closely in case he destroyed the legend.

Of course he might be right. It could indeed be the very mirror that the Winter King had used to foresee the future. Holly glanced at it again and felt the same disturbing pull. A breath of wind seemed to ripple through the still air of the gallery. The lights seemed to shimmer and the mirror glowed in its case as though it were alive. She shuddered, closing her eyes. When she reopened them the gallery swam back into her vision, all bright lights and clean modern lines. It looked normal, just an empty room with old objects in display cases.

"That brings us to the Sistrin pearl," Shurmer said, "for the crystal mirror was not the only gift bequeathed to Elizabeth by her grandmother. It was matched with a jewel of rare beauty and price." He waved a hand towards the miniature of young Elizabeth that was displayed in the glass cabinet. Holly saw that she was wearing a string of pearls with one huge drop pearl in the centre. The simplicity of the necklace and the radiance of the jewels suited the innocence of the portrait. Curiously though, the big pearl was shaped exactly like the crystal mirror. It was a pear shape, or teardrop.

"The Sistrin pearl was also said to hold great magic." Shurmer too, was looking towards the cabinet where the pearl gleamed at Elizabeth's neck. "It was supposedly a powerful talisman for good, but like the mirror it also possessed the power to wreak destruction if it was misused."

"Old pearls almost always have some sort of legend attached to them, though, don't they?" Holly said. "I mean, usually they have belonged to pirates or they are cursed or something. It was a very superstitious age."

"That is true," Shurmer said. "Certainly the Knights of the Rosy Cross believed the legends and used the pearl and the mirror together in their necromancy. They used their magic to create firewater, a medium through which the future could not only be seen but could also be transformed."

"That sounds rather dangerous to me," Holly said. "If you believe in these things…" She hesitated. "Well, you're meddling with forces you cannot control, aren't you."

"Yes," Shurmer said. There was an odd note in his voice. "Indeed you are."

"Was this what Ben wanted to know?" Holly asked. "The legend of the Sistrin pearl?"

Shurmer shook his head. "Dr Ansell already knew the history of the pearl," he said. "No—" His eyes met hers and Holly felt something akin to an electric shock. "Your brother wished to find out what had happened to the pearl after it passed out of the possession of the Winter Queen."

Holly felt even more bewildered. "Why on earth would he want to know that?"

"I have no notion," Shurmer said calmly. "He would not say. That was why I wanted to meet him. I thought that perhaps he had found it."

"*Found* it?" Holly felt completely bewildered. "I'm sorry, Mr Shurmer, I don't quite understand…"

"After the Winter Queen's death, the pearl disappeared," Shurmer said, "but unlike the crystal mirror it never reappeared. We do not know its fate. It is lost." He made a slight gesture and the light flashed on the expensive gold watch he wore. "It is the holy grail of collectors, Miss Ansell. Everyone wants to find the Sistrin pearl. I myself have sought it for forty years."

There was silence in the gallery. Holly could hear nothing except the soft hum of the air conditioning. She was very aware of Espen Shurmer watching her, gauging her every expression. She was not sure what was showing on her face. It had been astonishing enough to discover that Ben had been involved in some sort of family history research. Now to discover that he had been making enquiries about a long-lost pearl was extraordinary. It felt as though there should be a connection between the two but Holly could not imagine what it was. The story of the mirror and the pearl seemed no more than superstition and legend.

"You should know," Shurmer said, and Holly realised that he was picking his words very carefully, "that after Dr Ansell contacted me I did make some enquiries into his background and history." He spread his hands in a gesture of apology. "Forgive me, but I am a rich man and sometimes criminals will try to target my collection. Naturally I quickly realised your brother was no such person." His smile was disarming. "Yet equally I could find no obvious connection between your family and the Winter Queen to suggest why your brother might possess the Sistrin."

"Did you ask him?" Holly said. "Whether he had the pearl, I mean?"

"Yes," Shurmer said. His tone was pensive. "He was... evasive. He suggested we meet and I agreed."

There was silence. Holly tried to remember her conversations with Ben. None of them had involved anything as arcane as lost treasure. She thought about the mill. She had spent much of the day tidying it up and she had found nothing unusual or unexpected. The lack of clues towards Ben's disappearance had frustrated her.

"I'm very sorry," she said helplessly. "Ben said nothing to me. I really don't think I can help."

"No matter," Shurmer said graciously. "I would ask, though, that if you discover anything, you let me know?" He took a card from his inside pocket and passed it to Holly. It felt crisp and smooth beneath her fingers, the edges sharp.

"Oh, of course," she said. "Of course I will."

She stood up, suddenly wanting to be gone from this place, the supernatural stories and the crystal mirror's sinister gleam. It was easy to believe in superstition when she was encased in a world like the Ashmolean, where thousand-year-old tribal masks watched her with blank eyes as she passed and she could hear the whispers of history.

"I understand that you are most anxious to uncover the reasons for your brother's disappearance, Miss Ansell," Shurmer said quietly, getting to his feet too. "I hope that you find what you are looking for."

"Thank you," Holly said. "I…" She hesitated. "I'm sure he will turn up soon."

She saw the smile that touched Shurmer's eyes and knew that he knew she was lying.

"Let us hope so," he said. He held out a hand and Holly shook it.

"It was…very interesting…to meet you, Mr Shurmer."

"A pleasure, Miss Ansell," Shurmer said. He sounded as though he meant it.

Holly had already taken five steps away when she stopped and turned back. Espen Shurmer was standing where she had left him, beside the display case that contained the crystal mirror.

"What was the special power that the pearl was said to possess?" she asked. The words seemed to spring from her of their own volition. She was not even sure what had put them in her mind. Then, when Shurmer did not immediately reply, she added:

"You said that the mirror destroyed its enemies through fire. What did the pearl do?"

She saw it then, the flicker of disquiet in Espen Shurmer's eyes, and knew that for some reason he had deliberately kept this from her.

"Mr Shurmer?" she said.

"The pearl's power came from water," Shurmer said. "It destroyed its enemies through the medium of water."

Holly thought of the mill, of the splash of the stream running beneath the wheel and the lazy glare of the sun on the pond. It had to be a coincidence, and yet she felt a deep chill in her bones. She thought of Ben and for a terrifying moment her mind was full of darkness. There was the rushing sound of water in her ears and a pressure in her lungs that smothered her breath. Coldness gripped her limbs and there was fear that cut like a blade.

"The Winter Queen's eldest son died from drowning," she said slowly. "And her brother—did he not die after swimming in the Thames?"

"That is indeed so, Miss Ansell," Shurmer said. "Those who dismiss such magic as mere superstition are perhaps complacent."

A huge shudder shook Holly. If Ben truly had the Sistrin pearl, had it destroyed him too? She turned, practically running from the gallery, down the stairs and out of the main door oblivious to the curious glances of the people she passed. Her breath was coming in short bursts and she had a stitch in her side and when she reached the bottom of the steps she had to stop and steady herself against the wall.

Out in the street there were crowds gathering outside the theatre opposite, spilling into the road. The normality of noise and people and light slowly wrapped about Holly, banishing the mysteries of the museum. She straightened up and started to walk slowly towards St Giles, all the while wondering what had happened to her. Stories of cursed mirrors and legendary pearls, magic and superstition, were so alien to her that she was puzzled that she had entertained them for a moment. She used such ideas as inspiration for her engraving designs but she did not really believe in them. Or she had not, until tonight.

Now, though, she felt on edge, adrift, rocked by uncertainty. She told herself that in ten minutes she would be back at her grandparents' house and they would be bursting to tell her that they had had a message from Ben. He would be safe, he would be on the way home to Tasha and all would be well. Later, when all the fuss had died down, she would ask him about the pearl and Espen Shurmer, and he would explain that it had just been a casual enquiry as a result of something he had stumbled across in the family history...

Holly turned left into the Woodstock Road, heading for Summertown, walking briskly even though she was so tired. It was raining a little, the pavements slick, the raindrops running down the car windows and stinging Holly's face, blurring the city lights to an endless string of pearls that was finally swallowed in darkness.

7

William Craven had kept quiet about the soothsaying. Elizabeth was grateful he had held his tongue. At the same time she was ashamed he had seen her weakness. She owed him no apology for believing in the power of the mirror and the pearl, but she did regret revealing to him, however tacitly, her doubts in Frederick's ability to lead, to fight, to win back his lands. She had been weak and had shown too little faith. Time had revealed her mistake. Frederick's letters to her were full of joy and good news; Gustavus Adolphus had received him with all the ceremony due to a king and included him in his military councils. Plans were advancing for the retaking of the Palatine lands. Kreuznach had been reclaimed. Soon he would be sending for her to take their rightful place in Heidelberg once more.

Craven was Frederick's squire now and had been his constant messenger, carrying the news from the campaign in Germany and taking Elizabeth's more domestic correspondence back to the King. He had ridden in just as she had been about to set out from the palace that morning to hunt in the woods above Rhenen. Elizabeth had insisted that he accompany the party and give her the news as they rode. It had perhaps been unkind of her given that he was weary and travel-stained, and only three months before had been injured in the taking of the castle at Kreuznach. Frederick had commended him for his bravery, saying that Craven had been first through the breached walls and that the King of Sweden himself had praised him for being a fine soldier.

Elizabeth glanced at him now as they rode side by side through the dappled shade. They had outrun the rest of the hunting party who even now were crashing through the woods below, calling out, frightening away any deer in earshot. She had allowed her elder sons to join her that morning, but sometimes she despaired that they would ever learn the cunning and guile of the true hunter. Yet they were young still, and eager for the chase. She supposed she would reproach them more had they been timorous creatures who stayed at home whilst she rode out.

Craven's face was, as always, quite severe in repose. He made no attempt to entertain her or to chatter inconsequentially as so many courtiers did. Elizabeth wondered what it felt like to be him; to be so reckless of his personal safety that he would fight without reserve, without fear. It was no wonder that her sons admired him as a hero. They were uncomplicated boys, fired with the zeal to regain their inheritance. They wanted to be soldiers, understood nothing of politics and cared even less. A man of such straightforward convictions as William Craven commanded their loyalty.

"You have not yet told me the news from Munich," Elizabeth said. "I heard that my husband supped with the Duke of Bavaria."

"And wished you present, madam, to add beauty to the proceedings," Craven said.

Elizabeth laughed. "Frederick's words, I'll wager, not yours, Lord Craven. You are not known for your courtly address."

"As to that, madam," Craven said, "I can vouch that there are no beauties in Bavaria other than the scenery."

They were still laughing when the first of the hunting party broke through the trees into the dappled clearing. Elizabeth felt a wilful urge to wheel her horse around and dig her heels into its flanks, leaving them standing. Then she saw Charles Louis, his expression hovering on the edge of mutiny at the prospect of his mother outrunning him again, so instead she reined back and allowed them to surround her, chattering, and rode forwards decorously out of the shadows and onto the open hill.

From here there was a beautiful view of the little town of Rhenen, clinging to the hillside, and the curl of the river to the east. The sunlight twinkled on the gables of the hunting lodge Frederick had built, finished only the previous year. They'd had so little time to enjoy this place together before war had come again. Elizabeth felt a chill premonition that they never would.

The servants were spreading out a meal on a plateau in the shade of the trees. They scurried around unpacking boxes, setting rugs and cushions. There was glazed ham and pastries, roasted meats and red wine. Craven had gone to fetch a glass for her. She was about to dismount—Billingsley, her Master of the Horse, had come forwards to help her.

"Why such a long face?" she asked him, knowing full well

it was because she had chosen to ride ahead with Craven leaving him to watch over the Princes.

Billingsley flushed. He did not have Craven's easy way of responding to her comments, whether they were teasing or serious. He was too stiff and formal, conscious of his status and of hers too. She supposed William Craven ought to show a similar deference but he never did and she had given up expecting it of him. Besides, something about Craven's uncomplicated approach was refreshing. He told her the truth as he saw it. He could be blunt, but he was never disrespectful.

There was a sudden crashing sound of a branch falling and shouts from across the clearing where the Princes were playing hide and seek, climbing trees, their irrepressible high spirits toppling over into dangerous risk-taking. Elizabeth spun around in the saddle.

"Don't let them—" she said to Billingsley, but it was too late, one of the trees was rotten. The falling branch had been a precursor and now the whole trunk shook and with a roaring sound like the tide rushing in it fell, the branches clashing together. Some fool screamed. Elizabeth's horse took fright, rearing and taking her by surprise. She lost the reins and made a grab for the mane as the horse bolted, plunging back into the trees the way they had come.

Elizabeth saw a jumbled vision of images flash past: Craven, running for his horse, Billingsley, his mouth hanging open in shock, the servants frozen to the spot, the boys pausing in their shrieks of excitement to stare after her in horror. Then all hell broke loose behind her with screams and shouts, but all she could do was cling on for dear life, crouched low as the trees whipped overhead and the horse ran and ran, propelled onwards by its own panic until at last it slowed and then stopped.

She slid down to the ground and sat for a moment half lying, half tumbled whilst she caught her breath. Her first sensation was relief and her second, following swiftly, was anger. She was the best female equestrian at court, one of the best riders there was. Yes, the horse was skittish and high-spirited—even now she was shying at her own shadow, ears flat as she blew out her breath in great heaving pants—but Elizabeth had prided herself on the fact that she was one of the few who could ride her. Her pride had been richly served now.

There was no sound, no one calling for her, no noise of men or carts, nothing but the wind in the trees and the chirps of the birds, so loud they seemed to fill her ears. She reached for the reins and started to stroke the horse's nose, speaking softly to her, calming her until she too felt calmer. Soon she would be able to remount and try to follow her tracks back to the edge of the wood. It could not be difficult. She would find her way back to Rhenen. Besides, had she not always said she wanted to be alone? Now, unexpectedly, she had as much solitude as she could deal with.

The bushes rustled on her right, but it was only a bird foraging in the undergrowth. She got to her feet stiffly and, leading the horse, started to walk in what she hoped was the right direction. There was little sunlight through the thick canopy and the branches sprouted low, tangling with the thick and thorny bushes. Within a few minutes Elizabeth was hot and scratched and dirty, hungry too, and resenting the picnic left so far behind. Being alone was not as enjoyable as she had thought it would be. There was something unfriendly about the wood, its darkness and silence. It felt as though someone was watching her.

The horse picked up on her nervousness, flicking her ears, whisking her tail. When a noisy bird crashed through the leaves above and flew off with a startled alarm call Elizabeth thought she would bolt again and gripped the reins more tightly, but the horse was too tired. They both were.

The bird had been warning of an approach. Elizabeth could hear footsteps and turned sharply just as a man stepped onto the path in front of her. The sun was behind him and for a moment she could not see his face, then she realised it was William Craven.

"Craven!" she said. Her voice wobbled, betraying her. She wondered if he was going to berate her for poor horsemanship or make light of her headlong flight, but he did neither. His face was white and he looked afraid. He dropped to one knee and took her hand, kissing it.

"Madam! You are safe?"

"As you see," Elizabeth said. She felt shock and something more intimate that shocked her all the more. She resisted the urge to touch his bent head.

"Thank God." His voice had strengthened. He scrambled to his feet. "I was afraid for you." He corrected himself. "We were all afraid, for she set off at such a mad gallop with you. Everyone has been searching the forest."

"Then you had better lead me back to them," Elizabeth said. She looked about her. "I have no notion where we are. It was lucky you found me."

"You are almost at the edge of the trees." Craven had taken the horse's bridle, leading her between the trees, at the same time holding back the brambles and briars that snatched at Elizabeth's skirt. "You would doubtless have found your way back safely before too long."

"Nevertheless," Elizabeth said, "it was you who found me. I owe you a debt of gratitude, Lord Craven. Another one. As does my husband."

"Your husband?" Craven paused. They were on the edge

of the wood. "Yes, of course." His voice changed. "His Majesty would be distraught to know of your accident."

"There is no harm done," Elizabeth said. She looked closely at his face as she stepped past him, out into the sunshine and light and fresh air. "You, though," she said, noting the lines etched deep on his face, "you look as though you need a physician. I had forgotten you were wounded lately. Are you in pain?"

A smile lightened his expression, lifting the lines of anxiety from about his eyes. "I am quite well, thank you, madam." He came up to her and set his hands on her waist to lift her up into the saddle. They were very close together. Elizabeth looked up into his face, the strong line of his jaw, the cleft in his chin, the light in his hazel eyes. Something shifted inside her and warmed and she caught her breath on a wave of longing.

He looked down then, catching her desire, and suddenly he was close enough to kiss and she saw the heat in his eyes and for one long moment they stared at one another. Then he took a step back and lifted her, very gently, into the saddle and turned his back as he led the horse out onto the open hillside towards home.

8

Hester was waiting for Holly when she got back to Summertown. The house was warm and light. The smell of a casserole cooking reached her from the kitchen and made Holly's stomach rumble. Bonnie was waiting too, waving her feathery tail with the sort of enthusiasm she showed whether Holly had been away for an hour or a day. Holly felt her cold unhappiness thaw a little as she bent down to give the dog a cuddle.

"Hello, Gran," she said, smiling. "How are you doing?"

"Darling…" Her grandmother planted a firm kiss on Holly's cheek, one each side, and hugged her. She felt frail to Holly, her bones brittle beneath the cashmere jumper she wore. "I'm doing all right," she said, "but how are you? How did your meeting go with Ben's friend?"

"It was fine," Holly said lightly. She brushed her lips against her grandmother's cheek. It was dusted with pink and felt marshmallow soft.

"He hadn't heard from Ben, had he?" Hester asked, and Holly could hear the lift of hope in her voice.

"I'm afraid not," she said. She wasn't going to tell her grandmother about Espen Shurmer and the bizarre suggestions that Ben had been connected, however vaguely, to some sort of occult society. It was all just too strange to consider.

She watched her grandmother as she walked across the kitchen to reach for the kettle and turn it on. Tall, thin and ineffably elegant, Hester's shoulders were square and her back as straight as a rod. Army discipline, Holly thought. There was a picture of the Brigadier, Holly's great-grandfather, in one of the bedrooms upstairs. In it, he was whippet thin and the expression in his eyes suggested that he would not tolerate insubordination in the ranks or slumping in small girls. Holly wondered how much that discipline was helping her grandmother to deal with Ben's disappearance. She had had so much to bear over the years, losing her daughter and son-in-law and taking on their two children, and now having to deal with Ben going missing.

"Tasha rang," Hester said now, over the sound of the kettle boiling. "She hasn't heard anything from Ben either. His practice is in a complete tizzy. They've had to get a locum in."

"Of course," Holly said. "I hadn't thought of that." She realised for the first time that the ripples from Ben's disappearance would spread out much further than his family and immediate friends. She had rung round as many people as she knew, hoping someone would have had word from him, but she realised with a pang that she didn't know half of Ben's acquaintances. Trying to find him seemed a hopeless task.

"Tasha seems very angry and convinced he's gone on purpose to punish her for something." Her grandmother spoke without inflection but Holly could see the effort it cost her; her hands shook a little as she filled the teapot. Holly went across and put an arm about her and for a moment they stood close, their heads resting against each other.

"Do you suppose Tasha's right?" Hester asked suddenly. "That Ben was having an affair and has gone off with another woman?" She took two blue and white patterned mugs from the cupboard and warmed them with the spare water from the kettle. "I don't want to believe it, but I suppose it could be true."

"Gran, no!" Holly said. She felt shocked that her grandmother would even countenance the idea. "You know Ben wouldn't do something like that."

She saw her grandmother's brows lift slightly but she let the subject go.

"This is all Tasha's fault," Holly said, suddenly fierce. "Suggesting Ben was unfaithful. I'm so angry with her!" She had tried never to criticise Tasha to her grandparents because she knew that they had as delicate a relationship with her as Holly, but now she'd had enough. "Ben wasn't like that," she said. "He was very loyal. He would never run off without a word. Abandoning Florence and his work responsibilities… That's just not in character."

She saw her grandmother's shoulders slump and she gave her an apologetic smile. "I'm sure you're right, darling," Hester said. "This whole business makes me doubt my own sanity."

Holly nodded. "The trouble is that Tasha has told the police they were having relationship difficulties and so they don't think he is missing in the true sense," she said, fighting to keep the bitterness from her voice. "So they won't do anything to look for him." She spread her hands wide. "It makes me feel so helpless," she said. "I'm angry and frustrated and I don't know what to do."

Hester poured the tea and passed one of the mugs to Holly.

"If it weren't relationship problems they would imply he had run away because of something else," she said, with a sigh. "Financial worries, depression. They would suggest he might have taken his own life…" She looked up and Holly saw the fear in her eyes. It was so stark that she felt her heart miss a beat. "I do worry that might be true," Hester said simply. "I can't help myself."

"Gran…" Holly said. She was even more horrified now. "No. Ben wouldn't…" She stopped because she couldn't even form the words.

"Oh, well…" Hester's voice strengthened. "I'm sure I'm just being negative. We can't give up hope, especially so soon." She squeezed Holly's hand. "He'll be back soon, I'm sure of it."

Holly wondered if the words sounded a little more hollow each time someone said them and perhaps her grandmother felt the same because she turned away as though to shield her expression from Holly, like she was ashamed.

"Your grandfather is dining at Balliol tonight, so it's just us," she said brightly. "I hope you don't mind, darling? I think perhaps he doesn't know what to do with himself so he's trying to stick to some sort of routine."

"That's OK." There was a lump in Holly's throat. For so many years she had thought her grandparents invincible. It was frightening to think her grandfather was feeling as lost and confused as she was and that her grandmother was putting on a brave face. "I'll see him again tomorrow," she said.

"Lovely," her grandmother said. She opened the Aga and took out a battered-looking casserole pot. "It's lamb hotpot and beans."

"My favourite." Holly smiled at her.

They ate supper in the living room, with trays on their knees. The room was grand, but made smaller by the lamplight and the fire and the heavy curtains that blotted out the twilight.

"You don't mind a fire, do you, darling?" Hester asked. "I know it's been a hot day but I always feel the chill when night falls."

"As long as you don't mind me falling asleep," Holly said, stifling a yawn.

"Of course not," Hester said. "You must be exhausted. I don't suppose any of us have slept since..." Her voice trailed away. "We wondered if you wanted to stay for a few days?" she added. "Guy as well, if he's coming down..." There was an unspoken question in the words. "Or do you have to get back to London?"

"I'm not going back to London," Holly said. "Or rather I will, but only to arrange to have everything sent down to Ashdown. I'm going to live at the mill for a while."

Hester dropped her fork with a clatter. "Darling!" She looked appalled. "Is it really a good idea to uproot yourself from home like this? It could all be for nothing."

"I realise that," Holly said, "but I feel I need to be there."

"But..." It was unusual for Holly to see her grandmother lost for words. Before her retirement Hester had been a professor of mathematics; incisive, objective and able to pinpoint an issue and dissect it with forensic skill. "Please don't misunderstand me," Hester said now, very carefully. "I realise that you may want to be at Ashdown in order to try to find Ben. You want to be on the spot; perhaps it will help you to feel closer to him. But is this really wise?"

Holly sighed. She had been expecting a reaction like this but it was difficult to explain, especially when she didn't really understand the impulse herself. All she knew was that she had to be there. It felt right. It felt like the only place to be.

"I only know that I want to be at Ashdown at the moment," Holly said. "Guy and I are over." She met her grand-mother's eyes. "We were over long before this, if I'm honest. I just needed a jolt to make me see the truth."

"Again," Hester said, "not the best time to be making life-changing decisions."

Holly sighed. "Trust me. Please. Sometimes it's exactly the right time to see what is important and what isn't."

Now it was her grandmother's turn to sigh. "Oh, Holly."

"Don't tell me that you never thought I'd made a mistake," Holly said.

Hester looked reproachful. "Now you're putting me on the spot. But yes..." She shook her head, somewhere between exasperation and indulgence. "I did wonder. You're so self-contained I never thought you would marry anyone. I was very surprised when you got engaged. And I was even more surprised you chose Guy."

Holly demolished the last of the hotpot. She was astonished to find she had such an appetite. She hadn't eaten at all, hadn't felt like eating, for several days.

"I've wondered about that myself more than once since we split," she admitted. "Guy was nice." She winced. "Okay, that's not a good reason. He was funny, and charming, and we had a good time together. And that was all I wanted."

Hester smiled at her. "Guy was very likeable," she said. "It was easy to equate his charm with depth or character."

"Ouch," Holly said. "You really didn't like him."

"He wasn't good enough for you," Hester said with a shrug. "I'm old-fashioned, but I've always believed that as a couple you should be greater than as an individual—stronger, complementary... Guy didn't add anything to the equation. In fact I felt he took away from you rather than adding anything."

Holly rubbed a hand over her forehead. "It wasn't all Guy's fault," she said. She shrugged helplessly. "I thought what we had was good enough. All my passion goes into my work. You know that. It was one of Guy's complaints about me. It's true I'm selfish like that, I suppose. I didn't want a relationship that demanded too much of me."

She knew that Guy had wanted more than she was prepared to give. He had needed to be praised, worshipped and adored. The only thing that Holly adored was the diamond-tipped drill she used for her glass etching. She could not really blame Guy for the fact that when she *had* needed him he hadn't been inclined to support her.

"It's not selfishness," Hester said wryly. "Even before Ben vanished you had coped with so much. It's natural to want to protect yourself."

Silence fell again, but for the crackle of the fire and Bonnie's faint contented snores. "Oh, how I wish I could curl my legs up onto the sofa," Hester said. "Too old, I suppose—I might snap." She watched as Holly stacked the plates together and put them on the tray.

"Tell me about your decision to move to the mill. Are you really sure you want to live there?"

"Yes," Holly said. "It's affordable, it has a workshop on-site and if I work really hard I could probably set up a gallery as well and benefit from the tourists who come to Ashdown Park and Fran's café."

Hester smiled. "That sounds marvellous, but it wasn't exactly what I meant."

Holly avoided her gaze, rubbing her fingers over the smooth velvet pile of one of the cushions.

"You mean because of Ben?"

"And your parents," Hester said. "The place has so many memories."

"I don't really associate Ashdown with Mum and Dad," Holly said after a moment. "We didn't go there that often. To me it was just another holiday cottage." She swallowed. Her memories of her parents were sepia tinted now, as though she had known them a very long time ago. Yet time could not erase the ache of loss and the prickle of tears in her throat, all closer to the surface now because Ben's disappearance had made everything so raw again. If you loved you got hurt and the more you loved the more power it had to destroy you. For her it was that simple.

"Grief and loss are odd things," Hester said. "People imply you should get over them but that's the wrong terminology. They ease, I suppose, and smooth away a little and become a part of your life's pattern. The sharp edges do get dulled in time..."

"But every so often something will catch you," Holly said. "A memory, a place, a thought, and for that one moment the grief will be as sharp and terrifying as it ever was." She remembered how she had felt the day after Ben had gone and she shivered. She had never felt more isolated and alone in her life and she had turned to Mark to dispel that loneliness. Wrapped up in her own pain she had been selfish and she felt bad about that but it wasn't a night she was likely to forget.

Hester smiled at her, reaching out a hand to clasp Holly's. "This business with Ben has hit you hard," she said.

Holly did not deny it. There was no point in lying, and admitting that they were both feeling lost did not make them weaker. It drew them together more strongly. They sat in silence for a long peaceful moment and then Holly stirred.

"Did you know that Ben was doing some sort of family history research at Ashdown?" she said. "It doesn't seem very like him, does it?"

"Hardly." Hester looked mystified. "No, I had no idea. Are you sure? I thought Ben was bored by all that poking around in the past."

"So did I," Holly said, "but I wondered whether that was why Mum and Dad bought Ashdown Mill in the first place. Because of an interest in the history, I mean, or a personal connection to the place." She frowned. "I know nothing about Ashdown really but I thought I might try to find out what Ben was researching. It might...help. I don't know how, but you never know."

"You'd have to ask your grandfather if he knows anything," Hester said. "I think he did some work on Ashdown Park years ago. He was writing an article on mediaeval deer parks of Berkshire and Oxfordshire, or something equally obscure."

Holly smiled. Unlike Hester, her grandfather was the archetypal old-fashioned academic whose vagueness about life outside of his ivory tower had frequently driven his more practical wife to fits of irritation. Holly vividly remembered a trip to the supermarket with him when she had been about fourteen and her grandfather had seemed incapable of finding anything on the shopping list.

"Mediaeval?" she said now. "But I thought Ashdown Park was later than that."

"The house was," Hester said, "but the estate was based on a mediaeval hunting forest. I imagine there's been a mill on the site since the Domesday Book."

"I didn't know that," Holly said slowly. She thought of the thick ranks of trees, secretive and close, the gnarled oaks and fluttering beeches. No wonder there was an otherworldly atmosphere about the place. It was ancient. And the mill had been a part of that history for hundreds of years.

"I think the mill itself went out of use shortly after Ashdown Park burned down," Hester said. She cut herself a piece of Brie from the platter on the low table in front of her and nibbled at it. "That was in the early nineteenth century. Once there was no big house on the estate there was no need of a village to support it. Everything would have changed..." She shifted a little. "More than the house died that day."

It was an odd choice of phrase and it sent a shiver rippling up Holly's spine. A log broke apart in the grate in a shower of sparks. Bonnie stretched out towards the warmth.

"I didn't realise that the house burned down either," Holly said. "I don't suppose, as a child, I was curious about these things. I just enjoyed playing in the woods. I definitely need to find out more about it." She reached for a cheese biscuit herself, with cheddar, strong and smooth. "I assume they re-built the house though?" she said, her mouth full. "I saw it the other day. Tall, white stone, with a gold dome on the roof."

Hester looked startled. "Ashdown Park? No, it was de-molished after the fire. Surely you knew that? No house has stood there for two hundred years."

"But—" Holly stopped. She had seen the house, or so she had thought—the flash of white walls through the trees, the moonlight glinting on the windows. It was disconcerting to hear that what she thought she had seen was a ghost house.

Hester was looking at her with concern shadowing her eyes. She would have to back-pedal or her grandmother would be asking if she was so stressed and exhausted that she needed to see a doctor.

"I must have confused it with one of the other houses on the estate," she said. "They're renovating the old stable block and some of the other buildings, aren't they?"

"Oh, yes," Hester said. Her expression relaxed. "They've decided to convert it for housing. Mark Warner's company are managing the project."

"Mark?" Holly jumped. She could not help herself. "Do you know him?"

Her grandmother looked up quickly and Holly moderated her tone. The words had come out more sharply than she had intended.

"His godmother is a friend of mine," Hester said, after a moment. "Army connections."

"Oh, of course," Holly said. Something shifted in her memory and finally she realised why Mark had seemed so familiar. He had been on the cover of any number of newspapers a few years back, wearing dusty army combats, his smile a white flash in his tanned face, his eyes narrowed against a sun far brighter than an English one. A hero, the papers had called him, an army officer who had risked his own life to rescue one of his men injured under fire and bring his patrol safely out of an ambush. There had been pictures from Buckingham Palace too, when he had been awarded some sort of gallantry medal, his wife smiling as she hung on his arm, his parents speaking of their pride in him. The media had loved him. He had run the London marathon and hiked to the South Pole for charity with a team of veterans and one of the royal Princes. It had all been very high profile. But that must have been four years ago, maybe five, and since then Holly could not remember seeing his picture. He had dropped out of the public gaze and there had been nothing but silence.

He'd told her he had travelled with his job, which was a hell of way to describe his army career. And he had failed to mention that he was the developer who was converting the stable yard. She felt a stab of annoyance. If she had been economical with the facts then he had been almost as bad. She wondered about his wife and felt even more annoyed and upset.

Her grandmother was watching her and she quickly tried to compose her expression.

"You don't like him," Hester said, after a moment.

"We only exchanged a few words," Holly said. "Not enough for me to judge one way or the other." Her face burned. She hoped Hester would put it down to the heat from the fire. "Did his wife and family move to Ashdown with him?"

"He's divorced," Hester said. "No children, but he does look after his younger siblings, I think. Their father works abroad and their mother..." She shrugged expressively. "I forget what the problem was there. Anyway, I think Mark wanted a fresh start so he set up a company that specialises in old buildings and redeveloping historic sites like Ashdown Park." She sat forwards. "If you really are going to follow up Ben's research then maybe Mark could help you? I expect he's discovered loads of interesting documents about the place as a result of all the background he'll have done for the project."

"I wouldn't dream of troubling him," Holly said hastily. "I'm sure he's far too busy."

There was a moment of quiet.

"You really don't like him," Hester said.

"It's not that," Holly said. "I... We got off on the wrong foot." And that, she thought, must be the understatement of the year.

"I hear the development is going to be very exclusive," Hester said, pushing the cheese and the grapes towards Holly. "The place has been falling down for years, of course, so it will be a vast improvement." She paused. "I expect there were a few objections. There always are around housing issues these days and..." She paused. "Well, I remember your grandfather once saying that there are a lot of superstitions and legends about Ashdown Park."

"Superstitions?" Holly said, frowning.

"Stories, ghosts..." Hester waved a dismissive hand. "You know how much people like the supernatural." She drained her wine glass and placed it carefully on the table. Bonnie was having a dream, paws twitching, chasing rabbits in her sleep.

"I don't," Holly said, thinking of Espen Shurmer's stories

of the pearl and the mirror. She wondered whether one of the legends of Ashdown Park involved the Winter Queen's lost pearl. What had Ben discovered? Curiosity pricked her and something that felt like a lost memory twitched at the corner of her mind.

"Would you like anything else to eat?" Hester asked.

"Oh, no thanks," Holly said. "I'd burst. I've had too much cheese as it is. I'll make some coffee if you like, though."

"I'll do it in a moment," Hester said. She gave Holly an indulgent smile that somehow made her feel as though she was a child again. "Go and fetch your bags," she added. "I'll put the kettle on."

Later, in the comforting surroundings of the room she had occupied since she was a child, Holly pulled back the heavy curtains and opened the sash window to let in some fresh air. The room faced west and the faintest hint of sunset was fading from the May sky, a mere sliver of dark blue against the inky black of the night. The steady drone of cars still passed by on the Banbury Road. Holly drew the curtains together, wrapping herself in the warmth of the familiar room. Bonnie was already asleep on the rug by the bed.

There was a small shower room off the bedroom and Holly dropped her clothes in a pile, turned the shower on and stepped under the blast of water. She let the strength of it beat down on her head, closed her eyes and tilted her face up into the stream. The water was powerful—Holly visualised it as huge teardrops running down the side of the glass. She deliberately kept her mind clear of thought, concentrating on sensation alone, translating it into pictures, engravings in shades of grey.

She reached for a towel and stepped out into the bedroom, shivering a little as the air touched her bare skin. The wooden floor was cool and her damp feet clung to it slightly. She rubbed herself briskly and brushed her hair back ruthlessly from her face. The long, arched mirror on the opposite wall reflected her image back at her, pale and dark shapes, blurred at the edges, brown and white. Holly had always thought that she looked like a sparrow—pale skin, brown hair, hazel eyes and freckles that looked superimposed. She never tanned, just turned more freckled, like an egg. Her grandmother had said it was a throwback to her red-haired great-great-grandfather.

Oddly, after such a long and difficult day, she no longer felt tired. She slid a clean nightshirt over her head then prowled across to the bookcase looking for something innocuous enough to send her to sleep quickly. There were a handful of the children's adventure stories that she and Ben had devoured when they were young. On the shelf above were back copies of *The Georgian Journal* belonging to her grandfather. Holly was about to select one at random when her eye fell on a battered leather-bound volume with no title or lettering of any kind that was wedged into the corner. She took it out. The leather was smooth and worn under her fingertips. In the lamplight it gleamed deep green.

Curious, Holly opened it. The pages were stiff. The book smelled of faded lavender and old dust. At first she thought it was some sort of ledger, because it was handwritten in ink that had paled to brown over the years, the words swirling extravagantly over the pages. Then she realised it was not an accounts book but some sort of diary. There were pencil drawings too; on the first page was a delicately detailed flower, a pale faded mauve with long stems and tiny petals.

The Memoirs of Lavinia Flyte.

Written at Ashdown Park in January of the year 1801.

Holly jumped to read the familiar place name. She felt odd: a sensation of excitement gripped her, butterflies in her stomach.

A rectangular compliments slip fluttered to the floor and she bent automatically to retrieve it. There was writing on the back, Ben's neat black lettering. She recognised it at once. She had always teased him for having such neat handwriting when doctors were reputed to scrawl. It looked like a list of names.

William Craven.

Robert Verity.

Elizabeth Stuart.

Lavinia Flyte.

Holly turned the paper over between her fingers. Elizabeth Stuart, she thought, might be Elizabeth of Bohemia, although there were plenty of other people of that name. The other names were unknown to her.

At the bottom there was Ben's name and a question mark.

Holly turned the paper over again. There was a name on the reverse in blue gothic lettering: *The Merchant Adventurers.* There was nothing else; no address or telephone number.

She turned back to the text and read on.

I shall not say why and how I became, at the age of sixteen, the mistress of Lord Downes and embarked upon a life of vice. Or perhaps I shall relate it after all, for I suspect that a report of my amorous career is precisely the reason that many a reader will pick up these memoirs.

So here is my tale.

I was christened Lavinia Jane Flyte at St Andrew's Church in the City of London on 24th January 1783. My mother called me Lavinia because she thought it a pretty name. It means purity. Poor mama, what an inappropriate choice that proved to be.

Holly smiled. Head bent, still reading, she carried the book across to the bed and slid under the covers.

My father was a costermonger, selling fruit and vegetables from his stall in Covent Garden. How I grew to hate the smell of rotting fruit. It was as though it seeped from his very pores. Our poky little house in Bell Alley off Coleman Street stank too, of stale vegetables and dust and my mother's misery. I knew from the earliest age that such a life would not do for me and I planned to escape.

It was fortunate that I was very pretty. I make no bones about it. There is no place for false modesty in this account. My face and my figure were my key to fortune and I was determined to use them to full advantage. I had already observed that when I was on my father's stall we traded double the amount of wares that he would normally sell. Indeed, the gentlemen barely glanced at the fruit for they were too busy ogling me and I could encourage them to spend prodigiously. Perhaps there was less trade from ladies on those days, for they surely resented my beauty, but that did not matter to me. I do not need the good opinion of women to do well in my profession. Indeed, it would be positively odd if they bestowed it on me—or perhaps not, since I do them a great favour in entertaining their tedious husbands and sending them home in a better temper than when they left.

But I digress. It is a fault of mine, I fear, as will become apparent to you reading this memoir.

I had met Downes whilst selling him some oranges so, it was only a small step further to selling myself. He was handsome and young and spoke charmingly to me, and at that age that was all the incentive I required. I was desperate to get away from my father's house and Downes was desperate to have me, and so it came about.

Downes installed me in rooms at Oxford whilst he studied at the university there (I say he studied, but I saw little evidence of any great industry. It was all drinking and dancing and flirting, and most pleasant it was too). Alas, I had made a poor bargain, though, because this stripling lord was not of age and as soon as his guardian became aware of his infatuation with me he cut off poor Downes' allowance whilst his tutor threatened to send him down for immoral behaviour. Downes swore he loved me, but he started to crumble beneath this twin onslaught and soon he was begging me to tell him what he should do, for he said he would die if he could not be with me and yet he wanted his money too.

Fortunately, I had by that time learned a little of the ways of the world and realised that I needed to value myself more highly. I was not short of admirers and might catch a gentleman of greater wealth than Lord Downes would ever be. So it was that I solved Downes' dilemma for him by leaving his protection. The poor boy was heart-broken, but I imagine his distress was of short duration. As for me, I threw in my lot with Lord Gower.

Lord Gower was a gentleman of mature years and even more ma-ture fortune, who was easily able to keep me in the style to which I aspired. Despite the fact that he was a prosy bore and lamentably bad at pleasing me in bed, I do believe that I should have been devoted to him all my life were it not for the melancholy chance that he died within a six month. It was vastly inconvenient for me.

Sadly, Gower's heir was impervious to my charm and promptly evicted me from the pretty little house I had occupied in South Moulton Street. For a short while matters were most difficult for me. I fell further than I had risen and was obliged to find work in a bawdy house that delighted under the name of Madame de Senlis' Temple of Pleasures. Madame was no more a Frenchwoman than I, although she liked to pretend to all manner of affectation. Fortu-nately, my time there was short, but during those few months my amorous education was vastly expanded. I became proficient in the use of the birch. I learned how many men enjoyed the sight of two or more women disporting themselves lewdly together. I was celebrated for my ability constantly to recover my virginity so that once again it could be sold to the highest bidder. Useful skills all, but I felt I de-served more than this.

Help was at hand. One night during the season I was at the theatre and caught the eye of Lord Evershot. Evershot had no great personal claim to nobility or riches, but he had benefited vastly from the fame of his ancestor, the illustrious First Earl of Craven. Dying childless, the Earl had left all of his estates that were unentailed to the descendants of one of his sisters. This heir adopted the name Craven Evershot, but later the family dropped the Craven part entirely, which seems a little ungrateful. From such beginnings the Evershots had scaled the heights of the aristocracy. It gave them an air of being vastly pleased by their good fortune.

Evershot was a favourite of old King George, in whose service he had been, and was said to possess sufficient charm that even the Queen, notorious as she was as a high stickler, ignored his licentious and extravagant ways and considered him a fine fellow. I could never see the charm myself but that was nothing to the purpose. He was rich and tolerably handsome and quite young. He made me an offer that I refused. It was a dangerous gamble, for I had nothing to fall back upon. Fortunately though, Evershot was not the sharpest intellect and did not realise the weakness of my position. He made me a better offer and finally one that I was pleased to accept.

Evershot planned to take a house in Brighton and the thought of all those redcoats quite cheered me, but we had barely been there a sennight when a curious thing happened. My lord had a letter from the land agent at one of his estates that seemed to excite him inordinately. Immediately he announced that we were to go to Berkshire and would remain fixed there for a spell of time. In vain I protested that my portmanteaux were barely unpacked, that Brighton was highly diverting and that I could not bear the country. Evershot was adamant.

And so it was that in late January of this year 1801 I came to Ashdown Park.

9

"Gran," Holly said as she gulped down mouthfuls of scalding coffee, "do you know where Ben got this book from? Was it his or does it belong to Granddad?"

She had stayed awake later than she had intended, reading Lavinia's riveting account of her introduction into the low life of the high-class Regency courtesan. She'd hoped to find some reason for Lavinia's inclusion on Ben's list of names but other than a link to Ashdown Park there was nothing as yet. It was intriguing.

Hester, with the newspaper in one hand and her own cup of coffee in the other, looked at Holly over the top of her glasses. She was wearing a silk kimono of vivid design.

"Which one, darling?" She put the paper down on the kitchen table so that she could take Lavinia's diary in her hand. "I don't believe…" She flicked through it. "No, I don't think this is one of John's books. I've never seen it before. But you can ask him if you like. He'll be down in a moment."

"I wonder if Ben left it here last time he was visiting you," Holly said. "When was he last here?"

"I'm not sure when it was…" Hester murmured vaguely. "Oh, no wait." She looked up from the diary. "He was here about a month ago. It was the last time we saw him." Her voice wobbled a little, then steadied. "You think this might be his?"

"Well, it's all about Ashdown Park and the descendants of the First Earl of Craven," Holly said, "and it has a bookmark in with Ben's writing on it. I wondered if he might have left it here."

"Hmm." Hester was reading through the memoir again. "You know, there's something familiar about this…" She reached out and pulled her tablet towards her, typing in a few words. "Yes, I thought so!" She angled the screen towards Holly. *Lavinia Flyte—The Scandalous Diary of a Regency Courtesan, a true record as dictated to my trusted companion and maidservant Clara Rogers.*

"It's a published book," Hester said. "It was a huge bestseller in its time, apparently. It looks very risqué. I'm afraid it's probably all just salacious twaddle, darling, a complete fabrication."

Holly pulled the tablet towards her and scrolled down the list of books on display. There were a number of different editions of Lavinia's diary in print, and also various scholarly commentaries on the art of the nineteenth-century erotic memoir. The covers ranged from the tasteful—an elegant depiction of a boudoir—to the racy—a heaving bosom about to escape from the constriction of some very tight lacing.

"Goodness," Holly said. She clicked on the "look inside" button.

Written at Ashdown Park in this year of 1801.

I shall not say why and how I became, at the age of sixteen, the mistress of Lord Downes and embarked upon a life of vice.

"Oh." Holly felt deflated. Last night she had thought she had discovered something secret and unexpected. She had hugged the memoir to herself like a special gift. Now it appeared that the entire world knew about Lavinia Flyte and her diary. It had been published. It could not conceal any secrets. The brash flow of covers on the screen offended her. Not because she was a prude but because the handwritten diary with its delicate drawings of flowers and its flowing handwriting had felt too special to be no more than a sensationalist piece of erotica. Lavinia Flyte had seemed so real to her.

She looked dubiously at the plain green cover of the book as it rested on the table. "This is a handwritten version, though," she said. "Do you think it's the original?"

"That would be extraordinary," Hester said. "What would Ben have been doing with that?"

"I've no idea," Holly said. "Perhaps he found it at the mill."

An image came into her mind; the little hidden space beneath the window seat and a wet summer's day with the rain drumming on the mill roof.

"Holly! Come and see!" Ben's voice, urgent. *"Look what I've found!"*

She blinked. Had they really found the little green book in the secret compartment years ago, when they had been children playing at the mill, or had she imagined it? She could not remember.

"Do you want to see what your grandfather knows about it?" Hester asked. "Oh, here he is now. John, darling—" She spun around in her seat to address her husband, "do you know anything about this book? Holly found it upstairs. She thinks it may have been Ben's."

Again there was that small, telltale quiver in Hester's voice as she mentioned her grandson's name and John Hurley came across the kitchen and put both hands on the back of his wife's chair. He bent to kiss her; Holly saw her grandmother close her eyes briefly and rub her cheek against his arm, as though she was drawing strength from him.

"Morning, Granddad," Holly said, smiling at him. "I hope it was a good dinner last night."

To Holly, her grandfather had always epitomised the idea of a typical old-fashioned academic. He had thick salt-and-pepper hair, a slight stoop as though he had spent a long time hunched over his books, and he always wore a tweed jacket, even if it was a warm day. He matched the outfit with an air of slightly abstracted kindness that gave no hint of the steely sharpness of the mind beneath. Not for John the glamour and wanderlust of the television academic. He looked as though he belonged in Oxford's ivory towers and was determined to stay there.

"I certainly had too much after-dinner port," John said ruefully, rubbing a hand through his hair and making himself look even more dishevelled. "I should have learned at my age."

Meeting Hester's eyes, Holly saw the faint shadow of concern there. Many years before, her grandfather had been a very heavy drinker. Holly realised her grandmother was worrying that Ben's disappearance might push him into seeking that escape again.

John had picked up the memoir now. "Oh, yes, I remember this," he said. "It's an interesting document. I was going to get it authenticated for Ben but then when he left I couldn't find it."

"He'd put it on the bookcase in my bedroom," Holly said. She took the memoir from her grandfather, holding it close to her chest. "If you don't mind, I'll keep it for now. I'd like to carry on reading it."

"Of course," John said equably. Holly saw him exchange a look with Hester and knew they were both thinking she was eager to keep it because it was another tenuous link to Ben. Probably they both thought she was clutching at straws because in the absence of knowing what had happened to Ben they were all finding it hard to cope.

"What are you planning to do today, darling?" Hester asked. "Will you be going back to Ashdown?"

"Not today," Holly said. "I've decided to go back up to London for a few days. Not to make up with Guy," she added hastily, seeing an expression of wary surprise and relief on her grandmother's face. "I plan to pack up my stuff and make arrangements to move my workshop down to the mill. I wondered—" she looked at Bonnie, "whether you would mind having her for a day or two whilst I get myself sorted out?"

"We'd love to," Hester said, beaming.

"You should get a dog of your own, you know," Holly said. "They are very therapeutic."

"We couldn't possibly find one as lovely as this gorgeous girl," Hester said, stroking Bonnie's silky ears. "As long as we can borrow her sometimes we'll be fine." Bonnie thumped her tail in appreciation and agreement and when Holly rose to get ready to go the dog made no movement to follow her.

"Do you think she misses me at all?" Holly said, with a sigh.

"I'm sure she does," Hester said. "Give us a ring later and let us know how you're getting on."

It was still early, a Saturday morning, and the traffic was light, most of it heading into Oxford rather than out onto the M40. Holly rang Guy on the way to let him know she was coming. She didn't feel it was fair simply to turn up even if the house had been their shared home until very recently. When she got there the narrow cobbled mews and the tall slender house looked almost unfamiliar, even though she had only been away for a few days. It was an odd sensation, as though she had already moved on in some fundamental way.

Guy was waiting for her. He was in boxers and a stained T-shirt and had clearly only just got out of bed. He looked unshaven and not particularly friendly.

"I'm sorry about your brother," he said grudgingly, as though he had been rehearsing the words and thought he should be praised for his performance. "I thought he would have turned up by now." He paused, awkwardly. "I suppose they've started to think he might have topped himself…" His voice trailed away as Holly just looked at him.

The flat was in a spectacular mess. "I've been out most of the time," Guy said, by way of apology. "What d'you want to do?"

"I'll pack up all my stuff and take it back down with me," Holly said. The flat was Guy's, as was most of the furniture; it would not take her long. Looking about her, she saw how superficially she had made an impression on the place despite the time she had lived there, mainly because she had always been working. The cushions were hers as were a couple of the pictures. She owned one chair and some bedding. She certainly didn't own the toothbrush that was nestled next to Guy's in the bathroom but she ignored that. She wasn't going to pick a fight now.

Her workshop was a completely different matter. That was all hers and, as she let herself into the engraving studio and shop, she felt a sharp pang of loss and for the first time, questioned whether she was doing the right thing. Ben's disappearance had eclipsed everything else in her mind up until now. She looked around the shadowed interior, at the shelves laden with her stock, glasses and bowls and paperweights; at her long work desk and the drills standing idle and some of the old familiarity of her life returned again. She wanted to turn the clock back.

The problem was that she could not turn back time. Too much had happened. Ben was missing and she had changed. She wanted to be at Ashdown. She wanted to find out whatever it was that Ben had been researching. She wanted to find *him* somehow, through his work.

She could see that there were benefits in closing the studio. London rent was sky-high and for a number of months she had been struggling to make the payments. It wasn't that she was unsuccessful; she had a thriving small business, but expenses ate up so much of her profit. Perhaps it was time to move on somewhere different. The mill was a gift in the sense that she would have free accommodation and she certainly couldn't stay here, not now that she and Guy were over.

Back in the flat she told Guy she would be staying with a friend that night and saw his look of unconcealed relief. It was bizarre to feel that they had moved so far apart so quickly, and yet she thought they had actually never been all that close. For a while, their physical proximity had masked an emotional distance but now that pretence had been smashed to pieces.

"I forgot to tell you…" Guy was dressed now and looking as though he was ready to go out and hoping she wouldn't hang about too long. "A parcel arrived for you early this morning by courier. They woke me up, actually." He paused as though expecting Holly to apologise. "Anyway, here it is." He passed her a small padded envelope.

Holly pulled the flap of the package open. Inside there was a black velvet box and a stiff sheet of thick white writing paper.

She recognised the box at once and felt her heart do a

strange, sickening little lurch. Her fingers trembling slightly, she put it on the table and unfolded the letter. The paper felt smooth beneath her fingertips.

My dear Miss Ansell…

The writing was in ink, strong and black. Holly thought, irrelevantly, how rare it was to get a handwritten letter.

It was a great pleasure to meet you at the Ashmolean Museum last night…

"Holy shit." Guy burst out. He had taken the box from the table and opened it. Now he was standing there, his mouth hanging open, the crystal mirror in his hand. It looked tiny and fragile, but the diamonds shone with a hard glare in the morning sun.

Holly glanced up for a brief second but the letter called her back. There was a shaky nauseous feeling in the pit of her stomach. Her throat was dry.

You will, I am sure, remember me telling you the story of Frederick of Bohemia's crystal scrying glass, she read. *I have decided to withdraw it from the exhibition. Its place is with the Sistrin pearl; with you, Miss Ansell, for I am certain that in examining the cause of your brother's disappearance you will discover the pearl. I wish you success in your quest.*

It was signed Espen Shurmer. There was a short postscript.

The mirror is a gift.

Holly let the letter slip from her fingers onto the table, where Guy pounced on it. She grabbed the back of one of the kitchen chairs and sat down in it rather heavily. Guy was scanning the letter quickly now and when he spoke there was a new tone to his voice, excitement and disbelief jumbled up together.

"Is this for real?" he said. "Someone has *given* this to you?"

Holly looked at the mirror. It was lying in shadow now and somehow, in the ordinary surroundings of the kitchen, it looked diminished, shabby and half the size it had done when it had sparkled in its display case at the Ashmolean.

"Yes," she said. "I…think he has."

"Fuck!" Guy was staring at her. "Are those real diamonds?" He glanced at the letter again. "Who is this Espen Shurmer bloke?"

"He's a Dutch collector and philanthropist," Holly said. "He's an acquaintance of Ben's."

"Jeez." Guy sounded shocked. "I had no idea your brother knew such influential people. I mean… The diamonds must be worth at least half a million, probably more."

"I imagine so," Holly said. Her voice sounded odd in her own ears. She had never felt stranger, shaky, disconnected and only half comprehending. She touched the letter lightly with her fingertips. She had left the museum trying to persuade herself that the tale of the mirror and the pearl was no more than a garbled myth, a legend spun over hundreds of years, belonging to another time. She had tried to convince herself that it could have nothing to do with Ben's research.

The mirror is a gift.

She didn't want it. It was ridiculous that Espen Shurmer should have given it to her and that he would think it might help her find out what had happened to Ben. It was even more insane to think that she might find the Sistrin pearl.

Guy sat down opposite her.

"Hol," he said cautiously. "Do you think we should talk? About us, I mean? It's just that it's all happened so fast—"

The mirror lay between them, glittering in the sun.

"Guy," Holly said. "Really. You are so transparent."

Guy flushed. "I mean it. We've been together a while, we're good together. We were going to get married—"

"Except that we were always too busy to set a date," Holly

said, "which says something in itself." She touched the back of his hand lightly.

"Guy," she said, "I know what you're thinking, but I'm not going to sell the mirror. I wouldn't get rid of it and buy a better flat or an Aston Martin or a place in the Seychelles. That's not going to happen."

Guy was looking at her as though he had never seen her before. "What?" he said. Colour came into his face, hot and confused. "What do you mean you aren't going to sell it? What the fuck *are* you going to do with it then—keep it on your dressing table like you're Elizabeth the First?"

The words, spiteful and corrosive, seemed to spill across the quiet room and once again Holly felt a huge gulf yawning between them. It really was over.

"I don't want to keep it because I like it." Even as she tried to find the words to explain, Holly was aware just how inadequate they were. "It's an antique," she said. "It feels as though I've been given it in trust. I can't just get rid of it."

Guy shrugged. "Whatever." He stood up. "It's probably fake anyway," he said. "Clearly that bloke's barmy. And what did he mean about you wanting to find out about Ben's disappearance? You should leave that to the police."

Without another word he walked out of the kitchen and a few moments later Holly heard the bedroom door slam behind him. A beam of sunlight cut across the rooftop and played over the table, pinning the mirror in a ray of white. The diamonds sparkled with dazzling brightness. Yet it felt as though the air still hummed with Guy's antagonism, and remembering what Espen Shurmer had said about the destructive power of the mirror, it seemed to Holly that it had already started its malevolent work.

She did not feel as though she had received a gift. It felt more like a curse.

10

Elizabeth was having her portrait painted. There seemed to be little else to do. The weather was too inclement to walk, with a spiteful wind gusting in from the sea carrying grey drizzle with it. She did not feel like singing or playing or making music today. Last night they had held a masque and had danced and laughed and drunk and eaten their fill as though they were back in Heidelberg and the years of exile had vanished as if they had never been. It had felt a little mad, a little feverish, and this morning Elizabeth felt weary and heavy-eyed and all the pleasure had fled.

Perhaps they should not have been celebrating at all. A great victory had been won at Lutzen and Frederick was so close to regaining his ancestral Palatine lands, but the cost of success had been appallingly high. The Swedish King, Gustavus Adolphus, had died on the field of battle and at the moment of victory the Protestant cause had been plunged back into confusion.

It had been a strange year. In the spring Frederick's messages had been full of hope for the future but as spring had slipped into summer the tone of his letters had changed to melancholy. The advance on Heidelberg had stalled. He suffered from pain and deafness. Gustavus Adolphus would not grant him a command of his own and so he kicked his heels in idleness and frustration. Elizabeth had seen the pattern before; the way in which inactivity stifled hope, and confidence became mired in disappointment. Frederick travelled deep into his principality and his letters became gloomier still. Towns had been burned, devastated. His patrimony was ruined.

Elizabeth had felt so helpless. She and Frederick were accustomed to being apart; it had happened a great deal during their married life. Yet this time it felt different, more threatening, more dangerous. When Frederick had plunged into melancholy in the past she had been the one to cajole him back to good spirits or at least to lighten the burden. Now she was so far from him and she felt the separation in spirit as well as miles.

She also felt a new emotion, a sense of exasperation that Frederick could not be the strong, decisive ruler they needed. It felt horribly disloyal and yet it seemed she could not help herself. Dissatisfaction had lodged in her like a canker.

She had not seen William Craven since Rhenen. Others had taken on his role as Frederick's messenger. She did not know whether this was by his choice or Frederick's own. The gossip was that Gustavus Adolphus had offered Craven a command in his army, a most flattering promotion reflecting the worth the King placed on his skill and valour, which Craven had refused out of loyalty to Frederick. Elizabeth wished he had taken the commission; ever since Rhenen she had felt differently about Craven, too aware of him, too vulnerable to her feelings for him. They were feelings a queen should not have for her husband's squire, especially a queen such as she with a reputation for devotion and a hopeful brood of children.

It had been a shock to her to realise that she wanted William Craven. She wanted his strength and his certainty. She wanted his touch, his hands on her. She had been a faithful wife. She had never expected to want anyone except Frederick but she had never felt for him an ounce of the naked hunger she had for William Craven. It was a sickness, a fever. Whether she saw him or not made no difference. She thought it was because of the contrast between Craven's strength and Frederick's weakness, Craven's certainty and Frederick's indecision. But knowing the reason did not take away the longing.

She shifted slightly in the chair. It felt inordinately uncomfortable with the fat velvet cushions too thick and lumpy and the wooden arm digging into her side. Or perhaps it was just that she was feeling so restless today, uncomfortable in her own skin, uncertain, hopeful yet despairing that with Gustavus Adolphus now dead there was still a chance Frederick's lands would be snatched away once more.

Frederick had no such qualms. The letter he had sent her reporting on the victory had been full of triumph:

The Knights of the Rosy Cross have scried for me. The crystal mirror showed that I will regain all I have lost. Soon all shall be well, my love, and I will send for you...

Such promises should have made her happy, but Elizabeth did not trust the crystal mirror. Frederick, she thought, had made the mistake of believing that the magic that the pearl and the mirror possessed could be bent to man's will. She knew better. Old magic was not easily controlled and the trouble with prophecy was that it could be so blunt an instrument, promising much, delivering a sting.

"Majesty," Von Honthorst, the artist, said, half pleading, half irritated, and Elizabeth realised that she had been fidgeting with her pearl necklace, turning the Sistrin pearl in the centre over and over between her fingers. She wished that she had worn something different. It felt almost like a yoke about her neck.

"May I have a book to read, mama?"

Beside her was the fifteen-year-old Princess Elizabeth, her eldest daughter, wriggling and fidgeting on her cushion. The child was strange, preferring her book learning to hunting or games. Her daughter was not a true beauty, Elizabeth thought, at least not yet, although she might grow out of her youthful heaviness. If she smiled more it would be an advantage. She had inherited her grandmother's solemnity and her father's glum countenance. Still she was handsome enough to make a good match and now that her father would be Elector Palatine once more, Princess Elizabeth would be very eligible. It was time to start thinking of matches for her children...

The door flew open. With a growl Von Honthorst threw down his brush. Paint splattered. "Enough of interruptions! How is it possible to work when people are forever crowding around to petition you for favours, Majesty?"

It was not an importunate courtier who was hurrying across the chamber, though, but Doctor Rumph, black robes flapping, a letter in his hand, pages and pages of writing that he was waving in a frantic fashion. Elizabeth heard the chatter and hum of the outer chamber well up and then wane as the door closed behind him. There was a curious silence in the room. She could hear nothing but the tap of Rumph's shoes on the stone and marble floor and the sudden hitch in her breathing.

Something was terribly wrong.

She waited. Time spun out. It seemed to be taking Rumph forever to cross the floor to her.

"Mama?" Her daughter had turned towards her. The Princess' expression was questioning with a hint of panic. Von Honthorst had frozen still in the act of retrieving his paintbrush. He straightened up slowly. Elizabeth noticed the smear of paints, red and blue, drying on the floor.

"Come along, madam Elizabeth." The artist held out a hand towards the Princess. "You have sat very patiently and now you deserve an ice."

Elizabeth was still young enough to be charmed by the offer of a treat but she went with a long backwards glance at her mother.

"Majesty..." Rumph, in his agitation, had forgotten to bow. "I regret to inform you... The most shocking news..."

There was a pit of cold fear opening up beneath Elizabeth's breastbone. She could not breathe.

"His Majesty the King of Bohemia was taken suddenly with a pestilential fever..."

Elizabeth did not hear his words properly but she already understood their meaning. She would not see Frederick again. He was gone from her. She was alone, terribly alone, to face the future on her own.

The fear in her grew like a living thing, eclipsing all else, setting her shaking. Her breath would not come. She was suffocating. She clawed at her throat, snapping the string of pearls and sending them scattering across the floor in a cascade of iridescence. Dimly she could feel Rumph trying to support her, calling for help. The darkness beckoned to her. It was an escape and she took it.

"She breathes. There is still hope."

"The children... What do we tell them?"

"It is three days. No food, no water. Surely the end will be soon."

Elizabeth heard the voices but she had neither strength to move nor the will to do so. She floated, half-conscious, wanting never to wake. Figures moved about the bed, shadow forms. Time passed. She had no notion how much and no desire to return.

"Send for the chaplain. It cannot be long now."

There was a crash, the door banging open. It roused Elizabeth because it was so loud. Higgs was evidently anxious to hasten her into the next world. So often the chaplain was late; this time he was early. It would have amused her if she had had the will to feel anything but despair.

"My lord! You cannot go in there—"

Voices, louder. Hurried footsteps. There was a commotion about the bed, movement. It irritated her when all she wanted was the comfort of the darkness and silence.

"Majesty." She recognised that voice. It was William Craven. She must be dreaming. He had been with Frederick in Mainz. He could not be here.

"Madam. Wake up. Wake up, I say!" Craven's voice sounded rough with emotion, cutting through the fuss about her bed.

It was far easier to refuse than to obey him. She knew Craven could not have good news and she did not want to have to confront the bad, to accept that Frederick was dead and start trying to live again. Yet it seemed Craven would not leave her in peace.

"Elizabeth!"

No one ever used the Queen's name. There was a gasp of absolute horror from those courtiers gathered about her. But Craven was not done. He seized hold of her. His fingers bit into her shoulders. She thought he was going to shake her. Her eyes flew open in shock.

"Lord Craven!"

"That's better." Craven sounded grimly amused. "Where persuasion fails a lack of proper respect will so often provoke a response." He turned to confront the gaping court. "Fetch food and water for Her Majesty. She needs to build her strength. Hurry!"

Within seconds the chamber was cleared, all but for Dr Rumph who stood stiffly to attention like a soldier refusing to surrender his post.

"You bled her?" Elizabeth could hear the searing scorn in Craven's voice. "Then it is no wonder she is so weak."

She pushed herself up on to her elbows and tried to sit. It was true. She was as weak as a kitten.

"It's not Dr Rumph's fault," she said. "He did his best."

"You have no knowledge of medical matters, my lord." Rumph hated to have his authority questioned. He drew closer to the bedside as though to protect her.

"That's true enough," Craven said easily, "but I know what it is like to lose a great deal of blood and it does not make one stronger."

He strode across to the windows and threw the curtains wide. Light streamed in. Elizabeth blinked. Then he threw open the windows and she shivered.

"Enough!" she said. "Now *you* are trying to kill me." But it was too late for dying now. She recognised that the chance was past. Somehow she had to go on though even the mere thought of it exhausted her.

Craven turned back towards her and she saw the dust of the roads on him, saw too the lines of grief and tiredness that pulled his expression tight. He dropped to one knee beside the bed and took her hand.

"I am truly sorry for the loss of His Majesty," he said and she could hear sincerity in his voice. She knew that men had thought Frederick weak, ineffectual and no statesman. Craven had thought it too but it had not influenced his loyalty. Elizabeth liked that in him but it also shamed her. He had honoured Frederick with his service and now she had to honour Frederick's memory and put aside disloyal thoughts.

She gestured Craven to a chair by the side of the bed. He moved one of her dogs gently off the cushions and sat.

"Were you with my lord at the end?" Elizabeth asked. Her throat was dry and tight with tears but she would not cry.

"Yes." Craven's gaze was sombre, fixed on the shadows beyond the bed hangings. "His Majesty faced his death with true fortitude and noble spirit, madam. I have letters for you that he wrote in the days before…" He took them from his pocket, hesitated then laid them on the table beside the bed.

"He wrote of his love for you, madam, and instructed your children to obey you in everything."

The children. She had not even thought of them. She spent so little time in their company. Elizabeth's mind grappled with the necessity of speaking to them about their father's death. Charles Louis was Prince Palatine now, but he was still a child, underage. There was no possibility that he would succeed to the lands his father had struggled so hard to regain, not in this climate of war. Everything that Gustavus Adolphus had gained, everything Frederick had yearned for, could be lost now.

"You should go to them, the children." Craven was watching her face. "All of them. They are young and they are in grief. They need you."

It was more unasked for advice, more unwarranted interference. He expressed his views too freely. Yet she was too tired to rebuke him. Besides, someone had to deal with her directly, and never more so than now. She would need plain counsel in the days ahead.

Her attendants returned then, eager, with water and sweet wine, broth, bread and all manner of other food to tempt her. Craven withdrew to the outer chamber whilst they tended to her but she could still hear his voice. It comforted her. It felt as though he was the only stable thing in a world that was suddenly become unfamiliar.

She could not eat much but she soothed her parched throat and it felt good.

"I want to talk to Lord Craven again," she said when she had finished.

Her courtiers did not like it. She could see it in their faces. Craven was not one of them. He had overstepped the mark. Elizabeth could see that they already thought he had too much influence with her but she did not care. She waved them back to the edges of the room and propped herself up against her pillows, waiting for Craven to come.

He came back with the quick, impatient stride of a soldier. He had found time to wash at least, though he was in the same travel-stained clothes. Elizabeth could smell the dust of the journey on him, mixed with leather and horses, overlaid by the fresher scent of water.

"You came all this way to find me," she said, realising at last exactly what he had done for her, "when you must still have been on your own sickbed with the wounds you received at Lutzen."

"They are healing," Craven said shortly.

"And a brisk ride will have done them the world of good," Elizabeth said.

He smiled reluctantly. "I see you are yourself again, madam."

"Why did you do it?" Elizabeth asked. "Why did you come?"

She saw the moment when he realised just how difficult her question was and she waited to see how he would answer it. Would he turn it away with a light reply? Or would he deal honestly with her?

The laughter died from his eyes. He walked slowly towards the window, pausing with one hand on the sill. Elizabeth had had the servants stop the draught but the light still poured in, illuminating his face, his frown.

"Word came that you had died," he said. "They said that you had heard the news of the King's death and died on the spot."

"Fools," Elizabeth said.

"Yet not so far from the mark. If I had not woken you—"

"I would have regained my strength. Pray do not take the credit for saving my life."

She was lying now. She knew it and he knew it. He smiled reluctantly.

"Assuming that were the case," he said, "and you had rallied, you would still have been alone. Or so I thought." His voice had fallen. "Foolish of me." He made a self-deprecating gesture that encompassed the room and the hovering courtiers. "You are never alone."

"No," Elizabeth said. "But I can still be lonely in a room full of people."

He inclined his head. "So my mother said, when my father died. She was a strong woman with a mind as sharp as a rat trap yet she still missed him."

"I'm grateful to you," Elizabeth said. "Truly."

Craven shrugged. She could tell he felt ill at ease. Elizabeth wondered if it was the weakness in her, the vulnerability she felt now that she was on her own, that made her want to push him into acknowledging that there was more between them than simply the respect of a courtier for his queen. It was foolish of her. She knew she had to let it go. There could be nothing between a widowed queen and her late husband's squire, nothing that was not unseemly or scandalous.

"What will you do now?" she asked. "Now that my lord is gone?"

Craven looked surprised, as though he had not even considered the future. Other courtiers, she knew, would be scrambling for position elsewhere, deserting Frederick before his body was cold. They would scurry back to England, to her brother's court. She expected William Craven to do the same once he had had time to consider. It would be wise of him, and wise of her to let him go.

"I am your liegeman, Majesty," Craven said. "I swore my sword to your service many years ago."

"You promised allegiance to Frederick," Elizabeth said. "His death releases you from that debt."

He dropped to one knee by the bed, in front of the whole court. "What do *you* want of me, madam?" he demanded. "What is *your* command?"

I want you to stay.

She needed him but she could not say so. She could not make her feelings so plain.

"I think you should go to England," she said, forcing out the words, pinning on the brightest smile she could muster. "My brother has a great need of men such as you, Lord Craven. He will gain your wise counsel and you will also gain much in return."

"Advancement." Craven smiled, without mirth. "You know how little I value such things."

"I value them for you," Elizabeth said.

"Then I should thank you for your interest in my future, Majesty." He stood; bowed. He was going, and so soon. Elizabeth felt desolate and then angry with herself. This was what she had wanted. This was what she had commanded. Was she to abandon all dignity and beg him to stay?

Don't go. I need you…

It was impossible. A queen did not beg even when it was for her heart's desire. She should not want the things that were bad for her.

"I should be grateful if you would delay your departure by a few days so that we may talk more of my husband before you go," she said formally.

"Of course." Craven bowed again. "I will leave Your Majesty to rest now."

"Craven." Elizabeth injected some strength into her voice, to remind him once more who made the decisions.

"Madam?"

"Wait."

She waved the rest of her court away, watching as they massed like a flock of starlings at the end of the room, their excited chatter mocking the sober black of their mourning. She turned back to Craven and gestured him closer. She wanted no one to overhear this.

"His Majesty…" she said. "Did they bury him immediately?"

She saw a shadow touch Craven's face. "Yes, madam." There was unfamiliar hesitation in his voice. "It was the plague, you understand. We had to act quickly."

She did understand. No doubt that horrible report that Doctor Rumph had brought with him would detail it all, the fever, the swellings, the delirium. She shuddered, her mind shrinking from the thought of the pestilence ravaging Frederick's body. He had been so handsome when first they had met. She wanted to remember him that way, forever young, forever hopeful.

"There was the mirror studded with diamonds…" She

was so tired now that she needed to rest, but this was more important. "You know of it. The one that my lord and the other Knights of the Rosy Cross used for the scrying." She saw Higgs, the chaplain, turn towards her, ears straining to hear, and beckoned Craven closer still. "What happened to it?" She whispered. "What happened to the crystal mirror?"

At such close quarters she could see the gold flecks in his eyes, the shadow of his lashes, the stubble darkening his jaw. She felt a huge longing all of a sudden to be out in the fresh air and riding with him, shaking off the fetters of her role, being free.

"We buried the mirror with him, madam." Craven spoke without inflection. "I hope we did right. He wanted to take with him the miniatures of you and his highness Prince Charles and he asked for his sword and the insignia of the Knights of the Rosy Cross."

So Frederick had gone to his grave with the globe and compasses, the rosy cross and the mirror. Elizabeth knew she should be glad that they were all gone, buried, lost. Now it was over. They could be forgotten. The mirror and the Sistrin pearl together, with their false promises and dangerous enchantment, had wrought misery and destruction. It was good that the bond was now broken.

She lay back against the pillow, relaxing, her eyelids fluttering closed.

"Thank you, Craven," she said. "You may go."

She would sleep, she thought. Then when she was stronger she would ride to Leyden to see her children. She would manage very well without William Craven. He was just one man amongst many at her court. There was nothing special about him. She had no real need of him. He would go to England, where her brother Charles would honour him with titles and appointments. She would stay here to continue to push for Charles Louis to be recognised as his father's heir. They would do very well apart.

Or so she told herself, because she had no other choice.

11

"How's it going?" Fran asked.

It was only ten o'clock but it already promised to be a baking hot day. The door of the café was open, the tables and chairs arranged outside on the patio, stripy umbrellas shading the visitors. Fran was busy making sandwiches for the lunch orders from the building site, her fair hair bundled up under a white cap, humming under her breath as she worked.

"Can I help?" Holly asked. She was feeling lazy simply sitting watching Fran work. But it was relaxing too. The little café and deli was bright with sun and the smell of freshly brewed coffee was strong. Holly stirred her mug slowly, watching the swirl and ripple of the milk, breathing in the aroma. She had been in to see Fran the previous two mornings as well. She could see how this might become a habit.

Fran shook her head. "Thanks, but no thanks. Paula and I have it covered and besides, you look like hell. You need a rest."

"Thank you," Holly said. "I feel a lot better knowing that."

"I like what you've done with the posters of Ben," Fran

said. "It's a good idea. Someone might remember seeing him. There's no news, I suppose?" She caught Holly's expression. "No, of course there isn't. If there was you would be singing it from the rooftops."

"I'm doing everything I can think of," Holly said. "I've put out a call on social media and spoken to a couple of charities who help the families of people who go missing. And at least the police have started to take notice now. They've searched his house and the mill, and they've checked with all the hospitals."

"I saw them searching the woods again yesterday," Fran said. "And it was mentioned on the local news last night with a helpline number."

"Yes," Holly said. "Apparently there's been a good response. He's been seen just about everywhere from Dorset to Dubai."

"I suppose that's to be expected, isn't it?" Fran asked. "I mean if only one of those sightings is true then it has to be worth it."

"Yes, of course," Holly said. She wanted to feel optimistic but somehow she didn't. She was exhausted and flat. It had felt like such an effort to push forwards through the last few days. Even so she had kept busy, cleaning the mill from the attic to the cellars, tidying up the workshop and arranging her engraving equipment. She still fell into bed exhausted at midnight each night and was up at six to start all over again. She had done that for three days and wanted the place spotless before her grandparents arrived to deliver Bonnie that evening. It gave her focus and in an odd way, also strength.

There was no doubt, though, that the mill had lost its air of neglected whimsy and started to look clean and a great deal more cheerful. It was fortunate that it was already pretty much fully furnished, but there was no doubt the house benefited from the addition of her two deep armchairs even if their grey herringbone upholstery had originally been designed for the London flat. Seeing her possessions mingled with Ben's odds and ends had given Holly a curious wrenching feeling inside, a mixture of unfamiliarity, nostalgia and regret, as though the neat pattern of her life had gone fundamentally awry. She kept hoping there would be a knock at the door and Ben would walk in; time never altered the hope but over the days she could feel it changing from an edgy expectancy to a duller determination to keep going, as though she was settling in for the long haul.

On the table her phone blinked at her—a message. She felt her heart lift, as it always did, then sink dizzily back down as she saw it was only from her grandmother confirming arrangements for that evening.

Fran picked up her mug and came around to the table where Holly was sitting.

"Five minutes," she said, sliding into the seat with a little sigh of pleasure. "I need a rest." She fixed Holly with her shrewd blue gaze. "So how are you feeling? Do you think it's going to work out, you being here?" A small frown dented her forehead. "I mean, leaving aside all the complicated stuff, you always hated the country."

Holly was stung. "That's not true. I don't hate the country. I just didn't want to live in it."

"And now here you are." Fran put down her mug. "I suppose if it doesn't work out you can always go back."

"I haven't worked my fingers to the bone cleaning up the mill house for nothing," Holly said with feeling.

"I'm sure Ben will appreciate it when he comes back," Fran said.

Holly smiled at her. It was comforting that Fran had said "when" not "if" about Ben's return and she was grateful for it. There were no rules for situations like this and nothing to guide her. If she felt even a moment's doubt that Ben would return she also felt the most terrible guilt at losing hope.

"It's a lovely building, the mill house," Fran said. "A bit run-down, I suppose, but so full of charm. I'm not surprised Ben enjoyed spending time here. It must have been a nice break from inner-city Bristol."

"He wasn't here much though, was he?" Holly said. She savoured a mouthful of coffee. "I mean, it wasn't every week-end, or anything like that."

"He was here more towards—" Fran caught herself up. "More often just before he went away," she said. She frowned. "I wondered…" She stopped again.

"Well?" Holly paused, her cup halfway to her lips.

"I wondered if he was thinking of moving here," Fran said in a rush. "He didn't seem very happy with Tasha." She gave Holly a half-furtive look. "Did he say anything to you?"

"No. Nothing." Holly wasn't shocked any more, not after the things that Tasha had said, but she was taken aback that even Fran had noticed it. Had Ben told her stuff and she hadn't been listening? Had she made too many assumptions? Missed signs?

She put her cup down slowly. "I know there were problems but I find it so hard to believe," she said. "There wasn't someone else here, was there?"

"No, no." Fran avoided her eyes, tracing circles on the table with her finger. "Not as far as I know. It was just an impression I had. Ignore me. You know I have lousy intuition. It was just that he was suddenly here a lot, and Tasha never came with him, and so I wondered…"

"He told me he was coming here to do his historical research," Holly said.

Fran's blue eyes opened wide. "Historical research? Ben?"

"I know," Holly said. "But apparently Ben had been researching our family history and there was a connection to Ashdown Park."

"Perhaps Mark might know," Fran said. She eyed Holly closely. "I just thought we should get his name out there between us," she said. "I know you said it was a one-off and that you didn't want to talk about it—"

"I don't," Holly said.

A frown touched Fran's forehead. "This is a small village, Holly," she said, "and you are going to see Mark around. In fact I'm surprised it hasn't happened already. So you need to be OK with people mentioning his name."

"I'm fine with it," Holly said, not entirely accurately. "I'd be better with it, though, if you didn't keep going on about it." She looked out across the courtyard, where the red post office van had pulled up by a tiny, ancient postbox in the wall.

"That's Des," Fran said, getting up. "I'll make him a coffee to take away."

"How have people around here taken the plans for the new development?" Holly asked.

"Not too badly," Fran said, reaching over for a packet of cookies and ripping it open. She took one out and pushed the rest towards Holly. "They like Mark. He's very popular in the village because he helps people out with their building problems and stuff like that. All these old houses..." She shrugged. "They were never really built to last this long."

"Built for farm workers and now the last word in desirable country living," Holly said. "That's the way it goes."

Fran took the coffee over to the open door. "Des! Here you go!"

"Gran said that there are a lot of legends about Ashdown," Holly said. "Ghost stories and stuff." She was thinking of the glimpse of the house she thought she had caught through the trees, a ghostly presence in its former setting. It had seemed so real that night, and a couple of times since she had been convinced she had seen a flash of white walls or a gleam of the golden dome.

"So I've heard, but I've never seen anything myself." Fran sounded miffed. She loved the paranormal; Holly smiled as she remembered the time at college when Fran had been to see a hypnotist because she wanted to recover her lost lives and had come back saying that she had been Anne Boleyn.

"Mark could probably tell you more," Fran said. "He saw something quite spooky himself a couple of years back, up near the mill. It was the ghost of a woman running away through the trees. She had red hair, he said, and she was very young."

"That's very specific," Holly said. "Sounds as though he got a good look at her."

"Well, I expect it's all nonsense," Fran said vaguely. "Mark was drinking in those days—it was just after his marriage break-up—so he could quite easily have dreamed it all up in a drunken stupor and he's—"

"Standing right behind you," Holly finished even more dryly. She had forgotten how excruciatingly embarrassing Fran's habit of tactlessness could be. On the other hand she was grateful to Fran for eclipsing her own mortification on meeting Mark again.

Mark was standing at the counter, hands thrust into the pockets of a pair of battered moleskin trousers. A cream-coloured shirt had replaced the china blue one he had been wearing the last time Holly had seen him but the general effect was the same; broad shoulders, long legs, thick, dark ruffled hair. Her heart gave a little jolt in her chest to see him. She had wondered if the effect Mark had had on her before had only been a product of the strangeness of her feelings that day. Now she knew it wasn't.

"Mark!" Fran leapt up and kissed him on the cheek. "Sorry. I didn't see you there."

"I gathered that," Mark said. "You were in full flood, though I think you forgot to mention the bit about my addiction to prescription drugs as well as alcohol." He released himself gently from Fran's rather overenthusiastic grip. "How are you, Fran?" His cool dark gaze travelled over Holly and he gave her a slight smile. "Hello, Holly."

Holly liked the way he said her name and wished she didn't. She was a sucker for nice voices and Mark's was delicious, low, mellow and very smooth.

"Hello," she said. She wished she had thought of some sparkling conversational gambits in advance. Soon she would be falling back on some banality about the weather.

"Is there any news of Ben?" Mark was taking a battered wallet out of his back pocket and wasn't looking at her. She had the strangest feeling that although he was asking the polite question he didn't really want to know the answer.

"No," Holly said.

"Holly's moved into the mill," Fran put in brightly.

"Is that right?" Mark sounded indifferent.

Holly could feel her skin prickling with antagonism and something more. Fran threw her a beseeching look as though begging her to throw Mark an olive branch before the entire deli froze over.

"My grandparents are coming over tonight," she said. "They're bringing Bonnie back. I think you know them— John and Hester Hurley?"

"Sure," Mark said. "Mrs Hurley and my godmother are as thick as thieves."

"Army families," Holly said. "Like the mafia, only different."

"Well, I know what you mean," Mark said. He turned slightly away as though the subject bored him. So much for the olive branch, Holly thought.

"I was telling Holly that you know all the Ashdown ghost stories," Fran said.

"I heard what you said," Mark said.

Even Fran was not that bomb proof. She took refuge behind the counter and busied herself slapping butter on a roll.

"You'll give your customers a heart attack with that much fat," Mark said. He turned to Holly. "Fran was right when she said that I had a bit of a drink problem when I first moved down here," he said. "I was in a bad way. PTSD from Afghanistan, a messy divorce..." He shrugged as though it did not matter.

"I'm sorry," Holly said. She was startled by the abrupt disclosure. "That must have been very tough."

"Holly understands all about broken relationships," Fran put in.

"Sure," Holly said dryly. "I'm an expert."

"She's just split up with Ghastly Guy," Fran said. "We always thought he was awful but no one wanted to say so until now."

"Thanks," Holly said. "It's good to know that you were protecting me from the truth about my bad judgement."

She thought she saw a flicker of a smile touch Mark's eyes but it was gone before she could be sure. "I heard you'd moved down from London," he said.

"Of course you did," Holly said. Villages were like that. Everyone knew everyone else's business.

"I hope you don't find it too much of a culture shock," Mark said. "I used to travel a lot and found the change of pace difficult to adapt to at first, but it's a nice place. But, of course, you know that," he added. "You've been here before."

"People make the mistake of thinking it's sleepy around here," Fran said, "but they know nothing." She caught Mark's look. "Okay, so it's not Afghanistan. I realise that but at least you're unlikely to suffer from PTSD over anything in Ashdown."

Fran really was excelling herself today. Holly winced. Then she realised Mark had seen and misread her involuntary movement.

"You don't need to waste any pity on me," he said. "I'm over my particular traumas."

"Great!" Holly said. "Though I always think it's better not to confuse pity with empathy." She stood up, regardless of the fact that her coffee was only half-finished. "Sorry, Fran, I've got to go."

Fran looked bewildered, seemingly utterly unaware of the shimmer of antagonism in the air. "Why are you rushing off? We haven't had time to talk properly!"

Paula, Fran's business partner, bustled out from the back of the shop, wiping her hands on a tea towel. Her face was pink, though whether that was with the heat from her baking or the pleasure of seeing Mark, Holly was not sure. Paula had never struck her as a fluttery person before but she was fluttering now as she served Mark, tucking a stray strand of hair behind her ear, smoothing her apron, fussing with the coffee grinder.

"Your usual, Mark?" Paula asked, a proprietary edge to her voice.

"Thanks," he said. "Latte would be great." Fran came round the counter and caught Holly by the arm, pulling her back down into her seat. "Don't go, Holly," she urged. "Mark can tell you all about the renovation project while he's here."

Judging by Mark's expression, Holly thought he would enjoy that as little as she would.

"That's OK," she said quickly. "I really do have to get back to work."

"I've got to get back too," Mark said. "We've just found pipistrelle bats in the stables so there's going to be more delays whilst the ecological consultants do a survey."

"Wait!" Fran said. "Don't rush off!" She looked from Holly's face to Mark's studiously blank one. "We wanted to ask you about Ben's research, Mark," she said.

"I didn't," Holly said.

Fran ignored her. "Did you know that Ben was researching his family history?" she demanded.

"He did mention it to me." Mark had paused in the doorway, giving the impression that he was itching to get away. "I don't know much about it, I'm afraid." There was a complete lack of regret in his tone. "He came to the office a couple of times to look at our maps and some papers, and I pointed him in the direction of the Records Office but as to what he found out…"

"Perhaps your family is descended from the Cravens," Fran said, swinging around to look at Holly. "A lot of people come here looking for their ancestral roots."

She met Holly's gaze and raised her eyebrows. "What's the matter?"

"Nothing," Holly said. "I only just found out about the Craven connection to Ashdown House. I was surprised you knew, that's all."

Fran looked smug. "Oh, we all know about the Cravens around here. It's part of local history." She put her head on one side, studying Holly thoughtfully. "Hmmm. You don't really have an aristocratic look about you so perhaps you're just one of the local peasants like me… Mark though…" She grinned at him. "Yes, he's got the nose for it. Roman, do they call it? And those cheekbones!"

"Mark could be the model for a church memorial," Holly agreed dryly. "Carved in stone."

Mark gave her a look that brought the hot colour into her face. Okay, so he had not been cold and passionless when they had last met. Holly shifted in her seat.

"I don't think any of us can be descended from the Earl of Craven," she said a little at random, remembering Lavinia's memoir. "He didn't have any direct descendants. His estates went to a distant relative."

"Pity," Fran said. "It would really have been something if you'd been descended from the Winter Queen."

"What?" Holly said blankly.

"Elizabeth of Bohemia," Fran repeated. "She was married to William Craven."

"Elizabeth of Bohemia was married to Frederick of Bohemia," Holly said. "The clue is in the name."

Fran threw her a look that was half irritated, half triumphant. "Yes, she was, at first. She married William Craven after Frederick died. He built Ashdown Park for her. We know all about the Winter Queen here. Like I said, it's part of local history."

Holly stared at her. She felt a sudden chill ripple across her skin and shivered. The sun was bright and hot but she could not feel it any more. She felt as though she had been dipped in ice.

"We don't know for sure they were married," Mark said. "There's no proof."

"I didn't…" Holly's voice was husky. She cleared her throat. "I didn't realise that Elizabeth of Bohemia had any connection to Ashdown Park."

She remembered the name Elizabeth Stuart on Ben's list. So it had been the Winter Queen.

"She never came here," Mark said, "but it's true that William Craven built the house as a hunting lodge for her. She died before it was completed."

"Buried in Westminster Abbey," Fran said, adding with relish, "on a wild February night as a mighty thunderstorm crashed overhead. Buried with fire and water, as one of the chroniclers said."

"Fire and water," Holly repeated softly. The cold seemed to be inside her, intensifying, setting her shaking. Elizabeth and William Craven, the crystal mirror, the mill, the ghostly house, Lavinia's memoir, Ben's research... They were all threads in a pattern she could not yet see clearly but she knew it was there.

"Fran!" Paula was calling sharply from the kitchens. "You said five minutes and you've already been out there for ten."

"Oh, dear," Fran said. "I must learn to pull my weight. Mark—" She leaned an elbow on the table, "who would be the best person for Holly to talk to if she wants to find out more information? Is there anyone on your team who could help?"

"Oh, no," Holly said quickly, "I wouldn't want to bother anyone—"

"Relax," Mark said, a glint in his eyes. "I won't be volunteering. I don't have the expertise." He turned back to Fran. "What about Iain? He's been working with us on the restoration project here."

Iain, Fran's husband, was the county archaeologist but Fran dismissed him with a flick of the hand. "Iain's specialist subject is Bronze Age long barrows and the bones in them," she said. "I'm talking about the history of people who haven't been dead thousands of years."

Mark took a sip of his coffee and grimaced, reaching for a sachet of sugar. "Archaeologists don't just work on prehistory," he objected. "You know that."

"Honestly," Holly put in, "I don't want to put anyone to any trouble. I just wanted to know——" She hesitated, trying to find the words to explain why she felt such a strong need to continue Ben's research. Mark saved her the trouble.

"You desperately want to hold on to a connection to Ben," he said. "It's a common phenomenon when someone goes missing."

"Ouch," Holly said. It was true but he could have put it less brutally. She saw a flicker of regret in Mark's eyes. He opened his mouth and she thought he was going to apologise and for some reason that made her feel worse. She didn't want him pitying her because she was clutching at straws.

Her phone buzzed suddenly, urgently, in her pocket and she jumped, groping for it, feeling the customary lurch of hope and expectation. Fran, busy now with a couple who had just come in and wanted tea and walnut cake, had not noticed. Mark, though, was watching her with his unnervingly direct dark gaze and it felt to Holly as though he could read her thoughts. She deliberately turned a shoulder towards him. She felt vulnerable and edgy.

The text was from an old client enquiring about an engraving commission. Holly supposed she should be grateful that new work was coming in but as always when it was not Ben getting in touch, she felt a sick rush of disappointment.

When she looked up Mark had gone and Fran was standing hands on hips watching him walk away across the courtyard.

"Can't you just get past it?" she groused.

"What?" Holly said.

"The two of you," Fran said. "Mark all aloof and Mr Darcy-ish and you——" she waved her hands about in exasperation, "like a Victorian lady who thinks he's a bounder."

Holly laughed. "I guess we've discovered we just don't like each other very much."

"No." Fran pointed her butter knife accusingly at her. "That was not dislike going on there."

Holly sighed. Fran had known her a long, long time and for all her tactlessness she could be surprisingly acute.

"I just feel…awkward around him," she admitted. "It's hardly surprising. I treated him badly and I feel guilty about it and clearly he doesn't like me for it either."

"Hmm." Fran sounded unconvinced. "That's all true, of course—"

"Thanks."

"But perhaps you could build on it," Fran said. "Get together."

Holly shook her head. "I'm not in the market for a relationship. You know that." She got up and put her empty coffee mug down on the counter.

"I know," Fran said, her voice emerging, muffled, from the fridge. "Mark's had a rough time too. He hasn't had a relationship in all the time he's been down here."

Holly absorbed that for a moment. "So leave the matchmaking alone then," she said. She picked up her bag and slung it over her shoulder just as a group of walkers erupted through the coffee shop door, talking and laughing. "I'll see you later, Fran," she said. "I need to get back to the mill. There's still so much stuff to sort out."

"You know the shortcut back to the mill, don't you?" Fran asked. "Across the courtyard, take the path along the edge of the paddock and up to the Pearlstone—"

Holly felt a flutter of emotion beneath her breastbone, awareness, a sense of inevitability that stole her breath.

"Pearlstone?" she said.

"It's a sarsen stone." Fran was reaching for another roll, slicing it expertly and spreading the butter. "It stands by the path. You can't miss it."

"It's an unusual name," Holly said. Like a whisper, she heard Espen Shurmer's voice:

"The Sistrin… A powerful pearl said to possess great magic…"

Legend had it that the crystal mirror and the Sistrin pearl had been used together to conjure magic. Ben's disappearance had brought her to Ashdown Park where there was a sarsen called the Pearlstone. Could the sarsen be named for the Sistrin, the very pearl Shurmer thought Ben might have found and if so, did it offer a clue to the whereabouts of the jewel itself? She did not know. She was not even sure if she was being fanciful to imagine it.

Holly went out into the yard. The sky was a crisp pale blue with wisps of cloud shredded very high. There would be no rain today. Following Fran's directions, she crossed the cobbled stable yard and went through a gate into the paddock behind. A huge oak tree stood in the centre of the field with two horses sheltering in its shade. Both of them turned to watch Holly but neither moved towards her, as though they were too hot to be interested. The path climbed up the edge of the hill, a narrow chalky line between high grass and cow parsley and nettle. Elderflower overhung the path, just coming into white blossom. Holly had a sudden memory of her mother making elderflower wine in the kitchen of their house in Manchester. She could only have been six or seven at the time, and she had stood on a stool at the sink to help her mother wash the flowers. Hester had been there too, and the three of them had chatted and laughed as they worked, while the scent of lemon and sugar and the creamy floral smell of the flowers had mingled and filled the kitchen with sweetness.

She stopped walking for a moment as a sharp pang of nostalgia caught her. She thought about her parents every day but not usually with such acute emotion. When they had died the chasm of loss had been so vast she had not dared to explore it in case she fell apart and could not put herself back together again. She had tiptoed around it ever since, letting the years lay a superficial veneer over the hurt until Ben's disappearance had exposed the raw feelings once again. She wished she could talk to him. He would tell her she was not going mad, seeing ghostly houses, making patterns where none existed. He would talk about the power of memory and the way the mind made connections to explain things. He would tell her she was not insane but that there was something important here, threads she needed to connect to make the whole story. Then she would understand.

She started to walk with renewed energy up the path. She could see the cool edge of the wood beckoning and standing beside the path a huge grey sarsen, the Pearlstone. It was shaped like a pear with a rounded base and narrower top, exactly like an enormous version of the Sistrin that she had seen in the portrait of Elizabeth. It was therefore the same shape as the Bohemian mirror too.

The pearl, the stone, the mirror.

Now that she saw the stone, she remembered it from when she and Ben had played in the woods as children, though she had not known its name at the time. It had seemed even more enormous then and they had scrambled all over it and it had felt as ancient and immovable as time itself.

Holly hesitated then placed her hand on it. The stone was warm where the sun beat down on it, and surprisingly smooth against her palm, its surface yellow and green with lichen, the grey of the sarsen containing tiny flecks of silver. From here there was a view down towards the village in one direction and into the heart of the wood in the other, where a path disappeared into the green tunnel of the trees.

After a moment Holly let her hand fall, feeling foolish. There had been no visions or thoughts that had come to her in that moment to point the way towards Ben's work and the elusive Sistrin. But she could hardly expect a signpost. She needed to do some research. Even so, as she turned away from the stone, she thought she heard a whisper of voices far away and felt a memory stir that she could not pin down.

She carried on along the path, plunging into the wood's cool shade. On one side she could see a field full of huge white daisies. On the other the wood stretched away, a secret world of tangled paths and deep shadows. Holly had the strangest sensation of being watched but when she turned to look back through the trees there was only the Pearlstone, standing silent and tall, as it had done for centuries.

By the time she reached the mill she felt hot and sticky from the humidity of the day. She could almost imagine the splash of water over the mill wheel beckoning her to plunge into the pool to cool down but a drought had set in and there was no more than a trickle of water. The edge of the pool was thick with dust and dried grass. The sun was relentless.

Rather than letting herself into the mill she went along to the studio where all her equipment had been unpacked and set up. The wooden shelves now displayed some of her work—vases, paperweights, bowls. This was the place where she felt closest to Ben although there was no obvious reason why. When she had cleared the workshop a couple of days before she had scoured all the shelves looking for something—photos, notes, anything that her brother might have left there, but had found nothing.

But she did have one clue that Ben had left for her: Lavinia Flyte's memoir. She needed to do some work to start getting into a routine again, but later, when she had soothed her conscience, she would take out the memoir and see what it had to tell.

12

Ashdown Park, January 1801

What a horrible place this is! I swear I cannot bear it. It is so cold and lonely. We arrived here three nights past in driving rain to discover that the servants did not expect us and there were no beds made up, no fires and no food. Clara, my maidservant, declares she will take the first coach to the nearest town, but I fear she will be thwarted for no coaches pass by here. There is nothing but grass and sheep and birds twittering in endless chorus. Oh, and there are trees, a great forest of them that press close to the house like prison walls. I swear I shall die here, of boredom, if nothing else.

I became a courtesan because I discovered that I was good at it and because it is a well-paid profession, but at times like this I doubt my own choices. To be at the mercy of the whims of a man like Evershot, to go where he decides and do as he says is melancholy indeed. What other course is open to me, though? I suppose I could have stayed a fruit seller or flower girl but I wanted so much more. Or I wanted so much less; *less cold and poverty and drudgery. So I am a paid whore and must do as my protector demands.*

The laundry maid here at Ashdown considers herself too fine to speak to me, presumably because she only sells her services as a washerwoman rather than selling her body as I do. But the plain truth, dear reader, is that morals are costly. The price she pays is in blisters and chilblains on her skin from plunging up to her elbows in water, hot and cold. Her hands bleed; her arms are chapped and raw. She rises from her bed at four of the morning in the dark of winter while I sleep between the sheets she launders and wear the gowns she presses. So who is the fool there?

But as usual, I digress. Evershot seems curiously excited to be at Ashdown Park which is odd since it is such a benighted place. Naturally he tells me nothing so I do not know the purpose of our visit but he spends hours in the estate office scouring maps and designs from the earliest time the house was built. I know this because I possess a great degree of curiosity and contrived to pass the window one day and peer inside. Both Evershot and the land agent, a surly fellow called Gross, were leaning over a table strewn with papers and drawings. Evershot was so absorbed that fortunately he did not see me. I have already learned that he takes badly to my enquiring into his business so I keep my mouth shut as best I can. It is not my natural state however.

I have learned a little of the history of the house and of Evershot's illustrious ancestor, the Earl of Craven. This I have gained through a perusal of the books in the library, which clearly he never reads since some of them are uncut and all are thick with dust. I have also charmed the housekeeper, Mrs Palfrey, against her will since she believes me to be a loose woman. However she is another, like me, who cannot bear to have no one to talk to and so I asked her politely about the portraits that hang on the stairs and she told me all about the Evershot family. She was very proud to serve them, though for the life of me I cannot think why.

Let me see, what do I recall of that history lesson? I know that it was the Earl of Craven who designed this house as a hunting lodge in the seventeenth century. Apparently he was a great soldier and also the lover of the famously tragic Queen of Bohemia—known as the Winter Queen. I cannot say that I have ever heard of her—or of him, for that matter—but I can only imagine that his amatory skills were far superior to those of his descendant. Poor Evershot has been generously endowed by nature but alas has no understanding of how to use his gift to please me, and even less interest in learning. It is all about his pleasure and gratification rather than mine.

But yet again, I stray from the point. The Earl had monstrous huge houses built all over the place for he was excessively rich, but Ashdown was the house the Winter Queen chose because she wanted to live quietly in the country. Craven designed it to suit her taste in every particular. And then she died before it was completed. How melancholy and thoughtless that was. I so dislike unhappy endings! The Earl consecrated the house to her memory instead. He had no children to inherit, so all his wealth and estates went to his sister's son, John Craven Evershot. Thus the family rose to riches and titles and prominence without doing anything to achieve it other than to have been born under a lucky star.

I must stop now for it is dinner and Evershot demands my presence at table. He goes to the races at Newbury tomorrow with his mama, so I will have even less company than usual. It is deemed inappropriate for me to accompany him because I am too disreputable to be introduced to Lady Evershot. This is a woman whose standards of morality are decidedly lower than my own! Sometimes I detest the hypocrisy of society. Here am I, condemned for a life of vice because I chose to use the talents I had to better my place in the world, and there is Evershot who benefits from those talents—and believe me, he benefits a very great deal—and no one thinks the worse of him for it.

13

It was late afternoon and Holly was relaxing in an ancient deckchair in the garden. The sun was casting a net of light and shadow across the old brick wall. She had a glass of iced cranberry juice in one hand and a lurking sense of guilt that she was not still in her studio working, but finally the lure of the sun and the book had been too much to resist. She was waiting for her grandparents to arrive with Bonnie. There was a salad in the fridge, some new potatoes on the hob and a delicious cold spinach and blue cheese tart from Fran's deli to go with it. She felt modestly pleased with what she had achieved that day.

The light was so bright that Lavinia's sprawling hand seemed to dance across the bleached page, unreadable, so Holly pushed her sunglasses up on to her head, settled back in the chair and closed her eyes, thinking about the memoir rather than reading on.

Lavinia's grasp of history was probably both vague and un-reliable but Holly was sure now that there must be some truth in the gossip that there had been a romantic connection between the Winter Queen and William Craven, even if they hadn't actually married. It was curious watching the story unfold through Lavinia's eyes. Lavinia evidently cared nothing for her protector's noble heritage, pinning his less-than-noble behaviour down for clear-eyed scrutiny. Holly felt a great deal of sympathy with Lavinia whom she had to keep reminding herself was only eighteen. Lavinia came across as a hard-headed girl but Holly suspected that she was a great deal more vulnerable than she pretended.

There was something else about the diary that fascinated her, however. On her grandmother's suggestion she had downloaded both a published version of Lavinia's memoirs and also a book called *The Courtesan's Pleasure*, which was a racy biography of a number of high-profile women of the demi-monde. In it, Lavinia rubbed shoulders with the likes of Grace Dalrymple and Harriette Wilson. Holly had not had time to read Lavinia's biography yet and, in a way, although she was eaten up with curiosity she did not want to spoil the memoir by reading a more objective account of Lavinia's life. It would feel like reading the end of a book first. So she had put that to one side and had instead glanced through the download of the memoir. It had not taken her long to spot that the published version and the one she had found were two very different stories, and she had no idea why that should be unless Lavinia and Clara Rogers had simply decided to sex it up in order to make more money.

A slight breeze ruffled the treetops, setting the silver birch tree shivering and flicking through the pages of the memoir where it rested on the little metal garden table. It felt as though the story was beckoning her to read on, to discover more. Instead she got up and went back inside the mill, opening the lid of her tablet where it sat on the kitchen table.

She typed in "Earl of Craven" and pressed the search button. Lots of references came up—Wikipedia, various versions of the peerage, a list of paintings of the Earl looking handsome and haughty in black armour.

Holly changed her search terms to add the phrase Elizabeth of Bohemia. This time a motley selection of web pages and blogs appeared. A number of them coyly referred to an association between William and Elizabeth, described as "a lifetime's devotion." Holly read that Craven had served both Elizabeth and Frederick of Bohemia and had been Master of the Horse at Elizabeth's court in The Hague. When Elizabeth had returned to England after the Restoration of her nephew Charles II in 1660, she had gone to live in Craven House in Drury Lane in London. Various sources quoted Craven as Elizabeth's main financial backer during her exile and a courtier who had been dedicated to serving her for over forty years.

None of the reputable sources, however, seemed prepared to suggest that there was anything other than a respectful devotion between the Queen and her cavalier. Holly would need to delve deeper if she wanted to find out if there was any truth in the stories that Craven had been the Queen's lover or her husband.

The old-fashioned clock on the sitting room mantel chimed six times. She was about to close the tablet when one of the images caught her eye. It was a double portrait of Elizabeth and Frederick of Bohemia, facing each other, Elizabeth in deep mourning, Frederick in white. In Frederick's hand was a crystal mirror.

Holly shivered involuntarily. The mirror in the picture was instantly recognisable as the one in her possession, though it looked less battered, more alive somehow. The wood was smooth and gleamed with rich, deep colour. The diamonds in the frame sparkled. Holly found herself clicking on the image before she consciously thought about it. The painting proved to be in the National Gallery. It was by a Dutch artist and had been painted as a posthumous tribute to the Winter King. Elizabeth was the survivor, left to mourn his memory and continue the struggle alone. A little dog scrambled at Elizabeth's skirts. In her hand were two roses, one red, the other a withered brown.

Holly had studied symbolism in art as part of her degree. Roses, she seemed to remember, were associated with purity and the red rose in particular with martyrdom. The dog at the Queen's feet was a symbol of her faithfulness to the memory of her husband, who was presumably also portrayed by the withered rose.

There was a table behind Frederick on which were displayed a collection of objects: a bible, a skull, an hourglass, a compass and a globe. Yet it was the mirror that drew Holly's attention. She might have expected to see Frederick's reflection in the glass but instead there was something else… She leaned closer. The image was not a particularly high resolution and so the details were fuzzy but it looked like a crown. It could have been another symbol of Frederick's kingship or it could hold a deeper meaning, Holly thought. Espen Shurmer had said that the crystal mirror had been a scrying glass. It promised the world: titles, riches, fame. Yet a mirror also showed pure illusion.

The cold sensation she was starting to know enveloped her again then and she jerked back in her chair and shut down the screen. It felt as though the mirror was calling to her and it was the strangest sensation. The pull of it was strong. She barely noticed getting to her feet or moving across to the top left drawer of the dresser where she had put the black velvet box.

Would she see the future if she gazed into that pale glass? Would she see Ben's face and know that he was alive? Could the mirror give her the reassurance she craved from the moment she woke to the time each night when she put out the light? For a second the temptation was so strong that she stretched out a hand towards the box, intending to open it and look into the depths of the blue-white glass.

There was the crunch of wheels on the gravel outside and the sound of voices, doors slamming, then Bonnie burst into the kitchen, barking and waving her tail so vigorously it was in danger of knocking over the furniture. Holly shoved the box back into the dresser and pushed the drawer closed. She vowed to take the mirror and lock it away in the safe in her workshop, out of temptation's way.

"Darling!" Hester followed the dog in, her arms full of flowers. "A house-warming present," she said, kissing Holly. "Your grandfather has the wine."

They ate outside at the old iron table set in the corner of the garden where the evening sun warmed the old bricks of the wall and the pink climbing rose scented the air. Holly had been worried that it would be difficult for her grandparents to come to the mill, the last place that Ben had been before he disappeared, but they seemed to find comfort in its lichened walls and cottage garden.

"I always loved the old place," Hester said, inhaling the scent of the flowers with her eyes closed. "It's always felt a friendly presence to me, not inimical at all."

It was the closest they had come to anything that might cast a shadow over the mood and after the meal Hester took Bonnie for a walk in the woods whilst her grandfather helped Holly with the washing up.

"Have you had any time to pursue Ben's research yet?"

John asked. "I know it's only been a few days but you seemed quite keen."

"I am," Holly said. "It seems as though this historical stuff mattered to him so I'd like to see what I can find out. Unfortunately I don't have many clues—" She stacked the faded china plates carefully in the rack, "but I think it was something that involved the First Earl of Craven and Ashdown Park."

"Do you think it was some sort of genealogical connection?" John asked.

Holly shook her head. "I don't think so. You traced the family tree a while back, didn't you, so you would already know if there was one."

"True," John said, "although I only followed the direct male line. There could be any number of routes back to the seventeenth century." He paused, the drying cloth in one hand, the plate in the other dripping on the tiled floor. "Since the Earl didn't have any legitimate children it would probably be some sort of irregular descent and they are sometimes more difficult to find."

"Straight down the wrong side of the blanket." Holly smiled. "That sounds possible, I suppose. Did the Earl have any illegitimate children?"

"Not as far as I'm aware," John said. "I'm no expert on that period of history, though. I'd have to look into it." He noticed the plate in his hand and started to rub it vigorously. "I'll send you the family tree anyway if you're interested."

"Thanks," Holly said. "That would be great." She hesitated. For some reason she was reluctant to tell her grandfather about the Knights of the Rosy Cross and the legends of the scrying mirror and the pearl. Perhaps it was because he was so uncompromisingly the academic and with the Sistrin she was dealing with myth and magic. She didn't want John to destroy the stories with cold fact and logic. The link to Ben felt too important to her for it to be summarily dismissed.

John was watching her, though, and his gaze was shrewd and thoughtful, reading far more into Holly's silence than she had said. She wondered if he was going to ask her if there was something more troubling her, but in the end he simply said: "If you need my help with anything else, just ask."

"Thanks, Granddad," Holly said again. "Actually there is something else you could tell me." She rinsed the glasses under the tap and put them carefully aside. "I've got a guide book to the estate, the one the council wrote and produced." She saw John wince and laughed. "Okay, so it's not Gibbon's *Decline and Fall*, but it gives the facts about the history of Ashdown."

"Hmm," John said, eyes twinkling. "Does it include the story about the so-called marriage of the Earl of Craven and the Winter Queen?"

"It does," Holly said.

"There's no documentary proof for that," John said. "Only gossip and hearsay."

"I read that when Elizabeth came back to Britain after exile in The Hague, she went to live in William Craven's house in London," Holly said. "You can see why there might have been rumours about their relationship."

John picked up the cloth and absentmindedly polished the plate again. "She didn't stay there long, less than six months, before she moved to Leicester House."

"Rather like staying with a friend whilst you find your own place?" Holly suggested.

John looked startled at the analogy and then he smiled. "I suppose so. I think much has been made of their relationship because there is no hard evidence either way. Legend always prefers the more romantic tale."

"True," Holly said. "I just wondered if Ben's discovery had something to do with Craven and Elizabeth. If they had been married she might have entrusted something to him when she died."

"She left him various portraits and papers, I believe," John said. "I don't suppose she had a great deal more than that to leave, having been in impoverished exile all those years."

"I suppose not." Holly sighed. It felt like another dead end.

"How are you getting on with Lavinia Flyte's diary?" John asked, eyes twinkling. "It's not shocking you too much, I hope."

"The handwritten version is a great deal less racy than the published one I downloaded," Holly said, smiling. "I don't know if mine is just a first draft, but they certainly spiced it up later on."

John picked the book up and looked at it thoughtfully. "Interesting," he said. "I've done a bit of research myself since I saw you and I do know that the published version is largely a work of fiction—all erotic thrills and melodrama."

"I guessed as much from what little I've read," Holly admitted, "but this original is different. I'm sure it's authentic."

"Hmm," John said, clearly unconvinced. "Have you googled her?" he asked. "Lavinia Flyte?"

Holly had the feeling of disconnect that she always experienced when her grandfather made reference to technology.

"Um... No," she said. "I have bought a biography of her but I haven't read it yet. I didn't want to prejudge the memoir by reading up about her first."

"Well, I'm sorry if I've spoiled things for you," John said, "but perhaps it's better you know upfront rather than thinking you've discovered something authentic. I'm guessing that this—" he tapped the memoir "—is valuable in the sense that it's an early copy or perhaps even the original, but as a primary source it's very suspect."

"Wait a moment..." Holly groped for a chair, sat down. "I don't quite understand. Are you saying that Lavinia made everything up?"

"I haven't read the original, of course," John said, "but the published diary is generally considered to be pure imagination. Well, not so pure. But it was certainly successful. Lavinia and the maid both reputedly made a fortune from it. Lavinia was certainly able to retire from her profession on the proceeds."

"I...see," Holly said slowly. It felt as though the rug had been pulled from under her feet. She had been invested in Lavinia's story. She had liked her. Now she was not sure what to believe. Perhaps the next step was to read the biography after all, and discover what had happened to Lavinia after she had put not only her body but also her life up for sale.

She could hear Hester and Bonnie returning from their walk and got up, reaching for the kettle. "Poor Ben," she said. "I do hope he didn't put too much faith in Lavinia's stories."

"That was lovely!" Hester came in with a spring in her step, Bonnie all eager and alert by her side. "You are lucky to have some time here, darling—there are so many wonderful walks."

"I haven't had chance to explore them all yet," Holly said, "but I imagine Bonnie and I will have a great time."

"I brought you these," Hester said, holding out little bunch of pale blue flowers. "I don't suppose I should have picked them since they're wild—" regret tinged her voice for a second, "but there were loads of them and they looked so pretty. They're growing down by that big sarsen stone where the brook still runs."

"Water violets," John said, peering at them. "In folklore,

a quiet, dignified flower that is supposed to bring peace and reconnect people who have barriers between them."

"Is that so?" Hester's voice was warm. "Then let's pray that they help bring Ben home."

Holly went to the cupboard to take out a little glass vase.

"There," Hester said, as she filled it with water and arranged the flowers in it, "I knew that would look lovely."

"It's good that something still flowers in this heat," Holly said, "and that you found somewhere where the stream still runs." She peered more closely at the flowers. "I don't know much about wildflowers but they look a bit familiar. I know!" She reached for Lavinia's diary. "Look, there's a sketch of one here."

Sure enough the little sketch she remembered from the opening pages of the book was of a water violet. Lavinia had captured it beautifully, the long stem, the delicate tracery of leaves, the deceptively simple petals. Lavinia must have had considerable artistic talent, unless the mysterious Clara Rogers had been responsible for the illustrations too.

It was only later, when John and Hester had gone home and Bonnie was stretched out across the flagstones in utter contentment, that Holly wondered about the violets. Lavinia could not have seen them when she was at Ashdown Park because she had visited in the winter. Perhaps there had been a book of local flora and fauna in the library that she had copied. Or perhaps the water violet was special to her in some way.

Holly dozed too, in snatches of dreams, until the ringing of the phone brought her abruptly awake. She grabbed it, only to discover that it wasn't her mobile that was ringing, but Ben's phone, which she had kept charged and tucked away in the dresser next to the crystal mirror. She flew across the room to answer it and fumbled with the drawer, her fingers slipping in her haste, her heart pounding.

"Hello?"

She knew someone was at the other end even though they didn't speak. She could feel their presence in the silence. There was a sense of desperation to it that reached out to her.

"Hello?" she said again, more urgently. "Who is this, please?"

Suddenly there was a jumble of voices, quick, muffled, and then nothing else, only the stealthy click of the line being cut.

14

There was a new lady in waiting at the court, a sly, insipid creature called Margaret Carpenter whom the gentlemen seemed to find very pleasing. Elizabeth did not recall appointing her as one of her ladies but this was not surprising. Mistress Carpenter was the niece of very old friends and they would have assumed, as people did, that it was perfectly acceptable for Margaret to take up a place at the Wassenaer Hof. People assumed much. They had done so since Elizabeth's earliest days in Heidelberg, and she had always been too generous, too eager to please, to disabuse them.

She could remember vividly the days when she was first married and Colonel Schomberg, her steward, had stalked through her chambers at the castle, barking at the footmen to stand up straight and stop flirting with the maids, exhorting Elizabeth to be less profligate in her spending. Poor Schomberg. He had gone to his grave telling her it was better to be feared and respected than to be loved. She had tried, oh, how she had tried, to follow his strictures, but in the end she would always give too much away, whether it was money, jewels or her patronage.

Margaret's arrival had coincided with the return of William Craven from England. Elizabeth felt a hot wave of shame engulf her as she remembered how warmly she had greeted him. It had been several years and the surprise of seeing him without warning had banished all artifice. Her heart had leapt with pleasure and she had found herself smiling as he bowed over her hand.

"You came back," she said, foolishly, "I did not think—" Fortunately she had stopped herself before she had spilled too many secrets.

I did not think you would return to me...

It was a shock to realise how much she had missed him.

Then she had seen Margaret standing behind him. Margaret had dropped down into the deepest curtsey before her. Yet even through the pretty show of deference Elizabeth could sense the other woman's dislike. She was a good judge of character. She had met people who loved her, people who hated her, people who were poor at dissembling and people who were the best liars in the world, and she knew Margaret both despised her and was a very accomplished liar.

"Majesty." Margaret's gaze was lowered respectfully but Elizabeth saw the quicksilver upward glance full of flirtation that she flashed towards William Craven.

"Is this your wife, my lord?" Elizabeth asked coolly, knowing it was not. Craven had flushed brick red and stammered an introduction and Margaret had given a trill of artificial laughter that had held no amusement at all. Elizabeth knew it was a cheap revenge. Craven had stood there like a foolish, gaping schoolboy and Margaret was branded a whore, which was exactly what Elizabeth had intended when she had singled them out before the entire court.

Craven was not in love with Margaret, Elizabeth thought now, but he was addled by lust. She had seen it before, many times. The court was too small and the atmosphere too feverish for any affair to be kept quiet. And men were so often fools, losing cool reason in hot desire. But she did not like it. She realised that she had thought of William Craven as hers to command; that even if she could not have him herself he was still her liegeman.

She had tried to reason with herself. She was not her godmother, Elizabeth of England, who had kept her favourites dangling on a string like the puppets they were. She was a widow devoted to her husband's memory and her children's future, a stateswoman now. She was the one who had sent Craven away, because it was politic, because she did not trust herself. She could hardly blame him if he had found comfort elsewhere. Yet she did blame him. She was furious with him. The jealousy ate at her like a maggot in an apple.

She crossed to the desk, littered with correspondence from England, from her brother Charles, from Laud, the Archbishop of Canterbury, from her friend Sir Thomas Roe, all full of the intricacies of politics and diplomacy, the endless, pointless machinations of power and struggle. *Burn after reading*, Roe had written, but there was no fire. It was too hot a night. Elizabeth took the letter and held it to the candle flame, watching it curl and wither to ash. That, she thought, would prevent her enemies from being bored by the domestic trivialities of Lady Roe's life in the Northamptonshire countryside.

There was another letter, from her brother-in-law Prince Louis Philippe, Duke of Simmern, written in cipher. Louis Philippe warned of the imminent fall of the Palatine once again to the imperial army. Frederick's tomb at Frankenthal was in danger of being despoiled, opened, his body desecrated and dragged through the streets wearing a paper crown.

Elizabeth pressed a hand to her chest as though to push down the waves of nausea the image engendered. When she had first received the letter she had been violently sick. The passage of a couple of days had done little to calm the horror. Something had to be done, for Frederick and for the legacy buried with him. His body might be worth a fortune to the Emperor's propagandists but the value of the items buried in his tomb was incalculable.

She called a footman who came, yawning, from the door.

"Send for Lord Craven."

It was late; the court was abed. A vision came to her of Craven lying naked with Margaret Carpenter amidst his tangled sheets, drinking wine together and talking in intimately low voices as the candle burned down.

She snapped a quill between her fingers and the ink splattered.

"Stay," she said. "I have changed my mind. Leave him to his sleep. I will send for him in the morning."

"No," Craven said. "Absolutely not. I forbid it."

Elizabeth was amused. Her life had been hedged about by constraint from the earliest time even though most people would not have believed it to be so. It was a fact that there were more things a queen could not do than things that she could. Craven was demonstrating that now.

"You must see the necessity," she said.

Craven scowled. He looked angry and determined and it was oddly endearing. "I cannot say that I do," he said.

They were sitting in the scented garden behind the Wassenaer Hof. The palace's tumble of gables were silhouetted against a bright blue summer sky. Sun struck across the brass face of the sundial on its plinth in front of them. Elizabeth had chosen a place where they could be alone so that no one could overhear the conversation. It was not going well; in fact it was going worse than she had imagined and her expectations had not been high in the first place.

"Spanish troops are threatening to retake Frankenthal," she said. "The Swedes have given up all attempts to oppose them in Southern Germany—"

"I am aware of the state of the war." Craven forgot himself sufficiently to interrupt her. Elizabeth sighed inwardly. God protect her from men who did not care to be lectured in war craft by a woman.

"Then you will realise," she said carefully, "that if they take the town there is every likelihood that they will disinter my lord's remains and use them for their own purposes. They will parade his corpse through the streets, very likely dismember it and offer it every insult imaginable—" She broke off, hearing the quiver in her voice and not wishing to reveal her vulnerability. The previous night she had again been stalked by nightmares of all the terrible things that might happen to Frederick's corpse if Frankenthal fell to the enemy.

"I understand the necessity of preserving His Majesty's body from any insult." Craven's voice had softened. "Can the Duke not arrange safe burial elsewhere?"

"Nowhere is safe." In her agitation Elizabeth got to her feet and stalked across to the sundial, turning so abruptly that her skirts almost snapped the stems of lavender that overhung the path. The scent filled the air. She wondered when she had first started to dislike the soapy smell of it.

"Simmern is taking it...him...to Metz." It seemed ridiculous, macabre. Her brother-in-law was hauling her husband's corpse about the countryside as though it was a sack of firewood. "We agreed that Frederick should be reinterred at Sedan."

"Which is a good plan." Craven sounded easier, as though he thought he could talk sense into her. "Leave Simmern to deal with this, Your Majesty. You need have no involvement in it."

"You are not listening to me." Elizabeth rubbed some verbena leaves between her fingers. The sharp citrus smell banished the softer scent of the lavender and helped to clear her head. "I have to go to Metz," she repeated. "I have to take back the crystal mirror."

Craven stood up too now, irritation evident in the taut lines of his body. He ran a hand through his hair in a quick, impatient gesture. This time, though, he managed to keep a curb on his temper. "Majesty," he said. "If you fear the power of the mirror surely it is better to allow it to be reinterred with your husband?" His tone made it quite clear what he thought of the whims of superstitious women.

Elizabeth ignored the implied slight. "I was prepared to allow it to be buried with him whilst it was safe," she said. "But now—Craven, don't you see?" She spread her hands in appeal. "The coffin could be robbed on the way to Sedan. Or the Spanish could overtake the cortège. Anything might happen and if Frederick's body fell into the wrong hands only imagine what they might do to harness the power of the mirror. It has already wrought enough destruction. I cannot take this risk."

Craven had come up to her. He took her shoulders in his hands and held her still as he scanned her face, his hazel gaze as fierce and sharp as a hawk. She did not reproach him for his familiarity or move away from beneath his touch even though she imagined his hands on Margaret's bare body and that made her shiver.

"You really believe that," he said slowly. "You think it was the black magic of the Knights that was responsible for the loss of Bohemia and your husband's death and all manner of ills that have befallen you all."

"The Knights tried to harness the power of the mirror and the pearl and were punished for it," Elizabeth said. She knew Craven thought her a fool but she would never forget what it was like to look into the dark heart of the glass and see the visions she had seen. She had lost husband, eldest son, home and future. She knew how soothsaying could promise the world and then steal it away from you. Water and fire, fire and water... Both had taken a terrible toll.

"That is why I must go," she said. This time she did step away from him, as though to emphasise her words. "None but I can take back the Knights' treasure."

He was shaking his head. "It's madness," he said. "What if you were injured, or captured, or killed?" He threw out a hand. "Send me, Majesty. I will go to Metz and retrieve the mirror."

"You will come with me," Elizabeth corrected. "None but you. With your protection I will neither be injured nor captured nor killed."

She saw his jaw set hard. "You would trust me to keep you safe," he said, "and yet you would not trust me to retrieve the mirror for you."

Silence fell softly, split by nothing beyond sweet birdsong.

"Please do not tell me," Craven said, "that you believe that trinket would be a danger to me, that it might seduce me with its power." The sarcasm in his tone cut Elizabeth like a whet-ted knife. "Please do not tell me that you wish to spare me that peril when the truth is simply that you doubt my loyalty."

Elizabeth did not answer at once. It would be an insult to lie. It would be an insult to admit the truth. For it was true that she did believe the mirror would be a temptation to any man, and no matter how steadfast she believed Craven's fealty to be there was always a doubt in her mind. She knew how much magic could corrupt and the mirror's allure was not of this world.

"I trust you more than any man at court," she said truthfully. "I am surrounded by spies but you—" She paused. "You are the only one I believe to be wholly constant."

He gave a half-smile, which was fair since she had given a half answer.

"It is impossible for you to go," he said, more gently this time. "Surely you must see that? How long before anyone misses you? Are you to fool your entire court?"

"I had thought to pretend a putrid fever—" she began to say, but once again he shook his head with an impatience she would have reprimanded in any other man.

"Majesty, it simply will not do. To claim sickness would merely serve to draw attention. The court would be swarming with rumour and speculation. Everyone would be thronging your chambers waiting for news of your condition."

Elizabeth sighed. She knew he was right. Just for once, though, she had wanted to do something active. Sitting at her desk, writing letters, sending messengers, picking her way through the endless tricky business of diplomacy felt tedious and restrictive. Why was it only men who could take action?

"Send me," Craven said again. "You can trust me, Majesty."

He put out a hand and took hers in a strong grip. "I will not fail you," he said. "I will never fail you."

Her doubts flickered again like shadows crossing the sun. She repressed them.

"Thank you," she said, returning his clasp, interlocking her fingers with his. "I know I can trust you."

15

The phone call had been untraceable, number withheld. Holly imagined that the police would probably be able to discover who had called but as she had purloined Ben's phone she wasn't in a position to ask them unless she handed it over. She hesitated only because she wondered about the caller. There had not been anything that felt threatening about the call but she had felt that person's quiet desperation. She wanted to find them and, in an odd way, she wanted to reassure them. Except she could offer no reassurance.

She thought about it a lot the following day as she worked on the design for a set of glasses that she was producing for an anniversary present. The work was detailed and precise, the kind of thing she loved normally; the kind of thing that was supremely difficult when her concentration was shot to pieces as it was now. It was something of a relief when there was a tentative knock at the workshop door and a girl came in. She was skinny and beautiful, dressed in low-slung combat trousers, a cutaway green top and a pair of navy blue wedge mules; the girl Holly had seen at the bus stop on the day she had met Mark.

"Hi." She edged around the display shelves, walking in a slightly concave manner, like someone in a china shop. Holly had noticed that plenty of people did this. It was as though the presence of the glass made them uneasy. "Fran sent me. She said you might be able to help me." She was holding a plastic carrier bag, which she laid on Holly's desk. The contents were wrapped in tissue paper, which she very carefully unwrapped. Holly could see that it had once been a glass bowl. Now it was a jumble of shattered fragments. The faint, dusty sunshine slid through the studio window and scintillated off its spiky edges.

"Oh." Holly pushed her goggles up into her hair and bent to examine the pieces. "Oh, dear."

"Can you mend it?" the girl asked. There was hope and eagerness in her eyes.

"No," Holly said regretfully. "I'm afraid I can't. It's too badly smashed."

The girl did not seem surprised but her narrow shoulders slumped under the green top. "Bloody, bloody Joe," she said gloomily. "I told him to be careful."

"What happened?" Holly asked. Not that it made any difference knowing how the bowl had been broken. She could tell from looking at the shards that it had been a high quality piece, Caithness or Dartington Crystal perhaps. It would have been very beautiful.

The girl thrust her hands into the waistband of the combat trousers.

"Like I said, it was Joe's fault. He was messing about and he just bumped into the table and sent it flying. I'm Flick Warner, by the way. Joe's my younger brother. Older than me, I mean, but the younger of the two."

"Which must mean that Mark is your brother too," Holly said. She should have seen it at once. Whilst Flick's hair was blonde, she had the same brown eyes and breathtaking angles to her face that Mark had. On Flick, though, they were softened so that she looked spectacularly pretty but slightly sulky too.

"It's Mark's bowl." Flick looked awkward. "He won it for one of those charity endurance events he did. So it's really important, sentimental value as well as being expensive..." She trailed off unhappily. "I don't know what to do."

"Why don't you tell him what happened?" Holly suggested. "I'm sure he'd rather know the truth and since it isn't fixable—"

"But you could make a replacement, couldn't you?" Flick broke in. She blushed and Holly suddenly wondered if she was younger than she had thought. "It's just that I can't tell him." She knotted her hands together, twisting her fingers so the knuckles showed white. "Mark's great and I don't want to upset him. He'd hate me."

Holly smiled at the teenage overexaggeration. "Mark's not that scary, is he? I mean I know he can be a bit abrupt, but you're his sister. I'm sure he'd understand it was an accident."

"It's complicated." Flick was avoiding her eyes now. "I live with Mark during term time, you see, and Joe comes to visit some weekends from uni and neither of us want to piss him off in case he throws us out and we have to go back to living with our parents." There was an edge of desperation to her voice. "Don't get me wrong, Dad's fine but he travels a lot so it's just Mum and me, and trust me that is not a good combination..." She shrugged helplessly. "Could you help us out? Make something similar? That way, Mark need never know."

She fumbled anxiously in the raffia bag slung over her

shoulder. "Fran recommended you, you know, she says you're really good."

She saw the look in Holly's eye and rushed on. "Look, I've brought some photographs. I thought it was a good idea… So you can see what it was like—"

She tossed them onto the desk. Holly picked one up slowly, scanned it. It showed the bowl in all its glorious detail, down to the engraved lettering on the base, which stated that it had been awarded to Captain Mark Warner for completing the Antarctic Endurance Trek. It was decorated with beautifully engraved laurel leaves symbolising victory.

With a sigh Holly turned to another of the photos. It was a typical family snapshot—Sunday lunch or someone's birthday—and the family was gathered around a big walnut dining table with the crystal bowl in the middle. There was an older man wearing a grey suit, jovial smile and slightly strained expression and a gracious-looking lady in shift dress and pearls, who Holly guessed must be Mrs Warner.

"Didn't anyone ever tell you that honesty is the best policy?" Holly knew she was really too young to sound like somebody's mother, but she had to try. "It really would be better to own up…"

Flick grinned. She had pleasingly uneven teeth and an engaging smile. Holly could feel herself weakening.

"I'm frequently told that. I couldn't possibly let Joe get into such trouble, though."

Joe was also in the photo, lounging at the foot of the table next to a woman Holly did not recognise. Holly thought that he looked well able to take care of himself. Again there was the resemblance to Mark but in Joe's case he looked like a raffish eighteenth-century poet after a long night in the coffee house. Flick was sitting next to her father. Mark wasn't in the shot so perhaps he had been the one taking the photograph.

"Hmm," Holly said. "Well, I'd love to be able to help you but—"

"Great! We'll pay you—"

"But I shouldn't. It's unethical."

Flick screwed her face up. "I know! And I shouldn't be asking you, but—" She pushed her long, fair hair away from her face. "It's just that it's irreplaceable in the true sense, isn't it? I mean, we'd never get another one like it."

"No." Holly came to a decision. She put the photographs back on the table and sat down slowly. Her swivel chair was high, like a dentist's stool. She leant her elbows on her work desk and rested her chin on her hand. "Look, I'm sorry. I can't do this. I don't know Mark well but I'm willing to bet he would far rather know what had happened than you spend good money on a fake that will never look exactly the same anyway."

Flick's shoulders slumped. "I know you're right. Okay." She straightened. "I'll do it. Only—" She looked anxious. "You won't say anything to Mark, will you? It was stupid of me to think I could get around it like this but I'd rather tell him in my own way."

"As long as you do," Holly said, trying not to sound pompous. "And tell him it was Joe who did it. He shouldn't have left you in the lurch in the first place."

Flick's expression lightened and she gave Holly a spontaneous hug. "Thanks!" She backed towards the door, narrowly missing knocking over a box of paperweights.

"Oops!" Flick said. She cast a look around. "It's very different in here now, isn't it? You wouldn't know it was the same place."

She paused like a bird on the edge of flight and for a second Holly had the oddest sense that she wanted to say something else but then with a casual wave she was gone. There was silence for a long while and then a car door slammed; there was a roar of a powerful engine that sounded intrusive in the quiet. Holly caught sight of a flash of colour as a sports car shot off down the track to the village.

Shaking her head, Holly righted the box and went back to her work desk. She thought about Flick's hug and felt slightly bemused. She didn't think she invited closeness, not because she was unfriendly but because she was reserved. Flick must be the sort of person who rode roughshod over those kinds of reservations, which was lovely but surprising.

Or perhaps this was what life was like in the village. Really she had no idea. She'd never lived anywhere like Ashdown before.

Tomorrow she was determined to go down to Mark's office and ask very nicely if he could show her the maps and documents that Ben had been studying. Fran had been right. She did need to start behaving normally around him.

She reached above her work desk and opened the window shutters. Pale light filtered into the room. The wood was warm where the sun had beaten against it all day and the air in the workshop was still heavy with heat. Holly leaned over the workbench and picked up the glass she had been working on before Flick had interrupted her. She tilted it so that the light from window struck the glass. She was her own hardest critic, but she was pleased with the work. There was a pattern of honeysuckle beneath the surface, entwined and grasping upwards on woody stems. It reached towards her, forever blocked by the smooth glass. Holly turned the glass around and touched the letters cut into the other side.

"Anne and Henry," the inscription read. "Congratulations on 25 years of unmarried bliss."

Holly smiled. She loved the process by which she matched the gift to the recipient. In this case her client had been Henry's sister, who had told her that the couple ran a nursery and loved plants and nature, and preferred simple uncluttered styles to fussiness. Holly studied the pattern on the glass. It was pretty, perfect and ready to be packaged in the morning.

She pulled the workshop door closed behind her, wondering as she did so whether Flick Warner would summon up the courage to tell Mark what had happened to the glass bowl. She hoped so but she wasn't sure. There had been something fragile about Flick.

Holly walked slowly along the path to the mill. It was not much cooler outside but it was fresher. A slight breeze ran through the trees bringing with it the scent of cut grass and the call of birds.

Oddly, the door of the mill was ajar. Holly knew she had not left it like that and her heart started to race. She pushed it wide.

"Ben!"

Her call fell into silence. She waited a second then shouted again. There was no reply. She ran up the stairs, quickly checking each room. There was nothing, only Bonnie, standing and looking up at her enquiringly, wagging her tail in hope of a walk.

Holly sat down abruptly on the top step. She could feel the mad scramble of her heart start to subside and a wave of sick disappointment wash over her. Briefly she put her head in her hands. Perhaps she had been mistaken and had left the door off the latch. A cursory glance about the room suggested that nothing was missing, and Bonnie would surely have barked if there had been any intruders.

Slowly, feeling suddenly tired, she took Bonnie's lead from the shelf and they went out, taking a path that plunged deep into the wood. The path took them along wide grassy rides and through tunnels of lime and oak trees, crossing other paths, intersecting, dipping down through hollow ways that felt older than time. Bonnie played with her ball on a rope in the wide clearings. They arrived in the village and Holly saw that the door of the tea room was still ajar so she pushed it and went in.

"Fran!"

Fran looked up from the till. Her lips moved. "Seventy five, eighty… Damn it, Holly, I'd nearly finished and now it'll take me another half hour!"

"Stick it in the safe and count it up tomorrow," Holly suggested, coming inside and closing the door behind her. "How come you're so late anyway?"

"I got chatting," Fran said vaguely. "No worries—all I'm missing is the church roof fund committee meeting. They're getting terribly excited about the barn dance." She took off the ridiculously sexy glasses that she used for figure work and regarded Holly thoughtfully. "You are going to come, aren't you, Holly?"

"I have two left feet," Holly said. "Please don't make me inflict them on the unsuspecting members of the village."

"It'll be fun," Fran said. "Anyway, it's not until October. Plenty of time to learn the do-si-do." She disappeared into the stockroom and Holly heard the heavy clunk of the safe closing.

Fran re-emerged and started to pull down the metal blinds.

"Did Flick Warner come to find you?" she asked. "She said she needed a glass engraver."

Holly looked at her. There was more than a hint of curiosity in Fran's voice but she chose to ignore the hint. "She did. Thanks."

Fran narrowed her eyes. "So what's it all about?"

"Oh," Holly said, deliberately vague, "just an enquiry, but thanks for recommending me."

Fran glared. "You're short-changing me…"

"Yeah…" Holly grinned at her. "Client confidentiality…"

Fran snorted. "You just use that as an excuse for keeping secrets. Don't think I don't know!"

Holly raised her eyebrows.

"You've got a secretive face." Fran was on a roll now. "You should have been a bloody Trappist monk—"

"In another life, perhaps."

Fran closed the first blind with a metallic click and locked it. "She's had a lot of problems, that girl," she said. "They both have, Flick and Joe. Mark's been a star for taking them on. Actually I think it helped him too. Gave him something to focus on." She glanced at Holly over her shoulder. "How did it go last night?" she asked. Then, when Holly looked blank, she prompted: "With your grandparents? Weren't they coming over to take a look at what you've done with the mill?"

"Oh, yes." Holly smiled. "They like it. We had a nice time."

"Not too difficult?" Fran pressed. "I mean after Ben's disappearance I wouldn't have expected that any of you would want to set foot near the place."

"I would have thought so too," Holly admitted, "but I like it there. It's comforting, somehow."

"Great." Fran gestured towards the deli counter. "Look, would you like a hot chocolate? Hattie and Luke are with the childminder until six so there's plenty of time. We could take it outside as it's still warm."

"You've cleaned up already," Holly objected. "Won't it make a mess?"

"Hot chocolate with whipped cream is worth any amount of mess," Fran said.

"I'm starting to feel that all I do here is eat and drink," Holly said with a sigh. "Not that I'm complaining."

She went outside with Bonnie whilst Fran switched on the machine. The low hum of it mingled with the caw of the rooks nesting in the edge of the wood and the ever-present drone of the diggers at the building site. Mark must work long hours whilst his kid sister was running around the countryside in a flash sports car.

"Does Mark have a sports car?" Holly asked Fran when she reappeared with a tray complete with two mugs of chocolate, a pot of cinnamon sprinkles and a plate of cupcakes.

"Yeah," Fran said. "It's an Aston Martin. Racing green. He calls it the last vestige of his past life."

"It must be hell on these roads," Holly said. She took a sip of the chocolate. "Oh, that's good. Thank you, Fran."

"My pleasure." Fran sat back in the chair with a contented sigh. "Aren't these warm evenings gorgeous?" She turned her head and looked at Holly. "Have you found out any more about Ben's research, by the way?"

"I'm going to take a look at some of the papers he consulted tomorrow," Holly said. "I must say I was a bit surprised to find out that there was a link between Ashdown Park and the Winter Queen," she added. "I had no idea. I met someone recently..." she hesitated, "who gave me an artefact from Elizabeth's court in The Hague. A piece of crystal."

"Really?" Fran was lying back in her chair, face tilted up to the sun, eyes closed. She sounded sleepy. "You don't seem very pleased. Is it hideous? Give it away. Or better still, sell it on eBay."

Holly almost snorted into her hot chocolate at the thought of trying to sell the crystal mirror on eBay. *Pre-loved mirror decorated with diamonds, boasting a slightly dodgy reputation... Very beautiful if you like that sort of thing, may tell the future but may also bring bad luck...*

"I'd better get going," she said regretfully, draining her

mug. "I want to do some more work this evening. No, Bon Bon—" she pushed the dog's nose gently away from the remaining cupcakes, "not for you. I'll give you your tea when we get back."

"I'll stay here a bit longer," Fran said. "It's so peaceful." She opened her eyes. "Did you find your way back OK yesterday? The path by the Pearlstone?"

"Oh, yes," Holly said. "Thanks. It's a magnificent sarsen, isn't it?" She picked up Bonnie's lead and made for the stile that led to the footpath. "Thanks for the hot chocolate," she added, over her shoulder. "It was delicious."

The sun was low now, sparkling with golden radiance. It struck across Holly's eyes for a moment, completely dazzling her, then over the trees she saw the top of a bright white house with a dainty cupola crowned with a golden ball, so high that it seemed to sail against the blue of the sky.

"Are you all right?" Fran sounded concerned.

"I'm fine." Holly realised she was standing stock-still in the courtyard with both Bonnie and Fran staring at her curiously. She glanced back instinctively at the woods. No house stood there. There was nothing but the woods, sunlit and empty, nothing at all.

16

I raised the birch and belaboured Lord Hiscox about his plump posterior until it was rosy and heated and his lordship was begging me for mercy. Knowing that he required to be beaten in order to be roused I ignored his pitiful pleas for clemency and struck all the harder until his member jutted forth, painfully purple and distended, and I was able to give him the relief he craved. As soon as he was spent the others ran forwards to untie him and his place at the flogging stand was taken by Lord Carvel, so eager he was trembling with excitement.

Holly closed down the ebook and her screen went blank. She felt quite exhausted reading about all the flagellation that went on in Lavinia's brothel. The published version of Lavinia's memoir was an endless litany of sexual excess. From the rampant outrages of Oxford undergraduates to every conceivable fetish of the *Haut Ton* it romped along with no apparent plot or indeed moral to the story. The Lavinia of *The Scandalous Diary of a Regency Courtesan* was a happy prostitute who leaped from one liaison to the next, or several at a time. She bore little relation to the Lavinia of the handwritten memoir, and although some of the story was the same it was written in a parody of Lavinia's lively prose style and it felt like a cheap, exploitative copy.

She turned to the weighty tome she had picked up at Swindon Library after her chat with Fran. It was an analysis of sexual morals and mores in the late eighteenth and early nineteenth century and it mentioned Lavinia's diary a number of times, describing it as an attempt to cash in on her experience as a courtesan in order to make sufficient money to support herself in later life. Originally entitled, quite wittily, Holly thought, *The Transit of Venus*, it had gone through various editions and was generally considered to be one of the more explicitly erotic writings of the time. It did not try to present Lavinia in a sympathetic light or with any shred of good reputation. It was this, the author asserted, that had made *The Transit of Venus* a great deal more financially successful than the daring but relatively discreet diaries of other courtesans.

It was the comment about financing a retirement that made Holly wonder what had really happened to Lavinia in the end. Her grandfather had said that Lavinia had disappeared from the public view but that was the extent of her knowledge. She clicked on the Internet and keyed Lavinia's name into the search engine. There were a number of brief biographies of her; all of them claimed that she had retired to live abroad. There was no record of where she had gone or when her death occurred. No one seemed particularly interested, which felt odd. It seemed extraordinary to her that scholars had made such assumptions about Lavinia's retirement. But then they had only read the published diary, which ended with Lavinia disappearing into the sunset to live happily ever after on the wages of sin. No one but she—and perhaps Ben—had seen the original diary and realised how very different it was.

It had a completely different tale to tell.

Holly got up and walked over to the sink, filling the kettle and switching it on. The hiss of boiling water filled the quiet room. Outside dusk was falling. It had been another long, hot, dry day. As she waited for the tea to brew, Holly thought about the memoir. There was no doubt that the two different versions were a puzzle. Perhaps Lavinia had submitted the original to a publisher and they had thought it too tame and spiced it up. But Holly was certain that the published version was not actually Lavinia's work. She felt it deep inside; the "fake" Lavinia of *The Transit of Venus* was far too brash and superficial. She had none of the nuance of the diary. She was cold and dislikeable where the "real" Lavinia, for all her faults, was a warm and vulnerable woman.

Holly took her cup of tea back to the sitting room and picked up the original, settling back against the cushions, opening the book at the page she had last left off reading. Instantly she felt comfortable again, drawn back into the true story.

Ashdown Park, 9th February 1801

Someone has come. Something has happened in this deadly dull place. My lord has invited a gentleman to visit so that he may make an up-to-date survey of the estate. It seems an odd time of year to choose for such a project with the snow lying thick on the ground. It is even odder of Evershot to want yet more maps of his lands when he already has a dozen of them. However, I am past trying to understand his behaviour.

Mr Verity, the surveyor, is a very serious fellow with a horse whose face is as long as his own. The only dash of frivolity he betrays is in his apparel, which is very elegant; buff breeches and a blue coat that suits him very well. He rides out each day about the woods and hills, making small cairns out of stone and measuring distance with a peculiar squat piece of machinery. This much I have observed. I know no more as Mr Verity is silent the rest of the time, which makes for dinners no more entertaining than they were before his arrival.

In the beginning Mr Verity's presence seemed to lighten my lord's mood, which was very welcome. They would study the maps together and Evershot would often retire to bed in a state of high excitement and make love to me with great energy and little skill for a number of hours until in desperation I was ready to beg him to cease. I had no idea that the study of old maps could be so arousing to his senses.

Alas, his good humour did not last and for this I only had myself to blame. In my vanity I tried to win over our guest. Of course I did. The practice of flirtation comes naturally to me as breathing. I soon stopped for Mr Verity was impervious to my charms. There are women who claim that they can seduce any man living but clearly they have not met Mr Verity, for he appears to find his scientific instruments a great deal more attractive than any member of the opposite sex.

Even the mildest sign of flirtation was sufficient to send my lord into a jealous rage. He has an angry and possessive disposition and on the second week of Mr Verity's stay he took exception to some words we exchanged and positively dragged me from the room to berate me over it. After that he punished me long into the night with fearful games of his own devising. He has a particular liking for the crop and I am badly marked from it this morning. The ministration of my punishment drove my lord into such a frenzy of lust that I am bruised and sore as well. I had to send Clara into Lambourn to fetch ointment and I stayed in my room all day pleading illness, which was not so far from the truth. My lord seemed little concerned, for he went out hawking from dawn to dusk and did not send word to ask after me even when he returned. But I expect no more than this. I am bought and paid for, a commodity. To demand concern, consideration or even affection would be naïve and would only lead to heartache. My heartache, that is. Evershot, I am persuaded, has no heart to wound. He cares for nothing but material pleasure which, dear reader, probably makes him less of a fool than I.

Wincing, Holly put down Lavinia's memoir. Here was another example of the original diary differing greatly from the published memoirs; in the published version Lavinia had become intimately acquainted with Lord Evershot's penchant for BDSM from the start and participated enthusiastically in it. The tone of Lavinia's diary was, however, quite different. She did not complain of Evershot's practices but it was clear that he had hurt her badly and that she was in no way willing.

Holly imagined that the reality must have been so much more difficult to bear than the bald words of the diary suggested. Being the kept mistress of a rich aristocrat was not necessarily a privilege. Women could be abused in as many ways as men chose, men who thought it was their right.

Holly found she had wrapped her arms about her for comfort against the revulsion that gripped her. For Lavinia to be subject to the sadistic sexual whims of the man who had bought her was demeaning. She liked hard-headed, grasping Lavinia too much to see her humiliated by Evershot and that, she realised, was one of the reasons that the published diary angered her too. It was a travesty of the real Lavinia. It exploited her as much as Evershot had.

For a moment she was tempted to put the diary aside but that felt like a coward's way out. Not reading about Lavinia's treatment did not make it any more acceptable. Her heart ached a little as she picked the diary up and read on to the next entry.

Ashdown Park, 14th February 1801

It snows and snows and snows until all is obliterated in unending blankness. It is too deep for Mr Verity to make his measurements so he spends his time in my lord's library writing out complicated mathematical calculations. This delay in his quest frustrates my lord very much and then he vents his irritation on me. A bear with a sore head would be of sunny disposition in comparison.

This place begins to haunt me. On these dark winter days it is full of gloom. All the dead faces of Lord Evershot's ancestors gaze down at me from the walls of the staircase and landings in censorious disdain. I feel their eyes following me. There is only one of them that I like and it is a beautiful picture of the Earl of Craven with the Winter Queen. He is seated and she is crowning him with a wreath of laurel. He looks very handsome, but a little melancholy, whilst she is so very beautiful. Oh, to find a love like that! But I am no ingénue. I know love is not for me and indeed I should not want it for it addles the wits and leads to all manner of mad behaviour.

I have been reading about the Earl of Craven. The books I chose were by my lord's mother who has written several works of dubious quality. She fancies herself a playwright but I think she flatters herself. She has also written a family history not only reinventing her own story to erase those inconvenient infidelities to the late Lord Evershot, but also to give the family an even more illustrious pedigree than it already had. This may be as much a work of fiction as her plays but I found it entertaining enough.

She writes of the famous exploits of the Earl of Craven, that grand cavalier of two hundred years ago. He sounds most dashing. He saved the life of Prince Rupert of the Rhine in battle, he rescued London from fire and plague and he was the model of honour and virtue and gallantry. I quite believe that Lady Evershot is in love with him herself, or at least with the notion of him. She states quite plain that the Earl and the Winter Queen were married, though she does not say from whence she has gained this information. According to her they were wed secretly in The Hague during the years of the English Civil War and when they returned to England at the Restoration of the King in 1660 they lived together quite openly in London. Alas, though, some quarrel drove them apart, though not even milady's fertile pen comes up with an explanation for this. It cannot have been so very serious, however, for upon her death, the Queen left to Lord Craven her portraits and her hunting trophies as a sign of her regard for him. Those wretched antlers! They adorn every room of this house and make me think of the poor deer that gave their lives in the service of Her Majesty's entertainment.

Mrs Palfrey, the housekeeper, tells me in the strictest confidence that there were other royal possessions bequeathed to the Earl, including a famous cross of rose gold that had belonged to the King of Bohemia. With much whispering and furtive glances she told me of another treasure too, a pearl of great price that men spoke of softly because it was said to have the power to foretell the future. It is said that Lord Craven hid it for fear of men's greed and covetousness.

Now this made me think. Perhaps it is this pearl that my lord Evershot currently seeks for I hear the rosy cross was sold long ago to pay his gambling debts. Since he is the greediest and most covetous of men, it would make sense that he should be seeking to exploit his ancestor's riches. I will confess that finding a pearl of great price, or indeed any treasure, would certainly enliven our days here. Unfortunately Mr Verity is too discreet and Evershot too irritable to discuss their business with me, so I am unlikely to discover the truth. This is a great pity since my curiosity very nearly consumes me but I know I must hold my tongue. I do not wish to give Evershot further cause to whip me.

Holly put the book down slowly beside her on the sofa. She could feel a ripple of goosebumps over her skin as though there was a cool breeze blowing through the mill. For here it was: the reference to the Sistrin. Ben must have found it too when he was reading through the memoir. Like Evershot before him, he must have been on the trail of the Winter Queen's pearl. That would explain why he had read up about its history and contacted Espen Shurmer for information on its whereabouts. He believed Lavinia's memoir when she claimed the Sistrin was hidden at Ashdown Park.

Holly stood up, rubbing her eyes. It was very late but suddenly her tiredness had fled, banished by an excitement that gripped her hard. Had Evershot discovered the pearl's hiding place? She guessed that he had not since Espen Shurmer had told her it had never been found. But Ben might well have done.

She wanted to read on but her eyes felt tired and gritty now. She knew she needed to take a break but she was not sure she would sleep.

Drawings for a new set of engravings lay scattered across the kitchen table where she had left them a little earlier in the evening. She had decided to produce a set of glasses showing episodes from the life of Elizabeth, the Winter Queen. It felt appropriate to draw on aspects of Ashdown's history for her work now that she lived here. She had already sketched out the picture she remembered from those stories of her childhood, Elizabeth in a long hooded cloak escaping in a carriage, her baby in her arms, the towers and spires of Prague lost in the whirling snows. She had also started on one of Elizabeth being crowned Queen whilst the Gunpowder plotters whispered treason behind her. She decided to download a biography of Elizabeth's life, both to help her research further scenes for the engravings but also to give more background to the woman herself. She also probably needed a book about the Knights of the Rosy Cross. This was going to cost her a fortune.

Lavinia and Elizabeth; they were so different and yet it felt to Holly as though there were distinct parallels between them. Both had been strong women in their own way. Both had to an extent been lost from history. Both had stories to tell.

Holly took Bonnie's lead out of the kitchen drawer. It was time for their bedtime walk but she had become so accustomed to living in a city that she had forgotten there were no streetlights here. She had no torch and hadn't picked one up yet.

Bonnie bounded out of the door undeterred by the blackness outside. Holly followed more slowly. The light from the mill windows illuminated the uneven path, the picket fence, and the shallow empty bowl of the millpond where Bonnie was now eagerly sniffing around. The night was warm with the faintest shade of paler blue fading into the black night sky. No breeze stirred the trees tonight. A half-moon spun silver shadows through the trees.

Bonnie paused in her foraging. Her head went up, alert, ears pricked as though she had heard someone approaching. Holly listened too but there was nothing to indicate that a person or an animal was close by; no snapping of twigs, no footfall, nothing but deep silence. Very slowly, Bonnie's head turned as though she was watching someone—or something—walk along the path towards the mill. She was quite still and when the fur rose in a ruff along her neck and spine Holly felt the same pricking in the back of her neck too. Suddenly the silence and the darkness felt thick and oppressive. Atavistic fear breathed gooseflesh along her skin.

"Bonnie!" She wanted to shout but her voice came out as a dry croak.

For a moment Bonnie did not respond, then she looked at Holly and wagged her tail slightly. With one last lingering stare she trotted across the clearing to Holly's side. A tawny owl coasted down from the trees like a ghost.

Holly's heart was pounding. She spun around, making for the picket gate and the shelter of the mill. Through the close press of the woodland, for a split second, she caught a flash of white: a house glimpsed through the darkness, tall and pale and perfect in the moonlight, the golden ball on the cupola gleaming.

Walking quickly, refusing to look either to the left or the right, Holly marched back to the mill with Bonnie pressing close at her heels. She almost ran inside and slammed the door, thrusting the bolt home with hands that were shaking. The bright light, the ordinary familiarity of the room, seemed to make a mockery of the fear that had gripped her a moment before and she felt her heartbeat steady.

"Damn it!" Holly let out a sharp sigh, leaning against the table for support whilst her nerves settled. She was starting to feel as though she was teetering on the edge of sanity, seeing a house where none existed, getting spooked by Bonnie when all the dog had been doing was sniffing the night air, feeling as though Lavinia was starting to haunt her, flitting through her thoughts like a shadow. It was easy to let the darkness and the silence get to her when she was not used to the isolation.

She had not drawn the curtains and reached over the back of the sofa to twitch the old gingham pattern closed. As she leant across, something caught her eye, a set of initials, RV and a date of 1801 etched on the glass in the bottom right corner of the pane. She traced the writing with one finger, feeling the roughness of the scratches against her skin. The glass felt cold.

1801. That had been when Lavinia said the surveyor called Verity had come to Ashdown. And on Ben's list there had been a third name: Robert Verity.

Shivering for a third time she whisked the curtains together and shut out the night. The world shrank to the lighted room and suddenly she was ambushed with loneliness. Sometimes it was like this; the feelings came out of nowhere, overwhelming her, terrifyingly powerful.

On impulse she keyed in Ben's home number into her mobile. She knew in her heart of hearts that there couldn't be any news. Tasha would have told her. She just wanted to talk to someone who knew Ben well.

The number rang eight times before the answering machine came in. "Natasha isn't here to take your call at the moment..."

Holly pressed End Call without leaving a message. The recording didn't even mention Ben any more. It was as though her brother had been erased. She could feel him sliding away from her. No matter how she wanted to hold on to him, he was slipping from her grasp.

17

Wassenaer Hof, The Hague, August 1635

Elizabeth did not go down to the courtyard to wish Craven Godspeed. To do such a thing would have drawn attention to his mission, which they had both agreed would be a mistake. Craven was always running errands for her and so this latest trip of his had not been much remarked upon. He came, he went, and few people questioned him because he was not a man who offered or invited confidences.

She watched from the window of the gallery as his servants pulled the straps tight on his saddlebags. There was one woman outside making enough of a scene over Craven's departure to entertain the entire court. Margaret Carpenter, her pretty face puffy with tears, yet miraculously still appearing winsome, was hanging on to his stirrup and begging another kiss. Elizabeth was pleased to see that Craven looked irritated rather than gratified by this ostentatious display of affection. He said something to Margaret that set her face flaming and then he was gone, the echo of horse's hooves loud on the cobbles for a few moments before the sound faded and the babble of the wind washed it away.

"Madam."

Elizabeth jumped. She had not been aware that she was standing so close to the window that her hand had been resting against the leaded pane. She hoped no one had noticed. As she turned away she caught a brief flash of Margaret Carpenter's face uplifted to the window. Despite her earlier tears the woman was smiling, the sort of smile that told Elizabeth that she knew she had what Elizabeth wanted. Then Margaret pulled her cloak closer about her hunched shoulders and hurried to the door, head bent.

"What is it?" Elizabeth tried not to snap. She felt anxious; anxious that Craven's mission should be a success, anxious for his safety and, shamefully, still anxious about his loyalty.

"Her Royal Highness the Princess of Orange sends you an invitation to join her for a masque this evening." One of Elizabeth's ladies in waiting, Ursula Grange, had approached her and was curtseying, the invitation extended in her hand. Elizabeth felt another sharp stab of irritation. Masques and balls and plays… It felt as though all she did these days was write letters, have her portrait painted and indulge in merriment. She did not want to go to the Binnenhof tonight. The Princess of Orange had once been plain Amalia Solms, one of her own ladies, before marriage had elevated her to royal status. Amalia liked to consider herself the first lady of Dutch society now, and Elizabeth humoured her whims, but it was ridiculous really. Amalia was not of royal birth nor was she a queen. Elizabeth outranked her in every possible way.

She sighed. She knew how petty such quibbles were. It was a measure of her lack of true power that she gave them a moment's thought. And she knew she must accept the invitation. The dancing and the feasting and the merriment were as much a part of the role she played as the political diplomacy was. Frivolity was a cloak, a disguise. People were a deal more indiscreet around a queen they thought shallow and given over to pleasure. They spoke carelessly whilst she guarded her secrets.

"How delightful," she said, taking the invitation and dropping it casually onto her desk, where one of her monkeys seized it and started to rip the paper apart. "Please reply that I shall certainly be there."

Dancing whilst the Palatine lands burn again, she thought. She could imagine what her enemies would say about that.

Had they already seized Frederick's body? Were his bones even now scattered to the four winds and the treasures of the Rosy Cross stolen from his tomb?

She shuddered. There was a fire in the grate but she could not feel its warmth.

Fire.

She had told Craven to destroy the crystal mirror. She did not want it back. When she had been a child the mirror and the pearl had been a pair, never separated. In her innocence she had thought them no more than trinkets matched in beauty. Then she had witnessed their destructive power and she never wanted the two of them to be reunited. She wanted to destroy the Sistrin too, yet she found that she could not, and it was this inability to rule the power of the jewel that made her profoundly uneasy. For if she did not have the strength to resist the dark arts then how could William Craven be trusted to do her will? She did not want to doubt him. Yet still she did.

18

Mark's offices were not at all as Holly had imagined they would be. She had expected lots of wood, chrome and light pouring in through huge windows in the style of his house, a converted barn that Fran had pointed out to her a couple of days before. Here in the old stable yard, though, little development work had been done as yet. The office itself was signposted in a discreet corner and when Holly knocked a little tentatively on the door and stuck her head inside, it was cool and dark. It was also shabby. There was a rug on the wooden floor, worn so threadbare that the pattern was almost invisible, a few wooden chairs and a laptop on a battered old table. A door led through to a second room that appeared to be piled high with tottering towers of paper. The walls were rough and whitewashed. A rickety wooden staircase in the corner led up to a trapdoor in the ceiling.

Mark was working at the desk by the window, sketching out what looked like a design for a loft conversion. He looked up when Holly came in and she judged from his expression that he was about as pleased to see her as he would have been the plague.

"Hi," she said, determined to be light and friendly. "How are you?"

Mark stood up and stretched. There was something very physical about the movement and it plunged Holly straight back into memories of the night they had spent together at the mill. Despite the shadowy coolness of the room it felt as though heat was rising inside her. How did a man who worked at a desk get a physique like that? She remembered the outdoor trousers and desert boots. Probably he was a hands-on sort of boss. Fran had implied as much. And she needed to stop staring at him.

"You mentioned that Ben had come to have a look at some maps and plans," she said, rushing into speech when he didn't answer her. "I wondered if I could arrange to take a look at the stuff he was researching? I don't mean now," she added quickly. "Sometime convenient..."

When you aren't here.

Mark ran a hand through his hair. "It's convenient now," he said.

Great.

"I've got Bonnie with me," Holly said.

Mark smiled. It was the smile she remembered from the day they had met, high wattage, seriously dangerous. Her heart skipped a beat.

"Bring her in," Mark said. "This used to be the old estate office. There must have been hundreds of dogs in here down the years."

"It's not what I expected," Holly said, coming in and shutting the door. Immediately it felt as though all the air had been sucked out of the room. The impact of Mark's physical presence in so enclosed a space had her heart thumping. She struggled to keep control. Perhaps she had been naïve but she hadn't expected to be aware of him like this.

Bonnie evidently shared none of her awkwardness. She took herself off to the sunny, dog-shaped space beneath the desk where she promptly curled up.

"We're converting this bit last," Mark said, "once the rest of the site is finished. We have a smart office and showroom for visitors over the other side of the development but I like working here. It's…" He paused, shrugged. "It's authentic."

"And what you build isn't?" Holly said.

Mark winced. "You're very direct."

"Sorry," Holly said. She didn't want to get off on the wrong foot yet again.

"We use authentic designs and building materials to create a comfortable, modern and updated version of a period property," Mark said. "But if you'd prefer no bathroom and a primitive kitchen we can do that too."

"The facilities at the mill are quite basic enough for me," Holly said. She felt awkward, uncertain where to go, whether to sit and if so where. Mark however seemed impervious to the tension in the room. He had half turned away from her and was making a fuss of Bonnie who was gazing up at him with shameless flirtation, eyes half-closed.

"We made your brother an offer on the mill when we took on the contract here," he said. "We thought it would be a great addition to the development at Ashdown."

"Oh." That was yet another thing that Ben hadn't told her, Holly thought. "What did he say?" she asked.

"He wouldn't sell," Mark said, straightening up. "And he said half of it belonged to you anyway."

"That's right," Holly said. "It does."

"Family inheritance?" Mark cocked a brow at her. "I think Ben mentioned you used to visit here years ago."

"Yes," Holly said. She realised that her voice was husky. There was an ache in her chest. She cleared her throat. She certainly wasn't going to cry all over him again. Not after last time.

"Is there any news?" Mark said, then as she shook her head, "I'm sorry. It's very difficult, not knowing."

Holly noticed that unlike a lot of people he did not break eye contact nor shift uncomfortably when he spoke of Ben. Nor did he offer platitudes or tell Holly how she must feel. The matter-of-factness was easier to deal with than any amount of sympathy. She remembered that Mark had been a soldier and thought he was probably accustomed to giving people bad news, dealing with grief, looking it in the eye rather than shuffling away with half-hearted condolence.

"Thanks," she said. "Yes, it's pretty tough."

Their eyes held for a long moment and she felt her nerves tighten. It didn't matter whether or not she chose to ignore it; the connection between them was still there.

"Well," Mark said, "as I said before, most of the papers relating to the estate are held in the Berkshire Records Office. You'd need to go to Reading to look at those. I showed Ben this map—" He opened an old filing cabinet and took out a rolled-up paper, spreading it out on his desk. It was hand-drawn, with geographical features, historic monuments and other markers showing on the landscape. There was a house in the centre, tall, with a cupola on top and a golden ball. Around it the woods spread out, shaped like a rose, with eight sections like petals.

"Oh!" Holly was entranced. "How beautiful!"

"It's early nineteenth century, I think," Mark said. "The landscape was mapped shortly before the house burned down."

"I had no idea," Holly said. "No idea the woods are shaped like a rose."

"You don't see it when you are on the ground," Mark said. "Unusual, isn't it? I think it must have been deliberate. Although Ashdown was originally an ancient hunting forest, this shape was probably designed by the First Earl of Craven when he was building the house and pleasure grounds."

"RV." Holly traced the initials at the bottom of the map. "Robert Verity."

"Who?" Mark's voice had sharpened.

Holly jumped. "What? Oh—" She looked up. "The surveyor who mapped Ashdown Park in 1801 was called Robert Verity."

"How do you know that?" Mark said. He sat on the corner of the desk, one booted foot swinging. "I've searched everywhere for that information and there's nothing, no documents, no references."

Holly hesitated. "Ben found out," she said. "There's a diary. A memoir, I suppose…" She patted her bag. "I've got it here." She had been intending to nip along to the café after she had seen Mark and have a chat to Fran about Lavinia's book.

"May I see?" Mark asked. He hooked his foot around the chair and pulled it out for her. "Would you like coffee? It's not up to Fran's standard, I'm afraid."

"Tea, if you have it," Holly said, willing to accept the slight thawing in relations, watching him stroll into the inner office and flick the switch on the kettle. "Thanks."

When Mark brought the mugs back through she had taken Lavinia's memoir out and laid it on the table next to the map Robert Verity had drawn. The sun gleamed on the rich green of the cover of the book. "What a beautiful-looking thing," Mark said softly.

"It's the diary of a courtesan," Holly said. "Quite racy. She was called Lavinia Flyte. She was here as Lord Evershot's mistress at the beginning of 1801."

"When the estate was mapped," Mark said. "I see. May I?" He picked up the memoir and it fell open somewhere in the middle.

"'He took me to his chamber for several hours,'" he read, "'until finally we were interrupted by the steward who came knocking to inform his lordship that Sir Francis Bignall had called to discuss the purchase of a hawk. What a relief that was, for I fear that Evershot was inexhaustible in his sexual demands and after he had belaboured me for several hours I was near bored to death…'" Mark paused, looking up.

"I did warn you," Holly said, blushing. "It isn't an architectural manual."

"Evidently not," Mark said. His lips twitched. "Poor Lord Evershot; immortalised for his lack of prowess."

"The bit about Robert Verity is here," Holly said hastily, taking the book from him. Their fingers touched. She felt even more hot and bothered. She found the page where Lavinia described Robert Verity's work and handed it back.

"Fascinating," Mark said after a moment. "I wonder if Verity was a soldier, trained by the Ordnance Survey. They were mapping the whole of southern England around that time as part of the Napoleonic War defences. Even if Evershot hired him privately he could well have been in the military. I'll check that out."

"That would be really interesting," Holly said. "You hadn't come across the name before?"

Mark shook his head. "No. It's weird because we have all the maps and drawings and none of them were signed except with those initials. I'd given up hope of discovering who the surveyor was." He checked the date at the beginning of the book. "February 1801 was just before the house burned down," he said.

Holly gave a little shiver. It was warm in the estate office but suddenly she felt cold. Bonnie slumbered on in the patch of sunlight, unaware.

"How did it happen?" she asked.

"Apparently workmen were making repairs to the roof," Mark said. "They left a brazier untended and it overturned and burned the whole place down. It's said that the fire was so fierce that the cupola—the little domed tower on the roof—crashed all the way down through three floors and shattered the roof of the wine cellar beneath. We went down into what's left of the cellar when we were charting the estate—there's still blackened glass and stone lying all over the place."

Holly shuddered, closing her eyes. She thought of the beautiful white house swallowed by fire, the white house she could have sworn she had seen only the previous night. It had looked so real in the moonlight. Fire was a terrible thing, eating through the fabric of a building with terrifying speed, destroying everything in its path.

Suddenly her ears filled with noise; the crackle of flames leaping twenty feet into the dark sky, the groan and snap of timbers. She saw a tall chimney topple in a shower of stone. Something was falling from the sky, molten lead, like silver rain. She felt the cold burn of it against her cheek.

Fear caught at her throat, snagging her breath. It was sudden, visceral, the fear of the trapped or the hunted, death but a step away. For one terrifying moment she felt the heat and the darkness close in about her, smothering her, and then the sensation faded and she was left feeling hollow and empty.

She looked up and saw that Mark was watching her. "Are you all right?" he said. "You look as though you're going to faint."

"I'm fine, thanks," Holly said but she was cold and shaking a little, and Mark's hand closed over hers.

"Holly?"

"Sorry. I should have had breakfast." She freed herself and wrapped her fingers about the mug of tea, greedily seeking its warmth. She wasn't sure what had happened in those few moments. It felt oddly as though time and space had shifted around her and yet nothing had changed. The air in the old offices was dusty and still. Bonnie snored under the desk.

"Fire was so dangerous in those days when there weren't adequate means to put it out," she said. "It must have been horrific."

"The river had been running low that year because it had been a dry winter," Mark said. "There was a bucket chain manned by servants but strong westerly winds fanned the flames into a wall of fire. I imagine it was terrifying. I'm surprised more people weren't killed."

Holly looked up sharply, feeling the cold bite into her bones again.

"What do you mean, *more* people?" she said. "Did someone die?"

Mark nodded. "I'm afraid so. The library caught fire early on and burned hotter than an inferno, according to eyewitnesses. Lord Evershot was in there. They couldn't get him out in time and he burned to death."

Fire, Holly thought. *The crystal mirror.*

Lavinia had not mentioned the mirror in her memoir, at least not yet, even though it had also originally been part of the treasure of the Order of the Rosy Cross. Espen Shurmer had said that the mirror had been lost for centuries, supposedly buried with Frederick, whose tomb was never found. Yet Holly had the strongest sensation that the mirror had been at Ashdown Park and that on that fateful night when the house had burned it had been at the heart of the inferno.

19

Craven was several days late. He had ridden to within a mile of the city and walked the rest of the way. It had been a long journey with plenty of trouble. The countryside was alive with rumour. Marauding bands of Spanish soldiers, masterless men, ill-disciplined and violent, terrorised the villages. He had almost run into such a gang south of Liege and only by the greatest good luck saw their camp before he stumbled into the middle of it. It went against the grain with him to hide and to run rather than stand and fight, but this business was too important to risk. Only once had he been obliged to draw blood when three drunken cavalrymen had cornered him in an alleyway. They had been looking for trouble and they had found it.

Ahead of him was the Germans' Gate, a mediaeval castle with ridiculous little round towers that looked as though they belonged in a fairy tale. The yellow limestone gleamed in the pale morning sun. Craven did not like these foolish little continental toy castles that looked as though one blast of the cannon would send them toppling. He missed England. One day, perhaps, he would go back again.

The soldier, in French uniform, stepped from the guard-house and gave him a cursory glance. On foot, in a plain cloak, serviceable boots and a battered hat William Craven could pass for anyone—or no one. That was his skill. The soldier did not even notice the sword beneath the cloak.

"I have business with the Duke of Simmern." Craven spoke execrable French. His education had been much neglected, by his own choice, since he had preferred to join the army.

The soldier raised a supercilious brow and jerked his head vaguely towards the cathedral. "Sainte-Croix Square," he said. "Past the cathedral and on the left. The palace of Livier."

"Thank you," Craven said.

"He won't see you," the soldier said. "He sees no one—"

But Craven had gone. "English," the soldier said, and spat on the dusty cobbles.

Craven kept in the shadow of the buildings as he skirted the vaulted arcades of the Saint-Louis Square and took the narrow alley towards the cathedral. There was no point in drawing attention to himself and to his errand. Here the old timbered houses leaned close across the street like lovers long parted. The early sun tipped the tiled roofs with gold. The air was fresh and almost free of the stench of rottenness that would haunt the streets later when the heat increased.

The cathedral seemed to fly against the blue of the sky. Craven passed the east end without pausing to glance up at the stained glass and soaring buttresses. The streets were quiet in the early morning. He saw no one but a messenger in a livery he did not recognise, a merchant pushing a cart loaded with cloth and a mangy dog foraging amongst the rubbish.

The Duke of Simmern was still breaking his fast in his chambers according to his steward.

"Excellent," Craven said. "I'll join him."

The man looked askance. "Pardon, sir, but I doubt he would care for that—"

"Is that Craven?" a voice enquired from within the great hall. A moment later a man appeared through the arched doorway, a man of middling years whose hollow cheeks and serious mien made him look older. He shook Craven's hand.

"It is good to see you again, Von Rusdorf," Craven said. Von Rusdorf had been Frederick's first minister and since Frederick's death had belonged to the council that had administered the Palatine lands for Frederick's son. "Is all well?"

"As well as it can be trapped within these city walls with a corpse," Von Rusdorf said.

"Surely he is not here?" Craven looked around almost as though he expected to see a coffin propped in a corner. "Or do you refer to the Duke of Simmern?"

Von Rusdorf's face crumpled in horror. "Softly, Craven! You have no respect."

"I acknowledge it," Craven said easily. He stripped off his gloves. "Is there food and drink? I'm half-starved."

"We must talk privately," Von Rusdorf said. He shepherded Craven down the corridor, issuing instructions to the steward over his shoulder. "Bring refreshment to the parlour room and make sure we are not disturbed."

"Von Rusdorf!"

Craven felt the other man pause, stiffen. The Duke of Simmern was hurrying through the hall towards them still brushing crumbs from his chin as he came. Craven made a magnificent bow.

"Your grace."

Von Rusdorf gave a faint sigh. "This is Lord Craven, your grace. He comes from the Queen."

"Of course." Simmern's dark gaze appraised Craven. He felt quite comfortable under the scrutiny. This was not a man of any great power or moral fortitude though he might wish to pretend to both. Frederick's younger brother was in fact very like him; short, dark, with a handsome, melancholy visage, a hint of petulance about the mouth and more than a hint of indecisiveness in his eyes. Craven understood Von Rusdorf's sigh.

"You had no trouble on the road, I hope," Simmern said.

Craven's hand rested lightly on the pommel of his sword. "Nothing serious, your grace."

He saw a faint flicker of a smile touch Von Rusdorf's mouth. "It is the return journey to The Hague you need to fear most. Many men would kill for the goods you will be carrying."

"I know it," Craven said. Even so, he was not afraid. It was not an emotion he wasted time upon. It could paralyse a man and freeze his sword arm when he most needed it. Besides, it was too late to fear death when the sword was already at your throat.

The steward was still hovering. Simmern dismissed him with a flick of the hand and gestured to Craven to walk beside him. Tapestries covered almost all the walls, hunting scenes in vivid colours, making the narrow passageway seem all the more dark and closed. At the end Craven stooped to follow the Duke beneath the lintel of a low door. They were in a small room plastered white and set with plain wooden furniture. No fire burned in the grate and the morning sun could not reach them, making the room cold.

"I hope you are comfortable here at Metz, your grace," Craven said, doubting it. Simmern was an exile now just as his brother had been years before, thrown out of his family's ancestral lands by the advancing army of the Holy Roman Emperor.

"Her Majesty sends you her greetings," he added, withdrawing a letter from within his jacket.

"She is well, I hope." Simmern's query sounded perfunctory. He opened the letter and scanned it briefly before placing it on the table.

"Extremely well, your grace," Craven said, "and most active in arguing the case for support for her son in regaining his ancestral lands." He saw Simmern's eyes narrow and focus on him inimically. It was no secret that the Duke had been less than eager in promoting his nephew's interests. He had struggled in his dealings with the French, he had struggled in his dealings with the Swedes and now he had run away from the Spanish.

After a moment Simmern gestured him to sit in a particularly uncomfortable chair. "I am sure we all long for the day that Charles Louis comes into his inheritance," he said smoothly, "but alas, now that the Spanish threaten our lands once again..." He let the sentence hang as though it was a shrug, disclaiming responsibility.

"Hence the need to find a new resting place for His Majesty," Von Rusdorf put in anxiously.

"Of course," Craven said. "Her Majesty understands that need. She asks me to tell you that she agrees that you should take King Frederick's body to Sedan, to be interred in the mausoleum of his uncle, the Duc de Bouillon."

"That is impossible now." Simmern brought his open hand

down on the table with a slap to emphasise his point. "It is too dangerous. We had the devil of a job getting this far. Her Majesty does not understand the perils—"

"Her Majesty understands very well," Craven cut in swiftly. Hunger sharpened his impatience. That damned steward had forgotten his breakfast.

He fixed the Duke with a steely gaze. "She relies upon your courage as well as your goodwill to escort your brother's body to Sedan for dignified reburial."

Simmern was the first to drop his gaze. High colour mottled his cheeks. "Naturally I shall do my best," he muttered, "but there can be no guarantees in times of war."

"Her Majesty," Craven said softly, "would be extremely distressed to hear of the late King's body being taken by his enemies. I am persuaded you will not permit that to happen, Duke."

"Of course not," Von Rusdorf put in swiftly. His gaze travelled from Craven to the Duke and back again like a hunting dog anxiously scenting the air. "The Council will ensure His Majesty's safety, my lord. Have no fear of that."

"The Council must not know anything of the late King's reburial," Craven said. "The Queen entrusts that duty to you alone, gentlemen. For safety's sake the site must remain a secret."

"Preposterous!" Once again, Simmern could not restrain his anger. "I am not traipsing across the continent on a fool's errand for my sister-in-law's sake when I have other more important matters to attend to. I am not her flunkey!"

There was a silence. Craven allowed it to settle. Outside he could hear a faint peal of bells, the rumble of carriage wheels, the call of a street seller, all separate and distinct sounds. He prolonged the silence to a point where it was uncomfortable. Von Rusdorf fidgeted.

"Did I mention that the King of England takes an interest in this affair?" Craven said at last. "He wishes everything possible to be done to aid his unfortunate sister." He lifted his gaze at last to meet that of the Duke. "I am sure that King Charles will be interested to hear of your involvement."

Simmern flushed a deep, unbecoming red. Craven could see the man wanted to tell him to go fuck himself but did not quite dare. King Charles, quixotic and weak, had been as laggard in supporting his sister's cause as their father before him. That did not mean that it was wise to antagonise him, however.

"It is pleasing to hear that His Majesty is so eager to support our cause," Von Rusdorf put in hastily. "We had heard that he had offered his sister and her family a home in England—"

"Which the Queen would not accept, of course," Craven said. "She is completely dedicated to seeing her son regain his patrimony."

"She could do that from the comfort of her brother's court in England," Simmern muttered.

"Her Majesty would not wish to appear to be deserting her son's cause in Europe," Craven said.

Von Rusdorf's shoulders slumped. "Of course she would not," he said.

Craven hid a smile. Everyone saw Elizabeth and her stateless brood of children as a problem that they wished would simply vanish into thin air. But if Elizabeth was a thorn in the side, the dead body of her husband was even more of an inconvenience to his relatives. Poor bastard, even in death he was a liability.

"So," Craven said, as though there had been no dissension, "we are agreed then that you two gentlemen will deliver His Majesty to safe repose in Sedan. But before that is done…"

"You will rob his coffin," Simmern said.

Craven grinned. "Let's go," he said.

The first creak of the iron crowbar was followed by a splintering sound that echoed to the stone rafters of the crypt then fell back into dead silence. Although it was high noon and the sun was hot outside, here in the bowels of the church it was dim and dusty. Shards of sunlight struck across the floor from the sunken stained-glass windows.

Frederick's coffin rested on a slab alongside stone knights with blank, carved faces. They watched with incurious eyes as Craven inserted the crowbar beneath the lid once more and levered it upward.

Neither the Duke of Simmern nor Von Rusdorf was so stoical. Simmern had positioned himself a good twenty feet away as though distancing himself completely from the violation of his brother's coffin. His expression was one of polite distaste. Von Rusdorf hovered at Craven's elbow. He looked as though he might be violently sick at any moment yet he seemed transfixed.

"Stand back," Craven said tersely, as he drew his arm back for a third attempt. "I don't want accidentally to injure you."

The coffin nails succumbed; the lid fractured with a groan and Von Rusdorf leaped away like a cat whose tail was alight. Craven had not known quite what to expect. He had a strong stomach and Frederick had only been dead a couple of years and his body embalmed. In the event the smell was unpleasant but not overwhelmingly so, the scent of herbs and spices, once sweet and strong, now dulled by decay. Nothing could ever conceal the stench of death completely, though. Craven had seen men die in battle and peacefully in their beds and was not afraid of death but he did not like what it left behind. Frederick's face was the colour of wax beneath a discoloured silver crown. His skin was like leather that was dissolving around the edges.

Behind him, Craven could hear the sounds of Von Rusdorf retching and Simmern praying under his breath.

Averting his gaze from the corpse, Craven looked for the items he had been charged with retrieving. He ignored the sword clasped in Frederick's hands. The poor bastard had been no soldier in life, his sword stood for nothing in death. Instead he took out a soft velvet bag. The nap of the material was disintegrating. He could feel the hard lines of the golden cross through the velvet.

Elizabeth had asked that all the regalia of the Knights of the Rosy Cross be returned to her. All except for the diamond-studded mirror. That he was to destroy.

There was a sapphire ring on Frederick's finger. This, the sign that he was of the highest rank of the Order of Knights, was also the token by which some said that the brethren summoned the devil to their aid. Well, Craven thought, let Beelzebub put in an appearance now. It might give Von Rusdorf such a shock that it stopped him throwing up.

The ring was difficult to remove. Frederick's cold dead hand felt waxy in a way that Craven did not wish to define. The ring stuck and he did not want to pull too hard for fear of what might happen. Eventually he succeeded in drawing the gem from Frederick's finger. The enormous sapphire winked at him with cold fire. He shoved it into the bag with the cross.

That left the mirror. It rested face down on Frederick's chest, the carved wooden frame giving no hint of the dazzling splendour of the reverse.

Craven hesitated. He had seen Elizabeth's face when she had spoken of the mirror as accursed. He had heard the ripple of fear in her voice. She was afraid that the desire to see the future would tempt any man who laid eyes on it, that if they had the mirror and the pearl as well they would take the power of foretelling and use it for evil. The scrying mirror had ruined Elizabeth's life and her family's future. Driven by its power of prophecy, Frederick had risked all and lost. Elizabeth believed it the tool of the devil and decreed that it should never see the light of day again. That was why she did not want it back, why the mirror had to be destroyed. The mirror and the pearl could never be united for their dark power would be too great.

It was superstitious nonsense, of course. Craven reassured himself of that. Even though he remembered the vision of death he had glimpsed in the mirror he convinced himself he had been mistaken. Neither God nor the devil had been on Frederick's side. He had simply been unequal to the task before him. Elizabeth had deserved better.

Craven took the mirror in his right hand and turned it over. The glass was dull, barely reflecting his image in the faint light of the crypt. Then, just as he was about to stow it away, something moved in the heart of the crystal, something formless as mist that struck chill through his entire body. It happened so fast and the cold was so killing he almost dropped the mirror on the stone floor of the crypt.

"Hurry up, man!"

Simmern spoke impatiently but there was the shadow of fear in his voice.

As Craven turned to close the lid on the coffin, the mirror caught a beam of sunlight from the window. There was a flash: tongues of flame. Craven could have sworn they were blue, like lightning. He heard Simmern shout. Frederick's clothing was already smouldering, the material, laden with embalming oils, flaring into a blaze that leapt towards the stone ceiling of the crypt in an inferno of heat and light.

There was a sweet smell that stuck in the throat, making Craven want to retch. The sound of fire was all around.

"God in heaven!"

Simmern ran. Craven could hear his footsteps on the stone floor.

He slammed the coffin lid down. It was wood; he expected it only to add to the conflagration. Yet instantly there was silence. No sound. No light. After a moment he put out a hand and touched the wood. It was cold. He glanced down at the mirror in his hand. There was no flicker of a reflection from its milky surface.

Cold sweat was rolling down his face. He wiped it away with his sleeve and walked slowly toward the crypt steps. When he reached them he glanced back. The coffin lay where he had left it, no sign of burning, no scent of smoke, nothing.

"Christ Almighty, man! What happened?"

Simmern was at the top of the steps, Von Rusdorf, ashen grey, at his side.

"Nothing," Craven said. "Nothing happened at all."

"There was fire," Simmern said. "I saw it myself—"

"You saw nothing," Craven corrected. He stepped aside, gesturing to the coffin, shrouded in shadow at the base of the steps. "The light from the windows reflected off the mirror and created the illusion of a fire. That was all."

There was silence. The other men looked as though they wanted to call him a liar. Neither spoke.

"Here." Craven took a bag of coins from his pocket and held it out it to Von Rusdorf. "For the carpenter to nail down the lid. See that he does the job well and that he holds his tongue."

After a moment Von Rusdorf took the bag. The coins clinked softly. Simmern was still staring at the coffin as though transfixed by a ghost.

Craven pushed the bag with the sapphire ring, the crucifix and the mirror inside his jacket.

"You're leaving at once?" Simmern straightened, turning away from the crypt and its macabre contents. He did not trouble to disguise his eagerness and Craven smiled a little grimly.

"I am."

"Godspeed then." Simmern held out his hand with grudging respect. "Pray assure Her Majesty of my most humble and devoted regard."

With the closing of the crypt door, Von Rusdorf too had recovered some of his composure. "I shall send Her Majesty word when the King is safely interred at Sedan," he said.

Craven drew on his gloves. "Gentlemen. A pleasure."

He left Metz amongst the afternoon crowds of soldiers and merchants and travellers, crossing the bridge over the river Moselle unnoticed in the throng. In the centre he paused for a moment to look down into the water below. It ran sluggishly beneath the arches, grey-green and deep, and he thought of throwing the mirror into the depths and being rid of it immediately. This would be a foolish place to dispose of it, though. Someone would see him throw it in and go scrambling after. Or there would be a drought and it would be found in the mud when the waters receded. No, he would have to wait for a better opportunity.

For a moment he remembered the inferno in the crypt, the flash of fire from the mirror, the way that Frederick's corpse had burned as though it was on a pyre. He knew what he had seen.

He rode west with the sun in his eyes and the rosy cross heavy against his chest, and the mirror in his pocket seeming to weigh nothing at all.

20

I have changed my mind about Mr Verity. He may be a little serious but he is also a good man, a kind man, and God knows, I find kindness so rarely in the world.

This is what happened.

Last week I was obliged to leave the house and take some exercise in the grounds. There is nothing else left to do here or you may be sure I would not have resorted to anything so dull as walking. However, I found it a curiously pleasant experience. The day was fine— the snows have gone and tiny white flowers are piercing the ground. Mr Verity tells me they are snowdrops. They are extremely pretty.

But I get ahead of myself. What happened was this. My lord had ridden over to Newbury to visit his mama (he is tied to her apron strings by the need for money, if nothing else) so I decided to venture from the house and take a walk in the woods. Mr Verity had mentioned at breakfast that he would be surveying in the lower wood today but I did not seek him out. Well, perhaps I did just a little, for it is melancholy to be so much in my own company.

I came across Mr Verity in a clearing in the forest. There was a fountain there, a charming little thing that splashed and played amongst the frosty ferns and long grasses. Mr Verity told me that the First Earl of Craven had created it as part of the original pleasure grounds. He seemed a little reluctant to talk at first but I soon drew him out—I think I have mentioned that I am renowned for my charm and since we were alone Mr Verity was less stiff and formal. He seemed nervous, though, perhaps expecting my lord to leap out from behind a tree and challenge him to a duel for speaking to me, but after a while we were chatting like old friends and he told me all about the First Earl and his designs for the house and grounds. It was surprisingly interesting, though I confess some of my interest did spring from the way that the sun shone on Mr Verity's hair and turned it a very rich chestnut indeed, and the way it lit his hazel eyes. I had not noticed before quite what a handsome man he is.

I asked him then directly what it was that he and my lord were looking for in the woods but he turned my question aside with some answer about mapping the whole estate, which I know is falsehood. I did not wish to embarrass him, so I did not mention my wild idea that Lord Evershot was seeking treasure but turned the conversation to Mr Verity himself. He comes from an old family, sadly impoverished now, which was why he entered the army. It did not sound very interesting work, walking miles each day on reconnaissance missions and poring over a peculiar instrument that gives angles for some process called triangulation. I pretended to be fascinated however, and shortly after that Mr Verity shared his lunch of pork pie with me and asked me very kindly about myself, though he did blush when I spoke openly of my life as a courtesan.

Why pretend? I am as I am. And I do believe that after a little while Mr Verity did forget that I sell myself for profit for we chatted another twenty or thirty minutes about all manner of things from his mother's favourite recipe for whelks, which sounded unpleasant, to my maid's advice on how to treat a sunburned complexion, which I doubt he will find helpful. Finally I stood up to leave, realising that I was keeping him from his work.

Alas, at that point I had a most unfortunate accident.

As I was exiting the clearing I put my foot down what I assume was a rabbit hole and tumbled over in the most ungainly manner imaginable. I lay there, quite winded and utterly embarrassed. Mr Verity, in his kindness, was all thought and concern. He leaped across the clearing to help me, swung me up in his arms and carried me back towards the house. I did struggle—a little—and protested that he should allow me to walk, but he pointed out that I had lost a shoe and must be quite overcome by shock, which of course I was quite prepared to be since it meant that he held me tightly against his chest. What a wicked creature I am! But Mr Verity was so devoted and strong and protective whilst I cannot but imagine that if such an accident had happened to me whilst I was out walking with Lord Evershot, he would have left me floundering on the ground or barked at me to quicken my pace.

I slid my arms about Mr Verity's neck and clung to him, pressing myself tightly against him and burying my face in his coat. He smelled quite delicious and manly, and it was a great shame that he had to put me down before we reached the house in case the servants saw us and gossiped to Evershot. Mr Verity seemed quite breathless and red in the face when I slid out of his arms. He recovered swiftly enough and gave me a very creditable bow and said formally that he hoped I would feel much better soon. He hurried away back to his instruments and I saw Evershot's carriage approaching up the drive so I scuttled indoors before he could see me.

After that I contrived to spend time with Mr Verity whenever I could. I would seek him out in the woods or in the gardens or the library or wherever I might find him, purely for the pleasure of his conversation, of course. He is a fine artist and has taught me to sketch in *pencil and paint in watercolours. The flowers in this diary are designs I have taken from the books in the library, snowdrops and ragged robin (so curious a name!) and the water violets that in the summer grow by the millstream on the edge of the wood. How I would love to see the summer flowers but I think I shall be long gone by then. Either my lord will have found whatever it is he seeks here at Ashdown Park or he will have tired of the country, or he will have tired of me.*

I wish I had learned to ride, so that I might go out with Mr Verity on his explorations about the estate. There is so much I would wish him to show me. Coming from the city I do believe I have had my eyes closed to the beauties of nature until now, but Mr Verity can always make me see things anew. Alas it cannot be. In the first instance I detest horses. They have an uncertain temperament and they frighten me. Besides, although Mr Verity is a great deal more cordial with me now he is still as closed as a clam when it comes to discussing whatever it is he searches for. And if Evershot knew how much time I spend with Mr Verity, innocent as our association is, he would fly into a jealous rage.

21

"It doesn't sound very innocent to me," Fran said. "Lavinia is a minx. She knows she's leading him on."

"On the other hand I think she really does like him," Holly said, stirring her coffee thoughtfully. "Imagine you were stuck with an arrogant bastard like Evershot who treats you like dirt. Wouldn't you appreciate someone who was sincere and courteous? I think Lavinia likes Robert Verity more than she's letting on."

Holly had taken to discussing the latest chapter of Lavinia's diary with Fran whenever she dropped into the deli, which was turning out to be most days, morning or afternoon, or both. Working on her own, Holly found she needed the contact and it seemed that most of the rest of the village did too. Almost everyone dropped in at one point in the day or another, which was, Holly realised, how Fran maintained her impeccable flow of information.

"And I think our Mr Verity has a crush on Lavinia," Fran said, with a giggle. "Blushing like a schoolboy when she snuggled up to him. I bet he'd never met anyone like her before." She started to unstack the dishwasher. The smell of hot, squeaky-clean plates slid into the café.

"It must have been very difficult for him," Holly said. "What would it be like to be playing the gooseberry alongside Lord Evershot and his mistress? It sounds as though Evershot was a very possessive lover and if Robert Verity had a soft spot for Lavinia, witnessing her being abused and beaten must have been awful."

"There must have been a very weird atmosphere in that house," Fran agreed. "All those servants running around as well, watching, listening at keyholes, gossiping…it's all a bit creepy."

"Very claustrophobic," Holly agreed, "especially in the winter, miles from anywhere—"

"With no broadband or mobile phones," Fran finished.

Holly smiled. "I bet Lavinia would have loved the Internet."

"Perhaps if they'd had a mobile they could have summoned help quicker when the house caught fire," Fran said. She shuddered. "Ghastly about Lord Evershot."

"Don't waste your sympathy," Holly said. "It couldn't have happened to a more appropriate guy."

Fran stared. "It's not like you to be so harsh."

"I hate Evershot," Holly said. "He got what he deserved." As she said it she realised that it was true. There was a sharp, primitive anger lodged in her chest whenever she thought of Lavinia's lover.

There was a clatter of noise. Mark and some of his colleagues from the drawing office had come in and were milling around the counter trying to choose between chocolate brownies and vanilla cupcakes. Paula bustled out of the kitchen to serve them.

"She's trying to win him over with sprinkles on his coffee," Fran hissed at Holly across the table.

Holly smiled as Paula passed Mark a big takeaway cup she had clearly prepared in anticipation. "Best of luck to her," she said. She got up. "You're very busy today. I think you need this table. Great cake, by the way."

"My own recipe." Fran looked smug. "It's all home-baked stuff here."

"Holly?" Mark caught up with her by the door and held it open for her. "Can I have a word?" he said.

Through the melee of people at the counter Holly caught both Fran and Paula staring at her. Fran's mouth had formed a little "o" of speculation. Paula was looking very grumpy. Holly wondered if she was going to come over and snatch the coffee back. Fran had already asked her about her visit to Mark's offices the previous day. Naturally someone had seen her going in and probably timed when she had come out as well. This would stoke the gossip.

"Of course," she said.

"It's about Flick," Mark said.

Holly's stomach did a little flip. She had been wondering if Flick had come clean about the glass bowl. She looked up at Mark but the sun was in her eyes and she could not read his expression.

"Right," she said.

"She told me she broke one of my trophies," Mark said, as they stepped out into the sun-filled courtyard, "and that she asked you to forge a replacement."

"Almost," Holly said. "She told me your brother Joe broke the trophy and she asked me to forge a replacement. I'm sorry if that drops Joe in it, but I don't think Flick should take responsibility for something someone else did."

Mark let his breath out on a sharp sigh. There was a tight

frown between his brows. "No. Bloody Joe. He always lets someone else take the blame, and Flick's a soft touch. She's been covering for him since they were kids." He squared his shoulders; glanced sideways at her, an unsmiling look. "Flick said that you said you could have done it. Produced a replacement, I mean, and no one would have known."

"Technically, yes," Holly said. "Ethically, no." She groped in her hair for her sunglasses and slid them on. That was better. She had felt too exposed before under Mark's perceptive gaze.

"Look," she said. "I know you may think that I have no moral compass, and I can't really blame you for that, but—"

Mark put a hand on her arm and she stopped abruptly. "That hardly describes my opinion of you," he said. "Far from it."

"Oh." Holly blushed.

Mark drove his hands into his trouser pockets. "Look, can we leave us out of it for a minute? I was hoping you'd let me explain about my dysfunctional family. I..." He hesitated. "I wouldn't want you to think badly of Flick."

"I don't," Holly said. "I think Flick was terrified she'd upset you for whatever reason and so she thought I might help her out of a tricky situation."

"And you put her straight."

Holly shrugged. "Well, yes." She met his eyes. "I admit I was tempted to help. Your sister is very persuasive. But the thought of your devastating disapproval if you ever found out was enough to make me suggest to her that she tell you the truth."

There was an odd expression in Mark's eyes. "Do you mean that?"

"About honesty being the best policy? Yes, generally speaking."

"I meant about my devastating disapproval."

"Oh." Holly paused. "Well…"

The day seemed very quiet, only the sounds of the wood; the caw of the rooks, the soft hush of the breeze through the leaves, the trickle of the stream under the bridge. Holly had been flippant but now she realised that there had been more than a core of truth in her words. Just as Mark had not wanted her to think badly of his family so she wanted his good opinion too. Which was more than a little disconcerting.

"Sorry." Mark looked at her, then quickly away. "Forget it. I wanted to tell you about Flick. She lives with me at the moment because she had a major falling out with our mother a few years ago. They don't get on." He slowed his long stride to Holly's slightly shorter one, pausing to wait for Bonnie, who was sniffing curiously around the base of an oak tree. "Flick had problems in her early teens, shoplifting, that sort of thing. Dad travels a lot so he wasn't around much to help sort stuff out. I was in Afghanistan. Mum sent Flick to boarding school after she stole some of her jewellery. She said it was to help give structure to her life but really I think she just didn't know what to do with her."

"God, I'm sorry." Holly was appalled. "What a terrible thing to do—" She stopped. "I'm sorry," she said again. "I don't mean to criticise your mother when I don't know the full story but surely Flick needed help, not punishment?"

Mark nodded. "Yes, and of course it didn't work. Flick was even more unhappy, she took more stuff, so she was expelled from school and was sent somewhere else…" He shrugged. "I'd left the army by then but it was complicated." Holly looked at him. His gaze was shuttered, inward looking, the line of his jaw hard. "I couldn't help myself for a while," he said, "let alone anyone else."

"You're being very hard on yourself," Holly said.

Mark shot her a startled look. "Yes," he said slowly, "I suppose I am. PTSD is a hell of a thing to deal with, as I know now, but I couldn't shake the idea that I was just being weak."

Their gazes collided and Holly felt the impact of it all the way through her. To mask her reaction she walked on a little faster but she was very aware of him beside her now, his arm brushing hers.

"You did a lot of charity work," she said, to cover a silence that felt alive. "Was that before the PTSD kicked in?"

Mark shook his head. "I had it from the start. I'd dream in flashbacks and wake in the night shaking and in a blind panic but I tried to ignore it. Eventually that became impossible so I started to drink to blot it out." He shrugged. "I was a bloody awful mess. My marriage broke down because Carol got sick of the moods and the drinking. She had no idea what she would find when she came home from work. I can't blame her. PTSD and relationships don't mix. And all the time I was pretending everything was fine until finally it was so badly broken I couldn't pretend any longer."

Holly reached out a hand then let it fall back to her side. It startled her how much she wanted to touch him, offer comfort.

"When we had tea at the café that day I sensed there was stuff you were holding back," she said. "You talked about working in Norway but nothing about the army, or the building project."

"That wasn't intentional," Mark said. He corrected himself. "Well, it was in the sense that I never normally talk about this stuff." He gave her a glimmer of a smile. "Not even Fran could get it out of me. But I didn't mean to mislead you. When I got sober I did go to Norway. I have another sister, Kirsten, who's married to a Norwegian fisherman. I did some work with him for a while and then decided to come back here and set up my own company. The redevelopment is our first major project."

"Which enabled you to offer Flick somewhere to live," Holly said.

"That's right."

"No wonder she didn't want to tell you about this latest thing," Holly said. "After so much upheaval in her life the last thing she would have wanted would have been to upset or disappoint you."

The sun was bright and the air gentle and Bonnie scampered past, pressing her damp nose briefly to Holly's palm.

"Flick's been so much better living here," Mark said, "although she does relapse every so often. But yes, she's a bit fragile and I don't want things to go back to how they were."

"I'm sure they won't," Holly said. "Flick gave me the impression that she loves living here with you but I don't suppose the problems she's wrestling with are linear, if you know what I mean?" She was thinking over the past few weeks and how her feelings about Ben's disappearance had changed from day to day, plunging her from hope to despair in a breath sometimes. "If you are dealing with big issues then some days you're going to feel better than others."

"And some days you're going to feel very bad indeed," Mark said quietly, and Holly knew he was thinking of the day they had met. She drew in a breath but then realised she didn't know what to say. She didn't want to apologise. That made it sound as though she regretted what had happened and she didn't, not really, at least not in the sense of wishing it undone.

"Poor Flick is desperate to please everyone," Mark said, after a moment. "That's why she lets Joe take advantage."

"I've never met your brother," Holly said, "but he sounds as though he needs to grow up."

Mark shot her an amused glance. "Joe's only twenty. He's still finding his way. It doesn't help that he's insanely good-looking and has women falling all over him."

"You must find that a problem too," Holly said, deadpan.

Mark smiled, a sudden warm smile that made Holly catch her breath. Suddenly she felt very hot indeed. They reached the edge of the wood. It was a relief to step into the shade. The air was still warm and heavy but the sunlight, filtering through the leaves, was less fierce here. It was a path Holly had not taken before and it led along the old park pale of the mediaeval hunting ground. They didn't talk now and the silence prickled with all the things that were unspoken.

"This was the old icehouse," Mark said as they reached a clearing where the brambles and bracken beside the path had died back through lack of water, revealing a tumble of red brick. Holly paused to look at it. One corner was still standing to roof height and had an arched doorway leading to a set of mossy steps. The area was fenced off with rusty iron railings canted at a drunken angle, with cow parsley and grass sprouting between them. An ugly keep-out sign hung from the rails.

"What was an icehouse?" Holly asked. "Sounds a rather nice idea on a day like this."

"They stored the ice here for the big house," Mark said. "No freezers in the seventeenth century."

"I suppose not." Holly hadn't ever considered it. "Where did they get the ice from?"

"They cut it from ponds in the winter, packed it in straw and stored it underground," Mark said. "Then they brought it out to make desserts and ice cream and to put in drinks."

"That sounds very unhygienic." Holly peered through the railings. "I assume that's not a seventeenth-century sign?"

"The council fenced it off when they took the site on in

the 1950s," Mark said. "Kids used to play down there in the ice chamber."

"Health and safety," Holly said. "I wonder if the police have searched—" She stopped then, aware of the implications of her words. As each day passed it became more difficult to keep out the thoughts that Ben might be dead. They lurked at the corner of her mind like shadows and she had to work hard to stop that darkness rushing in. Now, looking into the dark entrance to the icehouse, she shuddered.

"Yes, they have." Mark's voice was very steady. He took her hand, his fingers interlocking strongly with hers. It felt comforting, close. She wanted to pull away but she wanted to touch him more. The strength of that need was a shock to her.

"Hi, Mark!"

Holly jumped back as though she had been scalded. Neither of them had seen anyone approaching through the dappled shade but now she recognised one of Mark's colleagues from the coffee shop, tall and gangly, a man whose flapping shorts revealed bony knees and whose tight T-shirt hugged a cadaverous chest.

"Greg," Mark said, nodding. "How are you doing?"

"Sweltering," Greg said, grinning. "You must be Holly," he added, extending an enthusiastic hand. "Sorry I didn't get the chance to say hello just now in the shop. It's good to meet you at last."

"Greg's our biodiversity officer," Mark said.

"Oh, badgers and newts and flowers?" Holly said. "Excellent."

"Well, there are no newts," Greg said, "as there's not enough water, but definitely badgers and various species of bird and butterflies and lots of unusual plants. Ashdown is a haven for wildlife."

"I see plenty of it," Holly said, "living on the edge of the wood."

"Fran said you're staying at the mill," Greg said. He fidgeted awkwardly. "I'm sorry about your brother. I'm sure he'll turn up soon."

Holly felt Mark shift beside her. "Thank you," she said. "Did you know Ben?"

"My sister introduced him a couple of months ago." Greg said, "He was in her shop one day when I popped in. The Merchant Adventurers." He corrected himself. "Sorry, it's called Marlborough Crafts now. Karen said the Merchant Adventurers confused the customers. I liked it though."

"It was a shop name!" Holly said. She was remembering the compliments slip she had found in Lavinia's diary and the fruitless hours she had spent trying to trace the name. "I never thought of that."

Both Greg and Mark were looking at her curiously. "It was just something Ben mentioned to me," she said.

"You should go and see Karen," Greg said. "Fran said you're a glass engraver. Karen is always looking to acquire high-end stock. I'm sure she'd be interested. I'll put a word in for you."

"Thank you," Holly said again. "That would be very kind of you. I'm just starting to check out new sales outlets."

"Well, then," Greg said. "I'll give her a ring. She's away for a couple of days but I'm sure we can set something up when she gets back." He gave Mark a quizzical look. "Are you heading back to the site office?"

"In a moment," Mark said. "I was going to show Holly the lavender garden."

"Right." Greg paused, looked from one to the other and then raised his free hand in a gesture of farewell. "See you in a bit then." He loped off down the ride.

"He seems nice," Holly said. "Sort of Tiggerish."

Mark smiled. "He's a good bloke."

"I think he wanted to come with us," Holly said.

"Probably," Mark said. He shot her a glance. "I didn't want him to join us. Do you mind?"

Their eyes met. Holly felt a flutter of sensation along her skin. She couldn't deal with this. She didn't know how. Her life was too complicated as it was.

"What's the lavender garden?" she said.

Mark laughed and took the change of subject but the glint in his eyes suggested to her that he had not let it go permanently.

"About fifty years after the house burned down the then Lady Evershot designed a garden on the site where it had stood," he said. "She laid it out according to the floor plan of the house, with lavender hedges marking where the walls, doorways and windows had been, and gravel squares for the rooms." He gestured to a little path that struck off at a right angle from the main ride. "It's this way."

He held aside a trailing strand of dog rose for her and Holly ducked beneath it, her shoulder dislodging a fall of petals as she followed Mark along the path. She knew she should be getting back to the studio. She needed structure in her day now more than ever, and she had always worked best when she kept to a nominal routine. She also needed to be wary. It was the enjoyment of Mark's company that was keeping her here and she knew it.

"How did you become a surveyor?" she asked. "Did you retrain after leaving the army?"

Mark shook his head. "I was in the Royal Engineers. I'd studied surveying and civil engineering, specialising in demolitions. This was a sidestep rather than a change, building things rather than blowing them up, I suppose."

Holly liked that. It felt very positive.

They came out from under the trees onto a broad, flat rectangular space with what looked like a pattern of lavender beds in the centre. The grass was mown very short here and the scent of it hung on the air, the sweetness fading in the heat. It mingled with the dry perfume of the flowers.

Holly walked through a gap in the hedge, her footsteps crunching on the gravel. Here was a circular planting pattern marking the rise of the staircase. It took up a quarter of the entire floor space. A long corridor bisected the house. Holly walked down it very slowly, hearing the buzz of the bees loud in the lavender. In the centre a stone sundial stood within an octagonal design. There were three large, square rooms making up the whole, marked out by lavender borders.

"What a beautiful idea," she said. "Commemorating the site of the house with a parterre garden."

"It is, isn't it," Mark said. He gave her a completely unguarded smile, sharing her pleasure, and her heart gave an erratic thump. "And what a stunning view from here. You can imagine how amazing it must have been standing on the roof terrace four storeys up."

Holly could. She could feel it. She could feel the sting of the cool air on her cheeks and the way the breeze ruffled her hair, plastering it against her face. The copper of the roof was hot beneath her feet and the little octagonal cupola was behind her, the sun glinting in shards of dazzling brightness from the leaded glass. On both sides the enormous chalk chimneys soared to the sky, the stone a smooth, bright white against the blue. She narrowed her eyes against the glare and looked out across the wood to the hillside beyond, with its weathervane pointing to the sky.

No road cut the green swathe of the valley at the foot of the hill. There was nothing there but a field scattered with grey sarsen stone and the slope of the downs as they climbed toward the horizon. A single rider was cresting the hill and cantering in the direction of the house, a figure in brown and blue on a chestnut horse against the vast green landscape...

Holly blinked and the vision dissolved and she could smell the lavender and hear the sound of a lorry labouring along the road and changing gear as it turned into the building site. One small fluffy cloud had crossed the sun, casting her in a brief cool shadow. She shivered.

"You look as though you've seen a ghost," Mark said.

"I thought I had," Holly said. She shivered again although the cloud had gone and the sun was hot. There was no rider on Weathercock Hill. "Vivid imagination," she said.

"What did you see?" Mark asked.

"I felt as though I was standing on the roof looking out across the valley," Holly admitted, wondering why she was telling him. She'd deliberately not told Fran or anyone else about the pearl or the mirror or anything else that might be construed as a bit flaky. She had enough to deal with without everyone thinking she was delusional.

"I could see a rider on the hillside. And there was no road." She shrugged. "Like I said, imagination. I'm sure that road has been there for thousands of years."

"No," Mark said. "The track from Lambourn across the Vale used to run further to the east. That road was only made in Victorian times." He raised a hand and brushed her jaw with his fingers. "I think you might be a bit fey, Holly Ansell."

Holly felt dizzy. There was a smile in Mark's eyes but there was heat there as well and then the amusement faded leaving nothing but raw desire. The rest of the world melted away and all she could see was him. She caught her breath.

"Mark—"

"I think about it." His voice was rough. "I think about that night. Every time I see you and plenty of times when I don't. So do you, don't you?"

Holly's throat was dry. "No. I… No."

"Liar." His lips touched hers. She was shocked by how much she wanted him to kiss her properly, for it to be like it had been before. The speed with which the sensation had come upon her was dizzying.

Holly put a hand against his chest and held herself away from him. "It was a mistake," she said. "We both agreed."

"I don't remember discussing it properly." Mark's cheek brushed hers, the stubble rough against her skin. She shivered.

"Neither of us do this sort of thing."

"There's never been a better time to start." Mark's lips were so close to hers that all it would take was for her to turn her head and she would be kissing him.

"I've never in my life had meaningless physical sex before I met you," Holly blurted out.

Mark laughed. "Just meaningful emotional sex?"

"Not much of that either." It was true. She had to rack her brains to remember a time when she had enjoyed anything in bed more than reading *The Engravers' Journal*. That was if she had even made it back from her studio with energy to do more than sleep.

She saw Mark smile and realised that she had just admitted to more than she had intended. A second later he had slid a hand behind her head and brought his mouth down on hers in a kiss that spun her straight back to that long, hot night in the mill. She kissed him back and it was everything she ached for, enough to make her forget all the confusion in her life, her tiredness and her fears.

Mark let her go and they stood staring at each other.

"This has got to stop," Holly said. She flattened her palm

more firmly against his chest and felt the strong beat of his heart. "I don't want to make things any more complicated than they already are," she said. She raised her gaze to his. "I would be using you to escape, to blot everything out. It would be wrong."

She saw the corner of Mark's mouth dip in a smile. "I could live with it," he said.

"We live in a small village," Holly said. "The gossip would be deafening. Besides, you have Flick to think about."

"And you have Bonnie."

Holly stifled a smile. "Be serious. I'm not looking for another relationship and Fran says you aren't either—"

"How helpful of her," Mark said.

"We need to be clear," Holly said.

Mark sighed; stood back. "Okay." His tone was smooth but she had the disconcerting feeling that it wasn't over. "You'll still need my help with your research, though, into Robert Verity and anything else I can discover about his work at Ashdown."

"You've changed your tune," Holly said.

Mark's smile deepened. She could still feel the heat shimmering between them. "Just trying to be helpful," he said. "I'll see you soon."

Holly was very conscious of him watching her as she walked down the avenue away from the lavender garden. She knew she'd done the right thing. Her emotions were in one big complicated mess at the moment and getting involved with Mark could only make that worse. All the same it was far more difficult than she had imagined to walk away.

22

The Palace of Rhenen, Netherlands, August 1635

"Is it done?"

"Aye, madam." Craven stepped out of the shadows of the line of poplar trees to join Elizabeth in a patch of speckled moonlight. She had insisted on this elaborate charade. They had been out hunting all day with the court but she could not speak to him then, nor take possession of Frederick's sapphire ring or the other relics. There could be no witnesses to the transaction. Absolute secrecy ruled the Order of the Knights of the Rosy Cross.

It was ironic then that the Queen had chosen this place for their meeting. With its avenue of trees that soared up into darkness it reminded Craven of nothing more than the vaulted depths of a cathedral. He could almost imagine Frederick's coffin lying between them in a blaze of fire. Except that he was not a man who indulged his imagination if he could help it and not when it conjured such images.

She would never know. He would never tell Elizabeth that he had seen the crystal mirror turn her husband's corpse to flame and ashes before his eyes. He would not reinforce her superstitions. What he had seen had been no more than a freak of nature; he had read about such manifestations when the sun shone off a mirror's surface. Science could explain most things.

"How did he look?" Soft moonlight fell on Elizabeth's face, sparkling on her hair, smoothing away the lines that cruel daylight illuminated, making her look young. She caught Craven's sleeve and he could feel the warmth of her fingers and her need for reassurance too.

"He looked…" *Dead.*

What was he supposed to say? There were no words that could bring her solace. Elizabeth and Frederick had been that most unfashionable and unusual of couples, a royal love match. Her pain was etched not only in the lines of her face but also in the cadence of her voice as she spoke of him.

Craven had never experienced such powerful emotion himself and was not sure he had the imagination ever to do so but he respected Elizabeth's loss because it was a part of her. She was too honest and open to love with reservation. When she gave she held nothing back, which was an invitation to hurt.

"Peaceful," he said. "He looked peaceful."

He had found the right words after all. She smiled at him, radiant, and his heart thumped. He reminded himself that he was doing this for her good, lying to her so that she would be free of the past, no longer haunted by the mirror, the pearl, the curse.

She let her hand fall but she did not step away from him.

"You have the items for me?"

"Aye, madam." He fumbled in the inner pocket of his

jacket. Now that the moment had come he found his hands were shaking. He felt like a felon.

"The cross." He passed the velvet bag that contained the cross of rosy gold. "The ring." The huge sapphire gleamed in the moonlight for a moment. If Elizabeth had any sense, he thought, she would sell that for a fortune and live off it for years.

"Thank you." He could not see her expression but her voice was full of gratitude. "What of the rest?"

"I left his sword," Craven said. "He was..." God forgive him another lie, "he was a soldier."

She nodded, her face grave, then she raised her gaze to his. Craven's heart lurched. This was the moment.

"And the other matter?"

"Is finished." He spoke curtly as though the tone would hide his guilt, convince her of his sincerity. "The mirror is gone."

"What did you do with it?"

Craven was silent for a moment. "It is better that you do not know, Your Majesty," he said. "That way you will not think on it."

"That way," Elizabeth said wryly, "I will always wonder."

"It was destroyed in a fire." Craven turned away, unable to give her the lie direct to her face. He walked across to the edge of the clearing. This hilltop, the "King's Seat" as it was known locally, had always been one of Frederick's favourite views. From here Craven could see the line of the Rhine stretching like a silver ribbon away to the west, towards Frederick's ancestral lands. He would never see them again now, though perhaps one day his sons would finally inherit.

"It destroyed itself," he said. He spoke with his back to Elizabeth, afraid he would betray himself if he looked at her. "It turned the power of the fire inward and burned up."

He put every ounce of conviction he possessed into the words and after a moment he heard her sigh. There was a soft rustle of skirts as she walked towards him.

"It is fitting that it should be so," she said simply, and Craven felt a huge rush of relief. He turned to face Elizabeth and she was smiling at him. She came up to him and put both her hands in his, standing on tiptoe to kiss his cheek. He felt the touch of her lips through his whole body.

"Thank you," she said. "You have done me a great service, William. I will never forget it."

He should have felt guilt then but he did not, only happiness because he had made her happy.

Elizabeth placed a hand against Craven's chest and tilted her head to look up at him. A strand of her hair brushed his cheek. She was so close Craven could smell her perfume and feel her warmth. In the dark, with the moon hidden by hurrying clouds now, he could see little of her yet his senses were acutely aware of her. He fought the attraction. He had fought it before, knowing it was wrong, that it could never be.

"Will you stay, now that you are back?" she said simply.

He would have given her half his fortune had she asked it of him. Hell, he would have given her all of it. A few minutes before he had been reflecting that he could never love as Elizabeth had loved Frederick. Yet what else could he call this feeling he had for her, this stubborn loyalty he felt? He knew it was an easy thing to fall in love with the Winter Queen. He had seen plenty of other men succumb to her charm. Even he, a dour soldier, was not immune to it. Elizabeth had charm and gallantry. She was a talisman, the embodiment of a cause. They pledged their lives to her because it felt like an honourable course of action. Yet those men were in love with a chimera. The Elizabeth he loved was real.

Love.

There was alchemy in the feeling. Even though he did not believe in magic he could feel the slide of emotion inside him. It was completely alien to him, unknown, unwanted, more frightening than facing the imperial army in battle.

He cleared his throat. "I am, as always, yours to command, Your Majesty," he said. He saw that she was shivering and slipped the cloak from his shoulders to wrap about her. She grasped it close, turning her cheek against the collar where it was warm from his body.

"What would I do without you, Craven?" she said.

"Let us hope," Craven said, "that we never find out."

Guilt for the lies he had told her pricked him again. *It is for her good*, he told himself. *I do it for her.*

A breath of wind disturbed the air, rippling through the poplars, raising a whisper. A dark cloud tracked across the moon and for a second the river gleamed red in the darkness, the colour of blood.

Elizabeth had seen it too. He saw the darkness come back into her eyes. "I feel so guilty," she said.

Craven jumped. The words echoed his own feelings so precisely that for a moment he thought she was accusing him of something rather than speaking of herself.

"You?" he said gruffly. "Why?"

She did not look at him. Her gaze was fixed on the distant silver ripple of the water.

"Everyone thinks me a loyal widow," she murmured, "and I am. I observe the rituals of mourning. I do my duty. Yet inside—" She pressed a hand to her breast. Her voice was so low now Craven had to strain to hear it.

"All I feel is relief," she said. "I am glad it is over. I betray Frederick's memory every moment of every day in my thoughts." She sounded desolate now, unable to bear the weight of her own perfidy. "I loved him so much," she said, "but over time it became too difficult. I became impatient of his failings. I thought him weak. God forgive me, there were times that I *despised* him."

Craven caught her hand. His heart was pounding. "Majesty," he said. "No one needs to know your thoughts. They are between you and God alone—"

"But can you understand the guilt, William?" Elizabeth broke in. "The weight of it? The endless pretence?"

Oh, yes, he understood the weight of guilt. The irony was that he could not tell her why.

"Majesty—"

"I wanted someone strong," Elizabeth said simply. "I wanted you, William. Every time you came to me with his letters. Every time I heard reports of your valour in battle whilst Frederick waited behind the lines for other men to win him his kingdom. That day when you saved me out here in the woods." He could feel her trembling, her passion restrained by such a thin thread. Any moment it might snap. The lust surged in him. He wanted her too, this Queen of Hearts, with all her charm and her beauty and her gallantry. He wanted to possess that.

And there was no noble reason restraining him, only his guilt, dark and monstrous and the thought that he could not compound his betrayal of her by making love to her when he had lied and lied.

He was grateful for the darkness that disguised how much he wanted her. He let go of her hand, not daring to touch her another second for fear he would crush her to him and take her here in the wild woods. Just the thought made his blood heat. He had only shreds of honour left but he held on to those.

"Madam," he said gruffly. "I am not worthy of your regard."

It was another lie for it did not matter to him that he was

the son of a cloth merchant and she a princess, but it was a convenient lie, and one she would understand.

For a second there was silence and then he heard her sigh. She stepped back and he felt her dignity fall around her like a cloak.

"Forgive me," she said, and her voice was cool again, all passion gone. "I am distraught. I spoke that way out of confusion."

"Of course. I understand."

So easily and with so few words were such matters as taking a lover—or not—swept aside. And as soon as she had turned away he wanted her all the more. He thought of her offering herself to another of her squires—Keevill, perhaps, or Erroll—and every possessive instinct in him flared. Yet he had turned her away, even if it had been for reasons he had thought worthy but which now felt hollow.

They rode back to the palace slowly and as soon as he had seen Elizabeth safe within he went to find Margaret. She was dining with friends, but he was in no mood to wait; he caught her eye and she excused herself at once and came out to him. Without a word he took her wrist and led her out of the chamber and down the curving stair to his rooms, kicking the door shut behind them, careless of the open shutters laying wide the labyrinth garden beyond the window. He slammed her against the wall and lifted her, pushing her dress up to her thighs. She was hot and eager as he slid into her, wrapping her legs about him, but even as the pleasure blinded him it was Elizabeth he was thinking of before his mind went dark.

23

Ashdown Park, 26th February 1801

*I*t has happened, as I knew it would. Robert and I are lovers. I
did not plan it. I swear I did not, for truly it is the most enormous
folly on my part for were Evershot to discover my perfidy he would
surely kill me. Yet oddly that knowledge adds spice to my clandestine
affair. It is most exciting. No, I must be truthful here, between the
pages of this book. It is splendid, and entirely wonderful. It is the
most delightful thing that has ever happened to me.

Unfortunately I have had to entrust my maid with knowledge of
the affair since she is the one who takes my notes to Robert and covers for my absence if required. Clara has been with me from the first
but even though we have endured a great deal together I do not trust
her. Whilst I pay her sufficient and she sees where advantage lies,
all will be well, but God forbid that one day she will choose to turn
coat. It is dangerous. I know that. But oh, it is worth it!

I adore Mr Verity. He has all the skill and concern for my pleasure
that Evershot lacks and so I tell myself that I deserve such an indul-

gence when I have to tolerate Evershot's appalling behaviour the rest of the time. Nightly Robert and I face each other down the long table in the dining room with Evershot sitting at the head and we converse so stiffly it would be painful if it did not hide a delicious secret. How strange and delightful it is to speak to Robert so formally when we are so intimate! Sometimes I could laugh aloud at the pleasure it gives me to address him as Mr Verity whilst I remember the sensation of his kisses and his hands upon my body. On these occasions we are careful not to touch nor betray ourselves with so much as a glance. It is most thrilling although I suspect poor Robert could manage well without the deceit. He is not a natural liar as I am.

On those days when I can slip away from the house, Robert and I meet at the old mill on the edge of the wood. The last miller left a month ago so the place is empty. I say he left but in fact he drowned in the millpond, which was extremely careless of him. Still, his loss really is my gain for the place lies empty now. I suspect it is full of rats but I do not care. When Robert and I lie together in the beautiful chamber above the mill wheel I forget all else in the pleasure of his company. Sometimes we do not even make love but hold each other and talk of everything and nothing, whilst the sun plays across the room in bands of glorious light and shadow and my heart fills with joy to be there with this man. If it were not so foolish I would say that I had fallen in love, but that is impossible. I know myself to be too shallow, too worldly, to commit my heart to any man.

Fortunately Evershot is distracted by courtship at present. He is paying his addresses to a Miss Francombe in the hope of winning her hand and, more to the point, her fortune. He goes from my bed to her father's drawing room with great regularity. Last week he came back unexpectedly early and I had mud on my shoes from the walk through the wood, which he remarked upon, and I was obliged to concoct a tale of an interest I had developed in studying the wall hangings in the church. Even I thought that he would see the ridiculousness of that but apparently he did not. I think he has no interest in me beyond the slaking of his lusts. In contrast Robert treats me like the lady I so singularly am not and it is a delight. So just for a little I shall indulge myself in this happiness...

Soon, too, I know Robert will confide in me what it is that Evershot seeks here at Ashdown Park. I know he trusts me now and as I am of so curious a disposition I simply have to know. Whatever it is, I hope he does not find it, for that would spell the end of Robert's time here and that is something on which I cannot bear to think...

24

Marlborough Crafts, previously the Merchant Adventurers' House, was a charming seventeenth-century town house in a prime position on the High Street. Holly stepped through the door and inhaled the scent of frankincense, lavender and old wood. The shop was elegantly laid out and she saw immediately what Greg had meant when he had said that his sister was only interested in high-quality crafts. There were exquisite scented candles, hand-painted cards and a mixture of other charming, eclectic and very expensive gifts.

Karen Hunter was waiting for her and came forwards, hand outstretched. Like Greg she was tall and angular, but she also had a white-blonde pixie crop and startlingly green eyes. She was as elegant and coolly confident as her environment.

"Hi, Holly," she said. "Come into my office." She led the way up a couple of rickety old steps into a back room and gestured Holly to a chair. "I don't usually stock glass," Karen said, "but Greg told me yours was wonderful so..." She smiled. "Show me."

Holly was desperate to ask Karen about Ben's visit but she wanted to get the business stuff out of the way first. It had been kind of Greg to give her an opening and she knew that if she was serious about locating her studio at Ashdown she needed to start looking for new outlets for her work. One thing she realised she had not thought about at all was what would happen when—if—Ben came back to discover that she had moved in. She knew she was deliberately pushing the thoughts away because they were too difficult to face. She was being a coward but just at the moment she didn't want to consider the opposite; what would happen if Ben didn't come back...

She took some engraved rose bowls out of her bag and unwrapped them. Karen picked one up, turning it around so that it caught the light.

"I'm not sure," she said, eyeing the engraved crystal dubiously. "I mean, they're very beautiful but they're a bit too traditional for what we do here..."

Holly nodded her agreement. She knew she had played it safe in showing Karen the bowls first. For all its old premises, Karen's shop had as bright and modern a vibe as she did herself.

"I can see it's not the sort of shop to sell old-fashioned engraved glass," Holly said. "How about this?"

She unwrapped a paperweight.

The piece had been inspired by a cold grey morning out on the River Thames. Holly had been crossing Waterloo Bridge and had seen the screaming seagulls whirling over the water. She had itched to capture their bickering madness in the glass. The finished result had been pleasing even to her. Paperweights were her favourite. She loved their roundness. It was intensely satisfying.

The soft cloth fell away and she thought she heard Karen

catch her breath as the light took the glass and struck back into her eyes.

"Oh!" Karen said. She looked up, her face bright with pleasure. "Now that is gorgeous. I love it. I'll take ten of those." Her expression clouded a little. "I know it's a small order but I can't carry a lot of stock..."

"No worries," Holly said. "I'm building my business up again from scratch so if people like them and tell their friends and I get more commissions, that's the best way I can build."

"I don't know how you make a living," Karen said.

"With difficulty," Holly said, truthfully. "But I'd rather do something I love than earn a fortune in a job I hate."

"I'd rather earn a fortune in a job I love," Karen said.

"Well, yeah," Holly said, laughing, "That would be nice."

Karen reached for the coffee pot and topped up their mugs. "Greg said that you live at the old mill on the Ashdown estate," she said. "Do you have any locally inspired engravings? They usually sell well." She opened a fresh packet of biscuits. The wrapper crackled and the scent of chocolate caught Holly, making her mouth water.

"I've done some glass panels engraved with the White Horse image, if you'd like to see one," Holly said. "I find the landscape on the Downs fascinating." She reached for her bag and brought out a slim panel of glass with the stylised lines of the Uffington White Horse trapped in midgallop, handing it to Karen.

"You're a rubbish saleswoman," Karen said, looking up from the panel with laughter in her eyes. "You should have shown me them first." She propped the little panel up on her desk. "That is stunning. They'll sell like hotcakes. It's such an icon."

Holly knew she was far too reticent in promoting her own work. She hated blowing her own trumpet and was shockingly bad at negotiating. From the shop came the murmur of voices as customers regularly came in and out from the High Street. Holly stood up and stretched. She could feel the buzz of the caffeine. The coffee had been strong.

"If you're interested in Ashdown Park you might like to see the rest of this building before you go," Karen said. "It was built in the 1650s, just before Ashdown House, although it was a Puritan merchant's house rather than a hunting lodge belonging to an aristocrat. We open it to the public on some days but you're welcome to have a quick peek now if you like."

"Thank you," Holly said. "I'd like that." She hesitated. She felt awkward under Karen's bright green gaze, as though she'd been keeping secrets.

"Actually I think my brother came here a little while ago," she said. "I'm not sure why, though I think he was doing some local history research. I wondered if you remembered him coming in—Ben Ansell?"

Karen frowned. "Ansell—wait, that's the guy who went missing." Her eyes narrowed. "I saw the article in the local paper but I didn't connect it. He's your brother? Greg didn't tell me your second name."

"Sorry," Holly said. "I didn't intend to be mysterious. It's just that I'm following up on some of the stuff Ben was doing and I think he visited here. He had a piece of paper with the shop name on it."

"Really?" Karen looked surprised and Holly's heart sank. She was not sure what she had expected but probably something along the lines of Karen immediately remembering both Ben and the reason for his visit. That had been naïve of her—or probably wishful thinking.

"Do you do mail order?" she said, a little desperately. "Perhaps he visited your website and ordered something online and they sent a compliments slip with it?"

"Yeah, that's possible," Karen said. She tapped the keyboard on her computer and immediately a spreadsheet rolled down the screen, lines and lines of orders, names and addresses.

"Here you are," Karen said, tapping a couple of keys. "Ben Ansell. Two months ago. Hmm..." She frowned. "He ordered one postcard. How odd. The postage cost more than the card itself."

Holly felt the same leap of excitement she had experienced when she had read about the Sistrin in Lavinia's diary. "Could you show me which one it is?" she said.

"I can do better than that," Karen said. "It's one of the portraits upstairs. Kitty Bayly. I can show you the original." She stood up. "Come this way."

They went out into the tiled hall. To the right there was a corridor and at the end a rather grand staircase. Holly caught her breath.

"Yes." Karen sounded slightly smug. "Greg says it's the spitting image of the stair at Ashdown, possibly even made by the same craftsmen. But I assume you knew that?"

"No." Holly felt a little dazed. "I mean I've never seen a picture of the interior of Ashdown House but I can imagine..." Her voice trailed away. Just as the view from the roof of Ashdown had come to her so vividly when she had stood in the lavender garden with Mark, so now she could imagine the stair at Ashdown rising up towards the cupola, the wide low rise of the steps, the curved elm of the hand-turned balusters, and the sturdy uprights of oak whose panels were decorated with a fall of carved fruit and flowers. There was the scent of beeswax polish in her nose and on the white-painted walls she could see those haughty aristocratic portraits that Lavinia had mentioned...

She blinked and the vision turned back into the Merchant Adventurers' House. There were no portraits on the wall and it was the smell of lilies that was overpoweringly strong where they stood on a polished table at the bottom of the stairs.

Karen was looking at her curiously and Holly said quickly: "The plasterwork ceiling is stunning. I was just wondering whether that pattern of shields and roses would work on glass."

"Come on up." Karen already had her foot on the first step. "There's more exquisite plasterwork on the first floor." She waited for Holly to join her on the first half landing.

Holly felt oddly reluctant to follow her. The wood of the handrail felt warm and smooth. Her fingers tingled from the contact. She almost felt afraid, as though she was about to step back in time.

Their footsteps sounded loud as they went up the steps, Karen chatting about the history of the house and the cloth merchants who had traded from there, but Holly barely heard her. She could imagine Lavinia ascending Ashdown's stair, the lamplight casting golden pools on the mellow wood, the sound of masculine voices and the clink of glasses coming from the drawing room below. On the first landing Lavinia would turn and look back and there would be Robert Verity in the shadows at the bottom of the stair, watching her...

It had not remotely surprised Holly to read that Lavinia and Robert had become lovers. It had felt both right and inevitable. Over the previous pages of Lavinia's diary Holly had traced the process by which Lavinia had fallen in love, because despite Lavinia's protestations to the contrary, Holly had thought she really did love Robert Verity. He was a true gentleman. He brought Lavinia gifts, talked to her, and treated her with kindness and consideration. Respect had been a rare commodity in Lavinia's life. It was no wonder that she found it irresistible.

They reached the first floor and she followed Karen into the parlour, which was bright with sunlight that poured through the oriole windows. The oak panelled walls were hung with portraits: a gentleman with a dark, watchful face wearing a rich lace collar and jacket with slashed sleeves, a lady whose ethereal silver gown made her pale face and blue eyes fade into insignificance beside the gorgeousness of her attire.

"Those are members of the Bayly family," Karen said. "They were the merchants who built the house." She frowned slightly. "I forget their names but the portraits are seventeenth century. There's a trust that runs the historical side of the house. I just manage the shop."

"You seem to have picked up plenty of historical information all the same," Holly said, and Karen smiled.

"It's difficult not to," she said, "working in a place like this. Besides, I love it. Buildings like this make the past feel so close, somehow, as though it's only a touch away."

Holly nodded. She walked over to the window. Below her she could see the bustle of Marlborough High Street through a prism of distorted glass and latticed panes. There was another portrait to the right of the window alcove but this one was very clearly not seventeenth century. It was a watercolour of a young lady in a white dress with a fur-lined stole of yellow silk and elaborately upswept blonde hair. Her eyes were hazel and her mouth had a soft curve.

"That's Kitty." Karen spoke from beside her. "She looks terribly sweet, doesn't she? She was one of the Victorian Bayly brides, I think. An heiress. They all married into money."

The name meant nothing to Holly and she felt a sharp pang of disappointment. She had no idea why Ben would have requested the postcard.

"She didn't have any connection to Ashdown Park, did she?" she asked. "I mean, she wasn't a member of the Evershot family or anything?"

"I don't think so," Karen said. "Maybe the local history group would be able to tell you more about her." She picked up one of a pile of postcards that was lying on the round walnut table. "Here's a postcard like the one we would have sent your brother."

Holly took it automatically. Kitty's shyly smiling face looked out at her from its gilt frame. She turned the card over. It had Kitty's name and dates, but it also had something else.

Kitty Bayly, née Flyte, 1801–1872.

Holly's stomach dropped with shock. She felt slightly dizzy. She looked into Kitty's hazel eyes and knew without an ounce of doubt that she was looking at Lavinia's daughter.

25

Holly was late for choir practice that night. She had come back from Marlborough buzzing with questions about Lavinia and her daughter, questions that were destined to be unanswered unless she could find a genealogist to help her trace Kitty Flyte's ancestry. There had been no mention of Kitty in the official biographies of Lavinia that she had downloaded, and certainly no references to a child in the erotic romps of the published version. The name Flyte was quite unusual, but she was facing the possibility that Kitty might be no connection to Lavinia at all. It was just that she had been so sure, with a deep instinct that could not be explained but felt rock solid.

There was, of course, Lavinia's diary, which might hold more clues to both Kitty and also the mirror and the pearl. Holly was very aware that normally she would have gobbled the book up long before now, but she had come to a point where she did not want it to end. She felt an ache inside when she thought about it finishing. Not only was it a link to Ben but it also felt like a connection to Lavinia across two hundred years and she did not want to lose that.

She let herself into the church through the vestry door, and stood for a moment in the cool before going into the nave, squeezing past the altos, and sliding into the spare seat on the pew beside Mavis Barker. Mavis had been in the church choir when Holly had been a child and she was still going strong. The choir itself had changed, though. There was a wider age range and a wider repertoire as well.

David Byers, the irascible choirmaster, gave Holly an impatient nod as she took her seat. The choir was in the middle of a medley of film music. Enthusiastic was probably the best way to describe the singing, Holly thought, but as she was as rusty as the next person she was in no position to criticise.

The music ran ragged and David cut them off with a chopping motion of his hand. A sigh ran through the choir, the sheet music fluttered.

"Basses, you're a quaver out again. We'll come back to that later. Let's try 'Any Dream Will Do.' Mark—from the top, if you don't mind…"

Holly looked up sharply. She had known Mark would be here—Fran had told her that she had persuaded just about everyone she knew to join the choir regardless of whether they were tone-deaf or not—but Holly had not seen him when she came in. Now she picked him out in the seats opposite, next to Fran's husband, Iain.

Fran leant forwards and dug her in the ribs with her songbook. "Wait until you hear Mark sing the solo, Holly. He has the most amazing voice—"

David Byers silenced her with one of his fierce looks and the pianist started again. Mark's tenor voice was the most sublime thing that Holly had heard in years. It wrapped around her, raising the tiny hairs on the back of her neck, setting her shivering. Beside her in the choir stalls, Mavis rustled the wrapping of her packet of Parma violets and leant forwards to offer Holly a sweet. She shook her head slightly, smiling.

Holly fixed her gaze on the shadowy arches leading down the nave. The air in the church smelled of warm dust mixed with the faint, cool perfume of lilies, and the light hung in a pale curtain between the stone pillars. Outside the sun had gone and the sky was fading to an ominous grey.

She missed the soprano cue and cursed herself. David's stern black gaze swept over, noting the mistake. Holly tried not to giggle hysterically. It was just like being back at school. It was a good job Fran was sitting behind her and they could not see each other.

The notes curled, entwined. Mark might have a stunning solo voice, but he was able to mingle in with the rest of the choir when required. Holly glanced at him again and saw with a curious twist of the heart that he was watching her. He smiled at her. She felt flustered, as though the air between them was alive. With an effort she broke the contact, snapped the invisible thread between them. She looked down at her sheet music, although she knew the song by heart.

"Let's try something else," David said irritably, when someone's mobile chirruped the theme of *Hawaii Five-O* and the choir dissolved into laughter. "Page twenty three—'Begin the Beguine.' One for the oldies amongst us."

They worked their way creditably through another four songs and finished just before nine o'clock.

"How great was that!" Fran enthused, threading her arm through Holly's. "I bet you're glad you're back, aren't you? Are you coming to the pub?"

The after–choir practice pub visit had been something of a tradition too, although at the age of nine Holly had been excluded from such adult mysteries. She glanced instinctively across the aisle to where Mark was chatting with Iain and Greg.

"Mark doesn't mind if we all go off and pickle ourselves in alcohol," Fran said cheerfully, following her gaze. "He goes home for a cup of cocoa."

"How decadent," Holly said. "I won't tonight, Fran, thanks. I've got an early start tomorrow. I'm due in Bristol at nine to talk to a big retailer about a contract."

"Okay." Fran might be tactless but she was hard to offend. "Hey, good luck! That would be fantastic."

A thought struck Holly. "Are any of the Craven or Evershot family graves here?"

"Graves?" Fran said.

"It is a church," Holly pointed out.

"Most of the family are buried at the church on the family estate outside Coventry." Iain had come up and slid an arm about Fran's waist. He was big, broad and fair-haired, dwarfing Fran's shorter figure. Holly had always imagined him as being in the style of the intrepid archaeologists who had journeyed to Egypt and beyond in the Edwardian era. There was an air of adventure about him even if he actually spent his time in Oxfordshire.

"The only thing here is the Craven memorial chapel," he said. "It's a bit dowdy and unexciting."

"I'd still like to take a look at it," Holly said.

"Leave it until daylight," Iain advised. "You can't see much in this half-light."

The church was emptying fast now. Mark had disappeared. Holly knew she should be going too. It looked darker than it should have done out in the twilight and she had a mile to walk.

Nevertheless she lingered as the silence fell and someone switched off the lights in the nave and she was left in the half darkness of the aisle. Here there were tombs of stone; not Evershot monuments, but their predecessors as Lords of the Manor, perhaps. The light was too dim for Holly to read the inscriptions. And here was the little Lady Chapel dedicated to the First Earl of Craven, Elizabeth's earl, with marble plaques and decorated hassocks and a window depicting him in full armour. He was mounted on a white charger against a background of what looked like burning buildings, his sword clasped in one hand and a cross in the other. The last light caught the stained glass of the cross, pouring a rosy glow across the stone flags of the floor like spilt wine.

Something moved behind Holly and she almost jumped out of her skin.

"Jesus!"

"Hardly." Mark's voice was dry. "Are you always this nervous?"

"I'm afraid of the dark," Holly said truthfully. "I thought you'd gone," she added, aware as soon as she said it that fear had loosened her tongue and made her give away more than she had intended.

Mark smiled. "I thought you had too. I'm glad both of us were wrong." He gestured to the chapel. "What are you doing in here?"

"Oh, just immersing myself in Craven history," Holly said lightly. "I think I'm becoming a bit obsessed." She pointed to the stained-glass window. "Why the burning buildings?" she asked.

"I think it's meant to depict the Great Fire of London in 1666," Mark said. "The First Earl of Craven helped to put it out. When many other aristocrats were fleeing the city he stayed."

"What a hero," Holly said. She stared at the portrait in the glass. It was in a very Victorian style, now she looked closely.

The Earl looked noble and austere, his long hair flowing, his sword clasped with grim resolve. The horse looked equally determined, just waiting for the word to gallop towards the flames.

"Speaking of heroes," Mark said, "I've been trying to find a record of Robert Verity. He's in the army record for the last decade of the eighteenth century. He served in Portugal and as I suspected, he was one of the officers mapping the country for the Ordnance Survey. He disappears from the record in 1801."

"Disappears?" Holly said. A cold breeze had edged a shiver down her spine. "You mean he left the army—resigned his commission?"

"No," Mark said. "There are no further mentions of him after early 1801, not in the censuses or any other documents. It's very odd, as though he vanished into thin air, but I'll keep searching."

Vanished like Ben, Holly thought, and felt a trickle of cold fear.

There was the creak of the church door opening and the sound of footsteps on stone, then Paula's voice, sharply from the shadows:

"Mark? Are you there? Do you want a lift home? It's going to rain."

Mark's hand tightened on Holly's arm, warning in his touch now. They both kept motionless, no sound but the faintest breath.

"Mark!" Paula sounded shriller now. "Stop taking the piss. This place is giving me the creeps, all these tombs and dead bodies..." There was a long moment and then Paula said something very short and rude under her breath before stomping off. The door slammed shut with what felt like a definite flounce.

There was a pause, the silence suddenly alive with awareness.

"That was very childish of us," Holly breathed. "We could just have said no thank you. Though I doubt Paula would have wanted to offer me a lift anyway," she added.

"She's got a sports car," Mark said. "There's only room for one." Holly heard him sigh. "Sorry. I know it was immature. I just get tired of blowing her out all the time. I don't want to hurt her feelings but I'm really not interested. Anyway, let's go."

"Yes, let's," Holly said abruptly. All the blank-eyed tomb effigies seemed to be watching her. Paula had been right; it was definitely creepy. She could imagine the tombs opening and the skeletons spilling out in a *danse macabre*. It would make a vivid piece of engraving though perhaps too sinister to appeal to any buyers.

The night felt different when they went outside. The sunset had gone, obscured behind a bank of cloud that was rolling over the top of the hill and piling darkness upon darkness. Lightning flickered along its western edge. The air felt heavy. Wind stirred.

"It is going to rain," Holly said. "Paula was right."

Mark checked the sky. "We might get back before it starts," he said. He led the way around the graveyard, the humps of the graves and their tumbled stones now lost in blackness, and started up the path to the Ridgeway.

"I don't know if you've noticed that the path leads straight to the south door of the church," he said. "It was the way the Evershots used to walk to church from Ashdown Park. Door to door."

"I'm surprised that they didn't take a carriage," Holly said. "Surely they should have impressed the villagers by arriving at church in style?"

"They were a keen sporting family, by all accounts," Mark said. "Perhaps they rode."

"It must be great to ride around here," Holly said. "You'd see the landscape from a very different perspective. Good for a surveyor," she added, when he glanced at her.

"It is," Mark said. He smiled his sudden, warm smile. "You're a very thoughtful person, Holly Ansell. And a very nice one," he added. "I can see why Bonnie likes you so much."

"Oh, dogs have the most terrible judgement," Holly said lightly. "Look at the way she fawns over you."

Mark laughed. "Carol always used to say that. Her parents had a German shepherd that barely gave her the time of day but was always following me around. It was embarrassing. I think that dog missed me more than the rest of the family when we divorced."

"How long ago did you split up?" Holly asked. The path had started to climb quite steeply now and she could feel her breath coming shorter.

"Four years," Mark said. "Carol went to New Zealand. She's got a new partner now. She's happy."

"And you?" Holly asked.

Mark's gaze came back to her. "I do all right. It's true I've avoided relationships recently. I've been focussing on the business. It needs a lot of investment in time and energy at the moment."

"It always seems more acceptable for a man to say that than a woman," Holly said. "I've had endless comments about putting my engraving career before marriage and kids."

"Yet you were engaged," Mark said.

Holly laughed. "That's why it's an ex-engagement. Trying to join my life with someone else's was a mistake. I'm not really cut out for it. Too independent."

The thunder was rumbling nearer now. The edge of the wood pressed close, a ragged ribbon of dancing trees as the wind rose. The first drops of rain were starting to patter down.

"Is it really about independence?" Mark said. "Or is it about not taking risks?" Then, when Holly did not answer: "I've had plenty of time to think about what happened between us the night after Ben went missing. I get that you were upset. That's totally natural. But there was more to it than that, wasn't there, Holly? You were trying to deal with something that was even more difficult to handle, something you were running away from. So you turned to me to escape."

The wood was alive with noise now; the thunder overhead, like a crouching beast, the rain falling hard on the leaves and softer on the forest floor. Lightning lit the sky and Holly shivered convulsively.

"I don't want to talk about it," she said. "I can't. It's too difficult." She looked up and met his eyes. "I'm sorry it happened."

"Are you?" Mark said. "I'm not."

He brought his mouth down on hers and it was exactly what Holly had feared and exactly what she wanted, the sweet rush of recognition, the sense of rightness, the hunger, all the things she had always avoided because they were too risky, all the things she wanted now with an intensity she'd never known.

They kissed until the world around her vanished and all she felt was heat and need. Her clothes were soaked and her hair was sticking to her head and she could feel rain running down her face and neck but all she felt inside was desire. She felt dizzy, aware of nothing but the giant oak that covered them with its shelter, the roughness of bark at her back and the coldness of the night breeze on her bare skin where Mark had moved her shirt aside to kiss her throat and the tender hollow above her collarbone. It was sublime, it was lovely, and the intimacy of it scared the hell out of her.

She wrenched herself away and steadied herself with one hand against the trunk of the oak. Everything was much too intense for her. It was going much too fast.

"I must get home before I drown," she said shakily. She stood on tiptoe to kiss Mark's cheek. "Goodnight."

"Wait." Mark put out a hand towards her. He shook his head sharply as though to clear his mind. If he was feeling anywhere near as poleaxed as she was, Holly thought it was no wonder. "You can't just run off," he said.

"I'm nearly back," Holly said. "I can find my way from here."

"That wasn't what I meant."

Holly knew what he meant. He wasn't going to let her just walk away. Not this time.

They fell into step, side by side, without any further words. A light glowed in the window of the watermill. It looked ordinary and safe, so different from how Holly felt inside.

"Thank you for seeing me safely home," she said.

Mark smiled. "I'll see you tomorrow," he said and kissed her, little more than a brush of his lips against hers, then again, a little longer, a whole lot hotter.

This time Holly watched him as he walked away through the trees and she thought of Lavinia, running through the snowbound woods to meet her lover, risking everything for an hour in his arms. She was starting to feel like that. She was starting to feel too much. And she didn't know what the hell to do about it.

26

Craven was tiring of Margaret. The sweetness that had seemed charming at first now felt cloying. She bored him. He told himself that it had nothing to do with his feelings for Elizabeth but he knew that was not true. Elizabeth was gold to Margaret's base metal. He hungered for her and the more he took Margaret the less satisfied he felt. Once upon a time Margaret's raw lust had been enough to satisfy him. She was prim out of bed and shameless in it, and he had liked the way she would do whatever he wished, match him and then exceed him. Now, though, he wanted her gone.

He sat up and reached for his day shirt. They had not slept much and he felt exhausted. He had chased his dreams of Elizabeth all night and felt empty and spent.

"William." Margaret placed a hand on his bare shoulder, staying him. "There is something I must tell you."

He drew away from her touch and pulled the shirt over his head before turning to face her.

"What is it?"

She avoided his gaze. Her slender fingers plucked at the coverlet, which was drawn up to her chest in a pretty gesture of modesty. This show of innocence would once have made him smile. Now he deplored the calculated sham of it.

"Well?" He spoke roughly, pricked by irritation.

"I am with child," Margaret said. "Your child," she added, evidently sensing that he was crass enough to raise the question.

The shock hit him in his stomach like a blow, stealing his breath. He wondered why he had never imagined this might happen. He had been thoughtless, careless. It had all been lust and excitement in the beginning, and then it had been habit and now... Now it was a disaster.

Margaret was watching him, biting her lip as though she was anxious of his reaction. Yet her blue gaze was watchful, not scared. Craven found his thoughts falling away from her to centre on the child. It might be a son, perhaps, an heir. It was not long since he had thought such things did not matter. It was interesting how quickly a man could change his mind.

He looked at Margaret again. She was pretty, well bred, presentable enough. She was not Elizabeth, of course; there was no depth to her, there was no compassion or sincerity, but he should not be comparing his mistress to the Queen. He could never have Elizabeth and Margaret would be a perfectly acceptable wife. Her family had no money for a dowry but he had plenty enough for both of them. And if this child were a daughter then that would be agreeable. A son would surely follow, and more children, a nursery full of them. And if there was no real love then that was the way of aristocratic marriages. The thought caused him an odd pang that felt like grief.

"We should wed," he said, realising too late that his tone

had an element of regret in it and that his words were not the most gracious of proposals. He tried to make up; took her hand.

"Margaret," he said. "Marry me."

"I do not wish to wed you." Margaret freed herself from his grip. She sounded very matter of fact, unsentimental. "I am already wed."

Craven's heart stumbled like a missed footstep. "What?" He felt confused and foolish. "How? When?"

"Years ago." She waved a slender hand in dismissal. "Lord Verity's son." There was a tiny pause. "He is insane."

Craven knew nothing of Lord Verity, or of his son and his insanity. His mind felt sluggish. All he could think was that he had not known. How was it that he had not known? He reached mechanically for his trousers, his fingers fumbling with the ties whilst his mind fumbled for the right questions.

"Who knows about this?"

"It's common knowledge." There was a shadow of scorn in Margaret's eyes. "But you never listen to court gossip, do you, William? If you did, perhaps you would have heard."

So it was his fault now. He rubbed a hand across his eyes. "Where is he?" He looked around almost as though he was expecting Verity to leap out of the chest.

"He stays in England, on his father's manor in Kent." Margaret was dressing now, quickly, efficiently, as fast as she had shed her clothes the night before. "I will need to return there at once now that I am with child."

Craven watched her, the nimble fingers tying her laces, fastening her hair, the cold efficiency and the calculation. Something hardened within him.

"And what," he said courteously, "will his lordship say when you return home bearing a child that is most certainly not his son's?"

"I imagine that he will be delighted," Margaret said evenly. "Robert is childlike, little more than a babe himself. It fast became apparent that he would never father an heir."

"I see," Craven said. He did. Suddenly he saw it all very well. This child would not be his heir. It would be heir to the Verity title and lands.

"And what do you want from me?" he asked. "Why did you even tell me you were expecting a child? Why not simply leave?" He sought to control his voice, sought also to control the fury that was building in him, hotter than a furnace. He had not known his own capacity for anger. In battle he was always calm. It was one of his greatest strengths. What he felt now though was harsh, ungovernable and white-hot. His hands itched with the urge to take Margaret by the throat and snap her slender neck with one turn of the wrists. He had lost his child before it was even born.

He forced himself to keep very still.

"I need money." She faced him squarely. "For my passage back to England."

"And you think I will pay? For you to steal my child away, my heir?"

A shadow touched Margaret's eyes, but what he read there was surprise, not guilt. "I did not think you would care," she said. "You never cared for me."

He could not deny that. He did not want to deny it. "A child is different," he said.

She did not flinch. "You should wed. Father a legitimate heir of your own."

"I thought," Craven said, with the first touch of bitterness he had allowed to show, "that that was what I was doing. With you."

She raised a shoulder in a half shrug. "I'm sorry, William." The words were conventional and he doubted the sentiment was more than hypocrisy. "But I am tied to Robert by law and the church. There is nothing that can be done."

Craven was not sure that he would wish to marry her anyway, now he had seen so deep into her venal soul.

"You will have to speak to my man of business about the money," he said. His voice was stiff. He moved across to the window and thrust back the curtains, opened the window wide as though the cold night air could banish the sickness in the room.

"There is no need to involve anyone else." Margaret spoke lightly. "You have in your possession a diamond mirror, a pretty piece. I could sell that to Meneer Bode on the Denneweg and it would raise sufficient money to fund my journey home—"

"No." Craven had crossed the room and caught her by the shoulders. He was not even aware he had moved until he felt the thin cotton of her chemise, and the fragile bones beneath.

"How did you know about the mirror?" he demanded.

There had been apprehension in Margaret's eyes but now there was curiosity and a speculation that made his heart lurch sickeningly.

"It's a secret," she said slowly. "I see."

"Don't be foolish." He let her go abruptly, turned away.

"Did you steal it from the Queen?" She was poised, on tiptoe, straining like a hunter scenting its prey. "I know it was once hers. I saw it in a portrait."

"Of course I did not steal it." Craven's voice rang with insincerity. Even he could hear it. "Why would I do such a thing?"

"I don't know." Margaret answered him seriously. "I'm not sure I need to know. But if Her Majesty is not aware of the theft then that makes matters simple for me. Give the mirror to me and I will not tell her what you did."

Silence. It felt thick. Craven could feel his heart thudding. That accursed mirror. He had intended to destroy it. He had told Elizabeth that he had. So many times on the journey from Metz to The Hague he had been about to cast it into a lake or thrust it down a rabbit hole and let the earth swallow it up. Yet he had not done so and he did not know why. He had told himself that he had no belief in its power and yet something—a superstition that he did not wish to admit to—had made him keep it alive.

Alive.

It was not a living thing. Yet it felt as though it were.

Margaret had taken it from the bottom of the Armada chest where he had hidden it, wrapped in a silken shawl, and was holding it up before her. He could see the candle flame reflected back at him and the sparkle of the diamonds as they caught the light.

"It's a fine piece," she said, with the satisfaction of a costermonger driving a hard bargain. "One of those diamonds alone would pay for my passage back to England a dozen times over." She was seeing her future in the mirror right enough, Craven thought, and it was all fat profit. She swung around towards him.

"So? Do we have an agreement?"

The mirror went dark. Margaret was half turned towards him and so she did not see, but Craven was transfixed. He stared into the swirling heart of the darkness. It was like a whirlpool, pulling him down until the cold and the grief closed over his head in a drowning wave. Then the mirror cleared and all he could see was the outlines of the room in the pale candlelight and all he could feel was emptiness.

He cleared his throat. "Take it then. Sell it. Only do it discreetly."

She gave him a look of contempt. "Of course. I have no wish to be arrested for theft like poor Mrs Crofts was when Her Majesty's father saw her wearing his gift of a necklace." She had already stowed the mirror within her bodice. "It's better this way, William," she said, suddenly. "The Queen would never have permitted us to wed."

"What?" Craven said. It seemed like an irrelevance. "I'm not sure that the Queen has the right to forbid my marriage," he said.

Margaret snapped her fingers so sharply he jumped. "You are naïve. She could withdraw her patronage, then you would discover what it is like to be without preferment."

"I take nothing from the Queen," Craven said slowly. "She is poor. She does not have anything to give."

"You took this." Margaret patted her bodice where the mirror lay against her heart. "And how curious that you should do so, you who are so virtuous and loyal." There was a sneer in her voice. "What did she do to you that you claimed such a revenge?"

Craven did not explain. He would not rise to her provocation, least of all tell her that he felt guilt and grief because Elizabeth had trusted him to destroy the crystal mirror and even now he did not understand why he could not.

After a moment Margaret made a sharp sound of derision.

"You had better hope she never discovers what you have done," she said, and it sounded like a curse. "I doubt she would forgive you for such a betrayal. After all, you are her creature." She came up to him and he could feel the fury tight in her body and see the brightness of it in her eyes and suddenly he understood, suddenly he knew. This was why she hated him; this was why she wanted revenge. This was why she was taking his heir.

"You belong to the Queen, William," Margaret said, "like her dogs and her monkeys do. She snaps her fingers and you come running. You are hers; you always were and you always will be."

27

Ashdown House, 1st March 1801

*M*atters are most difficult. Robert says that he cannot bear for me to be Evershot's mistress any longer. He is quite, quite passionate about it. He says he cannot endure to think of me lying with another man.

I should have envisaged this. My poor darling Robert is fathoms deep in love with me and has never espoused the light morals by which I live my life. We argued for what felt like hours until I was exhausted. When I told him I could not break with Evershot because I had no money he told me I was too good for this sort of life and that I should run away with him. He spoke wildly of how we should be married. If only we could, but it is folly, alas, and even more so now that I finally know the truth.

What I am about to relate is quite, quite extraordinary. I am not sure I would believe it had I not seen the evidence with my own eyes. It seems that Robert came to Ashdown Park deliberately. He had heard that Evershot required a surveyor and applied for the work because he has some distant connection to the family and wanted to see Ashdown for himself. Years back his great-great-great-grandmother or some such (I forget how many greats) was mistress to the Earl of Craven and bore a son. Or so his family history relates. So Robert and my lord are cousins several times removed, though one would never guess it for Evershot and Robert are as dissimilar as two men could possibly be.

Anyway, Robert tells me that the whole business was swept under the carpet since his great-great-great-grandmother was already wed and so the child was to all intents and purposes a Verity and in time he inherited the Verity title and estates. I did wonder what Lord Craven thought of this turn of affairs since he never had a legitimate heir of his own, but perhaps he was simply glad to avoid a scandal. History does not relate. But in time, of course, the Evershots rose high on the back of Craven's fortune and the Veritys, alas, fell almost as far as the Evershots had risen.

All Robert has to boast of the connection to the First Earl is some battered-looking mirror that has been in his family for centuries. Legend has it that it once belonged to the Queen of Bohemia, and is another of those mysterious treasures of which people speak but frankly if this is a piece of treasure, then I am a brass monkey. I never saw a more sorry piece, the glass is quite spotted with age and the wood all battered and worn. I suppose the diamonds are quite fine but they are dirty and dull and may be no more than paste for all I know.

Anyway, once more I digress. Robert came to Ashdown to see his ancestral home and when he arrived he discovered that it was indeed the Winter Queen's lost pearl that Evershot sought, for he too had heard the stories that it was hidden about the estate. Evershot made Robert swear by the most terrible oaths that he would tell no one of their quest. Naturally Robert, seeing the kind of man Evershot was, told him nothing of his connection to the Craven family, nor that he held the crystal mirror, for he knew it would go badly for him if Evershot knew.

They searched and searched for the Queen of Bohemia's pearl but they found nothing. Robert says that very probably the whole tale is naught but a myth, which is most unfortunate because the lack of success in his quest makes Evershot savage. Apparently he is not as rich as everyone had thought. His debts are pressing, his mama will no longer fund him and the heiress he was courting has betrothed herself to another so his mood is at all times vile.

Where does this leave Robert and I? In a desperate plight, I assure you. For here is poor Robert swearing undying love to me and begging me to elope with no thought for how his mama would feel were he to bring home a harlot as a bride and here am I trying to tell him it is impossible whilst secretly wishing it were not so. Yes, I confess it, I do love Robert with all my heart but the reality of our situation is that no matter how high he sets me, I am not good enough for him and I would be the greatest fool to believe otherwise.

Oh, if only matters were different! But alas, Robert could barely afford to keep me—I am very expensive—and it would do him no credit to wed me. His career would be blighted, his good name tarnished. There is no way out of the situation. I feel so miserable I could cry, and that is something I do rarely for it is ruinous to the complexion.

Holly was so engrossed in the diary that it took two attempts for Bonnie to rouse her. She pushed her nose into Holly's hand and dropped her lead neatly at her feet. Holly smiled and got up. It would do her good to get some exercise and it would also give her time to think about the latest revelations in Lavinia's diary.

She was going to read on to the end tonight. The compulsion to do so was too strong to resist. She wanted to know what happened. Unless there was some remarkable turnabout in the last few pages of the memoir it had never been found in Lavinia's time. Lord Evershot had sought it and failed. Holly wondered if Ben had been luckier.

Outside the air was warm and still, so still that Holly could hear the Ashbury church clock chiming across the fields. As she opened the gate she heard a step and looked up. For some reason she was expecting Mark and she didn't like the way that her heart dropped when instead she saw Greg Hunter coming towards her out of the wood. He raised a hand in greeting and loped up to them.

"Hi, Holly," Greg said. "I thought I'd come and take a look at your studio."

"Oh." Holly felt put out but she was not sure why. Generally she was happy to talk about her work and show people around her workshop, and she had been the one to suggest Greg come over in the first place. Greg had done her a huge favour in getting her the commission for his sister's shop and as a result of that she had already had enquiries from a number of other shops and galleries. Business was picking up.

"Of course," she said. Then, as Bonnie pressed closer: "Sorry, I was just taking the dog out…"

Greg checked his watch. "No problem. I hadn't realised it was past lunchtime. I've been working since first light today." He ran a hand through his hair. "There's a badger sett on the edge of the paddock and it's interfering with the laying of the new drainage pipes. But as the badgers were here first by about a thousand years we need to find a way around the problem." He gestured to Bonnie who was almost dancing with impatience to be going, "I don't want to hold you up so I'll come back some other time. It's just that Karen said your work was superb and I'd love to see it."

"That was kind of her," Holly said. She smiled at him. "Why don't you walk with us for a bit, if you're off duty now? I haven't had chance to thank you properly for the introduction to Karen. She's great, and I love the shop. It's got such a fabulous, eclectic mix of stuff."

Greg's face lit up. "It's really cool, isn't it? I knew your work would fit right in." He loped along beside her. "And the Merchant Adventurers' House is a wonderful setting. A real slice of seventeenth-century history."

"Karen said that you were very keen on history before you got involved in all the wildlife side of things," Holly said. She noticed that Greg blushed; his ears glowed pink. It was endearing.

"Oh, I loved history as a kid," he said. "All those castles and knights and swords."

"And buried treasure," Holly said.

Greg laughed. "I never found anything more exciting than a rusty bucket, though."

Bonnie was galloping between the trees, snuffling through the old leaves and scaring rabbits down their burrows. They walked down a shaded ride and out into a clearing. In the centre was a low wall of chalk and stone, tumbledown, over-grown, with a wooden seat beside it.

"There used to be a fountain here," Greg said. "It was fed by a spring but that ran dry years ago."

"All the springs have run dry this summer," Holly said. "The mill isn't the same without the water." She put a hand on the hot stone of the wall, feeling the warmth against her palm and the roughness of the broken mortar. A peacock but-terfly spread its wings to the sun. It was very quiet.

"I'd better get back," Greg said regretfully. "The next bus to Lambourn goes in ten minutes."

Bonnie raised her head and watched him go before return-ing to her rootling through the grass. Holly sat quietly, one hand still resting on the stone, feeling the heat of the sun beat-ing against her closed eyelids. The sounds of the birds and the traffic on the road mingled together until it seemed as though it rippled through her head like running water. Even though she knew the spring was dry it seemed as though she could feel the droplets from the fountain cold against her fingers. Yet she felt warm inside; she felt love, like a soft drift of blossom against her cheek. It filled her with a sort of wordless joy.

She opened her eyes.

Mark was standing on the edge of the clearing, Bonnie pirouetting around him in excitement. He bent absentmindedly to pat her head but he was looking at Holly. Holly felt her heart lift and she smiled spontaneously and Mark smiled back and she felt the same devastating wash of love she had felt a moment before.

Help.

Panic gripped her. This was not supposed to happen. She was getting confused. Lavinia's blazing love for Robert was taking over her mind.

"I thought I'd find you here," Mark said.

"What do you mean?" Holly said. She spoke more abruptly than she had intended. The intensity of the emotions she had felt had left her feeling completely disorientated and vulnerable.

Mark raised his brows at her tone. "Only that I met Greg on the path and he said you were here."

"Oh." Holly felt relieved at the banality of it. "Yes, sorry... I was daydreaming a bit."

Mark smiled at her again and she felt even hotter. "I was looking for you, anyway. I wondered if you'd like to come over to my place for Sunday lunch tomorrow? It's just a barbecue, nothing formal. Fran and Iain will be there and Greg and Paula and a few other people."

"I'd love to," Holly said, "but I sort of promised my grandparents I'd have lunch with them." She was taken aback at how disappointed she felt. "I haven't been to see them for a few weeks..."

"No problem," Mark said. "I should have asked sooner."

"I'll drop in afterwards if I'm back in time," Holly said.

She ran her fingers over the rough stone of the fountain. There was a date carved in the crumbling wall. Her fingers traced the numbers 1665. She remembered Lavinia making reference to meeting Robert Verity by a fountain somewhere in the grounds. She wondered if it had been here, in a very different time, with the snow on the ground and the bite of cold in the air.

"This was part of the original pleasure grounds," Mark said. "You remember I mentioned that Lord Evershot was remodelling them? He had men working on a series of tunnels and water mines to supply the fountains and pools."

Holly knelt down to push the grass and bracken away from the slab and uncovered the date stone. As well as the numbers it had a complicated arrangement of initials carved onto it, a *W* and a *C* and an *E* and an *S* with a design of leaves and stems shaped like a heart.

"William Craven and Elizabeth Stuart," Mark said, bending over to see. His shadow fell across the white stone. "I had no idea that was there. Cute, like carving your initials on a tree."

"He was besotted with her, wasn't he," Holly said. She let the grass spring back into place, covering the stone again.

"Do you know what happened to the first Lord Craven after the Winter Queen died?" she asked. "I know he never married."

"No, he didn't," Mark said. "He lived to a ripe old age but had no wife or child." Their eyes met and Holly felt her stomach somersault. "They say his heart was broken," Mark said. "He wanted no one but her."

28

It was odd how the loss of the mirror preyed on Craven's mind. He thought of it as a loss now, as though Margaret had stolen from him something that was legitimately his.

He had gone to all the goldsmiths and gem dealers in the city to try to find the diamond mirror and buy it back. It was not a job he could entrust to a servant. He went under the guise of looking for a pretty trinket for a mistress. But none of the merchants he spoke to appeared to have seen the crystal mirror and sometimes when he pressed too hard he saw the interest quicken in their eyes and knew he was in danger of giving himself away.

Each time he returned to the palace empty-handed.

And then Elizabeth summoned him one day. She was having her portrait painted and Craven felt a flash of irritation. It felt as though all she ever did was pose for these endless paintings; the martyred Queen reminding the world that she was still fighting for what was rightfully hers even if she used the paintbrush not the sword. He knew it was hypocrisy. She had told him so that night on the hill when she had offered herself to him, but now they had both retreated into formality. They both kept her secrets.

The portrait was almost finished and was not, to Craven's eyes, remotely flattering. The background of heavy gold brocade hangings and behind that the dull, flat greenery of the Dutch landscape set a sombre mood. Elizabeth was clothed in black widow's weeds, as she habitually was, with only the smallest touches of white at her neckline and sleeve. Craven found himself irritated again that she would not, after several years, throw off the black for something less morbid. He had once taken the liberty of saying that she should wear colours again only for Elizabeth to tell him very sharply indeed that a widowed queen's dress was as much about politics as fashion. She was the sober stateswoman on the European stage. It was difficult enough to get men to treat her with respect as it was, without giving them the opportunity to accuse her of frivolity and yet it felt as though she was smothering her own spirit under layers of funereal black, tying herself forever to Frederick's memory.

"Mierevelt," Elizabeth said to the artist. "Would you excuse us?"

The painter looked infuriated for a moment, as though he should not be subject to the whims of any sitter, no matter how royal. He dropped his brush with a clatter and stalked out, shutting the door behind him with a decidedly ill-tempered bang. In the sudden silence Craven could hear the panting of the small black and tan spaniel that was lying glumly on a cushion to Elizabeth's right. The dog featured prominently in the painting, pawing at Elizabeth's black skirts, gazing up at her with hope and the expectation of a sweetmeat. Craven snapped his fingers at it but the creature ignored him. Perhaps it was too hot to move. The room certainly felt airless.

"Oh, dear," Elizabeth said. "I expect he will send one of his students to complete the commission now. There is no one so ill-natured as an offended artist."

Craven moved across to the casement and pushed it wide. Now he could breathe more easily, even if the fresher air brought with it the unseasonable heat of early spring and the rotten stench of vegetables discarded by the palace kitchens.

"There is bad news," Elizabeth said. "The worst. It is as I had feared."

The light glistened on the pearls at her neck, a fine necklace that glowed with a soft lustre. Against their beauty Elizabeth's skin looked sallow, drained by the heavy black silk, age and lines and hardship showing. Craven felt a pang of pity for her and then felt angry. He had no right to feel sorry for her. She would not thank him for it.

"What is it?" he said.

"They have taken my lord's body," Elizabeth said. "It is lost. Simmern's party was attacked on the road."

Craven saw that her hands were shaking and moved swiftly to the table by the door, splashing a measure of wine into a glass and bringing it across to her. She took it with a nod of thanks but did no more than wet her lips before putting it down.

"Simmern does not know who took the body," Elizabeth said. "Robbers. Rough men, he thinks, illiterate jackals preying on travellers for money. Perhaps they did not even realise what it was they took. I think—" her voice faltered, "that the King of Bohemia's bones are probably even now scattered through the forest."

"Bloody incompetents," Craven thought savagely, and when he saw her smile he realised he had spoken aloud.

"I beg your pardon, Majesty," he said. "But in truth—" he smashed his fist into the other palm, "how could a group of trained solders fail to fight off a band of brigands? It beggars belief."

Elizabeth picked up the wine glass again. Her fingers clenched white around the stem. "Too late for regrets, Craven. I should have asked you to fulfil the commission instead. But for now—" She looked up. Her eyes were dark, strained. He wanted to go to her, gather her to him and soothe her fears. He kept quite still. Such intimacies would not be wise, nor were they permitted between them these days.

"We tell no one," Elizabeth said. "We act as though all is as it should be. We do not hand such a victory to our enemies. If they know of it we shall hear soon enough."

"I'll go to Germany," Craven said. "I can surely discover what happened—" he broke off for Elizabeth was shaking her head.

"It's too dangerous," she said. "If it were known that you were asking questions that information alone would make the spies of the Emperor suspicious. We leave matters as they are."

Craven opened his mouth to argue; closed it again. It was her choice. Elizabeth was the one after all who had to live with the images of her husband's corpse tossed aside by bandits eager for money and scornful of the respect due to the dead. She was the one whom, every day, would see the nightmare pictures in her mind's eye of the wolves feasting on his bones. She would always wonder and never know what had become of him.

"I am only grateful," Elizabeth said, "that you retrieved the treasures of the Rosy Cross before this happened." Her hand strayed to the huge drop pearl in the centre of her necklace. "Indeed, with the mirror destroyed I was disappointed such ill fortune could happen at all. The protection of the Sistrin has failed me."

With the mirror destroyed…

The sky beyond the windows had turned grey and the warmth had suddenly gone from the day. A wicked little wind was licking its way into the room, ruffling the drapes, causing the spaniel to raise his head and sniff the air.

"You know my opinion of such superstitions." Guilt caused Craven to speak more sharply than he had intended. "Cold steel, not spells and sorcery would have kept His Majesty safe."

Elizabeth did not contradict him but nor did she agree. She was still holding the pearl and there was an opaque look in her eyes that matched its mysterious iridescence. Craven had the sudden disconcerting feeling that she was using it to see the truth, to strip away his bluster and prevarication and see that he had failed her, betrayed her, and left the diamond mirror free to wreak its havoc in the world. Elizabeth, after all, was a member of the Order of the Rosy Cross too. She possessed the gift of prophecy if she chose to use it.

The instinct that she was reading his mind was so strong that he felt terrified, repelled, and had to repress a shudder. God help him, the thought of sorcery was turning him mad too.

He realised with a flash of despair that he would probably never know where the mirror had gone or what mischief it was perpetrating, until it was too late. His failure, his disloyalty, cut him like a sharpened sword. He had prized his reputation for unwavering fidelity as much as he valued his gift for decisive action and now he had destroyed one of the principles by which he lived his life. Worse, he had betrayed the love he had for Elizabeth by letting weakness rule him.

"There is something we must discuss," Elizabeth said. "A visit to my brother in England." Her tone had changed. It was business-like, regal, indicating that the previous subject was closed. Craven knew she would expect him to keep silent on the matter of the loss of the King's body as he kept silent on so many things. His discretion she took for granted. She had taken his loyalty for granted too and that had been a mistake.

"I am sending both Charles Louis and Rupert to my brother's court," Elizabeth said. "I have high hopes for them."

"I am sure that His Majesty will be impressed by both Princes," Craven said. Charles Louis, at eighteen, was already an adept politician with a clever, wary mind. Rupert was very different, energetic, impatient, quick to flare to anger but possessing dazzling charm for one so young.

"You will accompany the boys on their travels," Elizabeth said. She gave him an old-fashioned look. "I trust you to keep them out of trouble, Craven. You understand me? No complications, no distractions. Is that clear?"

"As crystal, madam," Craven said.

The visit to King Charles had a darker purpose too. Once more they would be begging for funds to furnish an army, trying to persuade both King and parliament to support Charles Louis' cause now he was of an age to fight for his German lands.

"I shall endeavour to keep them away from the ladies of your brother's court," he said.

Elizabeth's lashes flickered down, hiding her expression. Was she remembering the time when she had asked him to be her lover? Did she regret his rejection? He was startled to feel a sharp pang of lust. He thought he had mastered that particular weakness. Perhaps he needed to find a new mistress.

"If you are able to stop them bedding women then you are a miracle worker rather than a soldier," Elizabeth said dryly. "As long as it does not interfere with the purpose of the visit,

I will ask no questions. They admire you, William." She smiled. "I trust your influence on them."

"Madam." Craven bowed. So now he was to nursemaid Elizabeth's sons away from the brothels and bedchambers of London. God help him.

"You seem preoccupied today, William." Elizabeth had dropped the formality now. Her voice was soft. She had come up to him and placed a hand gently on his sleeve, her blue gaze searching his face. "Does something trouble you?"

"No, Majesty." With an effort Craven put thoughts of the crystal mirror from his mind. It was not so great a matter. Very likely Margaret had sold it or broken it or destroyed it for the jewels in the frame. And even if she had not, necromancy was for fools. He did not believe it; did not believe that it would continue to work its black magic to the detriment of Elizabeth and her family. Or so he told himself even as the shadows fluttered at the corner of his mind.

"You would not tell me even if you were troubled, I think." Elizabeth had moved a little away from him. She gave him a half-smile, quick and almost shy. "It is a great pity. I rely on your judgement and support so much, William, yet you take nothing from me in return."

If only she knew.

"It is not my place to burden you with my concerns, madam."

She ignored that. "Is it Mistress Carpenter?" She asked. "I heard she had left the court. You must feel…" she paused delicately.

"Absolutely nothing, I assure you," Craven lied, feeling the bitterness eat a little deeper as he thought of his child. He wondered how long it would be before gossip about Margaret's pregnancy reached the court in The Hague. He wondered if Elizabeth would work it out, count it up on her fingers, or ask him...

He doubted it. It seemed that if he was going to refuse to confide in her she was not going to be interested in his concerns. Her expression had hardened and she was reading a letter with rather determined concentration, excluding him from her notice.

"If that was all, Your Majesty," he said.

"It was. Go and prepare." She barely looked up from the letter. Sometimes she had all the stubbornness and petulance of her father.

So. He would go to England with Elizabeth's sons and try to make amends for his failure. He would raise men and money. He would fight for the Palatine cause again and he would defend Elizabeth's boys to the death. And perhaps death would be the best thing that could happen for in life he could never have her and she was all he wanted.

29

Holly and Mark walked back to the mill together through the wood. Bonnie galloped through the leaves and between the trees, circling them, racing away and then coming back, waving her feathery tail, full of bounce and happiness. Holly thought how easy and uncomplicated it was to be a dog.

"Do you have to get back to work?" she asked Mark when they reached the gate. "I mean, I wondered—" she hesitated, "if you would like to see my studio. If you're interested."

Mark looked surprised then so pleased that her heart missed a beat. "I'd like that very much," he said, and followed her in, stooping low beneath the old oaken lintel.

"I've got a bit of work to finish off, if that's OK," Holly said, "but please take as much time as you like."

She went back to her desk and picked up the piece she had been working on earlier that day. Mark walked over to the exhibition shelves and studied the fairy tale panels that were displayed there. When Holly had engraved a whole series of them for the children's section of the library she had done copies of a few for herself. There was Little Red Riding Hood with the wolf peeking at her from behind a tree, Cinderella running away from the ball and Snow White reaching out to take a succulent apple.

Holly watched Mark out of the corner of her eye; watched the fall of dark hair across his forehead and the hard, shadowed line of his cheek in the glare of sunlight, and something strange happened to her insides.

"These are really good." Mark's voice was quiet.

Holly dropped her drill and bent down to retrieve it. "Thank you." Her voice was muffled.

Mark traced the curve of the engraving with one finger. Holly repressed a shiver and bent back over her work. She had never experienced such a strong physical reaction to anybody and it totally threw her. She felt edgy and disturbed. Mark looked up. "How long did it take you to engrave all of these?"

"About two months," Holly said.

"And what's the going rate for a piece of engraving?"

Holly paused. "That depends on the commission. Those cost about a hundred pounds per panel."

Mark looked at her. He was shaking his head. "That seems absurdly cheap."

"Market forces," Holly said quickly, unable to keep a shade of defensiveness from her voice. "Places like museums and libraries can't afford to pay thousands for a piece of engraving, but they give me some small commissions and free advertising. So do individuals who want just one paperweight or vase. The larger pieces for companies and big organisations are more lucrative."

"Some of your images are so powerful it's disturbing," Mark said. "Very dark."

Holly thought of how she had planned to engrave an image of the Winter Queen fleeing from Prague with the snow falling around her and the life she had known tumbling away with it.

"There's a nice flower paperweight over there that's very pretty and not remotely dark, if that's what you prefer," she said.

"I don't," Mark said. "But I'm interested in what draws you to the dark side."

Holly shrugged. "It's more inspiring somehow," she said. "Poignancy and loss and danger interest me, at least in terms of my work."

Mark was looking at her. "You lost someone important to you," he said quietly. "I'm sorry."

"Ben and I lost our parents before we were in our teens," Holly said. "It was..." She hesitated to find the right word. "Terrifying."

Mark nodded. "And now with Ben gone..." He let the sentence hang.

Holly nodded. There was a lump in her throat. For a second her vision swam with tears. She still did not want to talk about it but she could feel those barriers weakening. Mark had asked. He had cared. She wasn't sure if that made her glad or nervous.

Mark had obviously seen her reaction and wasn't going to push her. He turned and picked up a paperweight. It was engraved with the image of a running hare.

"This is beautiful, Holly." There was something close to awe in Mark's voice that made Holly feel a prickle of pleasure. "I love the clean lines of it."

"Thank you," Holly said. "One benefit of living in the country—I've ample time to study the wildlife. I've done foxes and those beautiful birds of prey you see over the Downs."

"Red kites," Mark said. "Yes, they are stunning."

Holly switched the drill back on and picked up the glass she was working on. Steady hand, she told herself. Mark was walking slowly about the workshop. Despite the fact that her back was turned to him, his presence still disturbed her, breaking her concentration, distracting her.

"Damn!"

The glass fractured all the way around the top and broke off cleanly in a band half an inch wide.

"Neat," Mark said, picking up the glass bracelet, "but probably not what you intended to do."

"No." Holly gritted her teeth. The drill had hit a weak point in the glass on the annealing line, where the top edge had been sealed. It was entirely her fault that she had lost a piece of stock she could not afford to waste, because her hand had not been steady enough and her concentration had been flawed.

"Sorry," Mark said. "I guess I made you nervous."

"I'm not nervous," Holly said.

Mark's gaze collided with hers and suddenly it was difficult to breathe. Holly stood up, pushing her goggles onto the top of her head. She couldn't work like this.

"Fetching," Mark said, eyeing the goggles with amusement. "It reminds me of *Flashdance*. Are you going to get a blowtorch out next?"

"You're showing your age now," Holly said. "The paperweight is thirty-five quid, as it's you. Would you like to take it away now or shall I put it on one side for you?"

"I'll take it," Mark said, reaching for his wallet. "Thanks."

Holly opened a drawer and took out some deep blue tissue paper, expertly wrapping the glass and sticking it down with tape.

"I'm going to finish now," she said. "Would you like a drink? Tea, I mean, or a cold drink."

Mark smiled. "Sure. Thank you."

He waited while she locked the studio then followed her down the path to the mill door where Bonnie gave them a rapturous welcome as though it had been years since she had last seen them.

"Sometimes she comes into the studio with me," Holly said, "mostly when I'm doing hand etching. She doesn't like the noise of the drill much."

"I'm not surprised," Mark said. "If dogs can hear a sound several miles away, a drill at close quarters would probably drive them insane."

He stroked Bonnie's golden head and she tilted up her chin, closing her eyes in the most flirtatious gesture Holly had ever seen. Judging by Mark's grin he thought so too.

"What a hussy." He stroked Bonnie under the chin.

"She'll be rolling over for you soon," Holly said acidly. "You're irresistible."

Mark looked at her, raising his brows. She blushed. "Is cafetière coffee OK?" She was stammering now. "Or tea?"

"Actually, I'll have a cold drink if you have one, thanks." Mark had straightened and was looking around the room with professional approval. "It looks good in here. What have you done to it?"

"Cleaned it," Holly said. "I made some new curtains too. And waxed the table. That's about all."

"It looks a lot better than when Ben was here," Mark said. "It had a sort of unlived-in feel to it then. Sorry—" he added, catching her expression. "I seem to be channelling Fran's tactlessness."

Holly was surprised to find herself repressing a giggle. "That's OK. And I love Fran."

"I know," Mark said. "You don't have any trouble loving your friends and family, do you?" He looked at her.

"It's too late to help that," Holly said honestly.

"So it's just in romantic relationships that you want to keep aloof?"

The silence buzzed. Holly turned away and opened the fridge door. "Is lemonade OK for you? Home-made, though not by me."

Mark grinned. "Your grandmother?"

"She's famous for it," Holly said, handing him a glass. Their fingers touched. She tried not to jump.

"There's an evening reception at the new development in a week or two," Mark said. "It's mostly for the marketing guys, VIP stuff to gain publicity, and I wondered if you'd like to contribute a few pieces to dress the new cottages? A couple of vases, a paperweight or two, whatever you think would look good. It might get you some commissions and your work would look stunning in that setting."

He sounded nervous. He sounded as though he thought she might refuse. Holly's heart flipped. "I'd love to," she said. "Thank you."

"You'll have to come in early on the day to set up." Mark ran a hand through his hair. "We're running very tight on schedule and after the reception the houses will be up for sale—in fact most are already sold so I hope to hell we get it all done on time." He caught himself. "You're invited to the reception as well, of course."

"Gosh," Holly said. "Wow. Yes, that would be great."

"I'll introduce you to a few people." Mark smiled. "It would be lovely to show you the buildings anyway." His shoulders relaxed. "I thought you might like them—from a historical perspective, I mean."

"And to take a look at your work," Holly said. "Fran says your barn conversion is fabulous so I'm expecting something sensational."

Mark almost looked as though he was going to blush. "You'll see the house properly if you can drop in to the bar-becue at the weekend." He shifted. "I'd invite you back anyway, anytime, but I sense you're running scared." He tilted the glass of lemonade to his lips. Holly watched the muscles in his throat move as he swallowed. It felt very hot in the kitchen.

She realised she was staring and spoke hastily. "Won't you be too busy schmoozing all the VIPs at the reception to keep an eye on me?"

"I'd rather show you round," Mark said. He grimaced. "I don't much enjoy the schmoozing. I've done enough of that to last a lifetime. It's a necessary evil."

"And you do it so well," Holly said.

Mark grinned. "Don't believe everything you read in the papers."

"All right," Holly said. "I won't." She flipped open the cover of her phone. "What's the date of the party?"

"Two weeks' time," Mark said. "The 28th. Sorry it's such short notice. I'll drop off a formal invitation for you." He nodded to a big black and white photograph of a ruined ivy-clad tower that dominated the wall opposite the window.

"I've been meaning to ask. Did you take that?"

"I did," Holly said.

Mark stood considering it, cradling his glass in both hands. "It's great, very moody and atmospheric." He put his empty glass down on the worktop, still looking at the photograph. "Where is that taken? It looks familiar."

"It's the tower up on the Downs beyond Weathercock Hill," Holly said. "I took it a few years ago. It's almost entirely covered in ivy now. I'm not sure if people even know it's there."

"I know where you mean," Mark said. "It's on the OS maps. Did you know it's called Verity's Folly? I never thought of it before but I guess it was named for Robert Verity." He shifted. "Perhaps we should look at it. Any time you fancy a walk…"

Bonnie's ear pricked up at the word and she looked very hopeful.

"Now look what you've done," Holly said. "Sorry, Bon Bon. You've been out already today. A walk would be nice though," she added. "One evening, maybe, since it still stays light so late. I rather like that the folly is named for him," she added. "At least some trace of Robert Verity remains in the landscape even if he did disappear."

"I'm working on that," Mark said. "I've got a genealogist friend who might be able to help."

"I did find out a bit more about him," Holly said. "He was descended from the First Earl of Craven, down the wrong side of the blanket, allegedly. One of his ancestors had an affair with the Earl when they were in The Hague."

Her phone rang. She fumbled for it, feeling the familiar sense of hope and apprehension. She saw the caller ID was the bank and let it go to voicemail.

"Were you hoping for it to be Ben?" Mark's voice was soft.

"Always," Holly said, with a sigh. "I guess I should have got past that by now but…" She shrugged. "It's the not knowing that's particularly hard. The police keep Tasha informed as next of kin, but there's no news anyway."

She felt a huge rush of grief and misery, so sudden and shocking that it made her shake. She braced both hands on the worktop, breathing deeply to try to get it to pass.

"Sorry," she said, with difficulty.

"Don't," Mark said. His tone was fierce. "Don't apologise." He put his arms around her. For a moment Holly resisted the comfort, trying to draw away, but she was too tired and it was too tempting. She leaned into him and breathed in the scent of his skin and the smell of fresh air and sun, and felt the layers of protection she had wrapped herself in long ago unfurl a little more.

Mark smoothed the hair away from her cheeks and cupped her face. It was only then that Holly realised she had been crying.

"I did warn you," she said, trying to smile. It came out a bit wobbly. "I'm an emotional mess. I thought you would have walked away by now."

"I guess I have reserves of fortitude I didn't realise," Mark said.

"I wanted you to walk," Holly said.

"I know." Mark gave her a brief, hard kiss then tilted her chin up to look at her. "Are you all right?"

Holly nodded. "Yeah. Thank you."

"I'll call you later," Mark said. He paused in the doorway. "Just in case you were wondering," he said, his tone a little ragged, "I'd like nothing more than to go straight upstairs and make love to you but I'm determined to wait this time around."

He gave her another kiss and went out.

Holly felt as though her knees might just give way. She grabbed the edge of the worktop to steady herself and took a gulp of lemonade. The bubbles threatened to choke her. Putting the glass down she took a deep breath instead and waited for her heartbeat to slow down.

Breathe.

Whatever was between her and Mark was intense but that physical attraction was starting to run much deeper. She'd never felt like this before, never risked getting even close to it. Her instinct had always been to escape. Now she did not know what she wanted.

She went back into her studio, taking the rest of her lemonade with her. The air was still and warm. She knew she wouldn't be able to work to save her life. She couldn't concentrate. Instead she drew one of her sketch pads towards her and flipped it open, drawing in a few swift strokes the outline of a ruined tower bound with ivy, secret and shuttered.

She remembered the day she had taken the photograph. It

had been years ago and she and Ben had driven out to White Horse Hill and taken the path over the Downs and stumbled across the tower quite by accident. Ben had clambered in through the broken-down doorway to see what was inside whilst she had taken some photographs and then turned to view the whole broad sweep of the Downs, the sheltering copses clinging to the hillsides, the long view south and west to the distant hills, and the golden dome of Ashdown House glinting in the sun amidst its thicket of woodland.

Except that there had been no house and no golden dome, and she must have been imagining things then, just as she had years later when she had driven up the road and thought she had seen the house through the trees.

She dropped her pencil and pushed the drawing pad away. Memories. Imagination. She was starting to become confused as to which was which, what was real and what was not.

She thought of Ben again and the climb up to Verity's Folly and suddenly it was as though she was looking at that day in black and white, down the wrong end of a telescope, and that the picture was fading before her eyes. She could not remember what they had talked about, or where they went afterwards, or what she had worn that day or any of the brightly coloured details that she wanted to keep a hold of in order to capture Ben and hold him for ever. Like water, he was slipping through her fingers.

She thought of Lavinia's memoir then, and the postcard of Kitty. They were the only two slender threads that linked her to Ben's research. If she wanted to hold on to him she had to continue on that path. It was time to find out what had happened to Lavinia. It was time to read to the end of the memoir.

30

Ashdown Park, 3rd March 1801

*T*he most terrible thing has happened. Evershot knows. He confronted us this morning in the drawing room. At first he was calm as you please and I thought that all might be well, but soon his temper broke through and it was terrifying. I am almost certain Clara betrayed me, untrustworthy jade that she is. I expect he paid her well for the information and she, seeing an opportunity for gain, was not averse to taking it. Whatever the truth, Evershot dismissed Robert from his post, throwing his possessions out onto the gravel of the carriage sweep where they were soaked in the thawing snow. Robert was particularly distressed that many of his measuring instruments were smashed and broken. It was wilful cruelty on Evershot's part knowing how expensive such devices are and how little Robert can afford to replace them. All was lost but for the ugly mirror that belonged to Robert's ancestors. I saved it by hiding it in my skirts. Just in case the diamonds were real.

Anyway, the destruction wrought upon Robert's possessions was *as nothing to the violence with which he treated my poor beloved. Evershot's steward appeared with a horsewhip and threatened to drive Robert from the premises if he did not leave at once. Robert most bravely declared that he would not depart without me, whereupon the man set about him with the whip and then two others came and pushed Robert out of the door, locking it behind him.*

You may imagine the severity with which Evershot then turned on me, and the cruelty of his treatment of me. He dragged me up the stairs; the entire servants' hall had been roused by the altercation and stood watching and no one lifted a finger to help me. Of course they did not. They were all as terrified of him as I was. Or perhaps they felt that I deserved punishment for my deceit, if loving another man is dishonesty.

Once in my chamber Evershot tied me to the bedposts, stripped my clothing from me and whipped me soundly across my back and my buttocks, as he had done before. Even though I knew what to expect and tried to block out the pain it was excruciatingly dreadful. Anger gave his arm even greater force and he took such pleasure in hurting me. I did not cry out, for my anger matched his and I would not beg, but my strength deserted me and I think for a little while I fainted.

When I came to consciousness, sagging between my bonds, the most extraordinary thing happened. The door opened and my maid Clara appeared. She cast me a look of sullen triumph mixed with shame as she sidled into the room with a tray on which appeared to be some long plants with pointed furry leaves.

"You have found some," my lord said with evident satisfaction. "Well done. I was not sure they would be growing so early in the year."

He did not wait for the door to close behind her before he took the stems in a gloved hand and, coming over to where I hung in my bonds, started to brush them across my stomach and breasts.

At first I felt nothing. Then the sensation began, a stinging, burning, maddening itch that made my skin rise and turn a hot raw red. I could scarce bear it. I thought I would lose my mind at the vicious burn of pain. My back was throbbing from the whip and my breasts from the application of whatever this vile plant had been. It was torture.

Evershot cut my bonds and pressed me face down on the bed. What followed was as unpleasant as one might imagine, especially since my poor bruised and beaten body was pressed roughly against the covers with each thrust of his body into mine. He growled in my ear that I was a faithless jade and that I was his whore, no one else's, and that I was well paid to satisfy his lusts, not to service anyone else. Which was true, but still I do not think I warranted such treatment. He was unrelenting until at last he was spent and rolled off me with a groan leaving me lying there.

Holly put the book aside and put her face in her hands. She felt sick and distressed and blinded by fury, a fury all the more intense because it could have no target. Evershot was long dead and death was far, far too good for him.

Her hand was shaking as she took a glass from the cupboard and slopped some water into it. Was this why she had not wanted to finish the book? Had she known, in her heart, in her bones, that something so terrible was going to befall Lavinia? Had she been afraid to experience all of Lavinia's pain and grief because she knew it would be like feeling it herself, the echo of that violence and terror down the centuries?

She glanced back at the book, lying open on the table by the sofa. Lavinia had played with fire and had paid an appalling price for it. Yet surely this could not be the end. Lavinia deserved more, better than this ignominious dismissal. There was still Robert; he would not desert her. Holly was certain of it.

She picked up the book with her fingertips and a sense of revulsion.

Evershot sent for food and drink to fortify himself for further assault. Fortunately for me, he drank so copiously that he passed out, which gave me at last a chance to escape him. I knew that Robert would not desert me and that he would seek refuge at the mill and wait there for me. And so I made a plan. I would tie Evershot up and make my escape. I would rob him of anything I could take with me. Think what you will of me—it is the least Evershot owed me.

Although I was sick and bruised and heartsore, a tiny spark of excitement lived on in me. I have made my choice and I choose Robert. Perhaps it is folly to allow my heart to rule my head when all my short life I have been so careful to put material considerations before all else. Yet I feel this is no mistake. Robert is my soul's star. There. I admit it. I who once believed I had not a sentimental bone in my body! And oh, it feels so very splendid to love and be loved! It gives me the strength to endure almost any trial, for I know that at the end of it we two will be together and nothing will come between us again. Soon, very soon, we will be fled away together...

Impatiently Holly turned the page. There was only one more line.

Robert did not come.

The rest of the page was blank. For a moment, Holly stared at it, uncomprehending; then she quickly flicked through the remaining sheets of the memoir. They stuck together a little beneath her hasty fingers. They had the smooth pristine whiteness of the untouched. Lavinia had written nothing else at all.

Holly felt odd and disoriented. It was not merely that she felt a horrible, personal sense of betrayal that Lavinia had been abused twice over, beaten by Evershot and then abandoned by the man who had professed to love her. It was not simply that she wanted—needed—to know what had happened, to Lavinia, to Robert, to the child she would go on to have. She was also shocked at the speed at which Lavinia's life had unravelled. But then Lavinia had never had much security. One false step and she had lost everything: protector, lover, the roof over her head and the future of her unborn child.

With shaking fingers she turned to her laptop and brought up the published version of Lavinia's diary. Once she had realised that it bore little resemblance to Lavinia's original memoir, except at the beginning, she had not bothered to do more than flick through the pages. Now she searched them feverishly, looking for any reference to Ashdown Park or Lord Evershot or Robert Verity. Evershot certainly got a mention as one of Lavinia's cavalcade of lovers, and there was even a footnote to the effect that he had died soon after their liaison, but other than that there was nothing. There was no record of Lavinia's stay at Ashdown other than as a brief period of boredom in the country after which she separated from Lord Evershot and allegedly went back to London:

I bought my passage back to London in the only currency I had— my body, dear reader, should you be in any doubt—which involved a lusty encounter with a carter and two of his fellows in a barn near Reading. What energetic lovers they were!

There followed a lurid account of how, fortunately for Lavinia, a new brothel had opened and she took pride of place in it. She grew rich on the proceeds of sin and decided with a coy wink to the reader to turn respectable and retire.

If Holly could have thrown the book at the wall she would have done. She knew the account was scurrilous nonsense. She *knew* it. Someone—the perfidious jade Clara Rogers, no doubt—had taken the idea of Lavinia's diary and turned it into a fictitious memoir in the interests of making money. She had taken Lavinia's name and her identity and had got rich on it.

But what had happened to Lavinia herself?

Holly shut the laptop with a snap and wandered over to the door and looked out on the mill garden. It looked serene in the golden sunshine, yet she had never felt less peaceful. She felt sick and chilled to the soul. All along she had been fearful of an unhappy ending. From the first she had not only liked Lavinia for her self-interest and survival instinct, but had felt so close to her. Now it seemed that her worst fears had been realised. Lavinia's lover had deserted her. He had run off, according to the information Mark had found, disappeared from the army record, perhaps started a new life elsewhere leaving Lavinia abandoned to sink into the poverty from which she had come.

Holly let herself out into the garden. She felt sick and disillusioned and yet even as she cursed Robert Verity, it felt wrong. Instinct, stubborn and deep-seated told her that Robert would never willingly forsake Lavinia. She was not sure how she knew when she only had Lavinia's word on their entire relationship, and yet she was certain. She was sure they had loved one another with a deep, true love. Perhaps something had happened to Robert, preventing him from waiting for Lavinia at the mill. Perhaps it was fate's cruelty, not man's, that had separated them. If only there was a way to find out...

Amidst the tangle of misery she felt a spark of faith. Quickly she walked back to the memoir and flicked back to the beginning of the entry, checking the date. Then she opened her tablet... After Mark had told her about the fire she had read some old newspaper reports about it and made a few notes... Now she saw that the date of the fire was the same as the entry in the diary; 3rd March 1801.

Lavinia had planned to run away from Ashdown Park the night the fire had burned the house to the ground. Robert Verity had abandoned her that same day.

Holly needed to clear her head, to think. She took Bonnie's lead from the drawer. The dog bounded to her feet, eager, excited, following Holly out of the mill and into the wood. Chequered patches of light and dark lay across the path. It felt cooler than recently, a scent of sadness hanging in the air. Holly walked aimlessly for a while, her head a jumble of thoughts and emotions. It was only when she realised how dark the day had become that she finally looked up and realised that she was lost.

They were in an ancient bit of the wood she did not recognise. Stands of tall oak towered on each side of her. The ground beneath her feet was dry brown earth and leaves long dead that crackled as she walked. There was no other sound. The air was very still, heavy and dark.

Unusually, Bonnie seemed on edge and unhappy. They had barely reached the end of the stand of oaks when her head went up and she sniffed the air sharply, scenting something. She froze. Then she turned and ran, her shadow wavering between the trees until it was swallowed up deep into the wood. The rustle of bracken and bramble died swiftly. The dog was gone.

"Bonnie!" Holly was as much shocked as she was afraid. It was completely out of character for Bonnie to behave in such a way. She waited, listened. There was no sound. She spun around. Shadows were gathering now, the air thick with them.

"Bonnie!" She shouted Bonnie's name until she was hoarse but there was no sign.

Panic gripped her. She knew that when a dog was lost the best thing to do was to stay in the same place and wait for it to find its way back to you. Even so, she toyed with the idea of going home in case Bonnie had run back to the mill, but then she worried that Bonnie would come back here instead and not be able to find her. She thought about walking through the wood, calling Bonnie's name, in the hope that Bonnie would hear. And all the time it felt as though the darkness was deepening and the shadows were pressing closer and Holly could feel the fear tightening her chest and stealing her breath. In an odd way it felt as though time it-self was running out.

She decided to go back to the mill and wait there, but as she turned to retrace her steps along the path it felt as though the darkness was spinning dizzily around her, the shadows shifting and reforming, and for a terrifying moment she had no idea where she was. Then the world steadied and she saw again the tunnel of trees meeting overhead and started to fol-low it, still calling Bonnie's name, tripping over tree roots in her haste to get back.

Suddenly, she felt cold. Looking up she saw that the trees were bare and the sky above them was a darker black against their dark boughs. A crescent moon lay on its side, tangled in a web of branches. Beneath her feet there was snow, crisp and pale in the torchlight and she could hear water running. It was the sound of the stream that used to flow past the mill but had been silenced in the drought.

The path ended abruptly, the oaks falling back like senti-nels. She was on the plateau she had visited with Mark, only now there was no scented garden. Now a house rose, gleam-ing tall and white in the darkness, a house she had glimpsed several times before. She had to crane her neck to see the top, with its wooden balustrade, its decorative little cupola and the two soaring chimneys that stood out against the sky.

Ashdown Park, the little chalk mansion, as solid and real as she was.

Wild panic gripped Holly's throat. She put out a hand to steady herself and felt the roughness of the bark against her fingers. The cold was biting into her now. She had come out with only a light jacket on and it was not proof against the chill of late winter, nor the brisk wind that was blowing down from the hills.

Holly started to walk across the smooth expanse of snow

that separated her from the house. No footprints marred the pristine whiteness. She felt light-headed now, bemused, part of her mind taking in the sensory experience of the snow crunching beneath her shoes whilst at the same time wondering if she been right all along, it *had* all been a delusion, the result of grief and stress. She had been so deeply engrossed in the memoir before she had come out. It was entirely possible that she had fallen asleep and was dreaming, having walked into her own fantasy.

The house loomed over her now and she reached out and touched the smooth stone of the wall. It was cold against her fingertips and the chalk was slightly rough where age and wear had washed the stone away. It felt very real.

A light shone from behind a window on the ground floor. The doors at the back of the house were flung wide despite the cold, the drapes blowing outward in the wind. Holly felt the bite of snowflakes against her cheek. The moon had gone, lost behind a bank of cloud.

She could hear voices from inside the house; a man's tones; cold, and hard, and another; lower, indistinguishable. She was gripped by fear now, deep in her gut, a rising tide that threatened to obliterate everything. She crept closer, straining to hear the words, crossing the pool of lamplight falling from the window above.

"I found her at the mill, my lord."

"Waiting for her lover."

Evershot.

Holly did not know how she knew it was him, but her skin crawled with revulsion.

"Well," she heard Evershot say, and there was vicious amusement in his voice that made her feel sick, "she can go to join him soon, can't she, down in the pit? Just as soon as I've done with her."

Holly ran up the wide stone steps, through the open door-way and paused on the edge of the room. It was exquisite, a library with bookshelves the whole height of the wall and a plaster ceiling above, decorated with crowns and cupids and laurel leaves around the border. She saw the initials WC and ES entwined in the corners, picked out in gold leaf.

Evershot was standing by a grand marble fireplace, one arm resting casually along the mantel, a man who would have looked cool and handsome in normal circumstances but whose face was livid with fury, so much so that he vibrated with it, the air alive with violence.

Facing him were two people; a man Holly assumed must be the land agent, Gross, mentioned in Lavinia's diary. Standing quite still and quiescent in his grip was Lavinia Flyte. Lavinia neither moved nor spoke, but she was all ice and fire, her hazel eyes blazing in a face the colour of snow and her red hair falling in a vivid cascade about her shoulders.

Lavinia.

Holly could feel the pounding of her blood, feel Lavinia's grief and fury and frustration as her own, blinding, all-consuming, the loss of love and hope.

Robert Verity was dead. Lavinia had lost everything she cared for. She burned with the emotion of it.

"You killed Robert for the crystal mirror," Lavinia said. She stood a little straighter in the agent's grip, speaking directly to Evershot, as though they were alone. Her voice rang out clear and true.

"I did," Evershot said. He sounded bored. "For that and for having the temerity to bed my whore."

Lavinia did not even flinch but Holly did. She flattened herself against the doorjamb and watched, her heart thudding.

Evershot's face was illuminated by the fire, a lurid orange glow, half light, half shade.

"*I* have the mirror," Lavinia said. She raised her chin defiantly. "It will never be yours. Neither will the pearl. The Winter Queen's treasure is not for you. You have no claim to it."

Evershot made a lunge for her, but Lavinia was too quick for him. The crystal mirror was in her hand now. Holly saw it; saw the reflection of flames in its surface, like a vision of hell.

"Take it, you fool!" Evershot shouted as the land agent stood still, gaping, his grip on Lavinia loose with shock. "Don't let her—"

But it was too late. There was a roaring sound as though the wind had plucked off the roof of the house and was rampaging through. Fire flared outward from the face of the mirror in a curtain of orange and gold, the flames so fierce and sudden, scorching and scouring that Holly leapt back in terror. The room had gone in an instant, obliterated in a blaze so fierce she raised her arm to shield her face from the heat. She heard the land agent shout; heard the house crack and groan like a foundering ship.

Holly stumbled down the steps and out onto the parterre. Snow was falling harder now mingling with the sparks flying from the windows. The fire already had the house well in its grip. She could see flames leaping through the roof. She could feel the sting of cold and heat against her cheek, the cold burn of cinders she remembered from before.

There was a rush of movement and Lavinia was there. The crystal mirror was still in her hand. For a moment they stared at one another and then Lavinia ran down the lime tree avenue and away into the darkness.

Holly stood still, stupefied, then she ran too, plunging into the wood. Behind her the house illuminated the sky like a beacon. The noise of the fire faded away until all she could hear was the thudding of her heart and all she could feel was her breath bursting from her lungs.

She had no idea where she was any more, which time, which place.

The house was burning. Robert Verity was dead. She had seen Lavinia.

The jumbled thoughts raced through her head as she ran. The trees slipped by, rank upon rank of them, thicker than she had ever seen before, a prison, a maze. Then, abruptly, they opened out and she recognised where she was. It was the clearing in the woods with the fountain. Catching her breath on half a gasp, half a sob, she dropped to her knees, a stitch in her side, unable to go any further.

She lay still, panting, whilst above her the stars shone diamond sharp in the blackness and the light of the moon cut through the trees to dapple the grass and the images continued to flicker through her head like pictures on a dark screen: the house, Evershot, Lavinia, the fire, the crystal mirror...

She shuddered, sitting up. It had been impossible and yet so real. Was she losing her sanity? She realised suddenly that the air felt warm and that a pattern of leaves danced across the grass and rustled as they moved in the trees overhead. There was no snow beneath her. Wherever it was that she had been, she was back now. She could go home. A path ran directly back to the mill from here, if only she could find the right one. Everything would be all right, and Bonnie would be there...

She took a deep breath and scrambled to her feet. The stars above the wood had almost vanished behind a thin curtain of cloud drifting in from the west. There was rain in the air. She hesitated for a moment then took the second path on the left. She was sure it was the way home.

She was still shaking fifteen minutes later when she saw

the moonlight falling on the whitewashed walls of the mill. Then there was a bark and Bonnie came flying out of the darkness towards her.

"Bonnie!" Holly's legs buckled as she grabbed the dog tightly to her, hugging her with all her strength. Bonnie tolerated this with stoicism for a few minutes before pulling away and sidling down the path, an indication that she wanted Holly to follow her. Turning the corner of the mill, Holly smelled smoke and then she heard the crackle of a radio, voices, the splash of water. She stopped dead.

There was a fire engine on the gravel sweep by the mill-pond and a whole group of people hanging around outside the picket fence. One of them was Fran, who saw her limping down the track, and with a glad cry ran towards her and drew her into a bear hug.

"Oh, thank God!" Fran was squeezing her so hard Holly thought she would snap. "Where have you been? We thought you were inside! We thought you'd disappeared like Ben—"

"Bonnie got lost in the woods," Holly said. "I was looking for her." She ran a dazed hand over her face. "What on earth is going on?"

"There was a fire," Fran said. "In the studio. Mark reported it. He found Bonnie down by the stable yard and brought her back and when he got here he saw the flames and called the fire brigade." She pulled Holly towards the mill door. "It's OK, we can go inside. The fire was very localised apparently. They think it was a lightning strike. It destroyed one of the cupboards in your workshop but that's all. Everything's doused in water but your stock should be OK. It's a miracle, isn't it? Anyway, we should get you a cup of tea…" She was chatting, but Holly could not hear the words. Instead of following Fran into the house she broke away and went along the path to the workshop. It was chaos here, with hoses lying across the grass and everything dripping with water. Mark was standing in the doorway talking to one of the firemen. He broke off when he saw her.

"Holly," he said, and she heard the tension and relief in his voice. "Where the hell have you been?"

"I got lost," Holly said briefly. She walked past him into the workshop, where one of the firefighters barred her way.

"Sorry, ma'am, it's still not safe. We'll let you know when you can come in and assess the damage."

Holly said nothing. Over his shoulder she could see the charred pile of ash and wood that had once been a storage cupboard. There was the smell of smoke and water in the air. It caught at her throat.

"I don't suppose there's anything left," she said, but then she saw it, the faintest sliver of a reflection in the pile of ashes that had burned hotter than a furnace.

It was the crystal mirror, whole, undamaged.

Turning, she found Mark at her shoulder. He looked at her searchingly. "You're not OK, are you?" he said.

"No," Holly said wearily. "I just want everyone to go away."

She didn't know how Mark did it but within ten minutes the fire brigade were packing up, having assured themselves and her that there was no chance of the fire flaring up again, and all the onlookers had been gently encouraged to return to their homes.

"I expect they are all disappointed that the fire wasn't as dramatic as the one two hundred years ago," Holly said, as she shut the mill door behind them all.

Bonnie curled up on the sofa and yawned widely.

"I feel like that too, Bon Bon," Holly said. Suddenly she felt totally exhausted. Now that she was home, in the light and the warmth, reaction started to hit her and she began to shiver violently.

"I can go as well," Mark said, "if you'd rather be alone."

"No," Holly said instinctively. Then she blushed. "I... It's just... There's something I need to tell you."

Mark took her trembling hands in his. "You're frozen," he said. "Go and get in the shower before you do anything else. I'll make you something to drink."

"Mark," Holly said, catching his sleeve. "I saw the house. Ashdown Park. It was on fire. And Lavinia..." Her teeth were chattering. "I saw her too." She started to shake. "It was all so real," she said.

"Holly. Go and have that shower." Mark's voice was very calm. "We'll talk afterwards." He rubbed his chin. He hadn't shaved and the dark stubble shadowed his jaw. He gave her a gentle push towards the stairs.

The shower was hot. Holly welcomed the way it beat down on her head and her shoulders and yet she still felt cold inside. Evershot had killed Robert Verity and Lavinia had taken her revenge, burning the house to the ground with Evershot still in it. She wondered if the crystal mirror responded to negative emotion; whether it drew on hatred or jealousy and transformed them into energy.

Or perhaps she was just losing her mind, because while she had been watching the mirror destroy Ashdown Park it had been here at the mill, surviving another fire, magically untouched...

Holly turned off the shower and reached for a towel, wrapping it about her head and another around her body. Downstairs in the kitchen she could hear the clink of crockery and the sound of Mark talking quietly to Bonnie. It sounded reassuringly domestic and yet the darkness still lingered, crowding her mind. She knew what she had seen and it seemed madness but she knew it was not.

Shivering, she went into the bedroom, dropping the towel

and reaching for the robe that hung on the peg behind the door. She wrapped it about her, tying the belt, her hands moving automatically.

There was a tap at the bedroom door.

"I've brought hot chocolate," Mark said. He put the mug into her hands, wrapping her fingers about it. "You're still freezing!" He looked at her more closely. "You're also as white as a sheet. Did you hurt yourself?"

"No," Holly said. "It's not that." She sat down abruptly on the side of the bed. "I'm not mad, you know," she said, almost defiantly. "I know what I saw."

Some liquid splashed from the mug as she shivered. Mark took it from her and placed it carefully on the bedside table then took her hands in his again. The mattress gave slightly as he sat down beside her. "I don't think you're mad," he said.

Holly looked up and met his eyes. "But it is some sort of delusion, isn't it? People don't travel through time; they don't see visions!" Her voice was rising. "Not unless there's something wrong with them."

"Your coat was covered in ash and chalk dust," Mark said. "It was no delusion."

It took Holly a moment to understand and then the relief swamped her. "Oh, thank God," she said. For some reason she was trembling all the more now. "I didn't imagine it."

Mark put his arms about her and pulled her close to him. With her head against his chest she could feel the steady beat of his heart and felt warmth and strength flowing back into her.

"There's more I need to tell you," she said. "About the mirror and the pearl…"

"Later," Mark said. He tilted up her chin and kissed her. "Just now I think you need warming up." She felt him smile against her lips. "I hope you didn't like that coat too much," he added. "It's ruined." And he kissed her again.

Holly's stomach dropped crazily. She pulled up his T-shirt, running her hands over his skin, feeling the beat of his heart. He kissed her more fiercely, with heat and desire. It was so unlike the cool detachment that normally characterised him that it made her feel drunk. Her body ached for him. She dragged off her robe with hands that shook, pulling him down onto the bed with her, hearing his gasp as she fumbled with his flies and pulled open his jeans. His mouth was on her breast now; she could feel his stubble against her skin. It was all heat and blinding light and driving need, like it had been before but different too, tender, more real because with each touch she knew this was Mark she was with and it was him she wanted.

When he moved inside of her he had his fingers laced with hers and they kept their eyes open so that the connection was even more real and intense. Holly lost herself in sensation, felt the climax build and let it take them together. She felt the press of Mark's lips against the damp skin of her neck and when he pulled her into the curve of his arm she resisted the instinctive urge to pull away and let herself stay there, trying out the new feeling of intimacy. It was unfamiliar and yet it felt as though she had known this before, held him, loved him. The sense of recognition merged with her dreams until the terrible sense of loss she had experienced through Lavinia started to heal and she slept peacefully at last.

31

The Palace of Rhenen, Netherlands, October 1639

William Craven had done his best to get himself killed at the Battle of Vlotho. Elizabeth knew it instinctively but she did not understand why. She only knew that the thought that she might have lost him forever gave her such pain she could not bear it. He was as essential to her as breathing. She could not risk losing him again.

She watched him walk across the cloister gardens towards her. The day was mild and the sun warm. He looked so much older that she felt her heart stumble to see him. There was a grey pallor to his face, and deep lines were etched around his mouth and his eyes. She wanted to run towards him and throw herself into his arms. She had missed him so much.

"Majesty." Craven bowed, very formally and stood waiting for her to speak. She swallowed hard. There were tears in her throat, a weakness she seemed unable to control. Craven had been gone almost three years and she had thought of him every day. It had felt as though a piece of her was missing.

First he had gone with her sons on the visit to their uncle the King of England, to raise men and money to take back the Palatine lands. The fundraising had been successful but the subsequent campaign had not. They had lost the battle against the imperial army and Craven had been captured and imprisoned. Elizabeth had been frantic, not knowing his fate for the longest time, unable to get news.

"You are well?" She could feel the pitiful inadequacy of the words and the barriers that were between them. He felt like a stranger. Something had changed within him. She could sense it. He felt cold and distant and she did not know how to change that.

"I am well, Your Majesty." She saw a flicker of grim humour in Craven's eyes and knew he lied. How could he be, when he had been injured in battle and then incarcerated? He was telling her what he wanted her to hear rather than being honest with her.

She gestured for him to sit beside her on the stone bench. They were in the shade of an old apple tree that had been part of the nunnery orchards before Frederick had transformed Rhenen into a hunting lodge. Elizabeth's ladies hovered just out of earshot. There was always curiosity to see Lord Craven. He was a hero even in defeat, especially now that he had saved the life of the Queen's son.

Craven sat silent, his hazel gaze fixed on the sloping gables and pediments of the little palace. He was not making it easy for her, Elizabeth thought. But perhaps he was not making it deliberately difficult either. There was a new quality about him, a sense almost of desolation, as though he had lost something precious.

"I have messages for Your Majesty." Craven put a hand inside his jacket and withdrew a couple of letters. Elizabeth took them but laid them aside.

"Thank you," she said. "I'll read them presently. First I would rather know how you are. And Rupert."

"The Prince was well when I left Linz," Craven said. He fell silent again.

"Is he well cared for in his imprisonment? Does he want for anything?" Elizabeth lost her patience. "For God's sake, Craven, tell me the honest truth! Is it not bad enough that we have lost all hope of retaking the Palatinate now? If Rupert is sick, or broken in spirit as well, I would rather know than that you pretend."

He turned to look at her. Now he was smiling properly and she felt warmer at last, as though a few of those layers of stifling formality had been peeled away and they were approaching the friendship they had once known even if the intimacy she ached for was gone.

"Prince Rupert wants for nothing but his freedom," he said slowly. "You know what he is like. You might as well try to confine a hawk." He shrugged. "Arundel gave him a dog for company, a great big fluffy white creature that is devoted to him." There was a degree of humour in his voice now. "Rupert has also developed a certain regard for the daughter of his gaoler, Count von Kuffstein. I know that you asked me to ensure that he did not fall into any trouble but..." he spread his hands, "Not even I can undo the damage that Cupid's arrows inflict."

Elizabeth laughed. "You saved Rupert's life at Vlotho," she said. "That is enough for me. I shall never reproach you."

"Not for anything?" There was an odd tone in Craven's voice now. She noticed it; she almost stopped to question him but eagerness swept her onwards. She wanted to hear about Rupert. She wanted to hear how Craven had fought so valiantly and saved her son.

"I will never reproach you for anything at all," Elizabeth

said. "I swear it." She placed a hand on his. "But tell me how it was you came to save Rupert."

"I did nothing so dramatic, I assure you." Craven swept the claim aside. "His forces were surrounded. I came to his aid. He's a good soldier," he added. "He could be a great one if he learns discipline to match his courage."

"And Charles Louis?" Elizabeth asked. Charles Louis was her favourite but she knew few people shared her preference for him over his brother. As his father's heir he needed guile as well as courage. Where Rupert seldom troubled with tact, Charles Louis was skilled at playing all sides and was already an accomplished politician. His ignominious escape after Vlotho had been contrasted with Rupert's and Craven's heroic defence and refusal to leave the field, but Elizabeth was stung by the criticism of him for what else could Charles Louis have done? He was the Prince Palatine now even if he had not lands to rule over. It would avail them nothing if he were to be captured too, or worse, to die in battle.

"Charles Louis fought well," Craven said. No more.

Elizabeth smothered a sigh. "You were wounded, I hear," she said.

"A scratch."

"You always dismiss your injuries thus," Elizabeth complained.

"Because they are." Craven sounded abrupt to the point of rudeness. Elizabeth wondered if it was the pain of his wounds that made him so gruff. She bit her tongue rather than suggest it. If it were true he would give her an even more abrupt answer.

"You look ill." She abandoned courtesy and matched his bluntness. "I was going to ask if you wished to accompany me riding later, but I fear you would fall from the saddle at my feet."

"I think that possible." He sounded grimly amused. "Some other day, perhaps, if it please Your Majesty."

It pleased her very much to be with him even in this poor mood that she was prepared to sit there all afternoon talking rather than ride out.

"They wish Rupert to change his faith," she said. "They say they will free him if he converts to Catholicism."

"Then he will have a long imprisonment." Craven turned towards her and his expression softened. "Do not fear, Majesty. Prince Rupert will never swear allegiance to the Emperor. He is stubborn. If the Queen failed to persuade him when he was in England—and believe me his head was turned by so much attention accorded to him—then nothing the Emperor can do will make a ha'p'orth of difference."

"Then we shall need to broker his release in a different way," Elizabeth said. She felt a little comforted. She did indeed know her son and he was as stubborn as Craven said. "But how? They would not accept a ransom. They would not even allow you to pay a fee in order to stay with him."

"Trust me," Craven said. "We will find a way."

Elizabeth wanted to reach out then and touch him again, for reassurance, in hope that he was right. And for more than comfort. Her emotions felt jumbled but she knew she was tired of standing apart. A pedestal could be a lonely place.

She pulled her shawl more closely about her. The day was drawing cooler; the sun had gone.

"How was England?" she asked.

"Unfamiliar." A shadow touched Craven's face. "I felt almost a stranger there."

"I heard they gave you a degree from Oxford University," Elizabeth said. "Even with the paucity of your Latin."

That won her a laugh. "Your Majesty is correct," Craven

said. "It was the least appropriate honour they could have conferred on me."

"You could have stayed." After his release from imprisonment after Vlotho he had gone back to London with Charles Louis but neither of them had stayed there long. Charles Louis' return Elizabeth could understand; there was nothing to keep him in England. It was not his home. But Craven had estates there and responsibilities.

"I could have done." He sounded indifferent.

"Yet you chose to return here."

You chose to return to me.

She did not dare say it aloud after the way he had rejected her before. She was too proud. Which meant she would live on crumbs.

"There will be trouble in England soon." He was thinking of politics whilst she was thinking of love. His gaze met hers suddenly, sharply. "I dislike the way matters tend. The country is full of rumours." He glanced away from her, across the gardens. Elizabeth followed his gaze. Everything looked so neat, so precise, but it was an illusion of order. Both here and at home—if England could be said to be her home any more—there was turbulence close to the surface, chaos. Men disputed and argued with increasing fierceness. Soon it might spill over into physical bloodshed.

"They say there will be war in Scotland soon," she said, remembering the most recent letter from Sir Thomas Roe.

"There will," Craven agreed. "The Covenanters will not accept either the Book of Common Prayer or the imposition of Anglican bishops, and your brother—"

"Is a stiff-necked fool who does not listen to the counsel of reasonable men," Elizabeth finished dryly.

"Quite so, Majesty." Craven relaxed into a smile. "I am rebuilding the gatehouse of my castle at Stokesay. It is in the

Welsh borders," he added, seeing her look of puzzlement. "It is one of the few properties I own that is defensible, though it could not withstand a prolonged attack."

A quick fear chilled Elizabeth's heart. "Then you think the war might spread?" Was it not enough, she thought bitterly, that she had lost everything she had once owned? Must Charles squander his inheritance too, through folly and bad judgement? So many hopes had turned to ashes. So many lives had been lost. She shuddered that there might be more killing, more bloodshed, more hatred. This was not what she had wanted when she had grasped at the hope for a new, more equitable world, a world that the Knights of the Rosy Cross had promised. She and Frederick had wanted to foster learning and knowledge, healing and charity. Somewhere, somehow, that vision had been corrupted.

"I fear war may come to the whole of the three kingdoms." Craven's mouth was set in a grim line. "It is not much of a step from leading an army against the Scots Covenanters to facing a greater conflict."

"*Civil* War?" Elizabeth started to tremble. Nothing was more heinous than father fighting son, brother against brother. Her father, King James, had striven so hard for unity amongst his kingdoms. Could all his work be undone in one generation? She could not bear the thought.

"A melancholy prospect," she said, striving to keep her voice level. "A king set against his subjects is a terrible thing. Could Charles really take up arms against his people..." She let the words fade because she knew he could.

"I did not know you owned land near Wales," she said after a moment. "I have never been there. What is it like?"

"It's beautiful country," Craven said.

"Good for riding?"

"Not as good as my Berkshire estates." He smiled. "You would like those best, I think."

"Tell me more of your plans for your castle." It was a distraction and Elizabeth needed one. "Do you have any drawings?"

"I have one here." Craven took a parchment from inside his jacket.

Elizabeth leaned forwards as he unrolled the scroll. "That is a very small plan."

"It is a very small castle," Craven said. "Here is the gatehouse—" He pointed to a drawing of a wood and plaster building that looked for all the world like something from a fairy story of the middle ages and not, to Elizabeth's eyes, particularly defensible.

"And here is the inside of the main castle," Craven said. "I plan to create the most elegant panelled chamber for dining within the walls of what was the mediaeval solar."

"It's beautiful," Elizabeth said sincerely. She loved the ornate carvings and bright colours of the overmantel. "You are a builder, not a soldier now," she teased. "I can imagine you have many more grand designs."

"I do."

"I hope to see them all one day."

He looked up. Their gazes met. His hazel eyes were bright with sunlight and the pleasure of a project she could see he loved.

"I hope you will grace the room at dinner many times," he said.

So many possible futures, but she was afraid that none of them would come true.

Craven rolled up the scroll so his plans for the future vanished. "If your brother goes to war he will need soldiers. Fighting first, building when peace comes."

"You will go to support him?" Elizabeth asked. Her breath caught on an instinctive objection. She wanted to point out that he was older now, his sword arm would be slower and so would his healing be after injury. He had been wounded badly twice already. A third time he might not be so lucky.

Yet she knew it would be selfish to seek to dissuade him. Charles would need experienced soldiers and Craven's knowledge as well as his fortune would be of immense benefit to him. If she forbade him from going he would defy her and if she tried to persuade him it would be for her own selfish reasons, because she wanted to keep him at her side.

It was her destiny to lose William Craven. He was a professional soldier. He would answer a call to arms. She was destined never to hold him, always to let him go and so it would be better not to have him in the first place.

"You are an unusual man," she said. She spoke impulsively, lulled by the warmth of the sun and the heavy scent of the roses. "I have never met anyone quite like you before, William."

He smiled. "What am I like?"

She blushed. She was twelve years older than he was, widowed, the mother of ten children. She was a queen and yet she blushed. She could not find the words.

"You are..." She stumbled over it. *A soldier and yet a poet, even if your imagination manifests itself in stones and mortar rather than words or pictures or music. You are brash and yet assured. You are all hard steel and rough edges, cloaked in cavalier lace and velvet.*

She had met many men; smooth courtiers, politicians as slippery as eels, soldiers and fops, but she had never met a man like William Craven.

In the end she answered obliquely.

"I'm glad," she said softly, placing her hand on his. "Glad you returned."

She watched the smile ripple across his eyes again, such very beautiful eyes of the clearest hazel, honest and true. She felt a flutter of emotion beneath her breastbone. It was not the sweet, simple love she had felt for Frederick but a different sensation entirely, more complicated, edged with poignancy and yet still as strong.

"I wish you would not go away again," she said, "but I shall not seek to stop you. I would keep you with me always if I could."

He raised her hand to his lips. His eyes were full of emotion. At the last moment he turned her hand over and pressed his lips to her palm.

"Madam." He spoke gruffly. "You know that I do not—"

"I know you do not want me in the way I once wanted you. Yes." Her patience was at an end. There was only so much rejection a woman could take so she spoke without due consideration.

There was a short silence. Then she saw his lips curve into a smile. It was wholly masculine, the smile of a man confident in his own worth. "That was not," he said gently, "what I was going to say."

"Oh." She felt flustered, suddenly hot, a little dizzy and more than a little embarrassed. "I beg your pardon."

"Do not. But perhaps I should tell you what I was about to say."

Her dizziness increased. She was not sure she could breathe properly.

"I was about to say that I have to leave you, Your Majesty, because it torments me to stay here when I cannot have you. Why do you think I have been gone so long?"

Her ladies were so close, only just out of earshot, fluttering, curious. What could they read on her face? Or indeed from the way that their hands were now entwined? She freed herself, smoothed her skirts.

"You have changed your mind?"

"No. I always wanted you."

She risked a look at his face. He looked grim, not happy at all. What did he mean—that he wanted her, but he did not want to feel that way? Why was love so difficult?

"Yet you refused me before."

"Out of honour."

"And now?"

The self-deprecating smile touched his lips. "Perhaps I have no honour left for myself, though I should have more care for you."

They were talking quickly, in snatched breaths. It felt as though the air about her was on fire. She wondered that people could not see it, that they did not guess her blazing excitement. Yet she was an accomplished dissembler. She found she could converse with lowered gaze and thoughtful expression even when that conversation was about illicit love.

"I can take care of myself," she said.

"It is my place to protect you, not to put you in harm's way. But I wanted you to know the truth, Majesty."

"I will come to you tonight," Elizabeth said.

Heat flared in his eyes, quickly banked. "Majesty—"

"I have no notion how to arrange it," Elizabeth said honestly, "but I will."

She saw tenderness in his face then and her stomach dropped. "You have no experience of managing a love affair."

"Naturally not," Elizabeth said, with a quick flash of returning hauteur.

"Then perhaps you should leave it to me," Craven said. "I, alas, do."

"Not with any degree of discretion," Elizabeth said tartly.

He laughed aloud at that, with quick delight. Everything seemed so bright and brilliant about her all of a sudden, the day, her mood. She felt lighter than air, yet trembling with anticipation. She stood up.

"Tonight," she said.

He touched her hand then, so fleeting no one would notice and she thought:

This time it really will happen.

The afternoon dragged. She could not concentrate. She started several letters and tore them up. She felt restless, impatient. She snapped at her ladies. She almost snapped at her dogs.

The evening was worse. Time had started to run backwards. She was torn, half hope, half fear. She could not eat. Lady Douglas asked her if she had a fever, she was so flushed. She felt despairing. How had she even imagined that she could go to Craven's rooms, the Queen slipping past her attendants, down the long lamplit passageways to knock at a gentleman's door? It was impossible, ridiculous. She felt both relief and desolation.

She wondered if she should retire early. She wondered if she should retire late. She chose a most beautiful nightgown adorned with lace, taking it from the chest with a scent of lavender clinging to its folds. It felt as though everyone was watching her. She could not bear it and told them she had a headache and sent them away. Then she sat by the fire as an hour crept past and then another and the candle burned down and she knew it would not happen, that it had all been an illusion.

It was then that the loneliness, the misery, threatened to swallow her whole. She was alone, just as she had always been, just as she would always be. It had been no more than a fantasy.

There was a creak of a latch, a step in the doorway.

She turned, a hand at her throat, her heart threatening to leap from her chest, and there he was. Slowly, as though she was in a dream, she moved towards him and his arms closed about her, strong and sure. No one had touched her in so long a time; she felt starved for love. She was almost crying.

"If you have changed your mind—" she started to say, but he moved swiftly then, so fast she barely had time to draw breath. He swept her off her feet and onto the vast bed, following her down amongst the tumbled covers. Then he went very still, looking at her, touching her cheek gently with such reverence that she felt quite faint. She tilted up her face and he kissed her. It was a very long time since she had been kissed and it felt shocking, unfamiliar but delightful at the same time. She dug her fingers into the muscle of his shoulders beneath the jacket and drew him closer, sliding her arms about his neck now, pressing her fingers to his nape, giddy with physical sensation. She was young again, like a girl discovering love for the first time and it was wonderful. So she let go of the grief and the struggle and the years of hardship and lost herself in the moment, and for a little while everything felt fresh and new and joyful again.

32

Her grandfather was in the greenhouse when Holly arrived for Sunday lunch. She could see him through the glass as she walked down the mown path through the lines of broad beans and rhubarb; thick peppery grey hair, a little stooped as he bent over the pots of seedlings, but still broad shouldered and durable looking. He glanced up as her shadow crossed the window and his weather-beaten face broke into a wide smile.

"Holly!" The door was open and he gestured her inside, wrapping her in a bear hug. The tweed of his jacket was rough against her cheek and she felt a sudden huge wash of love for him, for both her grandparents, and hugged him back tightly.

It was the night after the blaze at the mill. Over breakfast she had told Mark about everything; the pearl, the mirror, Lavinia's diary, her visions. Mark had taken it with all the calm thoughtfulness she was starting to know very well. He had not told her she was mad. He had told her that the pattern would resolve, that they would work it out together.

Mark had gone back to the barn to get ready for the barbecue that evening and on the way into Oxford Holly had taken the crystal mirror to a friend who was an antiques dealer and had asked her to find an expert who could confirm its provenance. She had felt lighter as soon as it was out of her hands. Espen Shurmer had given it to her and had told her it should be reunited with the Sistrin pearl but Holly had seen for herself now the destructive power of the mirror and she felt deep down that the two should never come together. It felt too dangerous.

John held her at arm's length and scrutinised her with his shrewd blue gaze. "How are you?"

"I'm fine," Holly said. "How are you? You look well. Very tanned."

"Don't really need a greenhouse in this weather," John said. "I've grown salad leaves and calabrese and even given melon and sweet potato a go this year. With the heat the exotic fruit has done well too…" He waved a vague hand towards the garden, basking in the sun. The vents of the greenhouse roof were wide open but it was still hotter than a sauna in there, the air thick with a mix of herb scent and pollen that tickled Holly's nose and made her want to sneeze.

She picked a cherry tomato from one of the plants and put it in her mouth, closing her eyes as the sweetness of it burst on her tongue.

"Mmm. Delicious."

Her grandfather smiled indulgently as he picked up his watering can. "You can take a whole punnet of them home with you if you like."

"Thanks," Holly said. "I'd love to."

John looked up from the tender line of basil plants he was watering. "How are you getting on? Your grandmother said you were getting lots of new commissions."

"A few," Holly allowed. "Things do seem to be picking up. I've got a contract from a business in Bristol and I'm displaying some of my work at the open house for the Ashdown renovation project for a few weeks."

John smiled. "I'm so pleased, Holly." He hesitated. "I daresay we shouldn't worry over you, but—"

"I'd be upset if you didn't," Holly said, giving him another hug. "Have you spoken to Tasha about Ben?" she asked as she let him go. "Is that what this is about?"

John's eyes clouded. "It's over a month now." He moved the pots of basil around a little randomly, avoiding her eyes. "Some nights I can't sleep. Others I sleep like a baby and wake feeling guilty because I *should* have lain awake all night. I wonder where he's gone, if he's dead." He turned to face her and Holly saw the deep lines of grief in his face and the tiredness in his eyes. "I never say it to your grandmother," John said. "I shouldn't say it to you."

Holly could feel a lump in her throat. "You've been strong for us all for years. It's not a weakness to admit to feeling like this."

John closed his eyes for a moment. "Tasha's so practical," he said. "She says Ben's gone for good and we have to move on."

"It's her way of coping," Holly said. She felt a rush of sympathy for her sister-in-law. She had thought Tasha was cold and unloving but she could see now with time that they each had to deal with Ben's disappearance in their own ways. There was no right or wrong.

"I know," John said. He blinked rapidly. "She's just hard to comfort, you know? We can't get close." He rubbed a hand over his face leaving a smear of soil on his cheek. "Let's talk about something else," he said. "How have you got on with your research into Miss Flyte's diary—and the Winter Queen?"

"I'd hardly dignify it by calling it research," Holly said. "I have finished Lavinia's diary and I have discovered a few interesting things..." She paused. She wanted John's opinion on her discoveries but at the same time she knew she had become both possessive and protective of Lavinia. She did not really want to share her. She wanted to keep all her secrets safe. It felt as though it was a precious part of herself that she was hugging close.

"Lavinia was quite fascinating," she said now. "I believe she had a child, a daughter called Kitty who married into a merchant family in Marlborough. I saw her portrait last week."

She flicked open her phone and showed her grandfather the photograph she had taken of Kitty Flyte's portrait. Kitty could not have been more than eighteen or nineteen in the picture, she thought, the same age her mother had been when she had gone to Ashdown Park. Yet their two fates were very different: Lavinia, the courtesan; Kitty marrying into the rich respectability of the merchant classes.

"I don't know for sure who her father was," Holly said now, "but the timing fits with Kitty being conceived at Ashdown Park."

"Then surely it would be Evershot," John said. "He was Lavinia Flyte's protector, wasn't he?"

"It's not that simple," Holly said, thinking how inappropriate the word *protector* was to describe Evershot's treatment of Lavinia. "Lavinia was having an affair with Evershot's surveyor," she said. "He was called Robert Verity. Verity was supposed to be descended from the illegitimate line of William Craven."

"Ah," John said. "So there was an illegitimate descent, just as I imagined."

"Yes," Holly said tentatively. "Ben may have traced the connection too but I can't see that it's linked to our family tree in any way. There's no one called Verity in our ancestry, or Flyte for that matter."

"Keep searching," John said. "In my limited experience these things are tricky. Family relationships, even names, are not always as they seem."

Holly nodded. "There's certainly something odd afoot because Lavinia's handwritten diary—*my* diary—is completely different from the published version. I think someone stole the idea of the memoir, and Lavinia's identity, and published a fictitious version."

She had John's full attention now, basil plants forgotten. "Extraordinary," he said. "I must talk to the English faculty. Are you sure? I mean you've read both versions?"

"Rather too much of them," Holly said, thinking of the erotic cavorting of the published diary.

John rubbed his hands together. "Well, if you don't mind lending me the original diary I'd like to look into this," he said. "It sounds rather fascinating, a historical and literary mystery."

"I'm very happy to lend it to you," Holly said. "But I'd like to work with you on whatever piece of research comes out if it." She saw her grandfather's look of astonishment and spoke in a rush. "I know history isn't my subject, nor English for that matter but I've become rather fond of Lavinia and I want to be the one to tell the truth about her."

John's eyes twinkled. "A personal crusade?"

"Something like that," Holly admitted. "And whilst we're on the subject…"

John raised his brows.

"I know it sounds melodramatic," Holly said, "but the memoir mentioned lost treasure."

"The lost treasure of the Order of the Rosy Cross," John said. Holly gaped at him. "You mean you *know* about it?"

"I know that both Frederick and Elizabeth of Bohemia were patrons of the Order," John said. "Their court in Heidelberg was a centre for Rosicrucian learning. I hadn't thought of it before but I suppose the Rosicrucian treasure could have been hidden at Ashdown Park, given Elizabeth's connection to William Craven."

"I wondered if Ben had found some clue to trace it," Holly said. "Mark said he had been looking at maps of the estate and stuff like that, and an expert on the Bohemian court said Ben had contacted him for information." She paused but her grandfather simply waited, sharp interest in his eyes. "Then there's the fact that there is a standing stone called the Pearlstone on the edge of the Ashdown woods." Holly said. "It might be named for the Sistrin pearl, which was one of the treasures." Her face fell. "Except that the stone would pre-date the house and couldn't have been named after the pearl. Damn!"

"That could be easily explained," John said. His blue eyes now had the abstracted gaze he assumed when he was thinking.

Holly's heart did a crazy leap. "How?"

"There are plenty of places where a name is adopted later," John said. "There's an example near Ashdown itself, for that matter, Alfred's Castle. It's a hill fort named to commemorate the fact that King Alfred's battle of Ashdown against the Vikings took place nearby. But the name came later than the battle. It was only called Alfred's Castle in the eighteenth century." His blue eyes were bright. "Do you see what I mean?"

"You mean that the Pearlstone might have been deliberately named to connect it to the pearl," Holly said. "The names might have been given relatively recently. Perhaps... at the time the house was built? As a clue?"

"Exactly," John said, smiling.

"Wow," Holly said.

"It seems to me you've been very busy," John observed. "Is there anything else you have to tell me?"

"Only that the same expert Ben consulted gave me one of the Rosicrucian treasures," Holly said. "A crystal mirror."

John's eyebrows shot up into his hair. "Where is this mirror now?" he asked, with commendable restraint.

"I've lodged it with an antiques collector for authentication," Holly said.

John released his breath. "Very wise." He checked his watch. "I think you had better tell me all about this so-called expert and his crystal mirror over lunch."

Holly's lips twitched. "Yes, Granddad. I expected you to be a great deal more sceptical about the treasure," she added.

"I haven't lived for seventy-five years without coming across plenty of things I can't explain," John said mildly. "The Knights of the Rosy Cross was an odd sect. The members held all sorts of arcane beliefs."

"Prophecy." Holly nodded. "And reincarnation."

"Reincarnation is a fascinating theory," John said, "the rebirth of the soul in another body."

"It sounds exhausting to me," Holly said, "living and reliving a life over and over again."

"You have a very practical mind," John said affectionately. "There are different variations on the idea. One is that within your destiny there are different roads you can choose to travel, and that if you fail in some way the first time the pattern repeats in future generations. They inherit your spirit and your quest."

A ripple of wind seemed to run through the thick air of the greenhouse, shaking the tender stems of the tomato plants. It felt to Holly as though the sky had darkened and yet when she looked outside the sun was as bright as ever and the sky a hard, blistering blue.

"Within your destiny there are different roads you can choose to travel…"

She thought of Lavinia then and the choices she had made. Had she and Robert Verity been following a pattern set centuries before by Elizabeth and William Craven? Had the Winter Queen and her cavalier failed in a quest that had been passed down to their future heirs? Not many weeks ago she would have dismissed such an idea as fantasy but so many things had happened to shake her understanding of her world, so many links and connections had been revealed.

She watched her grandfather, his fingers stained with earth and pollen, as he laid each tiny tomato under the cloche and she thought about the complications of family and inheritance and love and destiny.

"Speaking of the Winter Queen and the Earl of Craven," John said, "I have something to show you." He adjusted the lid of the cloche carefully. "There. They should ripen nicely in there." He dusted his hands down the front of his trousers. "Come inside."

Holly followed him up the gravel path, between the fruit trees and in at the garden door. The house was cool and dark after the heat outside. A delicious smell of roast beef wafted from the kitchen. Holly could hear her grandmother clattering around with pots and pans and talking to someone at the same time.

"She's Skyping a friend in America, I think," John murmured. "Excuse me a moment whilst I wash the soil off my hands. I'll see you in the study."

He went down the passage towards the cloakroom whilst Holly turned right and went through the open door into the study, a square high-ceilinged room lined with bookcases.

She loved this room, from the threadbare striped rug on the floor to the tattered volumes piled up in the shelves in tumbling disorder. It was astonishing John could ever find anything at all.

"Now…" John had come in and was easing himself into the leather desk chair. "Take a look at this. I came across it the other day. It's called *An Allegory of Love* and it was painted by Sir Peter Lely."

He clicked on a tab on screen and a picture came up. Holly leaned on the desk to take a closer look. It was a painting of a man in a white silk shirt edged in blue, handsome, grave. A woman stood to the side of him in a russet gown that matched her hair. She held a laurel wreath in her hand. Three childlike figures with wings were grouped to the other side.

"William Craven and Elizabeth Stuart," Holly said. This was the painting that Lavinia had written about seeing at Ashdown Park, she thought. She remembered the heartfelt words in the memoir:

Oh, to find a love like that…

"Are those angels?" Holly asked.

"Cupids," John said, smiling. "Symbols of love. I think the painting gives lots of clues about their relationship. I don't know if Craven and Elizabeth were married but they were certainly bound to each other. Look—" John moved the cursor over the image, "one of the cupids has tied his wrist with blue ribbon. It was known as the *cordon bleu*."

"I thought that was for cookery," Holly said.

John laughed. "It is, but the phrase originated as an order of knightly chivalry. It implies that Craven was bound to Elizabeth through love and honour."

"She's crowning him," Holly said, squinting at the painted laurel wreath in Elizabeth's hand. The background of the painting was dark. It was difficult to see the details. "I thought laurel wreaths were a symbol of victory."

"Victory, peace and wisdom," John said. "Laurel is also a symbol of marriage, so perhaps this is the closest they ever came to acknowledging the marriage publicly." He turned away from the screen to view Holly directly. "There's something else though. You may remember me telling you that the Rosicrucian Order believed in reincarnation? The laurel is a symbol of regeneration and future life."

"The life they had and the lives of the generations to come," Holly said. "Yet a little while before Elizabeth died, they parted," she said. "I wonder why that was."

"I believe they quarrelled," John said. "It was the gossip of the time." He clicked on another link and a few lines of text came up. "Not Pepys," John said, "but a lesser diarist called Tremaine. He was at the theatre one night when Elizabeth and William Craven were present." He moved out of the way so that Holly could read.

To the theatre where the entertainment on the benches far exceeded that on the stage. Her Majesty the Queen of Bohemia left in the middle of the performance. It seems she has quarrelled rather badly with that old cavalier Craven, perhaps because his former mistress was in the audience too. Reports have it that Her Majesty has left his protection and is to be the tenant of Lord Leicester instead...

"Oh, dear." Holly pulled a face. "I wonder if that was the mother of Craven's illegitimate son, or another woman?"

"Tremaine doesn't say, unfortunately," John said, "but I'll see if I can find any other references."

He turned away; closed down the screen. "Poor Elizabeth," he said. "Just because you may believe in soulmates and destiny it doesn't mean you aren't human and fallible."

"And poor William Craven too," Holly said. "After so

many years of devotion it must have been unbearable to lose her."

John stood up slowly, as though his bones ached. He reached for her, drew her in for a hug. He smelled of pollen and warm wool and soil and Holly's childhood and she hugged him back, feeling the tears prick her throat.

"Better to risk all for love than to be too afraid to try," John said, "in my opinion." He let go and smiled down at her. "Remember that, when the time comes."

33

The baggage train filled the courtyard outside and spilled out of the gates onto the road. Craven was not the only one leaving for England. A number of gentlemen had pledged themselves to Elizabeth's brother's service now that the three kingdoms were tearing themselves apart in civil war. But Craven was the only one Elizabeth did not want to see go. Her court was in uproar, her life falling apart and re-forming again into a different pattern. Yet all she could think was that this really was the end. Craven was leaving and she would only see him again on the far side of war, if at all.

She could not hold him. She did not have enough to offer. She never had had anything to offer a man who was impatient of idleness, a soldier who needed a cause, who always had to be active. He could not sit by in The Hague playing cards or attending masques or having his portrait painted. She had seen how it drove him to madness. Even when they had gone hunting together, riding out fast and hard, she had sensed that for him it was not enough. Even when he had been in her bed and it was sublime, it was only the respite of an hour or so.

He came to take his farewell of her. He was dressed for travelling, plain, serviceable. They had not even discussed his departure. It had been accepted that he would leave for war and she would watch him go. It did not matter that he was her lover. Other loyalties came before that.

"Majesty." He bowed and took her hand for a formal kiss. She looked in his eyes and saw he had already left. He was a soldier. He had a job to do.

"Be careful." Her heart was cracking in two.

He nodded and released her.

She had so little time and so much pride. She watched him walk across to the door.

"William!" She could not stand it a moment more.

He turned.

"Don't go," she said. Her words tumbled out now. "I don't want you to go. Stay here with me. Please. I can't imagine what it would be like without you." She did not dare look at him, not when she had thrown aside all her pride just to make him see the truth. She *could* imagine it, the bleakness without him, the emptiness, but the further words stuck in her throat.

There was a moment of absolute stillness.

"Elizabeth," he said.

"I don't just want you as my lover," Elizabeth said. "It's not enough. Marry me."

He looked winded beyond shock. It was so comical she had to stifle a laugh. Yet it was no joking matter. With the words out she realised how much she wanted to bind him to her forever. To take him as a lover for a couple of months, or

even years, was not enough. His was the strength and counsel she relied upon. She could not risk losing that on a lovers' quarrel.

He glanced quickly around. In the bustle of departure it
seemed that no one had heard. She suspected that plenty of
people knew of their liaison but Craven had always been
scrupulous of her reputation, never showing the slightest familiarity in public.

He crossed the room to her and took her hand again,
tucking it through his arm, walking with her casually down
the length of the room and out onto the gallery. He did not
speak. It felt so informal, certainly ordinary enough to fool
her courtiers. Yet he covered her hand with his and that was
not casual at all. He did not speak and she did not dare glance
up at his face.

At the end of the gallery was an antechamber, no more
than a storeroom, cold and full of old travelling chests and
the smell of dust. She felt him glance back and then they were
through the doorway and he closed it behind them.

The room was so small they were almost touching.

"Elizabeth…" There was so much emotion in his voice
and yet he seemed uncertain what to say. Fear seized Elizabeth then. He was going to tell her that soldiering was his
life, that he could not break his pledge to support her brother
simply so that he could stay with her. It was not honourable.

He was going to say that he cared more for war than he
did for love.

"I'm sorry," she started to say, but he shook his head.

"Don't be." His voice was fierce. His hand came up to cup
her jaw. "I did not know—"

"Did not know that I loved you?" She felt astonished. How
could he have lain with her night after night when she had

poured out all of herself and her love to him without restraint and not realise that she cared for him above all else?

She placed a hand against his chest. She could feel the beat of his heart against her palm. "Marry me," she said again.

"Elizabeth," he said. "You are a queen. It is impossible."

"It is possible to lie with me as a mortal sin and yet refuse to wed me with honour?"

She saw the struggle in his eyes. "It is not that." He sounded angry. "Do not demean yourself or what we have by speaking thus."

"Then why refuse me?"

"Because of the disparity in our rank! Because you are a queen whose cause can only be diminished if she is seen to have married beneath her." He threw out a hand in exasperation. "Surely you can see that as well as I?"

"You have always considered yourself the equal of any man," Elizabeth said.

Craven made a sound of frustration. "This is not about what I feel. This is about what other men think."

"But you love me."

"Of course." He looked baffled that she should question it and the simplicity of his response made her smile. In the end it really was that simple.

"Then you must wed me." She had never been so sure of anything in her life.

She saw the darkness gather in his eyes as though he was going to argue again and she pressed her fingers against his lips to silence him. She did not want to hear any more objections. There could be none. "Hush," she said, standing on tiptoe, kissing him.

Footsteps passed close to the door, voices; the rattle of keys, discovery so close and so dangerous.

"Say you will." She was teasing him now, her spirits as light as a girl, dizzy with renewed desire as they kissed and kissed.

"I won't go to England," he said, resting his forehead against hers when it was over, breathing hard. "I will stay here with you."

She felt triumph but hot on its heels was an echo of melancholy. She had made him choose and he had chosen her. She pressed closer to him to drive out the sadness and the guilt. And when she felt his resistance melt and he shifted to hold her more firmly she felt nothing other than relief for she knew that she had won.

34

"Happy birthday!" Fran said, grinning from ear to ear as she plonked a sponge cake with chocolate icing down in front of Holly. One modest candle shone in the centre. Clearly Fran had not had enough to supply the other twenty-eight, or perhaps she was just being tactful for once. Not that Holly minded being almost thirty. Not much.

"I couldn't arrange for you to have hot sex as a birthday present," Fran was saying, "so chocolate is the next best thing."

"Fran!" Holly glanced around to make sure that they were the only two people in the café. Fortunately for once they were.

"What's the matter?" Fran said, opening her blue eyes wide in a very innocent fashion. "You don't like chocolate?"

"No," Holly said. "Yes." She picked up the fork and dug it into the cake. Cream exploded out of the side. "Mmm," Holly said, closing her eyes as she licked the fork. "That's better than sex, not the next best thing to sex."

"Really?" Fran paused in whisking a quiche mixture. "I thought you and Mark were together now?"

"Fran!" Holly dropped the fork with a clatter.

"Well?" It was impossible to embarrass Fran. She leaned over the counter, eyes bright with expectation. "How is it going?"

"Fine," Holly said. *More than fine.* She felt hot thinking just how fine it was. "Have some of that cake," she said. "It might stop all the questions."

"Huh." Fran sounded put out but she pulled a slice of cake towards her anyway and dug in. "I expected more than that."

"Dream on," Holly said.

It was mid-morning and once again the sun lay in bright lozenges across the tiled floor of the coffee shop but the weather was cooler, rain never far away. The water was rising in the millpond again. Only the day before, Bonnie had gone in for a swim.

"Wasn't that a great barbecue yesterday?" Fran said, cutting herself a lavish slice of the chocolate cake. "Thank God the rain held off. I'm so glad you were able to drop by in the evening, Holly. You're part of the village now whether you like it or not." She paused. "You did enjoy it—didn't you?"

"It was very nice," Holly said. She had driven back from visiting her grandparents in the late afternoon and had gone over to Mark's barn conversion. The day had been mellowing into a clear, warm evening and all Mark's guests were equally mellow through good food, drink and sunshine. Flick had fallen on her like a long-lost sister and dragged her over to sit with her on a long swing seat between two ancient apple trees. There had been a lot of laughter and conversation long into the evening and Holly had almost forgotten about Ben, about the constant ache of his disappearance, until Flick had asked for news and the ache had flared into vivid life again.

This was how it was, she supposed, the circle of loss and doubt and not knowing, until perhaps at last something happened to bring release. She wondered how people lived with the not knowing for year after year. She could not imagine it.

"When Mark said he was inviting a few people around I didn't think he meant the whole village," Holly said. "Everybody seems to know everyone else." They had all been so welcoming, she thought, so much a community. It was her fault if she felt she did not quite fit, that she was an observer on the edge of the crowd. She still preferred the anonymity of the city to a place where people shared their damson jam and stories of their plumbing issues. It all felt a little too claustrophobic for her but she was learning.

"Mark's house is pretty spectacular," she said.

"I love it." Fran gave an envious sigh. "All those glass walls and open views. He did all the work himself, you know, and it's a great advert for his company. Hey," she waved her fork in Holly's direction. "What did you think of Joe? I saw you chatting."

"He was exactly as I imagined him to be," Holly said, laughing. "Spoiled." Mark's younger brother had come over from Bristol University and arrived even later than she had, making the sort of entrance usually reserved for rock stars, amidst much swooning from Flick's friends.

"He is pretty to look at though, isn't he," Fran said.

"If you like the Regency poet style," Holly said. She shook her head indulgently. "He's cute. Charming, but he's just a boy. Whereas Mark is more..."

"Mark's a man," Fran said dryly. She smiled. "Mark didn't like Ben much, you know," she said. "I'm so glad that didn't get in the way for the two of you."

"What?" Holly looked up, startled. "What do you mean, he didn't like Ben?"

Fran looked confused. She gathered the plates together with unnecessary clatter, stacking them, her face turned away.

"They didn't seem to have much to say to each other," she said. "That's all. I wondered…" She stopped, shrugged. "I guess you can't get on with everyone."

Holly didn't reply. She felt odd, disorientated. She realised that she had somehow assumed that Mark had liked Ben—surely everyone liked Ben—but now she thought about it he had always been cool about him. He asked if there was any news, he gave her support and understanding, but he had never said that Ben was a good bloke or anything else she might have expected. Yet she knew Mark well now and that meant that if he had disliked Ben she knew there must have been a good reason for it.

"Forget it," Fran said now. "Hell, Holly, you know me, I am so tactless. I didn't mean to cause a problem. Anyway, I'm probably wrong."

"No," Holly said slowly. "No, I don't think you are."

The shop bell pinged. Fran quickly painted on a cheerful face. "Hi, Mark! We weren't talking about you. Not at all. It's Holly's birthday. Would you like some cake?"

"Please help yourself," Holly said, "before I eat it all."

"Thanks," Mark said. He bent and kissed her cheek. "Happy birthday." He gave her his long slow smile, full wattage. Holly thought she might spontaneously combust.

Holly could see Fran looking at them. It made her feel ridiculously self-conscious. She stood up. "I'd better be getting back," she said. "Thanks so much for the cake, Fran."

"Are you having a birthday party?" Fran looked hopeful.

"I hadn't thought of it," Holly said.

"We'll organise one for you," Fran said. "Next weekend."

"Don't bulldoze her," Mark said mildly. "Not everyone sees the village mafia as a good thing."

"It's really sweet of you, Fran," Holly said. "Thank you."

Fran shot Mark a self-satisfied smile. "See?"

Mark sighed.

Holly's phone rang. She fumbled for it, trying to dampen down the familiar rush of mingled hope and nausea. She recognised the Oxford code but not the number. Not Ben.

"Holly?" The woman at the other end sounded warm and very pleasant. "This is Eleanor Ferris about your mirror."

"Eleanor!" Holly said. "Gosh, thanks so much for getting back to me so quickly." She could feel her heart beating hard. The phone slipped a little in her hand.

"It's a most interesting piece," Eleanor said. "I'll be sending it back to you with a full report but I thought you would want to know a little about it now. The wood is willow and dates from about the sixteenth century and the glass is most certainly original Bohemian of a similar date. The reflective surface is badly worn, of course, and urgently needs restoration." There was a note of hesitation in her voice. "I checked the records you suggested and it does correspond to the descriptions of the crystal mirror belonging to the Winter Queen, albeit those are rather scant. There is just one thing..."

"Oh?" Holly's heart missed a beat.

"It's the diamonds," Eleanor said. "At some point in its history, probably in the early nineteenth century, someone took the original diamonds and replaced them with stones made of paste. They are worth nothing at all."

"Right," Holly said. Her mind spun at the implications. "Worthless. Thank you."

"I hope that's not bad news," Eleanor said, a little anxiously. "I mean, the mirror is still worth something because of its probable provenance, and also the quality of the crystal, but it's not original, if you know what I mean."

"Yes," Holly said. "No, it's not bad news. It might be quite good news, actually."

She slid the phone into her pocket.

Lavinia, she thought. It had to be. Her spirits lifted. She did not know what had happened to Lavinia after the fire but if she had sold the diamonds she would have been rich enough to start again. Perhaps that was what had paid for Kitty's dowry.

Fran was busy serving a couple of customers and didn't look up from the counter but Mark paused as he opened the coffee shop door and smiled at her. Holly made up her mind quickly. She stood up.

"Mark," she said, "I know you're busy but could I drop by later and discuss something with you?"

Mark raised his brows. "Sure. You can discuss it with me now if you don't mind walking back to the office with me."

"Thanks," Holly said, grabbing her jacket. Fran caught her eye and gave her a saucy wink. Holly rolled her eyes at her.

"Have a great time!" Fran sang out, buttering a scone with extra vigour.

"No one needs a town crier with Fran about," Holly said with feeling, as she closed the door and they started to walk slowly across the cobbled courtyard towards the old stable yard.

"Do you mind?" Mark asked. He shot her a sideways glance. "That everyone knows, I mean."

"No," Holly said, realising that she didn't mind at all. She blushed. "No. It's…fine."

Mark smiled at her again. "What was it you wanted to talk about?" He took the top off his coffee and took a deep swallow. "Ah, that's good. I've been up half the night working on the stuff for the open house."

"I won't keep you long," Holly said. "I just wondered…"

She hesitated. "This is going to sound weird but..." She stopped, shivering. They were in the shadow of the buildings and a chill breeze was blowing down from the hills. "I wondered if you disliked Ben," she said in a rush.

She felt Mark tense beside her. There was a guarded expression in his eyes. He did not answer for a moment.

"I didn't know him well," he said. His gaze was on the far horizon and Holly suddenly felt a distance opening up between them, as though he had quite deliberately taken an emotional step away. Then Mark's gaze came back to her and he gave her an apologetic smile.

"I'm sorry," he said. "I guess Ben and I just didn't have much to talk about."

Holly struggled with that. She knew she ought to understand; it was exactly how she had always felt about Tasha. Sometimes people didn't click and that was all there was to it. Yet it felt as though there should be something more.

"There must have been a reason," she said. "I mean, you're not the sort of person to take a dislike to someone over nothing."

She waited but Mark neither denied it nor explained. His mouth was drawn into a tight line and there was tension in the lines of his body.

"I..." he started to say, but then there was a shout from across the courtyard, cutting into the moment. They both turned.

Greg was hurrying towards them, shirt flapping. "You need to come over to the farm conversion, Mark," Greg said, giving Holly a quick nod. "They were putting in some pipework and they found a body—"

There was a buzzing in Holly's ears. The day suddenly seemed too bright, the yard spinning like a top.

"Greg, for fuck's sake!" Mark grabbed her tightly to stop her from falling. He sounded absolutely furious. "Holly—"

"I'm all right," Holly said faintly.

"Oh, God, I'm sorry." Greg looked utterly stricken. "I didn't mean... It's not a body, it's some bones. Hundreds of years old, Iain said. And some tools with it, or instruments, or something. I dunno. Shit. Sorry. I didn't mean—"

Mark ignored him, steering Holly over to the corner of the yard where she sank gratefully onto a wooden bench.

"Put your head down," Mark said. "You'll be OK. It's shock."

"I know." Holly waited for the sickness to subside. She felt hot and sweaty and yet at the same time so cold she was shivering.

After a moment, Mark crouched down beside her and touched her arm. "How are you doing?"

"I'm fine," Holly said, sitting up, taking a deep breath. "Sorry about that."

The shock was fading but she could remember it like a beat through the blood. Perhaps not knowing about Ben was better. At least there was hope, not the dead thud of realisation that he was never coming back.

"What did Greg mean when he said there were instruments with the body?" she said, remembering the scramble of words.

"I've no idea," Mark said. He was frowning at her. "Farming tools, perhaps, if it was a burial, although it sounds too late for that. Don't worry about it." He put out a hand and helped her to her feet. "I'll take you back to the café. You need a glass of water. Then I'll go over and find out what's going on. I'll let you know."

"Okay," Holly said. "I'll get a bottle of water, but I'm coming with you." Her legs felt shaky and the day still seemed too bright. She felt exhausted. "It's just that I think I know who it might be," she said. "The bones, I mean. I think it might be Robert Verity."

35

Wassenaer Hof, The Hague, April 1646

"Elizabeth!"

Craven barely waited for the scurrying attendants to close the door behind them before he slapped down his gloves on the table and stormed across the room, shedding his cloak carelessly on the way. He had come straight from the stable without stopping to wash the journey from him. Times had indeed changed.

Although she had been expecting this, Elizabeth raised a hand protectively to her throat. A wife, she supposed, should be accountable to her husband over the slander of her good character, even when the wife was a widowed queen and her husband a commoner. She remembered with something like nostalgia the diffidence with which Craven had first taken up his role as her spouse. She had led. He had always followed.

"Good evening, my lord." She tilted up a cheek for his kiss cool as spring water. "I trust your journey went smoothly?"

She reached for the bell on the table. "Shall I call for refreshment? A glass of wine?"

She saw Craven check his temper, ease out a sigh.

"Thank you. In a little, perhaps." He took the chair beside hers. The room had ceased to vibrate with his anger but there was still a hum of it in the air.

"Elizabeth," he said again. "What the devil is going on? Is it true that your son has killed de L'Epinay? How in hell could you have let this happen?"

Elizabeth swallowed hard. It was difficult to explain and Craven had a right to anger but she felt a dual sense of shame at her behaviour and resentment that he could question her. It was uncomfortable, like indigestion.

"Yes, it is true that de L'Epinay is dead," she said carefully. "Philip is hot-headed—" she dismissed her youngest son's waywardness as lightly as she could. "He thought that the Chevalier de L'Epinay had been too familiar in the way he spoke of me..." She shrugged awkwardly, seeing the way that this would inevitably lead her. "De L'Epinay taunted him and Philip took it badly. He was defending the honour of his house—"

"By slaughtering the man?"

Elizabeth flinched. "Please! There was a duel, a quarrel, high words were exchanged, it all escalated out of control..."

"And no one had the sense to stop him before it was too late."

"You were not here," Elizabeth said.

"Can I not be absent for even a month?" Craven did not sound flattered, as she had hoped. He sounded furious. "Where is the boy now?"

"He fled," Elizabeth said. "The authorities are out to arrest him."

"Naturally. He murdered a man."

"William." Once she had welcomed his plain speaking.

Now it hurt a great deal. "I need you to help him. That was why I sent for you."

"We'll talk of that in a while, perhaps." He dismissed her plea with a wave of the hand. "This other matter—de L'Epinay's slander of your reputation. How did that come about?"

Elizabeth's heart sank. If she did not tell him there would be plenty of others who would make sure he heard what had happened, and in the most damaging and undignified way possible. Yet she bristled at having to explain herself.

"The Chevalier called here at the court to pay his respects," she said. "He was witty, amusing. I saw no harm in receiving him."

"You were bored."

"I appreciated the Chevalier's company, that is true. He was entertaining."

"He called often."

"I... Yes, I suppose he did."

She knew he had. Every day, de L'Epinay would come to wait upon her and she had been flattered by his attentions. It was mortifying to admit it.

"He had a most unsavoury reputation."

"I had not heard of that."

She had not. She felt a fool.

Craven shifted irritably in his chair. "Damn it, you know how people talk. Everyone is saying he was your lover."

"They talk because they have nothing better to do." She laid a hand on his arm, half pleading, half restraining. She understood that his honour was injured here. She had managed to damage them all through her folly.

"William, you know there could be no truth in it," she said soothingly. "The idea is absurd. I love no man but you."

His gaze rested on her and for a moment she felt frightened because it lacked the usual warmth.

"If you were to acknowledge our marriage publicly," he said, "that might alleviate the scandal."

Elizabeth felt a rush of anger. "It would only make matters worse! Then they would say I was a woman who marries one man in secret and flaunts another in public!"

It was the wrong thing to say. She knew it as soon as the words left her lips but she could not call them back. Craven sprang up, walked away from her.

"Foolishly I imagined you had sent for me because you needed me by your side as your husband." His voice was deceptively quiet. "Yet I see I was mistaken." He swung back to face her. "Let me guess... Your only desire is that I help Philip escape the law for his crimes. You wish me to see him safely abroad, to take him to England, to go with him and ensure his future. You are sending me away again."

For a second it stole Elizabeth's breath because it was painfully true. "I only thought..." She floundered. "You are so good at dealing with such matters."

"I pay for difficult things to go away," Craven said brutally. He came across to her. "What did you imagine—that I would squire your reckless son around Europe to save his skin?" The fury in his voice frightened her. "Is that all I am to you? A means to an end?"

"You have always protected me and those I love." She was lost now, driven back on the truth. "I thought you would help me." The quiver in her voice, the tears in her eyes, were not entirely false. "William..."

For a second she thought it would not work, her power was gone. Then he swooped on her and pulled her into his arms, kissing her fiercely, violently, as though to drive away the doubts and the sharp words. Sometimes in the past they had ended arguments this way. She knew it aroused him to have her, a queen, submissive to his touch and she had exulted in it too, abandoning herself to him. Now she shook to feel that same response, washing away the anger. She forgot everything, her tiredness, the lateness of the hour, the bitter words, and let herself be taken on the rising tide of passion. His strength, the repressed violence in him, found its match in her, kiss for kiss and touch for touch. If this were his price she would pay it gladly.

Later, lying beside each other in the half dark, they ate and drank and talked.

"I have a cousin," Craven said, "Robert. He is a few years older than Philip, very sound, very steady. I will arrange for him to accompany the boy to England. He will make him a good squire and keep him from further harm."

It was not good enough for Elizabeth but she knew when to leave the discussion. "Thank you," she said.

"I am too old to go travelling myself any more," Craven said, and she knew that was as close to an apology as she would get.

"You are scarce an old man," she teased, reaching for him, kissing him.

The servants took away the empty dishes and left them and she wondered, between William's renewed caresses, why this was not good enough for him. Everyone knew they were wed. It was accepted; understood. Even if it was not openly acknowledged he was known to be her husband. She could not give him more. Could he not see it would undermine her and her fight to secure the future for her sons? She was the daughter of one king and the widow of a second and he, for all his dash and bravery was no more than a commoner. They had so much. In the beginning that had been sufficient for him. It had been more than enough. Yet increasingly it seemed that had changed.

36

There was already a crowd of people in the farmhouse garden, standing around a trench, which Holly presumed the water company had been digging when they had found the bones. It stood next to a slab of stone, which had been uncapped to reveal a tunnel below.

In addition to the engineers, who were standing around chatting and smoking as they watched, there were two men from the building site, armed with spades, and a whole straggle of others. Greg was there; he shot Holly a shamefaced look when he saw her but she smiled at him and his face lightened. Some of the villagers had come to watch, including Fran who had her coat collar turned up against the threatening rain and was chatting to a neighbour and dispensing coffee from an urn set up on a makeshift table.

"Iain rang to tell me what had happened," she said. "They needed supplies." She hugged Holly. "What on earth are you doing here? You know—" A comical look of horror slid across her face. "Oh, God, you know it's not Ben, don't you? They're just bones. Probably eighteenth century, Iain says."

"Yes, I know," Holly said. She broke off as a police Land Rover bumped along the track and turned into the drive.

"They always have to turn out if bones are found," Fran said. She shot Holly another deeply sympathetic look. "This can't be good for you, Hol. Go home—"

"I'm fine," Holly said. "I wanted to know who it was. I think it might be Robert Verity."

Fran stared at her. "Who? Oh, the guy Lavinia Flyte was having an affair with? Really? Why?"

"He disappeared," Holly said. "It's just a hunch, but I wondered."

Iain had waylaid Mark and they were talking to another man whom Holly did not recognise.

"That's Nick Frazer," Fran said, waving a hand towards them. "He's the bones specialist. He'll be able to date the skeleton accurately to a year or two."

Holly shrank within her coat. The wind was rising, driving the rain across the clearing. Was this where Robert Verity had died, hurrying up the path to the mill to meet Lavinia, shivering in the biting cold of winter, having lost everything that mattered to him? Had he been hoping against hope that she would be able to escape and run to him? What plans had he been making to save her, what hopes for their future together? Holly thought of the land agent, waiting in the dark, and shuddered.

"Here, get this down you." Fran passed her a mug. "You look frozen."

"Thanks, Fran," Holly said. She huddled deeper within her coat and sipped the steaming liquid. She couldn't taste it, but at least it was hot.

"Interesting," Iain said, coming over to return two empty plastic cups and pick up fresh ones. "There's a water mine down there that's been blocked up a long time. The chalk and clunch wall was unstable and we think it eroded and washed the bones through, or we might not have found them."

"Are they going to bring the body out?" Fran asked.

"Once it's been photographed in situ," Iain said. "Mark's going down there with Nick. He'll do a quick recce of the tunnel as well, whilst Nick examines the bones."

"No!" Before she could help herself, Holly had started forwards, dropping her coffee on the grass. The fear she had felt was instinctive and powerful. "He can't," she said. Then seeing Fran's look of astonishment, "Mark can't go down there. I mean… It's dangerous… There's water and the tunnels might be unstable…"

Mark had half turned when she had cried out and now he came across to her taking both her hands in his, regardless of their audience. "Are you OK?" he asked. Fran's expression had moved on from surprise to intense speculation.

"Yeah." Holly made an effort to pull herself together. "Sorry."

"I know what I'm doing." Mark's voice was very level. "It's all right, Holly. It'll be quite safe."

"I know," Holly said shakily. "I know you will. It's just…" She couldn't explain the vicious feeling of terror that had gripped her. She imagined everyone would assume she was on edge because there were too many resonances with Ben's disappearance but she knew that was not the reason. The emotion that had seized her had been all about Mark and how she felt about him. Or were they her feelings? Was she confusing Lavinia's passion for Robert with her own emotions? She no longer knew.

"Just be careful, all right?" she said, fiercely.

Their eyes met and Mark nodded, unsmiling.

They had put a rope ladder over the side of the well. Holly

watched as first Nick Frazer and then Mark went down. There was a palpable sense of tension around the group now.

"Well," Fran said, in an impatient aside. "Do you want to tell me what all that was about?" She paused and when Holly did not immediately reply she said: "If you tell me now you're not in love with him, Holly Ansell, I'll call you a liar to your face."

Iain's radio crackled. "Go ahead, Mark," he said.

Fran shot him a look of irritation. "Iain, this is important!"

"I can confirm it's the entrance to a water mine." Mark's voice crackled across the airwaves. "Thirty feet deep, about three foot wide, brick, arched, late seventeenth century but with later additions. The wall that blocked it up was probably early nineteenth century and not very well put together."

"Mark said that Lord Evershot was redesigning the pleasure gardens in the early nineteenth century," Holly said to Fran. If Evershot's men had been digging out the mines, she thought, there would have been no quicker and easier way to dispose of a body than in one of the pits they had already dug out. They could have taken Robert Verity and thrown him down the shaft and sealed him in there to lie alone and forgotten for two hundred years.

The radio crackled again. "We have the body." Nick Frazer's voice this time, steady and unemotional. "Hard to tell detail down here in such a dark and enclosed space. We need to bring him up." There was a pause. Holly could hear the indistinct mumble of voices in the background but not the individual words. Apprehension, anticipation, breathed gooseflesh down her spine. "Definitely male, probably about thirty years, rough dating suggests early nineteenth century." There was a pause. "Is Holly there?"

Iain passed the radio over.

"Hi, Nick," Holly said. She could feel herself holding her breath.

"Mark said to tell you that you were right," Nick said. "There's a pentant here, lying underneath the body. We think it must have been in his pocket before the material rotted away. It's a type of navigational instrument," he added. "The sort a surveyor would use and it dates from about 1800. Oh, and I would say he was definitely murdered. There's a blow to the head that would have killed him instantly."

37

They buried Robert Verity in Ashdown churchyard on a grey afternoon a week later when the trees that sheltered the plot were tossed by a cold wind from the northeast. The grave was in a corner, sheltered by a group of sarsen stones that had made up the circle of megaliths called the Sistrin.

A number of Mark's colleagues attended including the team who had raised Robert Verity's body from the pit. Mark had researched Robert's army record and requested military honours, and he was buried with the union flag draped on his coffin. Holly had loved Mark for that; for the care and thought he had put into making special this loneliest of farewells for a man out of his time. Even so, it felt sad and sombre, and Holly huddled under Fran's black umbrella as the rain started to fall. She watched Mark's face; he looked forbiddingly handsome today in his black funeral clothes and she wondered suddenly how many times he had stood beside a grave for a fallen comrade. She slid her hand into the crook of his arm and he covered it with his and gave her a faint smile.

"I wonder what his family thought," Fran said as they walked slowly back down the uneven path, through the black iron gates and out into the car park. "Robert Verity wasn't an orphan, was he? There must have been people who wondered what had happened to him after he just disappeared."

Holly had been thinking about that too. She had not told Fran, or anyone else other than Mark, that she thought it was Lord Evershot who had murdered Robert Verity since she could not explain how she knew, but on the basis of the remains and the pentant found on the body plus Lavinia's memoir, they had agreed it was likely to be him.

"The family line ended with him," Holly said. "According to the records, no one knew what had happened. He just disappeared."

"It's so sad though. For Lavinia, I mean," Fran said. "She lost the chance of a future with him, didn't she." She glanced at Holly. "I like to think they would have been happy together. From what you told me, they were soulmates, like Elizabeth Stuart and William Craven."

"That's why I'm longing to know what happened to Lavinia afterwards," Holly said, with a sigh, "but I can't find anything out."

"Why not come back to the café for a cup of tea?" Fran asked. "We could raise a toast to Robert Verity."

"I'd love to but I have to get back to work," Holly said. "I've got a commission for an anniversary present I'm working on." She hugged Fran. "I'll see you later."

Back at the mill, though, she felt restless and upset, unable to concentrate. She picked up various pieces of work, made mistakes with them and put them down in exasperation. Only a tiny slip of the drill here or a millimetre's inaccuracy there would spoil the work. Probably no one else would notice, but Holly knew and she could not sell pieces that were less than perfect.

She took Bonnie out for a long walk on the Downs, where the sharp wind was colder still and chilled her face. They passed Verity's Folly, shuttered with ivy and overgrown with nettles and grasses. Holly could not tell if her sadness was for Robert's death or because of Ben. He felt so close to her here, where she could almost hear the echo of their child-hood shouts and laughter.

Back at the watermill she managed to do a couple of hours of work, then took out her laptop intent on trying to make more progress with her investigations into the complicated tangle of relationships that had connected William Craven and Robert Verity. She was searching Internet genealogy records for the woman who had been William Craven's mistress, the one Lavinia had said had borne his illegitimate child and been Robert's great-great-grandmother. Lavinia had said that the crystal mirror had come to Robert as a family heirloom. It was a reasonable supposition then to imagine that Elizabeth had given the mirror to William Craven, and that for some reason he had given it as a gift to his mistress. Holly wondered if Elizabeth had known. The thought troubled her. Craven had by all accounts been utterly devoted to Elizabeth. How had a piece of such value, of reputed magical power, fallen out of his hands?

By dint of persistent searching rather than anything else she uncovered rumours of various mistresses during Craven's time in The Hague at the court of the Winter Queen, but only one name—Margaret Carpenter, not Margaret Verity. There was one reference to her in the 1630s and then she had disappeared. So Holly went looking for Margaret Verity instead and found a woman whose birthdate was slightly differ-ent, who had married in the late 1620s John, 3rd Lord Verity.

A note in the text of the document recorded that John Verity was rumoured to be insane but that he and Margaret had produced one son, Robert, to carry on the family name. Digging further for information, Holly found a rather florid and diverting Victorian history of the barony. The author clearly disapproved of Margaret and had referred to her as a "woman of light morals." There were, he said, rumours about her fidelity, in particular during a period of time she had spent at the court of the Winter Queen in The Hague in the 1630s.

"She was said to have consorted with a number of lovers and to have borne a son to Lord Craven, but as his lordship never made any claim on the child he was recognised as heir to the Verity title," the historian wrote frostily.

Holly closed her laptop, cutting off the bright white light from the screen. Night had fallen whilst she had been working. She had been so wrapped up in her research that she had forgotten to turn on the lamps.

She sat quietly for a while and thought about William Craven and Margaret Carpenter. So much of what she had found out could only ever be rumour and speculation. It was the secret history that slipped through the gaps of the record.

On an impulse she called up the ebook again, wanting to see if there was any reference as to what happened to Margaret Verity. She missed it on the first read-through as it was in a footnote, but on a second read she saw the tiny lettering at the bottom of the page:

"John, 3rd Baron Verity outlived his spouse by fourteen years. She died in the Great Fire of London of 1666, the only aristocrat to do so, found in her husband's house near Bridewell, overcome by smoke but without a scratch on her."

Holly stood up a little stiffly and crossed to the windows to pull the curtains closed. She snapped on a lamp and the room immediately swam into comforting light. It was impossible not to wonder whether the crystal mirror, with its reputation of bringing destruction through fire, had wreaked some kind of macabre revenge on Margaret Carpenter.

It was pouring with rain again outside, the drops beating against the old tiles of the roof, gurgling in the pipes and splashing from the mill wheel into the pond. The wind was rising too. The mill mechanism creaked and groaned like a foundering ship. Suddenly there was a crash below Holly's feet. She felt the floor shift. Bonnie woke up, raising her head, poised to bark. There was another sound, a sliding, scraping crack of wood giving way.

"Damn."

Holly knew what had happened. The increase in water over the wheel had loosened the mechanism down in the machine room below and something had come free. Perhaps a spar on the wheel had broken. It was old and rotten and she had been nagging Ben to get it fixed for years. It had happened once when she had been a child. She remembered her father opening the steps down to the cellar, the smell of old wet wood and musty cold that floated up from the dark depths, the chill that had touched her skin like clammy fingers and the thick sense of gloom like a living thing. She had vowed at the age of seven never to go down there, but now she had little choice. If she did not check the mill might flood.

Cursing under her breath she grabbed her torch from the dresser and made her way into the pantry. A trapdoor in the floor led down via an iron ladder into the machine room. That much she knew.

It was hard to lift the door. It was heavy and seemed to have stuck firmly shut. In the end she had to get a crowbar from under the sink to prise it up. Immediately there was the stench she remembered, the stagnant air and the damp cold. She pressed a hand over her face and tried not to breathe in the noxious smells. Tentatively she switched on the torch and peered down the shaft. She could see nothing below but fusty darkness. Cursing even more she leaned over the edge and shone the beam around, trying to work out where the walls were and how far down it was to the floor. It felt as though she was peering into an empty void. She knew that the sensible thing would be to climb down the iron ladder but it looked rusty and dangerous and she felt fear welling up in her throat as though she was seven again. She did not want to go down there. She did not want to see the monsters lurking in the shadows…

She told herself not to be so stupid. The police had been down here only a couple of weeks ago when they had been searching for Ben. There was nothing to fear.

Holly set her foot to the first rung of the ladder. It shifted alarmingly under her weight. She hesitated for one fatal second and by then it was too late. She felt her feet go from under her and she fell in a bone-jarring, bruising tumble, down into blackness.

Debris was falling around her, showering her, dust filling her nose and choking her. She landed hard, and with a splash. The torch, which she had been clutching for dear life, rolled away.

Grabbing it with hands that shook even more now, Holly tried to sit and promptly banged her head on what felt like a curving roof. Through the pain in her skull she forced herself to breathe calmly, hearing the blood pounding in her head and waiting for the dust to clear from her lungs. She knew she was not trapped. There was no need to panic. In a moment, when she stopped feeling so sick and dizzy, she would be able to find her way back to the hatch and scramble out.

She flicked the torch back on and looked around. The beam had never been particularly powerful and now the torch was making a disturbing hissing noise. The water must have got into it. She was afraid that the beam would flicker and go out.

The pale light picked out a roof of arched brick closer above her head than she had expected. The ladder had come away from the wall and was dangling a few feet above her head in a sickening fashion. To her right were broken spars of timber and the remains of what had once been a door. Holly had not known it was even there, let alone where it led. It looked like another water mine. The water was lapping through the jagged opening, dark and cold, rising all the time.

She shone the torch through the gap and saw a long, narrow passageway that stretched away into darkness. At the end of it was a pool of water unnaturally flat and glassy that reflected the light back at her like a mirror.

It felt then as though a breeze moved along the tunnel, ruffling the stagnant water into tiny ripples, stirring the surface to reveal something gold. Holly focussed the torch on the flash of colour and it grew stronger, floating closer, links in a chain that seemed to ebb and flow with the tide, until it washed up beside her. Holly put out a hand and touched it. The golden chain was battered and barely recognisable and the clasp, where once an enormous pearl had hung, was empty.

The edge of the beam of light caught something else then, something paler and horrible, and what looked like a face. With a strangled cry Holly recoiled, almost dropping the torch for a second time. The light flashed across an arm, hanging like a dead weight in the water, casting grotesque shadows against the brick wall of the tunnel, lapping closer all the time.

Nausea grabbed Holly. There was a sickening fear in the pit of her stomach but it was as nothing to the sudden inexplicable sense of evil that paralysed her. The presence of it grew until she felt as though she was being swallowed in darkness. She could hear the roar of water in her ears and smell the scent of death. She felt as though she was drowning, sucked down into the depths until she could no longer breathe. Her lungs were bursting. She was suffocating in water, a great flood of it racing to claim her and break over her head...

Somewhere high above her she heard Bonnie bark sharply, over and over, and the sound pulled her out of the nightmare and somehow she forced her trembling legs to move. The torch went out and she left it behind, scrambling across the waterlogged floor, reaching for the first rung of the steps, not caring that they swung wildly as she hauled herself up, desperate, shaking, thinking of nothing but the next handhold, slipping, wrenching her muscles, clinging on in desperation until finally she pulled herself out of the hatch and collapsed onto the kitchen floor.

She lay there, sick, winded, her heart pounding, whilst Bonnie licked her face. Eventually she sat up and noticed that she was completely drenched as though she had swum through a flood. She gave Bonnie a huge hug and staggered to her feet, leaving wet footprints across the floor as she ran for her phone and called the police.

This time there was nothing patronising about PC Caldwell. She had obviously been trained in how to deal with shock and how to speak to bereaved relatives. Death was something firm, something definite that she had seen and understood. It was not like missing persons where there was nothing to focus upon.

She sat at the kitchen table whilst Holly, clean and dry now but chilled to the core, lost count of the number of mugs of tea everyone put in front of her. PC Caldwell spoke softly about how sorry she was, how it seemed that the recent rains had broken through the wooden panels that had separated the machine room below from the millstream outside. She talked about tunnels and water mines and how Ben must have fallen down a shaft elsewhere and his body had remained hidden until the recent weather had set the mill race running and washed him down to the pool. The words passed over Holly in a jumble of noise.

They had taken Ben's body away and PC Caldwell had told her, trying to be kindly, no doubt, that there was not a scratch on him and they were sure it had been an accident, the chalk soil crumbling away beneath his feet on the path nearby so that he had fallen into the tunnels and been knocked unconscious and drowned in less than a foot of water.

"Just like you almost were," Fran had said, shuddering, but Holly knew there was more to it than that. She had felt the evil that enveloped her. She had sensed the destructive power of the water and the Sistrin pearl. The gold chain sat on the table beside her now. No one had commented on it because it looked like a battered old relic you might have found—and ignored—at a car boot sale. But Holly had seen it around the neck of the Winter Queen in more than one portrait with the Sistrin in the centre. She did not know where the pearl was now but she knew that Ben had had the chain with him when he had died.

The door of the mill opened and Mark came in. He came straight across to Holly and took her in his arms, holding her tight. His mouth was against her hair and his arms were close about her and Holly felt a helpless wash of love sweep through her.

"Are you all right?" Mark's hands were hard on her shoulders as he held her away to look at her face. "Holly—"

"I'm fine," Holly said, shaken as much by what she had seen in his eyes as what had happened. Mark opened his mouth to say something else but there was a step behind him, a flash of movement and Flick was there, her long fair hair hanging loose about her face in soaking strands, her expression pinched and scared.

"Flick," Mark said sharply, "I told you to stay at home—"

"I had to come," Flick said. She drew herself up, pale and defiant. "It's time I told the truth." She turned to Holly. In the silence that followed Holly noticed all the little things; that the cuffs of Flick's corduroy jacket were starting to fray, that her nails were painted but bitten down, that her slender fingers were shaking. She looked at the same time older and much younger than her nineteen years, an adult and yet simultaneously a frightened child.

Suddenly Holly knew exactly what Flick was going to say, and she started to shake too.

"Ben and I quarrelled on the night he died," Flick said. Holly saw her throat move as she swallowed convulsively. "I pushed a note under the door, asking him to meet me out on the path on the far side of the millpond. I threatened to tell his wife about us if he refused to see me."

Holly saw PC Caldwell's jaw drop and she made a grab for her notebook.

"You were having an affair with Ben?" Holly's words came out as a whisper.

"I loved him," Flick said. "I was crazy about him. He told me all about his research, how he was looking for the Sistrin pearl, and about William Craven and Elizabeth Stuart and the diary he had found belonging to that girl who was here with her lover. He said they had been soulmates, destined to be together through time and that we were the same, special, bound together. But that night—" Flick's voice caught on a sob. "I wanted to go into the woods with him but he wouldn't go beyond the pond so that he could still see the mill. He wanted to know Florence was safe. And I suddenly saw… I realised…" She gulped. "It was all a sham. Just words to seduce me, you know? It was all empty, meaningless stuff to get me into bed. He was never going to leave Tasha or risk losing his child. I was so angry with him—"

"Flick," Mark said, and there was clear warning in his voice. "Don't say anything else."

Flick's head went up.

"I didn't kill him," she said clearly. "He tried to buy me off with that—" She nodded towards the battered gold chain on the table. "Said it was special, that it had belonged to the Winter Queen. I just swore at him and shoved it back in his hand and then I ran away. And that was the last time I saw him."

There was a silence. Even PC Caldwell was sitting, pencil poised, having written nothing in her notebook at all. Holly saw her give herself a little shake and reach for her radio, speaking in a low voice, calling for backup. Fran was whiter than a ghost, her mug of tea tilting perilously, forgotten in her hand. She looked stricken and ill, and for once she had nothing to say.

Holly looked at Mark. His eyes met hers for a moment and she thought she saw the shadow of regret there, of apology.

Mark had known, she thought, and she felt a dull thud of betrayal and understanding. She could see all too clearly now why he had disliked Ben so intensely. He had known that Flick and Ben had been having an affair. He had not told her. In fact he had done a remarkable job of hiding both that knowledge and his feelings from her.

Holly got up and walked past him without a word, and went out into the dark.

38

London, May 1661

London looked so different. Elizabeth's memories were golden girlish dreams full of pageantry and pleasure; the river had glittered in endless sunlight, the tables had groaned under the weight of the feasts and the fountains had run with rose water. She had left England in love and sunshine. She returned to it under the cover of darkness, her ship slipping up the river from Gravesend. She stood on the deck despite her ladies warning her of the pernicious danger of the sea air. Here and there along the bank a light showed, but most of London was shrouded in night.

Craven had sent a carriage for her, of course, and an entire fleet of smaller coaches to carry her luggage. She smiled at the ostentatious display. He, of all men, should know how very few possessions she had left. She was tired now though and the soft cushions were very welcome to her aching bones. She had no urge to raise the blind and look out on London.

She could hear the sounds of the city, so different from The Hague. They were familiar yet strange at the same time, poignant and yet exciting, stirring up the past, promising an unknown future. So many years had gone by, so much had changed, so many loved ones lost. Craven, though, was steadfast, unchanging. Her heart eased a little at the thought that he was waiting for her.

The carriage turned and at last she leaned forwards and lifted a corner of the blind to see a long straight avenue of elms and a wide set of gates, all illuminated by torchlight. As the carriage swung into a courtyard she had the strangest illusion of grandeur, all this for her, as though she was still honoured and revered rather than the last relic of a lost generation.

A sudden shower of hail rapped on the roof and she jumped at the noise. The door swung open to reveal the cobbled yard awash. Craven himself was waiting to help her down.

"Majesty." His bow was exquisitely formal, his hand steady in hers when she, the veteran of so many more important occasions, suddenly trembled. "Welcome back to England."

"With weather such as this there can be no mistake," Elizabeth said. "November in May."

A ripple of laughter ran through the phalanx of servants drawn up behind Craven who were already shivering and sodden. Elizabeth drew her hood up and allowed Craven solicitously to usher her across the yard and in at the door of the house. She had a confused impression of a wide expanse of brick, with high doorways and elegant carving. The carpets were thick and silenced the steps. It felt warm and comfortable.

"I will take you up to your chambers, Your Majesty." With a jerk of the head Craven indicated to the servants to fall back and leave the two of them. Elizabeth noted that not by a flicker of expression did any one of them show their surprise.

"You have your servants well-trained," she said, laying a hand on his arm as they ascended the stair side by side. "Either that, or..."

"Or?"

"Or they know."

He sighed. "Elizabeth, everyone knows that we are wed. They have known it for years." There was an edge of steel beneath the smile in his voice. "All they wonder is why you refuse to acknowledge it."

Here it was, and so soon. Years ago it had been she who had pressed for the marriage. Craven never ceased to remind her of that, remind her that he had been the one who had spoken of her queenly duty, of the gossip and scandal that would inevitably follow were she to wed a commoner. She had ridden roughshod over all his objections, so anxious had she been to keep him by her side. Yet she was the one who had seen fit to keep the marriage a secret for the past nineteen years.

Colour stung her face. All the warmth and comfort she had felt to see him faded. "We have spoken of this," she said. Her voice felt stiff. "You know that all I have left to me now is my royal status—"

"Which would no longer be diminished were you to admit to our marriage." He sounded weary, the same arguments rehearsed and rehashed into staleness down the years. Charles Louis had regained the Palatinate now and England had a restored monarchy. Craven saw her work as done.

She could not remember how long their first flush of passion had lasted but it had been wonderful, like rain falling on parched earth. Each time they had parted and come back together it had felt exciting, illicit, as though they really were still lovers rather than husband and wife. That passion had faded with time and age but much of the sweetness had remained. He still made her feel safe. She was still sure of his loyalty after all these years. She did not want to quarrel.

"It pains me to hear that your status is all you value," he said.

His words flicked her on the raw. "It was not my intention to belittle what you mean to me," she said.

"Yet you value your standing higher."

Her head ached sharply. She wondered how it had come to this. She did not understand why he could not see her point. She wondered if it was sheer masculine pride that blinded him to the fact that she had a greater purpose to fulfil; that as a queen her place was on a grander stage than he could offer. She remembered the French ambassador's words to her when she had left The Hague. He had told her that her role now was to secure affection for the whole of the royal family, for her nephew Charles, so newly come back into his kingdom, his grip on the throne still insecure. She had to charm those who did not yet know her and remind those who remembered her that she was still the Queen of Hearts.

When she did not reply, Craven said, a little dryly:

"I think that you underestimate my popularity here in the capital. A public acknowledgement of our marriage might burnish your status rather than lessen it."

She knew that there was some truth in that. He was a hero and their story was a romantic one. People were sentimental. Charles would give him titles and honours, perhaps even a dukedom. Yet at the end of it he would still be the son of a cloth merchant and she would still be too proud to wish to be reminded of that. It was strange how her mother's barbs still stung after so many years. She could imagine Queen Anne standing here now, taunting her for her choices. When first she had married Frederick, Anne had mocked her for choosing a mere prince. Now her second husband was a man whose fortune was built on sheep.

The old slights still had the power to hurt. Ten years or more ago she had heard gossip at her court that Craven had paid her late brother fifty thousand pounds for her hand in marriage and she had been incensed to be spoken of as though she was some cheap bargaining chip in a loathsome deal made for men and arms. It had been the first time she had regretted their marriage and something had been broken that day that she could never get back.

Yet through war and bloodshed, the loss of brother, sons, more friends than she could care to count, all the seemingly endless trials that life had put her through, Craven had stood by her.

"Let us not speak of this now," she said. "I am tired and it is late."

She saw a grim little smile touch his lips and alongside the tiredness felt almost a desperation that matters were so awry so soon. This was a homecoming. It should have been happy.

A servant was approaching down the stairs; there was no time or opportunity to talk even had she wanted to do so. Lack of privacy had always been a saving grace as well as a curse.

"Of course, madam." Craven, the consummate courtier now, opened the door of a suite of rooms at the top of the stair. "These are your chambers. I trust that you will be very comfortable here."

Materially, there could be no doubt about it. There were formal reception rooms with exquisite plasterwork, a boudoir hung in pale green velvet, dressing room and bedchamber, richly carpeted, the warmth of the fires blazing. Here there were no threadbare covers or battered furniture to mock her poverty. There was even a replica of the hunting tapestry from the palace at Rhenen, made new in vivid colours.

For a moment she could not believe it and she felt the tears sting her throat.

"Oh!"

"Do you like it?" Craven looked boyishly pleased with himself, all ill temper gone now. "I asked an artist fellow to sketch it and had the design made up here in London."

Elizabeth ran her fingers over it, feeling the thickness of the weave, taking in the brightness of the colours. It was like looking back through a window onto a life that had gone. She was not sure if it made her feel happy or sad.

"You are so kind." That at least she could say with all sincerity.

Her ladies were coming now. She could hear their voices upraised in pleasure as they marvelled over the luxury of their new accommodation.

"You had better go," she whispered to him.

Once, she thought, he would have argued. He would have shot the bolt, taken her in his arms, made love to her. Now, with exquisite formality, he took her hand in his and kissed it like a courtier, and then he was gone.

39

The police were questioning Flick. Mark had stayed with her for moral support. Holly went out into the walled garden, through the picket gate and out to the millpond. Now that it had started raining again there was a pool of water lying in the dip, its silver surface reflecting the moon. It seemed odd to Holly that there could be so little water here when it had flowed fast enough through the mill race to break the wall down and wash Ben's body back. But she was not entirely sure now that there had been a flood. It had sounded like one. It had felt like one, but when the police had gone down in the cellars there was only a puddle. Not enough to drown her. Not enough to cause so much damage.

Holly sat down on a huge sarsen stone, put her hand in her pocket and drew out the golden chain. She could remember seeing it in one of Elizabeth's portraits, the Sistrin glowing in the clasp. Now the pearl was gone but it seemed its power remained in the chain that had bound it.

Well, it had not taken her but it had wrought destruction. Holly looked out across the wood. For so long she had linked Ben's disappearance consciously or unconsciously to the magic of the mirror and the pearl. It was a shock to see that actually it had come about through the destructive power of love, just as Robert Verity's death had. Flick had loved Ben desperately. Holly could see that now. Flick, struggling and unstable, knew no half measures when it came to love. She was not like Holly, careful to take no risks, to avoid hurt. Holly remembered the grief she had seen in Flick's eyes when she had come to the studio and the studied carelessness with which she had always asked if there was any news of Ben. She must have been tormented in so many different ways. Fragile, alone, carrying a secret she was too afraid to share... Holly felt so furious, so lost and angry, yet she could not sustain her anger with Flick. It was like hating a butterfly.

But Ben... Ben had not been the good guy she had thought him. The sick anger rose in her. She wondered how she could have been so blind. Tasha had told her Ben had been having an affair and Holly believed her to be mistaken. Worse she had thought Tasha disloyal and uncaring. She remembered her sister-in-law's brief softening into tears that day at the mill when she had come to collect Flo. Now she understood that Tasha's tears had been as much for the loss of something irreplaceable as they had been born of anger with her husband. Even Hester had not been unaware of Ben's faults but Holly had not listened to what her grandmother was saying. She had ignored their doubts because she had been so sure. She had had absolute faith in him.

There was a step behind her and she turned to see Mark walking slowly towards her. He stopped a good distance away and she understood that.

"Is Flick OK?" Holly asked. "Have the police finished talking to her?"

She saw the flash of expression in Mark's eyes, the surprise behind the utter exhaustion. "She's doing all right," he said. "Thank you." He drove his hands into his pockets. "They've almost finished. I'm going to take her home in a minute."

Holly nodded. She turned away to look back across the wood.

"I knew Flick and Ben were having an affair," Mark said. "I'm sorry I didn't tell you."

Holly felt a great weariness fill her. It was laced with pain. "Why didn't you?" she asked.

"If I had believed for a moment that Flick knew what had happened to Ben I would have told you," Mark said. "I would have told the police even though it would have killed me to do it. I'd asked her if she had seen him that night and she denied it and I believed her."

"I know it wouldn't have made any difference to the fact that he was dead," Holly said numbly, "but if Flick had told the police where she had last seen Ben it might have helped them find his body." She looked up at him. "I'm trying, Mark. I'm really trying not to be angry but..." Her voice shook. "You *knew* how I felt. I was in pieces! Every time that damned phone rang I hoped..." She stopped and took a breath, trying to calm herself. "Why didn't you say? I even asked you if you disliked him!" She jumped up, the fury in her suddenly a bright and vivid thing. "I gave you the chance to tell me," she said, "and you weren't honest with me."

"No," Mark said. His tone was flat. "I wasn't honest with you. I hated Ben. He was having an affair with my kid sister, knowing how vulnerable she was, knowing he was married and that Flick was burning up with the desperation of loving him. I asked him to leave her alone. I practically begged him. Hell, I wanted to kill him myself." He shifted; ran a hand through his hair. "Sorry, but I did. Especially when he told me that he loved Flick—but not enough ever to leave Tasha and Florence to be with her. That's not love, at least not in my book. He was cheating all of them."

There was a silence but for the soft splash of the water over the mill wheel.

"I do understand that," Holly said, after a moment. "Of course I do." She felt cold inside with the knowledge of the depth of her brother's betrayal. Flick had got herself into a terrible situation but Ben was more culpable in her eyes because he had been older, married, a father... His disloyalty was everything Holly hated and suddenly she was struggling with such anger and misery that she had to press a hand to her mouth to keep the tears in because she didn't want to cry in front of Mark, not now, perhaps not ever again.

It was too late. Mark had heard the catch in her breath and she realised that she had no defences against him. She was completely vulnerable. She had let herself trust him. She loved him. She could not hide.

"Holly." Mark's voice was rough. "This was why. This was why I didn't tell you." She heard him sigh. His tone softened. "You had Ben on a pedestal from the first," he said. "He didn't belong there. He was human and fallible like the rest of us. But I felt I couldn't tell you all that. I didn't want to strip away your illusions about Ben when you were so desperate not to lose him."

You had Ben on a pedestal...

Tasha, Holly thought dully, had said the same thing. Guy too, and even Hester. But she had not been listening. She had not wanted to listen.

"You shouldn't have protected me," she said dully. "I'm a big girl. I would've been able to cope. I always cope on my own."

"I don't doubt it," Mark said. "You're strong and you're brave, Holly Ansell. One thing I know now, one thing I learned fast, was that you are nothing like your brother. But I didn't want to hurt you. And I didn't *want* you to be on your own. I wanted you to be with me. So," he said, shrugging, "I made a mistake."

"Yes," Holly said. "Yes, we both did." She looked up. "You'd better get back to Flick. She really does need you."

Mark looked at her for a very long moment and then he nodded. When she looked back he had gone.

Ben's funeral was as different from Robert Verity's as it was possible to imagine. The church was packed with people and it felt to Holly more like a social gathering than an occasion for mourning. A lot of Tasha's celebrity friends were there looking cool in black, wearing dark glasses. The press were encamped outside.

Holly knew that Hester and John were finding it difficult. This was not a farewell to a grandson they knew, it was like the funeral of a stranger, usurped by people who did not know him.

Holly had already let go of one aspect of her brother's memory. Ben had not been the man she had believed him to be. Mark had been right: she had set him on a pedestal and refused to see any wrong in him and that had blinded her to what he had truly been. Now that those illusions were gone she could see Ben had been a man like any other, a man who had made mistakes, had got himself in too deep, perhaps. She had felt more kindly towards him after that, her bitterness and anger with him settling into regret. Love was starting to edge back around the corners of her feelings for him. In time, she hoped, she would be able to think of him with generosity again as well as love.

She drove Hester and John back to Oxford after the service, before returning to Ashdown. It was the open house that night at Mark's building development, and she was determined to be there. There were things she had to say to him.

First, though, she had a quest to complete.

Back at the mill she changed out of her black trousers and jacket and into her work clothes, and went along to the studio. The rain was heavier now, drumming on the roof in an insistent beat, dripping from the gutters onto the path outside.

Holly switched the lights on, flooding the workshop with artificial brightness. She had everything she needed—gloves, an artist's respiratory mask, chemicals, a hammer, a screwdriver. On her workbench lay the crystal mirror with its false diamonds dull, its reflection opaque. Eleanor Ferris had sent it back to her a few days previously with a long report. Since then, Holly had been racking her brains as to what to do with it. She had thought that perhaps the correct thing to do would be to send it back to Espen Shurmer along with the golden chain, but she hesitated to do that. Shurmer had wanted the mirror preserved, reunited with the Sistrin pearl, but Holly knew deep in her heart that that would be too dangerous. She had to destroy the mirror before it could wreak any further harm. She did not know if she would ever find the pearl but she did know the mirror and pearl could not be allowed to coexist. Taking up the screwdriver she inserted it between the glass and the frame, carefully prying the two apart. The glass came out with surprising ease, lifting free. Holly placed it carefully on a piece of lint-free cloth. It was exquisite, perfectly cut, as clear and unblemished as the day it had been made.

She realised that she had been holding her breath as though expecting something to happen. She had expected it to defend itself. Yet it lay quiescent on the cloth. It was almost as though it knew its time had come.

Slowly, methodically, Holly applied paint stripper to the silvering on the back of the glass. She had expected it to take hours for the silvering to peel away and yet it seemed to dissolve almost instantly, melting, disappearing and leaving very little trace. She washed the glass again, in distilled water this time. She was not sure why she was going to so much trouble when she was going to smash it and yet it seemed important to make it beautiful again.

She picked up the little hammer. The crystal mirror was no longer a mirror. It was a piece of wood and a piece of glass, the two parts separate now, unable to reflect anything, the future or the past, for good or evil. Holly raised the hammer intending to bring it down with the slightest of taps that she knew would smash the glass to smithereens.

She paused. For a brief second the glass seemed to shimmer before her eyes, dazzlingly bright. She lowered the hammer. This was Bohemian crystal, over three hundred years old. She could not break it. It would be a criminal thing for an engraver to do, a betrayal of her craft.

As she stared at the glass a picture started to form in her mind, a rose with eight petals on a slender stem, fragile and beautiful. She could take the glass and etch the symbol of the Knights of the Rosy Cross on it as a memorial. She could turn the mirror from an object of power and danger into something beautiful. She would change its purpose and give it new life.

The glass started to glow again then, ripples of flame running across its surface. Holly saw the flash of images like the flickering of an old black and white film: men hooded and cloaked within a ring of fire, Ashdown Park burning... Cold ate into Holly's bones and she gave a convulsive shudder.

She raised the hammer and brought it down hard and the glass shattered into a million fragments.

40

Her nephew Charles came to visit her. Once he knew that he would not be required to make any financial provision for her he was quick to pay his respects. It amused Elizabeth to see how attentive he could be when he saw how much her popularity grew with each passing day. Where he called others followed. It was a virtuous circle and soon she was dining with the Duke of Ormonde at Kensington and visiting Lady Herbert at Hampton Court, receiving calls from ambassadors, going to the theatre or to masques at court. It was pleasant enough; she disliked the licentiousness of the court and thought her nephew a lecher but she was old, a different generation, and her values were not theirs. Rupert was in England too. He had returned before she had, in fact, and was a popular member of his cousin's circle. The ladies adored him and it was, Elizabeth thought, mutual.

Craven House was a cocoon of luxury. There was a garden

to walk in on the fine days and a library to read in on the inclement ones. She was pampered. She wanted for nothing. It was easy to sink into the pleasure of it.

Craven was building again. He had his estates restored to him now, and he had lost no time in starting a grand plan of improvement. The scale of his ambition was dazzling.

One day he brought two men to see her. She was tired that day with a headache and a sharp pain in her chest that stole her breath. She was little inclined to meet strangers but when she saw them she realised that she had met them both before, in The Hague. Sir Balthasar Gerbier was the consummate courtier, wily, charming, slippery as a fish. Gerbier was all things to all men: courtier, spy, diplomat, artist and now an architect. With him was a youth Elizabeth remembered, Craven's godson and, at one time, a page in her household. Captain William Winde was diffident where Gerbier was expressive, stolid where Gerbier was quicksilver. Yet of the two men she far preferred him.

"Gerbier and Captain Winde are to build you a house," Craven said, drawing Winde forwards whilst Sir Balthasar flourished a ridiculous bow and kissed her hand. "I have an estate in Berkshire, at Hamstead Marshall. It was once a royal demesne and it will be again. We plan—"

"A palace!" Gerbier exclaimed. "A marvel to rival the beauty of your castle in Heidelberg, Majesty! Magnificent!"

"You expressed a wish to live peacefully in the country." Craven was looking pleased with himself. Her wish truly was his command. She felt a flash of irritation that Craven thought her so easy to please, and then reproached herself for her ingratitude.

"I did," she said. It had been a careless remark when she had been tired one day, her bones aching from the damp of a dismal London in the autumn rain.

"There is to be a hunting lodge too. You love hunting," Craven reminded her. He beckoned Winde forwards. The young captain unfolded a set of papers, spreading them across the walnut table, moving aside the book Elizabeth had been reading.

"Ashdown Park," Craven said. "It is set in the best hunting country. It will be built from chalk, white like your mother's palace at Greenwich, your Majesty."

"It looks top heavy," Elizabeth said, staring at the drawing of a tall, square house with four floors and a roof terrace. On the top was a dainty-looking cupola with a very big gold ball. How like Craven to crown his plans in gold.

"It is pretty," she said quickly, seeing Winde flush red. "Like a doll's house."

"It is the latest style, Your Majesty." Gerbier had pushed the younger man aside and was pointing enthusiastically to the plan. "The continental influences… See, we have pediments and a balustrade and the hipped roof—"

"Like the Wassenaer Hof," Elizabeth said, and felt a prick of nostalgia. She smiled at Winde. "I like it. I shall look forward to seeing how your plans progress, Captain. Sir Balthasar."

It was a dismissal. Both architects looked disappointed. Did they expect her to talk about stone and mortar, architraves and quoins? But Craven had not noticed her lassitude. He was still enthused.

"Perhaps in the spring we could pay a visit," he said, "and see how the building work progresses. They have opened the quarry already, and are taking sarsen stone too, for the foundations, from an old fort across the fields…"

Elizabeth was not listening. Spring seemed far away. She liked London. She did not want to be immured in the country, where nothing happened. She had had forty years of living an empty life. If she moved to Berkshire everyone would forget her, whereas here she was celebrated and courted and it was very fine.

"In the spring," she said. "Yes, let us go. Of course." And she knew she would not.

41

The building development looked completely different from how it had been in the days running up to the open house. Then there had been an air of mild panic. Dust sheets were still on the floor and over some of the furniture. Last minute paint had been applied and tiles grouted. To-night, though, the wide gates of the former stable yard were flung open and lanterns lit the way to the show houses. It looked exactly what it was: elegant, luxurious, new life given to wonderful old buildings. Holly could feel the buzz of excitement in the air as she made her way across to the entrance. Ideally she should have arrived earlier to dress the house but she doubted that Mark expected her to turn up at all. She had butterflies in her stomach at the thought of seeing him. There was so much to say. She hoped he would want to hear it but she could not be sure.

She had brought Bonnie with her. When she and Mark had discussed the open house they had agreed that Bonnie would add the final touch, lying picturesquely in pride of place in front of the Aga on the stone-flagged kitchen floor in the converted laundry house. Bonnie could turn a house into a home.

Most of the guests had not yet arrived and through the lighted windows Holly could see Fran and Paula setting up the buffet. She clutched her cardboard bags of vases and paperweights nervously and knocked at the door. A harassed looking PA let her in and directed her to the cloakroom, leaving her free to wander around placing the glass where it would show to advantage and also enhance the setting, an engraved panel here, with the light shining through, a paperweight there, elegantly placed on a wooden windowsill.

She stowed her bags and took Bonnie away from the temptations of Fran and the canapés. Guests were starting to arrive now. Holly knew Mark was out in the hall greeting them and she stayed out of sight. She didn't want to ruin his big night. Later there would be time to talk.

It got busy quickly. People dropped in to ask her about her work. A tutor from the local college gave her his card and asked her to call about running a course in their art and design department. One of Mark's competitors suggested that in future she dress their show homes instead and offered an outrageous sum of money to poach her. Several people took her cards and promised to ring for commissions. Everyone admired the dog.

It was an hour later when she saw Flick come in, sipping a glass of champagne, looking pale and ethereal in a silver shift dress. She was chatting animatedly to Joe but her eyes were tired. Holly wondered if she had not been sleeping. Today, the day of Ben's funeral, must have been particularly difficult for her, having no part, staying away, pretending.

Holly had guessed Flick might be there and had been on the lookout for her; she knew she needed to speak to her first, even before she talked to Mark. Suddenly, though, she felt inadequate, afraid to say the wrong thing. Flick was looking both stricken and terrified and Joe was watching them warily, and suddenly Holly understood that this wasn't about her and that nothing except unconditional love would be enough to reassure Flick. Holly wasn't demonstrative, she never had been except with closest family and friends, but she put her own glass down with a snap and walked over to Flick and hugged her tightly.

She felt Flick's surprise melt within three seconds and then she was hugging her back so tightly that Holly thought she might choke.

"Hey," she said, feeling Flick's hot tears scald her neck, "stop that. You look too good to ruin your mascara."

Flick gulped and laughed and hugged her again, and then Joe was smiling and stooping to kiss her and Flick was talking and wiping the streaks of make-up off her cheeks. When Mark walked in they didn't see him for a moment and then Flick stopped talking and Holly looked up. She felt a moment of panic.

"Holly," Mark said, "I didn't think you would come." His tone was careful, guarded.

Holly raised her chin. "I said I'd be here," she said. "I don't let my clients down."

She saw a flicker of amusement in Mark's dark eyes. "That's very professional of you," he said gravely.

"Also," Holly said, taking a quick breath, feeling her heart start to hammer, "I need to talk to you. I know it can't be now, but maybe later?"

"Why not now?" Mark said.

Holly felt her stomach drop. All around them the party buzzed with excitement, voices and laughter. She waved an arm around to encompass the room and everything beyond. "Because of *this*," she said. "Because it's important—"

"Some things are more important," Mark said. He caught her wrist. "Come with me."

"I'll look after Bonnie for you," Flick called after them.

"And I'll look after the guests," Joe said. "Especially the good-looking women."

Mark steered her across the stable yard to the corner where the estate office sat in darkness. Moonlight lay across their path, broken by the scudding clouds and the whispering shadows of leaves. It was quiet, the sounds of the party floating across to them from a distance. Mark held the office door open for her and Holly walked inside and immediately felt enveloped in the past. The slow ticking of the clock could have been any time. The light from the lamp illuminated a corner of the room with warmth.

Mark waited for her to speak with the same contained stillness she had grown to know, but this time there was the burn of emotion in his eyes and the line of his shoulders was tense. Holly wanted to touch him then, but there were things she had to say first.

"I wanted to say that you were right," she said. "I did idolise Ben. I couldn't see any wrong in him." She hesitated. "I'm sorry, Mark. It must have been absolute hell for you, knowing what was going on, wanting to protect Flick. Then I came along, asking questions, stirring things up. I'm surprised you even spoke to me when you realised who I was."

Mark shook his head. "It wasn't like that," he said. "I liked you from the start." He gave her a look. "Hell, that must have been quite obvious. But you were struggling so hard with Ben's disappearance. I admired how gallant you were and I felt I couldn't do anything to destroy the belief you had in him." He sighed. "Bad decision."

"I've made mistakes too," Holly said shakily. "I tried to keep you at arm's length because I was scared of what there was between us. It was there from the start, the chemistry and the sense of connection. I just didn't want to face it because I was scared of risking everything and losing it again."

"Sweetheart—" Mark smoothed the hair away from her hot face. "You had reason."

"But in the end logic and reason don't make you happy," Holly said. Her voice wobbled. "I love you. If you still want us to have a relationship…" She stopped.

"Yes," Mark said, before she had barely finished speaking. "I do." He pulled her to him. His mouth came down on hers.

"I love you too," he said against her lips. He pulled her close into his side, his arms around her, her head resting in the curve of his shoulder.

"Hell, Holly," he said, his mouth against her hair. "If only you knew."

Holly tilted her head up to look at him. "Knew what?"

"What it's been like for me," Mark said. "From the very first moment I saw you."

That stole Holly's breath. She shook her head slightly, bemused. "What do you mean?"

"I felt it too," Mark said. "The sense of recognition, the affinity." He pushed a hand through his hair. "It was a shock," he said mildly. "I'd been down here a few years, I'd had PTSD and got wasted, I'd lost my marriage and taken on looking after my siblings. I'd foolishly thought nothing else could happen…" He spread his hands in a gesture of surrender, "and then I saw you and this feeling just hit me. It was as though I knew you, as though I'd always known you. It felt as though somewhere along the line I'd lost you and as soon as I saw you I wanted you back."

He pulled her down to sit next to him on the old sofa.

"But you were Ben's sister," he said. "And Ben was missing and Flick was all messed up… I told myself it was better to keep my distance. Except that I couldn't. I'd never felt such a strong physical attraction to anyone. At first I tried to pretend that was all it was, but I knew it was more."

This kiss held everything; gratitude, passion, promise for the future.

"Come on," Holly said, taking Mark's hand, pulling him to his feet. "We have to get back to the open house."

She held him tightly and for once she did not think of the past. This was her choice, to be with Mark, here, now. This was her life to live. She remembered her grandfather telling her to be brave, and smiled.

42

London, January 1662

The theatre at Salisbury Court was full that night with the audience preening and jostling like so many peacocks in the boxes and galleries. Elizabeth loved the noise, the dazzle and the excitement. This was what she enjoyed about London; it was alive. There was light, music and spectacle enough to entertain her forever. No need to dwell on all she had lost. This was her restoration too, just as it was Charles'.

The opera was *The History of Sir Francis Drake* by Sir William Davenant. Elizabeth thought it an amusing if slight piece, the dashing Sir Francis painted in heroic light through his adventures off the coast of South America. The music was rousing, but the audience was there as much to be seen as to watch or listen. The candlelight reflected on the radiance of jewels and the blush of satin. They chattered, restive and shifting, like a sea of iridescence.

Seated to Elizabeth's left, Craven seemed enthralled and

heartily entertained. His enthusiasm was childlike and endearing. Hers was waning as the play progressed and she started
to entertain herself instead by seeing how many of the audience she could name. She had not been back in London
long but her acquaintance was extensive. Hertford, Killigrew,
the Castlemaines... Her gaze slid to the woman at Barbara
Castlemaine's side. There was something familiar about her,
something in the upward angle of the neck, something in that
fading blonde prettiness, the ringlets too young a style for her.
She thought it was a face from her time in The Hague—yet
that was odd because all those men and women who had been
a part of her court had hastened to visit her at Craven House.
This woman had not.

The woman raised her gaze to meet Elizabeth's and to hold
it. A small smile played about her mouth. With the slightest,
most stealthy of gestures she slid her hand into her pocket
and took something out. For a moment Elizabeth could not
see what it was amidst the soft pink folds of her gown. Then
there was a sparkle, a dazzling flash of light. Across the theatre, across time, the crystal mirror shone, the diamonds in
the frame bragging their ancestry, the crystal itself glowing
with the inimical light she remembered.

Elizabeth felt cold; faint. She stared. There could be no
mistake. Beside her Craven laughed at some wit in the play
but she could not copy the audience's roar of humour. The
sounds came to her from far, far away. Her face felt stiff. She
could not smile. It felt as though her heart had stopped. The
mirror, here, some twenty-five years after Craven had sworn
it had been destroyed.

Then she remembered. The woman. Margaret Carpenter.
The mistress she had tried not to hate because it was beneath
her dignity as a queen. There had been a rumour that Craven had wanted to wed Margaret before he had discovered

she was already married. Had the mirror been his love token to her? Had he rescued it from Frederick's grave and sworn it was destroyed only to give it to this woman so lightly, so carelessly?

The chill seemed to have seeped into every inch of Elizabeth's body. She could not hear the words of the opera. The music and laughter faded. She was trapped within the dazzling spiral of the mirror that she had thought dead and gone and now found to be alive. The misfortunes of the past years toppled over her then like a flood. Three of her sons lost, her brother's kingdom all but ripping itself apart, lands and dominions burned into barrenness, everything lost and so much death and slander and grief.

She felt such a fool. Through it all she, blinded by trust in Craven's loyalty, had believed his protestations that the curse of the mirror and the pearl had been lifted. She had thought the mirror destroyed and the bond broken.

She had to get out. Suddenly the heat of the theatre, the press of the bodies, the smell of humanity was too much for her. She struggled to her feet. Immediately Craven stood too, all gallantry, solicitous for her comfort. She could not look at him.

She barely waited for the carriage door to close on them before she burst into speech. It was not calm and dignified. She sounded like a fishwife in the market.

"That woman… Your *whore*… She has the mirror. I saw it. She has the mirror of crystal that was once mine!"

She saw Craven flush with confusion; he looked utterly bewildered and she wanted to scream at him.

"Margaret." She gasped a breath. Her heart was hammering. Or perhaps it was breaking. She was not sure. There was such pain in her but the fear of the mirror was eclipsed utterly by her sense of betrayal. "Do you remember her?" She bit the words out like poison. "The woman you wanted to *marry*? The one you gave my mirror?"

She saw the precise moment that understanding slid into his eyes. He turned ashen.

"I thought—" He stopped. "I thought she had sold it."

So he did not even have the wit to deny it. The carriage rumbled and jerked through the streets, making her feel sick.

"You gave it to her," she said.

"She took it to pay for her carriage back to England."

"Back to present her husband with your bastard child."

He said nothing. She could feel the jealousy welling up in her, the spite that she had tried so hard to master all those years ago in The Hague. She had thought those dark emotions banished by love and trust, but now the trust was broken.

"It was all a lie," she said. "My faith in you."

"Elizabeth," Craven said. "Don't be foolish."

She could feel everything starting to unravel now but the fury was alight in her like a fire consuming everything in its path. She was seduced by it; it felt good to find a reason for all the misfortune, to know who and what to blame. This was the explanation for the disaster that had blighted their cause.

"You betrayed me." She was shaking so hard her teeth were chattering. "I trusted you! You swore loyalty to me and you broke it. I had belief in you and you proved false. You knew the mirror's power—"

Craven lost his temper. "And you knew I always thought that superstitious nonsense."

"That was not your decision to make!"

Craven's hazel eyes were stormy. He grabbed her by the upper arms, his grip fierce. She winced. "Elizabeth," he said. "I gave up everything for love of you! I abandoned my allegiance to your brother's cause in order to be with you. I put you before all else, even before honour." He released her so suddenly she almost fell from the seat. "And in return—" He turned away, "you value me so little you would not even admit we are wed."

Old wounds, old grievances. They spilled their corrosive poison over everything until it withered and died. She looked at Craven's face, so familiar to her, so dear, and felt her heart snap.

The coach jerked to a halt in the courtyard of Craven House. A blank-faced servant stood ready at the door but neither of them made any move to alight.

"I must beg your hospitality for tonight at least," Elizabeth said stiffly. "On the morrow I will find some other place to go."

She saw his shock. He had never imagined it would come to this but even as he was putting out a hand to her in a last gesture of appeal she had gathered her skirts and was stepping down from the coach, turning her back on him, a queen back in her rightful place, above him, untouchable.

And the curse had completed its work.

43

"I've got something for you," Mark said. They were having a breakfast of coffee and croissants under the apple tree in the orchard garden. It was the sort of late summer day that would burn hot at noon but cool down with a hint of autumn later. The seasons were starting to turn, the trees in the wood slipping from green to gold.

"What is it?" Holly felt drowsy with warmth and love, happy and sad, all mixed up.

Mark reached for a folder he had laid on the seat next to him. "I've found Lavinia," he said. "Or rather my friend did. Harry, the genealogist?"

"You found her?" Holly put her cup down sharply. "I didn't know you were looking for her."

Mark looked shamefaced. "It seemed so important to you to know what had happened to her so I thought I'd ask Harry to try. I didn't tell you because I didn't want to get your hopes up. Harry thought the prospect was pretty unlikely. Anyway, it took him a bit of work but he got there in the end." He held the piece of paper out of her reach as she made a grab for it. "I think you'll like this. I hope so."

"Tell me then," Holly said.

"Right," Mark said. "Well first of all, you were correct that Kitty Flyte was Lavinia's daughter although by the time Kitty married into the Bayly family her mother had changed her name to Jane Flyte and long given up her first profession. She was a very successful milliner."

"Lavinia became a milliner?" Holly was so surprised her mouth fell open.

"She set up in Bath in 1802," Mark said. "She features in the trade listings every year. Very gradually she built up a respectable name and a reputable clientele. Her designs were much sought after and she made a lot of money."

"Well, I'll be damned," Holly said. Lavinia had put her sharp mind and acquisitive nature to work on making a fortune in a very different way from writing erotic memoirs. Holly felt incredibly proud of her. What a girl.

"It's expensive setting up in business," she said slowly. "I'm more sure than ever now that Lavinia sold the original diamonds from the mirror to reinvent herself and give Kitty a good education and start all over again."

"Yes," Mark said. He smiled at her. "I think you're right."

"I don't suppose we'll ever know," Holly said. "Nor whether Robert Verity was her father."

"Not for certain," Mark said, "but I'd like to think he was." He looked at the piece of paper and then up at her. "There's something else," he said slowly. "I'm not sure how you'll feel about this."

"Go on," Holly said.

"Kitty Bayly had seven children," Mark said. "Amongst them was a daughter called Helena. Her husband was a man called John Darcombe. They were a military family, quite a distinguished one. He died young, in battle, and Helena was left to bring up her young family alone." Mark was watching her face, his eyes gentle. "They continued the military tradition. The most recent Darcombe was a Brigadier. It's a name I imagine you know?"

"Yes." Holly wrapped her arms tight about her, feeling the shivers run over her skin. The world was spinning, the pattern changing, re-forming.

"Darcombe was my grandmother's maiden name," she said a little shakily. "Her father was Brigadier Robert Darcombe."

"Yes," Mark said. "You are descended from Kitty Flyte and possibly from Robert Verity too. And via him from William Craven."

Holly smiled ruefully. It was no wonder that she had not been able to find Kitty on the Ansell family tree. The descent had not been in the male line. It was all those strong women, Lavinia taking her daughter and forging a new life, Helena bringing up seven children alone, Hester taking on her orphaned grandchildren and giving them new hope, who had carried Lord Craven's legacy down to the present day.

"There's just one other small thing," Mark said. "Lavinia herself was descended from Elizabeth and Frederick of Bohemia. Henry was really chuffed when he discovered that."

Holly stared. "What? How?"

"From what I gather, Elizabeth's sons were a philandering bunch," Mark said. He grimaced. "I should know. My family were descended from one of the other lines ourselves and it wasn't a legitimate descent either, but straight down the wrong side of the blanket from Prince Rupert," Mark said. "I'd never paid much attention to the family history before all this, but…" He let the sentence hang and Holly knew what he was thinking. William and Elizabeth, Robert and Lavinia, all connected by fate and blood and destiny and spirit.

"So whom was Lavinia descended from?" she asked.

"Elizabeth and Frederick had a son called Philip," Mark said. "By all accounts he was a bit of a bad lot; he killed a man in a duel and was forced into exile and after that he became a soldier of fortune. He died in battle at only twenty-three, but not before he had fathered a child on a camp follower, a woman called Jacqueline Fleet. Fleet became Flyte over time, I guess, but there was never any hint by Lavinia's generation that they had royal antecedents."

"No," Holly said. "I imagine Lavinia would have made the most of it if she had known. She would probably have persuaded George III to have given her a pension, or something." She sighed. "I see now what Flick meant," she said, "when she said that she thought that she and Ben were part of the chain. She really believed that they were the lovers in this generation of the story. She thought they were destined to be together." Her eyes met Mark's. "I'm so sorry," she said.

"Yes," Mark said. "Poor Flick." He reached out and touched her cheek lightly. "Because she was wrong, wasn't she. There were two lovers who were destined to meet in this life, just as William and Elizabeth, and Lavinia and Robert, had done before. But it wasn't Flick and Ben."

"No," Holly whispered. She could see the pattern now, whole, beautiful. "No," she said again. "Those lovers were you and I."

Mark's fingers linked with hers, long and strong. "Shall we see if we can get it right this time?" he said.

"We can do our best," Holly said.

Flick had not been awake to share breakfast with them but now Holly saw her coming towards them down the drive, her high wedge heels scattering the gravel. This morning she was dressed down in leggings and a long shirt that was at least three sizes too big. She still managed to look elegant.

"How does she do it?" Holly sighed.

"It's in the genes," Mark said, with a smile.

Flick waved and quickened her pace, wobbling all over as though she was about to fall. She looked all leggy and edgy, like a deer, poised on the edge of flight. The whole atmosphere around her felt as though it was suffused with nervousness.

"Holly," she said, "could I have a word?"

"Of course," Holly said.

"I'll go and—" Mark waved a hand vaguely towards the house.

"No," Flick said. "Don't go, Mark. I need you to hear this."

She sat bolt upright on the very edge of the seat. She was fidgeting with something she had in her hands, a book wrapped in a plastic supermarket bag. She held it out to Holly.

"This is yours," she said. Her gaze fell. "At least...it was Ben's. He was the one who found it."

"Ben's?" Holly said. She took the parcel from her and slid the book out of the bag. The leather was smooth and worn under her fingertips. In the light it gleamed deep green. It was the same shape and size as Lavinia's diary but instead of the lavender and old dust smell of the memoir it smelled of damp and simultaneously, curiously, burning.

"Careful," Flick said, as she opened it. "It's very fragile."

Holly turned the page. She could feel her heart beating fast. The sound filled her ears. At the same time she had a strange sensation of time spinning backwards again to a March night in 1801 when Lavinia had planned to rob Lord Evershot and run away, and Robert Verity had disappeared.

The writing was practically illegible. Part charred, part blurred by water damage, it swam across the page in a riot of numbers and formulae and the odd scattered word here and there. The date 1801 and the words "January" and "downs" and "stone" were the ones that leaped out at Holly from the disintegrating pages.

"Robert Verity's notebook," she said. She looked up from the disconnected words on the page to look at Flick. "Where did you find this?"

"I took it from the mill," Flick said baldly. "I stole it." She looked at Mark. "I'm sorry, Mark." She carried on talking, quickly, jerkily, not looking at either of them. "I just wanted something of Ben's. A memento. You know what I mean. I—" She studied her hands, locking the fingers together until her knuckles gleamed white. "It was so hard, not knowing, not telling anyone. I needed something of his just to keep, to hold." A tear rolled down her cheek and she dashed it away. "I'm sorry."

Holly shifted along the seat and put her arms about her. "Hey," she said. "It's OK."

"I took it that day I came to see you about the bowl," Flick said. "I don't know where Ben found it but I knew he kept it in a drawer in the dresser." She scrubbed at her eyes. "I hope it wasn't important. The notebook, I mean."

Holly's eyes met Mark's. "No," she said. "It doesn't matter at all."

Flick put her head on Holly's shoulder and cried as though her heart would break and Holly held her tightly feeling Flick's hot tears soak her jacket. Over Flick's shoulder she could see Mark turning the pages of the book, studying diagrams in Ben's handwriting, annotations and drawings.

"I'm probably going to do this a lot." Flick drew back, sniffing. "I'm so sorry for everything. But I do love you, Holly. You are the best." Silently Mark passed her a handkerchief and she gave him a watery smile. "I'll go now," she said. Her gaze darted from one of them to the other. "I guess you have stuff to discuss."

Holly squeezed her hand. "You'll be all right?"

"Yeah," Flick said. "Thanks." She took a breath. "I'll never forget him."

"She's very lovable, your sister," Holly said, watching as Flick's slender figure walked away, head bent. "And she's very generous with her love too."

Mark took her hand. "I'm not surprised she loves you," he said gruffly. "You have been more forgiving and generous than either of us had a right to expect."

He released her. "Look at this." He handed the book to her.

Ben had created a most perfect line drawing of the house, tall, elegant, gracious with its soaring roof and little golden ball. Beneath it was a line in his neat handwriting:

"The Sistrin was concealed in the cupola."

Holly caught her breath on a gasp. "So Ben did find the pearl's hiding place," she said. "He must have worked out its location from Robert Verity's calculations."

She fumbled in the pocket of her jacket and took out the battered gold chain. "Flick said Ben tried to give this to her. She refused to take it and he had it with him when he died." She looked up and met Mark's eyes. "But where is the Sistrin itself?"

Mark smiled. "I think you'll find it's somewhere at the mill," he said. "Although perhaps not quite in the form you might expect."

"What do you mean?" Holly said.

"I think Ben found the pearl in the wine cellars," Mark said slowly. He touched the links of the gold chain very lightly. "This looks as though it's been badly damaged. You remember me telling you that the cupola fell all the way down through the house during the fire?"

"Of course," Holly said. "The pearl necklace would have

been buried under a load of rubble when the house burned down."

"The cupola falling into the cellars smashed a lot of bottles as well," Mark said. "There was red wine sediment all over the floor."

"Pearls will dissolve in wine." Holly was gripping the edge of the table tightly now. Her heart hammered in her throat as they pieced together the last elements of the story.

"Do you think the Sistrin was destroyed?" she asked.

Mark shook his head. "Not completely. But it must have been damaged and if it lay in the acidic wine for any length of time it would change colour and lose its lustre—" He stopped. "What is it?"

"I know where it is," Holly said shakily. "I found it the very first day I came to Ashdown but I didn't realise…" She was thinking of the little secret compartment in the window seat in the bedroom and the misshapen yellow stone she had found in it.

The day was quiet, but for the call of the birds in the trees and the run of the stream.

There was silence between them for a couple of moments and then Holly started to laugh.

"It is the ultimate irony," she said. "There was Lord Evershot looking all over the estate for clues to the hiding place and all the time the Sistrin was above his head. Literally. And he never knew."

She stood up, scooping the Sistrin's chain into her hand. "There's something I need to do," she said. "Come with me?"

They walked back to the mill together. Mark waited by the door as Holly went up to the bedroom, opened the lid of the window seat and reached in to take out the pearl. It sat in her palm, shrunken and yellow, without light or lustre, its beauty lost. Yet Holly knew that the sheen of it might have gone but the power remained.

They walked over to the gate and both leaned their elbows on it. The Ash Brook ran alongside the track here and, Holly could hear the soft splash of the water. Soon the mill-pool would be full again and next summer the dragonflies would return and the parched earth would turn the lush green she remembered from her childhood.

When she had first come to Ashdown Park she had not imagined that she would be here to see the summer come around. She had not thought that far ahead. She had not wanted to, she had not dared. Half in fear, half in hope she had perhaps believed that Ben would have come back by then and she would be back in the city where she belonged, with the noise and the people and the rain splashing onto hot pavements and making them smell of dust.

She looked at Mark who was resting one elbow on the gate now and gazing out across the stubble fields where the rising sun was turning the mist to gold. He turned and looked back at her but he did not smile and she knew this was where her final choice was to be made.

She waited; listened, and felt love, like a fall of petals against her cheek again, and she heard a whisper:

"Be happy." It was Lavinia's voice, Lavinia's last gift to her. She took Mark's hand and held it tightly.

I will love you until the end of time.

They did not speak for a long time. When Mark finally let her go Holly took the Sistrin's chain and held it for a moment in the palm of her hand, nestling next to the pearl.

"I think Elizabeth would want it to be destroyed," she said.

Mark nodded. "Close the pattern," he said.

They walked a little way down the track to where the brook plunged beneath a small stone bridge. Holly threw the chain and the pearl as far and as hard as she could over the edge and into the water. For a moment the sunlight gleamed on gold and then it disappeared. When she leaned her hands on the worn stone of the parapet and looked down into the water there was nothing. Both the chain and the pearl had gone.

"The current runs fast here," Mark said. "There's a spring that joins the stream just by the bridge. Legend has it that the water comes up from the heart of the earth. If anything has magic..." He paused. "Well, I'd say that it was this water."

He put his arm about her and Holly rested her head against his shoulder, feeling the strong and steady beat of his heart.

"It's over, isn't it?" she said.

"No," Mark said. He bent to kiss her. "It's just beginning."

44

She dreamed about the house on the night before she died.
In the dream she felt as insignificant as a child, a miniature
queen clad in a cream silk gown embroidered with gold. The
collar prickled the nape of her neck as she craned her head to
gaze up, up at the dazzling white stone of the house against
the blue of the sky. It made her dizzy. Her head spun and the
golden ball that adorned the roof glittered and plunged like
a shooting star falling to earth.

She knew now that she would never see it. Her story finished here in the lonely luxury of Leicester House. The cavalcade of crowns and glory, exile and defeat, love and loss was
at an end. First, though there was something she had to do.

She knew now, at the last, that love was the most powerful magic of all.

She sent for William Craven. She entrusted the pearl to
his hand with her undying love. And so her story closed and
a new one opened.

★ ★ ★ ★ ★

*Keep reading for an advance look at
Nicola Cornick's new novel,*

THE PHANTOM TREE

HOUSE
OF
SHADOWS

NICOLA CORNICK

Reader's Guide

GRAYDON
HOUSE

The story of the secret marriage of the Winter Queen and her devoted cavalier

It was the house that was the start of it all. It sits beside a lonely road over the hills, nestling down in a hollow in the woods. You drive past and see a quick flash of tall white walls and the golden dome on the roof shining in the sun, then it's gone. For years I would pass by and wonder about that house and its history. Although it was open to the public to visit, it never seemed open on the days I was free and so it remained a mystery to me.

Then I left my office job to become a full-time writer and I was looking around for things I could do alongside my writing. I liked to get out and meet people and I loved history. An advertisement caught my eye—the National Trust needed people to act as guides at Ashdown House. I signed up. So began my long love affair with Ashdown.

There's something about Ashdown and its history that captures you as soon as you walk through the door. It's a little gem of a house, tiny, a perfect square, built on the four cardinal points of the compass. It has a stunning marble-and-white-stone hallway leading to a huge oaken stair that ascends four flights to the roof, and on the top sits a little glass cupola topped with the golden ball. It's like a doll's house or something from a fairy tale.

Once I started to research the history of Ashdown House, I discovered that the story behind it is equally compelling. The idea that William, First Earl of Craven, had the house built for Elizabeth Stuart, the Winter Queen, is a fascinating one. The house is full of her paintings and other reminders of her. Visiting is like looking through a historical mirror into her life.

I'd known for a long time that I wanted to write a book involving Ashdown House, and when I found out about the possibility of a secret marriage between Elizabeth and Lord Craven, I was hooked. Even though I was writing fiction, as a historian I wanted to keep as closely to the facts as I could. Luckily the true story of Elizabeth's life reads like a novel!

Elizabeth Stuart was the sister of King Charles I, who had married a German prince in 1613 when she was sixteen years old and gone to live in Heidelberg. Her husband's rule as King of Bohemia ended in battle and exile after only a year, and Elizabeth lived in The Hague in Holland for forty years whilst fighting to regain her husband's patrimony for her son. Elizabeth and her husband, Frederick, were also famously devoted to one another and when he died in 1632, she was said to be inconsolable.

In Frederick's entourage was a young man (twelve years younger than Elizabeth) called William, Lord Craven, the son of a fabulously wealthy cloth merchant who had been Lord Mayor of London. The Cravens originated in the North of England and in only two generations had risen from being agricultural labourers to having fortune, titles and royal recognition. William

Craven Junior was a soldier renowned for his courage and loyalty. He supported Frederick's attempts to regain his ancestral lands with money, soldiers and his own sword. After Frederick's early death, Craven became utterly dedicated to Elizabeth's cause, saving the life of her son Rupert in battle, financing her exile and remaining at her side during the turbulent years of the English Civil War.

When Elizabeth was finally able to return to London with the restoration to the throne of King Charles II in 1660, it was Craven who provided her with a place to live—his palatial mansion in Drury Lane, London. Craven lived there, too, and escorted Elizabeth about London, to the theatre and to visit her nephew King Charles. She held court at Craven House, and the unusual domestic arrangements (Craven was known officially as the Master of the Queen's Household) gave rise to a great deal of speculation and rumour as to the relationship between them. But they were both hugely popular with the people of the City of London. Elizabeth was viewed as a romantic heroine and Craven as a loyal and courageous war hero. He began ambitious building projects for Elizabeth in the form of a "palace" in Berkshire called Hamstead Marshall and the hunting lodge at Ashdown Park. However, there is no happy ending to the story, for Elizabeth died before Ashdown was completed, leaving to William Craven her portraits, her hunting trophies and her private papers. He remained close to her children and in particular to Prince Rupert, whose illegitimate daughter he cared for after Rupert's death.

Of course no convenient marriage certificate exists—or has been found—to confirm the existence of a marriage between Elizabeth and William Craven, and we are left to draw on circumstantial evidence as well as historical rumour. In the case of William and Elizabeth, there is one particularly beautiful piece of evidence in the form of a painting called The Allegory of Love by Sir Peter Lely, which shows the two of them joined by cupids and features many other symbols of love and devotion.

In addition to the intriguing possibilities of the secret marriage between Elizabeth and Craven, there were so many other historical facts in the story that were stranger than fiction. Elizabeth and her first husband, King Frederick, were members of the Order of the Rosy Cross, a secret sect that believed in magic and the power to foretell the future. I was astonished when, during the course of my research, I discovered that one of my own family had also been a Knight of the Rosy Cross. It drew me in even more closely to the story I was telling. Then there was the mystery of Frederick's tomb.

After he died, Frederick's body was lost just as I describe in the story, and no one knows where it is to this day. Perhaps one day, like King Richard III, his resting place will be rediscovered.

The Sistrin pearl, which features so strongly in House of Shadows, is based on the Bretheren, a famous drop pearl inherited by Elizabeth of Bohemia from her grandmother Mary, Queen of Scots. It features in some of the paintings on display at Ashdown and, just like the pearl in the story, is said to be cursed. The beautiful pearl necklaces that Elizabeth's daughters wear in their portraits caused something of a diplomatic incident in the nineteenth century. Together the strands formed an eight-string necklace, which was eventually inherited by Queen Victoria, a descendent of Elizabeth through her youngest daughter, Sophia. However, one of the strings had been lost in the seventeenth century when Elizabeth's daughter Henrietta was buried in her wedding dress, wearing the string of pearls. Victoria decided that she wanted the eighth string back and wrote to the authorities in Romania, where Henrietta was buried, asking them to open her grave and remove the necklace! Unsurprisingly the request was refused.

Another element of my research into the Craven family that influenced the development of the story was the connection between the Cravens and the author Jane Austen. I discovered this when I was looking at the later descent of the Craven title and their relatives in Berkshire. Not only did the Cravens and the Austens intermarry on several occasions through the Georgian period, but Jane herself drew on a couple of members of the family as character inspiration. It is believed that John Willoughby, the scoundrel in Sense and Sensibility who breaks Marianne's heart, is based on William, First Earl of Craven, who was a typical Georgian rake. In her letters, Jane comments on the shocking news that William Craven has installed his mistress at Ashdown House. The mistress in question was Harriette Wilson, the famous Regency courtesan, and it was fascinating to find her link to Ashdown House. Harriette would, of course, later go on to write her scandalous memoirs and attempt to extract money from her lovers in return for leaving them out of the account, which prompted the famous occasion on which the Duke of Wellington said "Publish and be damned!" William Craven also refused to pay and as a result Harriette described him as extremely tedious, a man who habitually wore an unattractive cotton nightcap and droned on about his estates to anyone who would listen. In actual fact, Craven was extremely charming, although, as Jane Austen hinted, possibly not in possession of a strong moral compass. He was extraordinarily extravagant; he married an actress and sailed his own armed yacht in the English Channel during the Napoleonic Wars in the hope of engaging with the French Navy. Harriette's relationship with William was behind the story of Lavinia and Lord Evershot in House of Shadows.

With such a wealth of history to draw on, it was an utter pleasure to weave together the strands of House of Shadows, keeping the story as authentic as possible whilst also using historical imagination to fill in the gaps. Although in the book

Ashdown House has been destroyed, in real life of course it still stands, a beautiful little white "palace" dedicated to the memory of Elizabeth the Winter Queen and full of her portraits, each room echoing with memories. It's wonderful to be able to show visitors around the house and even more amazing to work in such a place where the past feels so close and there are so many stories to tell.

CHAPTER 1

Alison
Marlborough, Wiltshire, the present day

She saw the portrait quite by chance, or so she thought.
It was eight weeks to Christmas and the rain-sodden streets of Marlborough already glistened in the gaudy light of the decorations that were strung from buildings and lamp-posts. The wind was strong that night and the illuminations swung back and forth, scattering shadows and shards of colour over the late-night shoppers below. A Victorian market was being held in the town square and the air was thick with the smell of grilled sausages and hot soup. It made Alison feel hungry.

She put her head down and increased her pace against the fine rain that slicked the pavement. She hated this sort of faux-historical event with rosy, smiling stallholders dressed up in costume. Beneath the crinolines and jackets, they had on their thermal vests and long johns to guard against the cold. They had waterproof boots and raincoats. They thought this play-acting was fun, a jolly celebration of Christmas past.

She remembered past Christmases very differently: the bone-sharp cold, the damp, the chilblains and the hunger that had hollowed her stomach. Even though she had been trapped in the present day for so long now that time had started to blur, some of her past she could remember with utter clarity. Pain, sickness, violence, death had been a raw reality. Someone thrust a toffee apple under her nose in an invitation to buy, and she shuddered and turned away, picking up her pace along the pavement.

There was a creaking noise high above her, a flap as the wind caught the edge of an inn sign and set it swinging.

The White Hart.

She stared at the image of the majestic white stag as it swayed backwards and forwards in the wind. Its head was raised proudly. Around its neck was a golden crown. It was strange how the most potent and magical of Savernake Forest's symbols survived into this brash and modern world. There were traces of history everywhere—in street names, on inn signs, in old tracks and ancient hedgerows, buried walls and tumbled gravestones. Scratch the surface and it was there.

Alison had seen a white hart in the forest once. Her cousin Edward Seymour had said that the Queen had wanted to come to hunt it, the hart being the ultimate hunter's trophy and Elizabeth being a queen who collected such things. Perhaps she had come to Wolf Hall after Alison had left. She did not know. There was no record of a royal visit, but then so much fell through the cracks of the past.

The fresh blast of air from the Downs to the north brought with it a softer scent, of mingled herbs and flowers, wild garlic, basil and lavender, taking Alison straight back to a long-lost summer in the garden at Wolf Hall and the smell of sun-warm brick and hot grass. She had not been happy in those days but still, the sense of loss and dislocation hit her fiercely and gave her no time to prepare. There was too much that was familiar here in Marlborough—the town, the inn, the memories. She should have realised that coming back to Wiltshire was a bad idea. But she had had so little choice.

Breathe. Accept. Wait.

The wave of dizziness and nausea retreated a little. Alison found she was leaning against a wall between two shops, rather like a drunk steadying himself as he tried to weave his way home late at night. Awareness returned to her, the smooth coldness of a drainpipe against her clutching fingers, the chill sting of the rain and the heavy, greasy smell of the street market.

She was standing in front of a shop she had not seen before. High Street shops came and went, of course, and it was a good ten years since she had been in Marlborough, maybe more. She tried not to count most of the time.

The shop was actually an art gallery, all high-tech lighting and huge windows, its modernity blaringly incongruous in the middle of Marlborough High Street's olde worlde charm.

Most of the paintings Alison could see through the window were equally strident, highly coloured, swirling patterns in oil with huge price tags and no artistic merit in her opinion. Not that she knew much about art. She drew for pleasure and had done so since she was a child, but she had no training and no technique to speak of.

To the right of the enormous bow window was a pastoral scene with a spotlight trained on it. It might have been an antique. Alison could not really tell. Below the canvas ran a broad white shelf that stretched along the full length of the showroom. There were a number of smaller paintings displayed there, mainly portraits, and she knew at once that they were old, sixteenth century, to judge from the style and the type of clothing. There was King Henry VIII, painted at the moment his glorious, golden youthfulness was changing into something more watchful and inimical. When Alison had been a child, his name had been used to frighten them all into obedience: "Behave yourself or old King Hal will come to get you." When she had been young, she had had no idea what he had looked like but her imagination had supplied the image of a monster. She had seen hundreds of pictures of him since, of course. The English were proud of their infamous spouse-murdering monarch. Distance had lent the sort of affection to his memory that had never been felt in her own time.

It was odd seeing Henry now, a relic, a throwback to her past. It unsettled her.

Alison's gaze travelled on to the next portrait on the shelf, that of a woman, standing, her hands folded demurely in that style so beloved of artists who wanted to persuade the viewer that Tudor womanhood was modest and decorous. The display light cast a shadow across her face. Alison strained closer to see. This was no one as instantly recognisable as Henry and yet there was a familiarity about her. It was a face she knew.

Mary Seymour.

Alison's breath stopped. There was a tight pain in her chest and a buzzing in her ears. Mary. After all this time.

She had never given up hope. It wasn't in her nature to despair, although she had come very close to it so many times. All the history books—those that mentioned Mary Seymour at all—said that she had died as a child. Alison had known that was not true but she had never discovered what had happened to Mary after she had left Wolf Hall.

Help me, she had said to Mary all those years ago. *Help me to find my son. I'll come back for him. Leave me word…*

She had not begged, precisely; her relationship with Mary had been too prickly to allow her to show that vulnerability. She had phrased it as an order, but Mary had known. There had been a bargain between them. She had helped Mary escape Wolf Hall and, in return, Mary had promised to help her.

Mary was the key to finding Arthur. She always had been and so Alison had held tenaciously to the belief that one day she would see Mary again.

And now she had.

Suddenly she felt faint with shock, trembling, tears pricking her eyes.

"Are you all right?" Someone was addressing her, a woman with a plastic rain hat and an anxious expression. She spoke in the tones of someone who feels obliged to offer help but sincerely hopes it isn't going to be needed. Alison forced a smile.

"I'm fine, thanks. I tripped over the edge of the pavement and winded myself for a moment."

The woman's sharp gaze scanned her face.

She thinks I'm drunk, Alison thought. She took a deep breath and pinned the smile on tighter. "No harm done," she said. "Thanks for stopping to check."

"Well, if you're sure…" The woman was already moving away, duty done.

Alison found that her hand was resting against the windowpane as though reaching out to touch the portrait within. She let it fall to her side and straightened, then pushed open the door and stepped from the dark street into the bright interior of the gallery. For a moment the harsh light dazzled her. Out of it came the figure of a man, summoned by the bell on the door. He was elderly, greying, with a stoop and leather elbow patches on his tweed jacket, but his eyes were bright, vivid blue, and he seemed to crackle with life and energy. Alison felt it at once, that force of personality that some people seemed to project effortlessly, lighting up everything around them.

"Can I help you?" He sounded surprised that anyone should have dropped in on a wet late-autumn evening.

"That portrait of a lady," Alison said. "The Tudor one…"

"Beautiful, isn't it," the man said.

Alison was taken aback. Had Mary been beautiful? Perhaps she had, although Alison had never thought so. She was the one whom men had admired. She had been curves to Mary's angles, rose to her sallow. She looked at the portrait again, trying to be dispassionate and to ignore the stirrings of old jealousy. She had never liked Mary. In the beginning, she had hated her with a child's simple hatred. That had grown into a more complicated set of emotions as she grew up, but they had never been friends. They had been too different and too far apart.

The woman in the picture had features that were neat rather than beautiful: a long nose but delicate and not disproportionately so, arched brows above eyes of an indeterminate dark colour, a slight smile on the pursed pink lips. There was only the faintest hint of the hair colour beneath her Tudor gable hood, though Alison knew it to be red brown, like her mother's. Mary's gown was of sumptuous gold and green velvet embroidered with pearls. She looked to be a woman of substance. There were pearls, too, on the hood and a space where one was missing. That was typical of Mary. She would not have noticed.

She realised that the man was waiting patiently for the question she had not yet articulated.

"It's lovely," she agreed. "The artist must have been very talented."

She saw him smile and realised that she had not quite been able to repress the spite. Mary grown up, or at least on the cusp of womanhood, made her as jealous as Mary the child had once done.

She sighed. None of that mattered. What was important was that Mary had survived. Thrived, in fact, by the look of it. And that was good because Mary was the key. Mary had promised to leave word of Arthur for her, and Mary never broke her promises.

Alison felt it again then, the dizziness that was a mixture of hope and terror. She could not let herself believe that this time she would find Arthur. The crash of despair that had followed each time she had failed had been almost too much to bear.

"...unidentified." She realised that the man had been speaking all the time that she had been lost in the turbulence of her thoughts.

"Sorry," she said. "Did you say that the artist has not been identified or the sitter has not been identified?"

Now he was looking at her with concern. She caught a glance of herself in the mirrored wall behind the sales desk, all wet rat-tails hair and pallid complexion. No wonder he was fidgeting with the display in front of him, fussily moving an ugly ceramic vase two inches to the left whilst he waited for her to take herself off. She could hardly fit the profile of a potential customer.

"The artist is unknown," he repeated patiently. "The sitter is Anne Boleyn."

"No," Alison said. She cleared her throat. "Sorry, but that isn't Anne Boleyn. It's Mary Seymour."

"It is Anne Boleyn." The man was still smiling in a rather determined fashion. He was charming. She didn't deserve such tolerance. "Tudor portraits aren't my forte," he said, "but I do know that this is a newly discovered portrait of Anne, authenticated only recently." He pointed to the background of the painting. It was dark and the shapes drawn there were difficult to decipher. "Can you see the box?" he asked. "It has her initials on it." Then, as Alison frowned, leaning forward to peer into the depths of the picture: "*AB.* For Anne Boleyn."

The box. *Her box.*

Alison could see it, now that he had pointed it out. It sat on a ledge to the right of Mary's head, only the very faintest sheen on its patina showing in the dark background. It would have been easy to miss, this clue, this promise.

See, Alison, I did not forget you. I have your workbox here, safe for you.

She looked back at Mary's painted face, at the slight sideways glance that led the viewer's gaze to the wooden box and the bold initials. It had been made of walnut, she remembered, worn smooth over the years by the touch of her fingers. She had loved that box, storing any number of inconsequential items in it: her thimble, a length of ribbon and a scrap of lace. She might have kept Edward's love notes in it had he written her any, but he had not.

"My godson could tell you more about it," the man said. "He was the one who discovered the portrait. He's written a book about it. He's speaking at the festival tomorrow night."

"Festival?" Alison said. She tried to get a grip. She felt strange, jittery. Although the shop was almost aggressively modern, she felt closer to the past than she had done in years, disorientated and confused.

"There's a literary festival running all week," the man said. "Adam—my godson—is talking about the painting and about the Tudor court." He nodded towards Mary, serene under the dazzling lights. "It's all very exciting. Apparently, there aren't many portraits of Anne Boleyn."

"And this isn't one of them, I'm afraid," Alison said. Rain was seeping down her neck, making her shiver. Or perhaps the shivers were coming from elsewhere, somewhere far deeper inside.

There was a pile of flyers for the talk spread in an artful fan on the white shelf beside the portrait. She bent to pick one up.

"'Adam Hewer,'" she read, "'historian, author and presenter, unveils the face of Anne Boleyn. Don't miss this exciting event, exclusive to the Marlborough Festival.'" There was a picture of a book cover for *Discovering Anne Boleyn* and a photograph of the author: *Adam*.

Alison sat down abruptly in a flimsy-looking white plastic chair that she thought was probably part of an art installation. It creaked.

"You look quite done up," the gallery owner said kindly. "Can I get you a cup of tea? It helps, you know."

"I'm fine," Alison said automatically. "Just a bit tired."

Odd that it should be Adam, of all people, who should be the one to lead her to Mary. Or perhaps it was not odd at all. That sense of time shifting, the lure of the brightly lit window, the portrait... It had not happened by chance. When it came to fate and time, she did not believe in coincidence.

She needed to think. She had to get away from the bright lights that were making her head ache with the buzz of too many discoveries, made too quickly. She dropped the flyer back down on the shelf, where the edges curled up slightly in the heat of the lights.

"Thank you," she said. "You've been very kind but I'd better go now."

"Alison?"

Adam's voice stopped her where she was, two steps away from the door. She turned slowly. It had not occurred to her that he might be there, listening, and now she felt a prickle of annoyance that he had not made his presence known sooner.

He looked older than she remembered, but not by much.

It was a good ten years since they had met but annoyingly Adam seemed to have aged better than she felt she had. He was tall, well built, with brown eyes that were a startling contrast to his fair hair, and had an air of restless energy that was familiar to her. With a sudden tug of the heart, she realised he had become the man she had glimpsed in the boy she had known.

After they had split up, she had shied away from following Adam's career, although she did know that he was one of the new generation of TV historians, celebrity academics who travelled to exotic places to present the past in new and vibrant ways. As a breed, they were young, good-looking, photogenic and formidably bright. Apparently, they made history accessible. That had always felt a painful irony to her. History was not accessible at all; at least she did not find it to be.

Adam came out of the office at the back and into the bright lights of the gallery, casual, hands thrust into the pockets of his trousers. "I thought it was you," he said. "How are you?"

He was smiling. Alison remembered the public-school charm, so like that of his godfather, which could smooth over the most awkward of encounters. It had bowled her over when first they had met, reminding her painfully of the life she had left behind. She had clung to something that felt familiar in an alien world only to find that there was no similarity between Adam and the men she had known in her past.

Now she felt a disconcerting echo of that teenage confusion and she was cross with herself because there was a flutter in the pit of her stomach and a whisper of what might have been. Stupid, because what might have been had already happened: a youthful affair that had burned itself out.

"I'm good, thanks," she said, matching his effortless courtesy with what felt like abject gaucheness. "Just down here for a few days. I work in London now. But you—" She gestured awkwardly towards the flyers. "You're doing well. TV shows, writing..."

She knew she sounded inane but he merely inclined his head. "Thanks."

"It's what you always wanted."

She saw a flicker of expression in his eyes then, gone too quick to read. He said nothing. Alison was starting to feel hot and anxious. It had been a stupid thing to say. She knew nothing of what Adam wanted these days. She had barely known him ten years before and if she had realised she was going to meet him again today, she would have been better prepared.

Butterflies fluttered again, trapped, beneath her breastbone. She needed to give herself some time and space to think. Adam's godfather—in an unusual breach of courtesy, Adam had not introduced him—had moved away, pretending to rearrange the paperwork on the sales desk, but she knew he was listening, wondering.

"Well..." She waved a vague hand towards the door. "I really must go. Good luck for the talk tomorrow. Not that you'll need it, of course."

"I heard what you were saying," Adam said, ignoring her words. "You don't think this is a portrait of Anne Boleyn."

Alison felt a sharp pang of disappointment, followed swiftly by a sort of anger at her own obtuseness. This was why Adam had come out to speak to her. It was not because he had wanted to see her. It was because she had raised questions about his work. The anger pricked her into speech.

"It's a portrait of Mary Seymour," she said, "the daughter of Katherine Parr and Thomas Seymour."

Adam paused for a moment, studying her face. There was a tight frown between his brows now. Alison waited for him to contradict her. She was already regretting her words; she should have gone back to the hotel, thought about what had happened, decided on what she should do next, rather than blurt out a statement that would only make Adam want to know more.

"I thought Mary Seymour died as a child?" Adam said.

Kudos to Adam, Alison thought. Most people had never heard of Mary Seymour, let alone knew what had happened to her. She did not know herself. Until tonight, her search for Mary had drawn a blank. She had hunted her through books, archives, museums and galleries and had found next to nothing. Mary's had been a life almost completely lost from history. But the one thing that Alison did know was that Mary had not died as a child.

She shifted, aware of Adam's acute gaze resting on her. "She definitely survived into adulthood," she said.

"I assume there is evidence to support that?" Adam leaned against the edge of the sales desk and folded his arms. His tone was not disbelieving, but there was more than a hint of challenge in it. Alison felt a flutter down her spine. This was precisely the sort of conversation she should have avoided until she got her head together.

"I've seen other portraits of Mary," she said. "I know a bit about her. I researched her for some work I was doing..."

She could sense Adam's puzzlement. One thing he did know about her was that she was no historian. When they had met at summer school in Marlborough, she was a sullen teenager with a sponsored place on a tourism course. He had just accepted an offer to read history at Cambridge.

"Genealogy," she said quickly, forestalling his next question, making it up as she went along. "I was looking for some stuff on my family tree and found Mary. There's a distant connection between us."

She felt as though she was digging herself in deeper rather than out.

"Genealogy," Adam repeated. His gaze was narrowed intently on her now. He looked as though he didn't believe a word. "You never talked about your family," he said slowly. "You told me you couldn't leave them behind fast enough."

"That's how I felt at eighteen," Alison said. "People change." She fidgeted with the strap of her bag. "Look, forget I mentioned Mary at all. You've got a talk and a book…"

"And a TV programme," Adam said dryly. "All based on the premise that this is a portrait of Anne Boleyn, not Mary Seymour."

Alison felt a flicker of sympathy for him. The discovery of a new portrait of Anne Boleyn was quite a coup and would bring Adam lots of publicity. She had planted a seed of doubt in his mind now and even though he knew she was not a professional historian, he could not risk making a highly visible mistake.

"It was authenticated," Adam said now, almost to himself. He straightened and pushed away from the desk, then took several strides across the gallery before turning back towards her, all repressed frustration and energy. "We found it with some other Tudor artefacts," he said. "There was no doubt about the dating. Then there was the box with the initials on it…"

"The box still exists?" Alison cut in quickly. "The one in the portrait?"

Adam stared at her. "Yes. Why?"

"Oh." Alison moderated her tone, realising she had sounded too eager. "I thought there might be something interesting in it, that's all. Something to do with Mary, I mean."

Adam was still watching her. It was unsettling. She had always thought she was a good liar but now she was starting to doubt it.

"There were some items inside," he agreed. "If that is indeed Mary Seymour in the portrait, I suppose they might have some connection to her." He did not elaborate and Alison knew it was deliberate. There was no reason why he would satisfy her curiosity.

Her heart was thumping. She could feel herself shaking. She knew she should not push this now but desperation was driving her harder than she had ever known it. Mary seemed only a breath away. And Arthur... What clues had Mary left her to Arthur?

"Where did you find the box?" she asked, and she could hear the quiver in her voice.

Adam shook his head. There was a faint smile playing about his lips now.

"I'll trade you that information, and more," he said, "to see the genealogical research you've done on Mary Seymour."

There was a small, deadly pause.

Alison knew she was trapped. She could not see any way that she could show Adam the work she had done on tracing Mary without disclosing her own history. He had been right: she had not told him a single thing about her family. She had never spoken of them. But they were all there on the pages of notes she had so painstakingly compiled. The Seymour family tree linked them together, tangled as the roots of the old oaks of Savernake Forest. They were all there: she, Edward, Mary, Arthur...

The silence stretched out whilst her mind scrambled for a solution, but then Adam shifted and smiled a condescending smile that made her itch to smack him.

"I thought not," he said pleasantly. "There is no research, is there?" He ran a hand through his thick, fair hair. "Look," he said, "I don't know why you've suddenly turned up after all this time, Alison, but there's really no point. I moved on a long time ago—"

"What? Wait!" Alison drew back. "Are you implying I'm here because I wanted to see *you*? I didn't even know about your talk!" She threw out a hand, narrowly missing the ceramic vase. "I came in because of her," she said, pointing at Mary's picture. "It was nothing to do with you—"

"Whatever." Adam raised one shoulder in a half shrug. "I'm not interested."

"Fine," Alison snapped. "Then I hope you don't find that some other person more academically credible than I blows your Anne Boleyn theory to smithereens."

She pushed open the door of the gallery and stepped out into the driving rain. She thought she heard Adam call after her as she slipped out into the dark but she did not wait, pulling up the hood of her jacket and hunching deeper inside it when the wind caught her with its icy edge. The disconsolate re-enactors were closing down their stalls and heading to the pub. A woman was wheeling a pushchair erratically across the pavement and was dragging a small child along with her other hand. He had toffee apple smeared across his face and was screaming.

Emotion pierced Alison deep inside where the hurt and the loneliness were locked away. She shuddered, blocking out the child's scrunched-up face and the mother's harassed scolding. Only fifty yards further along the wet pavement was her hotel. A small bay tree stood shivering in a planter on each side of the door. She hurried inside.

She'd chosen somewhere modern and exclusive rather than one of Marlborough's more traditional places to stay. She'd always found that embracing the present was the best way to keep the past at bay. Except that in Marlborough tonight the past had swept back like a dark tide.

She was still shaking. She knew that rationally she could not blame Adam for thinking that she was only trying to stir up trouble, but rationality had nothing to do with the fury and frustration that welled up in her now. She felt the hot prick of angry tears against her eyelids. She had waited so long for word from Mary, each time she failed to find her, absorbing the blank wall of silence and the bitterness of defeat. And now here was Mary—and the box—and Adam was thwarting her attempts to get closer.

The winter storm was gathering, sending litter skipping along the gutters, dimming the Christmas lights with a fresh downpour of rain but, inside, the hotel was warm, opulent and lit discreetly by lamps with striped beige and cream shades. A smiling receptionist handed Alison her key. So often, Alison found light and warmth—the most basic trappings of modern life—gave her comfort and made her feel safe. Tonight, though, they only served to emphasise her sense of dislocation. So did the impersonal luxury of her room.

She dropped her soaking jacket on the floor and lay down on the bed, staring at the orange glow of the streetlights beyond the windows. She knew she did not have much choice. Adam had information she needed. He had the portrait, the box, possibly other artefacts connected to Mary. She had been waiting for five hundred years for news of her son. She could not let the chance slip now.

CHAPTER 2

Mary
Wiltshire, 1557

Alison Banestre and I were cousins of a kind. We were both orphans. There the bond between us began and ended: Alison, my enemy.

We made a bargain, she and I. She helped me to escape; I helped her to find her son. It is entirely possible to bargain with an enemy if there is something that you both want and so it proved. Thus we were bound together through time.

We met at Wolf Hall. I came there in the summer of fifteen hundred and fifty-seven, in the fourth year of the reign of Mary the Queen. I was a Mary, too, cousin of the late King, Edward, daughter to one dead queen and niece to another, with a famous name and not a penny to pay my way. I was ten years old and I already had a reputation for witchcraft.

"The child is possessed, your grace," the cook at Grims-thorpe told the Duchess of Suffolk when, at the age of five, I was found sitting under a table in the kitchens, holding a posset that had curdled. "That cream was as fresh as a daisy only a moment ago."

"Mary broke my spinning top!" one of my Seymour cousins wailed one day when the wooden toy was found to have split neatly into two halves like a cut pear. "She put a spell on it!"

That was the first time I realised that I possessed the magic. He had been tormenting me and I had hated him; the anger had boiled over within me and I had wanted nothing more than to teach him a lesson.

I did not want such power, though. I wanted no more than to be ordinary, accepted. My mother, many years before, had been within inches of arrest for heresy. Witchcraft was but one strand of such blasphemy and dissent and the thought of following her fate terrified me. Yet I could not escape. It came with me to Savernake, the whisper of witchcraft, wrapped like a cloak about me, for I was different, other, an outsider, whether I wished it or not.

My name is Mary Seymour. I was born at Sudeley Castle but have no recollection of my nursery there, hung with red and gold, for almost as soon as I came into the world my mother left it. I'm told that my father had never anticipated that she might die in childbirth, which is odd since it is a common danger, particularly for a woman such as my mother, Katherine Parr, who was past the age when it was wise to have a first child or indeed perhaps a child at all. But she was giddy for love of him and he was giddy for love of himself, so I imagine they gave little thought to the consequences of their infatuation.

I was born. My mother died. My father professed himself to be so stunned by grief that he could not think straight. However, he knew enough to realise he did not want the burden of a baby daughter, so he took me to London and abandoned me in the nursery of my aunt and uncle, the Duke and Duchess of Somerset, where I might have cousins with whom to grow up. It was a good plan, if a self-interested one, and it might well have turned out quite differently had it not been for his overweening ambition, which toppled over into treason.

My earliest memory was of being unwanted.

"What is to become of the Lady Mary?" My governess, Mistress Aiglonby, was the only one who, in the chaotic aftermath of my father's arrest for treason, pressed for my family to continue to care for me. I can still hear the wail of her voice rising above the sound of my belongings being packed away into boxes. I had no real sense of what was happening. I remember tipping my set of skittles out of the box again, spilling them all over the floor and tripping the nursemaid up as she ran about trying to fold my clothes into a bag that was too small. She was red of face and flustered, and looked near to tears.

"Lady Mary cannot stay here." It was my aunt, the Duchess, who spoke. She had no warmth in her, least of all towards me.

"I agree it would be difficult to explain to her in the future that her uncle signed her father's death warrant." Dearest Liz Aiglonby. She could be tart when she chose. She had been one of my mother's maids before she became my governess. Her family were ambitious for preferment at court but that did not prevent her from defending me like a lioness.

"That was not my point." The Duchess' tone had chilled still further. "Let her mother's kin take her in."

"The Parrs do not want her."

No one wants her.

My skittles had been a present from my father. They were carved into the shape of men, painted to look like sailors. I took one in my fist and neatly struck off the head of another with it. Or so I am told. In truth, I probably remember nothing of this, being too young, although it feels as though the memory is real.

"Lord Seymour suggested her grace of Suffolk…" Mistress Aiglonby sounded hesitant now and my aunt gave a brusque bark of laughter.

"Why would he do that? I thought he liked her?" Her voice changed. Malice rang clear as a bell. "Mayhap the rumours are true and she did refuse him and this is his revenge."

"Her grace was a close friend of the late Queen."

"Which does not mean she would wish to be saddled with her penniless child."

Yet to the Duchess of Suffolk I was sent, like an unwelcome gift, trailing my retinue of nursemaids, rockers, laundresses and servants.

Lady Suffolk was renowned for her piety but this did not mean she possessed generosity of spirit as well.

"The late Queen's child is too expensive for me to keep," she told anyone who would listen, but no one *was* listening, not really, not even parliament, which eventually restored to me all that was left of my father's property. This was practically nothing. So my expensive household was dismissed but for a few servants, and Lady Suffolk sent me to her castle at Grimsthorpe in Lincolnshire since I could live more cheaply in the country than in London.

I loved Grimsthorpe. The castle had been neglected since the visit of the old King, Henry, some ten years before, and its rooms smelled of stale air and damp and secrets. There were locked doors and tumbledown walls, rambling gardens and endless woods under wide blue skies. Best of all, no one cared what I did, so no one interfered. One of Liz's brothers came to tutor me sometimes, and Liz herself tried to instill in me the skills and lessons appropriate to a lady, but I was a stubborn child and had no interest in learning. I think that the Duchess of Suffolk might have tried to betroth me young had I even the smallest dowry but as I had nothing but notoriety, she knew no one would want to wed me.

How long my idyllic life at Grimsthorpe might have continued I do not know, for when I was eight years old the Duchess and her fierce Protestantism fell foul of the Bishop of Winchester and she vowed to leave England for fear of persecution. There was no question that she would take me abroad with her. For a couple of years, I was shunted from pillar to post, from London to the country, from north to south, from court to church and back again. I was a nuisance. Queen Mary declared that I should be sent to one of my father's manors. Liz Aiglonby staunchly maintained I was too young, that I was the Queen's ward and her responsibility. Mary said dryly that as the Seymours had begat me so to the Seymours I should go.

My uncle Somerset had followed my father to the executioner's block, so it was left to my cousin Edward, as head of the family, to provide for me. He and I were united in disgrace, the Seymours fallen further than they had ever risen.

It was then I first heard the whisper of that name: *Wolf Hall*.

My first sight of the place was on a day of bright sunlight, but once we were within the forest of Savernake, the sun vanished into darkness and the track seemed interminable and lonely. It felt as though we were arriving at the end of the world.

"What sort of a name is Wolf Hall?" Liz asked as she placed my clothes in the big bound chest in the chamber I was to share with my cousin Alison. We had been welcomed warmly enough on arrival with bread, a little butter and some fruit, although it was closer to dinner than breakfast time. Dame Margery, the housekeeper, had then shown us to my bedchamber and had vanished, although Cousin Alison had remained. She sat in the window, where the pale light seemed to shimmer on her flaxen hair. I had never seen anything so pretty in my life.

Liz sounded suspicious, I thought, as though she expected a wolf to appear from behind a tree and gobble her whole. She disliked the country and thought its inhabitants unruly and unpredictable, whether human, feathered or furred. Nor did she like Wolf Hall itself. The rambling old manor was even more run-down than Grimsthorpe had been, and here I was less than no one and Liz, consequently, nothing at all for all her London connections and service to the court.

"Wolf Hall is nothing to do with wolves," Alison said. She sounded faintly patronising. "It comes from the ancient Saxon name for the estate."

"Saxon!" Liz said. Her family had come over with the Norman King William. Her sniff of disdain left no room for doubt that she considered the Saxons even more barbaric than the present inhabitants of Savernake Forest.

Alison smiled, tossing her golden plait over her shoulder. She looked very Saxon herself with her cream-and-roses complexion and her blue eyes. There was a look of the late Queen Jane about her, or so I was told. Except that Queen Jane was pious and demure and Alison was never that.

Alison and I were only distantly related, but at Wolf Hall, I had already discovered that we Seymours were all jumbled up together, called cousins regardless of our relationships, abandoned here because there was nowhere else for the sprawling offshoots of the family to go. There were half a dozen of us children and I never worked out how we were connected other than through rejection or loss. There were two babies in the nursery; whose they were, I never discovered. Closest in age to me was a boy of seven, but from the lofty heights of ten years, I considered him negligible. Then there was Alison, two or three years older, and above her in the pecking order a sullen youth who boasted that he was soon to be sent away as squire in a knight's household.

Liz had turned her back as she laid out my linen shifts in the trunk. These had been worked with fine white lace and I saw Alison's gaze narrow on them and something cold and hard and inimical come into her pale eyes as she looked back at me. She could not have looked less like meek Queen Jane then.

"Those are very beautiful linens indeed," she said.

"The Lady Mary is dressed as befits the daughter of a queen," Liz said.

Alison's cornflower gaze swept over me. "Only beneath her gown," she said.

Even though I was only ten years old, I was adept at reading what went on in the minds of men—and women—for my fate had often depended upon it. I knew that Alison resented me, that for all my notoriety and poverty, she was jealous because I had fame even though it was not of my own seeking. I was also adept at smoothing over discord, so I slid from my chair and went over to her.

"Would you show me the forest?" I asked.

She looked scornful. "It would take days for you to see the forest." Her sharp gaze pinned me down. "We are forbidden from venturing there. It is dangerous."

"Why?"

There was a sudden silence and I realised that she did not know. She had never asked.

"It just is." Her head was bent. I could not see her expression. Her busy fingers were sorting through the skeins of thread in her workbox. She put aside the ones that drew my gaze—the red, the gold, the blue—and selected the brown and the black. "Besides, we have no time for idleness here.

455

We clean and cook and sew and tend the garden and dairy and a thousand other things beside."

"Are there not servants to do such tasks?"

She gave a snort of laughter. "So speaks the Queen's daughter. No, *your highness*—" her mouth curved into a sly little smile "—we do not have that luxury here, at least not when Sir Edward is away. In his absence, we make shift for ourselves."

I bit my tongue before I could make reference to Cousin Edward. Already she found me presumptuous. I would do nothing to antagonise her further. Instead, I slipped out of the bedroom when Liz's back was turned. I knew Alison would tell her she had no notion of where I had gone and if I got lost in the dangerous forest she would not mourn me.

I had not been at Wolf Hall long enough to know which chamber was which, but I ignored the blank doors staring at me and trod softly down the stair. Patterns of light and shade speckled the steps. The wood creaked beneath my feet and I hesitated, but no one came. I was accustomed to sliding away on my own, gone like a ghost. Although I had been hedged about by servants from the earliest age, I still managed to be a solitary child.

To my left was the great hall with its sloping stone floor, swept clean this afternoon and smelling sweetly of rushes. Behind me the chapel door, heavy studded oak, forbidding, warning of retribution within. But ahead was the passage and, at the end of it, the door was open into the garden and I was drawn irresistibly outside.

The gardens at Wolf Hall proved a delight, a tangled land of enchantment full of overblown roses and secret paths. Beneath the trees of the orchard I could see a harassed-looking goose girl trying to round up her flock. She was flapping as much as they. Over in the stable yard, I could hear the chink of harness and the murmur of voices. The air was full of scent and heat, and I wandered at will, lost in the pleasure of it.

The garden led to the wood. There was a half-open gate covered in ivy and a path beyond. Naturally, I followed it. I say *naturally* because I am drawn to the forest. I don't know why; people say it is a lonely, lawless place, but to me it is a safe haven in which to hide. One path led to another and another, some overgrown tracks, other wide avenues lined by trees that looked like the entrance to a manor far more majestic than Wolf Hall. I went where I willed, following a butterfly here or the sound of water there, running through the dappled shade, discovering new delights.

It was growing dark. I realised it suddenly, knew I had been out for a long time because I was hungry. There was a damp chill settling on my skin. The trees that had enchanted me now threw long shadows. The rustle of the leaves sounded too loud. The air felt still and watchful.

I had no notion which way was the road back.

Distantly, I heard the sound of hoof beats. My hopes lifted, for where there was a horse and rider there might well be a track leading to Wolf Hall. I scrambled through the undergrowth, pushing aside bracken and nettle and grasses, fighting my way towards the noise. With each step the night seemed to close in. The hoof beats were growing louder and, as I stumbled out of the clutch of the thicket and onto a wide avenue, they seemed to fill my head and make my entire body pulse. The earth shook. I fell, dizzy and sprawling, and lay there in terror, waiting either for the shout of fury from the rider or the crush of the horse's hooves.

Neither came.

The beat in my head eased a little and I dragged myself up onto one elbow and stared into the engulfing shade. Down the long avenue, I could see the white shadow of a horse galloping hell for leather. In the saddle swayed the figure of a woman. She looked as though she was about to fall at any moment. Her cloak billowed out behind her, a fine velvet cloak laced with silver thread, and on her head… But she wore no hat and she had no face because above the line of her collar she had no head, nothing but white bone gleaming in the last light and deep red splashes of blood.

There was a jumble of light and voices about me. I was not lost in the forest but lying in a bed. The tip of a feather pricked my cheek and I turned my head against the pillow. There was candlelight. It was night, and I felt hot and sickly and wretched.

"Already nothing but trouble…" The lamentation floated far above my head. I recognised Dame Margery's voice. "Only here for two minutes and already we have had to send out a search for her and pay for a physician—"

"Pass me the bowl and the cloth." Liz this time, sounding snappish. "You heard what he said. She has the fever."

"She has only herself to blame, wandering around the forest alone! She's like her father was, reckless and foolish. She does not think about the consequences of her actions."

"She is a child who got lost, that is all." Liz was starting to sound frayed. I thought it unlikely she would defend my father, whom she had never liked. It was my mother to whom she had been devoted.

"Babbling about phantom horses and headless women!" Dame Margery was not so easily appeased. "It sounds like witchcraft to me."

"It's fever, no more," Liz repeated. I heard the rustle of cloth as she stood. "I need fresh water."

"I'll come with you." Dame Margery sounded hurried now,

as though she did not wish to be left alone with me for fear of enchantment. "Alison can watch over her for a moment."

I had not realised that Alison was there. I opened my eyes a crack. She saw the flicker of movement and immediately she was at my ear.

"I hope you are satisfied, your highness." She smelled of peppermint and sweat. Her whisper was fierce. "Thanks to you, I have to share a chamber with the babies now whilst you lord it in here alone. I wish they had not found you!" Her face hung over me like a big red, angry moon.

"It's true, there are phantoms in the forest," she said. "I think it was the black shuck you saw, a huge dog that brings death and madness to all that see it."

"It was a horse." My lips were dry. I felt hot, feverish, and my head was full of the nightmare but I was still stubborn. If I were to be terrorised by a phantom at least let it be the right one.

"A horse and a dead woman?" She laughed. "Mayhap it was Queen Anne Boleyn you saw then. If it had not been for *your* aunt Jane, she would not have lost her head. Maybe she is coming for you in revenge."

The sound of voices and the lifting of the latch warned her. She scrambled away and when Liz and Dame Margery re-entered the room, she was sitting on the window seat all prim and quiet.

"She sleeps," she said sweetly. "May I go now?" And with that she slipped from the room, leaving me with my feverish nightmares.

Darrell came to me that night as I was tossing and turning in my sleep. Darrell had been my companion from the earliest time. He was more than a daydream or an imaginary friend. I knew from the start that he was as real as I, that we could talk to each other in images and thoughts and ideas.

Such things are natural to children. We do not question. I did not know who he was. I assumed we must be related in some way, such gifts so often connecting members of one family, but I had so many relatives and when I looked around at the sprawling network of my Seymour cousins, not one of them felt right. He told me his name was Darrell and even though he knew I was called Mary he called me Cat because he said I was small and fierce. I loved him; it was simple and comfortable because I had always known him. He felt almost like another aspect of myself, closer than close.

"*Cat. Are you there?*"

The words came to me, as they had always done, as a whisper sliding into my mind, calling me. From earliest childhood it had happened like this, first in blocks of colours and images in my mind and then, as I grew older, in words and emotions.

"*Where are you?*"

I ignored him, turning a shoulder as though he was in the room and I was shunning him. When I had been obliged to leave Grimsthorpe, I had called to him for comfort but he had not replied. I had been hurt, needing him and the comfort his presence brought. Yet sometimes it had been like this. He slipped back and forth through my life and sometimes when I needed him, he was gone. This was the first time he had spoken to me since I had left Lincolnshire and it was contrary of me to sulk when he was the one person who could make me feel better.

"*Cat?*"

"I am at *Wolf Hall*." I was short with him.

I felt his puzzlement before it cleared like rain clouds running from the sun.

"*Savernake? Why?*"

"*They sent me away again.*" I was sick and feeling sorry for myself. I felt him laugh. Unforgivable.

"*Poor Cat.*"

I sent him the mental equivalent of a rude gesture I'd seen the servants make and felt him laughing harder.

"Such a lady."

"Go away."

He sobered at once, sensing the genuine misery beneath my ill temper.

"I'm sorry. Is it very bad?"

This time I sent a shrug, a hardy sort of a feeling. It was bravado. He knew I was homesick and lonely and unhappy. He could sense it. I could not keep him out even when I wanted to do so. Yet I also knew that not so many years before, he, too, had been sent from home. I had sensed his loneliness and isolation. I had tried to get him to tell me about it—had he gone to another household for his education? It was the way life ran for the sons of noble households and sometimes the daughters, too. He would tell me nothing about himself, though, not then, not ever. He was a mystery to me.

"There's the forest to explore. You love the forest."

The thought felt eager and so like a boy, trying to offer solutions. If only he knew how much the forest had cost me already. Nevertheless, I had softened towards him. I could not help myself. He always made me feel better. There was comfort in his presence and I no longer felt so alone.

"Yes. I suppose so."

He sent me a boy's hug, clumsy, affectionate. I smiled. The warmth of it soothed me, lulling me back into sleep.

"Goodnight, Darrell."

"Goodnight, Cat." Goodnight, goodnight…

I slept.